The Beach Hut

About the Author

Leah grew up on the Dorset coast and has been a barrister for almost ten years. She is a graduate of Curtis Brown Creative's Novel Writing Course. She lives in Hertfordshire and is currently working on her second novel for Hodder Fiction.

The Beach Hut

Leah Pitt

**HODDER &
STOUGHTON**

First published in Great Britain in 2024 by Hodder & Stoughton
An Hachette UK company

This paperback edition published in 2024

1

A CIP catalogue record for this title is available from the British Library

Paperback ISBN 978 1 399 72654 2
ebook ISBN 978 1 399 72655 9

Typeset in Plantin light by Manipal Technologies Limited

Printed and bound in Great Britain by Clays Ltd, Elcograf S.p.A.

Hodder & Stoughton policy is to use papers that are natural, renewable
and recyclable products and made from wood grown in sustainable forests.
The logging and manufacturing processes are expected to conform to the
environmental regulations of the country of origin.

Hodder & Stoughton Ltd
Carmelite House
50 Victoria Embankment
London EC4Y 0DZ

www.hodder.co.uk

In loving memory of Nan,

Who taught me to type.

Prologue

That day
10.30pm
Matilda

The bonfire coughed, illuminating the row of brightly coloured beach huts behind us. The flames cast shadows on the hut fronts, like dark figures moving across the patios. Perhaps the figures were watching us.

Perhaps they were watching me.

This was a mistake. I shouldn't have come.

Through the darkness, the waves whispered from the shore. Caitlin was dancing near the fire, vodka sloshing around the bottle in her hand. Tom cheered loudly, but Dev's eyes were fixed unblinkingly on Caitlin as she lifted her arms above her head, sun-bleached hair falling across her face. Next to me, Kip leant over and passed another beer to Sophie. She took it, reluctantly. The boy beside Sophie slid a hand up her thigh: a flash of panic crossed her face.

Later, they would tell the police it had been the perfect summer. That there had been no warning signs, no hint of a storm on the horizon.

If only we had noticed the shadows that crept up the beach towards us.

If only we had known it would all go so horribly wrong.

I

Chapter One

Now

Sophie

Starlings swoop in the evening sky as Harry heaves my bag onto the faded wooden deck and peers up at me, his thin white hair caught in the salty breeze.

'Been a long time since I've seen you down here, Sophie.'

Twenty years, to be exact, but I don't say this. My eyes are gritty with tiredness and my neck aches: all I want to do right now is reach for the bottle of middle-shelf Malbec I bought earlier and blur the edges of my life.

Out of the corner of my eye, the row of beach huts stand shoulder to shoulder, flashes of familiarity here and there, even after all this time: the hollow clack of wooden wind chimes from the Parkers' patio, the black fishing buckets outside old Harry's. Tom's hut, painted a soft cream, next door to . . . I tear my eyes away, my stomach giving a painful lurch.

Harry hasn't moved.

'Holiday, is it?'

'It's being sold. There's stuff to clear, that sort of thing.'

The long look he gives me says he doesn't buy this excuse.

'Seems a shame. Nice hut, this.'

'It's never used anymore. Better someone else enjoy it.' My tone is hard, clipped. I am already longing for the anonymity

3

of London: no one ever asks questions voluntarily. The fresh, briny air is making my head swim with tiredness.

'Real shame,' he repeats, with a click of his tongue. 'Hardly any of the original owners left anymore, just these City people who come down here demanding better phone signal.' He shoves his hands into his jacket pockets and squints at the shoreline, past the gently rising sand dunes, towards the bottom of the headland.

'Never been quite the same after what happened to that girl.'

I know where he is looking and I turn away, not wanting to see it reflected in his watery eyes. I don't need to be reminded of how her body was found, lifeless on the sharp rocks. Somewhere, up on the headland, there is a plaque dedicated to her. Matilda.

Harry probably thinks I am cold, not gazing mournfully out at the waves alongside him. As if he knew her. The breeze billows inside the hood of my waterproof, flapping against my ears as I stand, waiting.

At last, the old man pulls his gaze away from the shore and gives a sigh.

'I've got fish to see to. You look after yourself.' He walks away, back towards his hut.

Finally alone, I sit down on the deck and look out at the beach where I spent all my summers as a child. Despite my mood, it is a beautiful evening. Navy-pink clouds hang low over the slumbering waves and the tide is out, leaving a swath of glistening wet sand and clumps of seaweed in its wake. The beach is long, divided at intervals by lines of tumbling grey and white rocks, an obstacle course for daring children.

For most people, arriving at a wooden chalet on a quiet beach like this would be a balm, a peaceful break. It was once that for me, a long time ago. Now I don't know what it is. A wave of sadness breaks over me. *Stop it. Pull yourself together.* Getting to my feet, I rummage around in my handbag for the hut keys. They are still looped through the smooth piece of wood Dad attached them to. After unlocking the stiff doors, I step inside.

She's back.

I watch closely as Harry sets her bags down in front of the blue hut. No husband, no kids. Just her.

Sophie Douglas. She looks different, but I would have recognised her anywhere. I don't forget details. Not about her. Not about that summer. The wild brown hair she had as a teenager has disappeared; replaced with a sleek bob. Very London. Her expensive leather brogues are out of place on the sandy deck. I hear she's a real success now.

The white wine I was sipping on my own deck – so crisp a moment ago – now tastes like acid. Looking down, I am surprised to see I am pinching the skin of my right forearm. There are two small marks there now, like a snakebite.

My gaze turns towards the huts on the left, dotted along the curve of the sandbank. Most of the families who owned huts during that summer have gone. Those who remain seem to have moved on. Forgotten. Tossed into the sea, the memories sinking to the darkest depths, where the light doesn't touch.

My pulse quickens.

I have not forgotten.

Sophie Douglas will not have forgotten.

Chapter Two

Now

Sophie

When I wake the next morning, it takes me a second to orientate myself. I briefly anticipate the warmth of Nick's arms; then the sound of breaking waves washes over me, reminding me I am not at home in London, burrowed in my soft sheets. I am alone, under a musty duvet on the sofa-bed I didn't bother to wipe the sand from. Soon, Nick will be boarding his flight. Perhaps he will be sat next to some attractive, single woman. Will she notice his wedding ring? Or will he have removed it by now?

I swing my legs out of bed. The morning light pushing through the blinds has a pearly quality, promising a warm day. Reaching for my phone, I automatically tap the email icon. Unread messages flood onto the screen and my chest tightens. I go to open the first email, but then notice the 'Out of Office' banner at the top of my inbox. The pre-set message reads: *I am currently on leave. In my absence, please contact Keith Mansfield. Many thanks, Sophie Douglas, Senior Publicist.* I grit my teeth. *This is ridiculous.* All because of a few chest pains and some shortness of breath that turned out not, as I had assumed, to be a heart attack, but according to the doctor, panic attacks due to chronic stress. Before I knew it, the pushy new HR Director had signed me off with words like 'wellbeing' and 'burnout'. I hesitate. *It won't hurt to check a few emails. Just in case.* I was nervous about how Melissa, my over-eager junior, would handle our more demanding clients. We had targets to hit, after all. A bit of help here and there wouldn't hurt, just to ease Melissa into it.

I am already drafting a response to the first email when I remember Nick's question right at the end: *do you even like what you do, or do you just need to control everything?* I put the phone down, angry at his imagined chastising, angry at myself for thinking about him.

Standing in the middle of the hut, I inhale the mildew that clings to chair pads and sleeping bags. All the memories of running into this hut at the start of summer flash around me like tiny, silver fish. While everyone else jetted off to seemingly exotic locations like Corfu, my parents would be waiting for Anna and me at the bottom of the school steps, red Defender groaning with camping mugs, instant hot chocolate and jelly shoes. We would throw off our uncomfortable school loafers as Dad sped down the coastal road towards the sandbank and Mum passed us packets of Haribo, sticky with the July heat. Owning one of these beach huts – the kind you can sleep in for the summer, complete with small kitchens and mezzanine floors – was like living a parallel life a lot of the time. I would finish the school year as boring, uptight Sophie and start the summer as Fee: shell-gathering, fish-gutting merwoman.

Who am I now? In this neglected hut, the window shutters still closed. It feels as though only a heartbeat ago I was at home with Nick and his steady, solid presence. Now at the age of thirty-five I am back to where I started, trying, as I was then, to understand where my place is.

Chapter Three

Then

Sophie

'Stones for sale!' my sister hollered at the top of her voice. 'Stop *yelling*,' I hissed, embarrassed. Anna ignored me and carried on with her sales tactics. It mostly involved shouting loudly at each passer-by, who would quickly decide that 50p for a hand-painted rock was worth paying for some peace.

It was the beginning of summer, and, though we didn't know it, the year that everything would change.

I had decided that this was *my* year: the year I would finally transcend the rank of girl to woman. I had done my time in prepubescent purgatory: I had spent exactly fourteen summers already on this small stretch of beach and this summer I was swapping pigtails for artfully cut-off denim shorts and tankinis for skimpy bikinis. I wanted to be *noticed*.

I was getting noticed, alright, but in the worst way: hanging out with my little sister while she made extra pocket money and embarrassed me in front of all the new families renting out huts this summer. At ten, Anna had no interest in social status or boys; all she cared about was selling enough painted rocks to tourists to keep her in sherbet spaceships and gobstoppers. I huffed in irritation and folded my arms, wondering why I hadn't seen any of the older, cooler lot yet. Maybe they were all hanging out together somewhere.

'Fee!'

Matilda bounded along the beach towards us, kicking up sand as she went. When she reached me, we grinned at one another, breathless with excitement and a touch of nervousness. It was always this way with beach friends: come September, we would wave goodbye, returning to autumn school uniforms and new pencil cases, unsure when we would see each other again. I often wondered whether Matilda, so confident and chatty, had changed during the school year. Perhaps she wouldn't want to be friends with someone like me. It was a relief to see that she looked almost identical to the last time I had seen her, though her blonde hair was longer and she had grown even taller, now towering over my five foot two inches. She was beautiful, but she was still Matilda.

'Nice hair,' I said. Matilda grinned, a bright, beaming smile.

'Thanks. Nice boobs.'

I let out a splutter and crossed my arms, blushing furiously.

'Tildy!'

She burst out laughing and tugged my arms away from my chest.

'Don't be daft! Come here.' She pulled me against her and lifted the chunky polaroid camera attached to a leather strap around her neck.

'Why do we always do this *before* I have a tan,' I moaned, already readying my face for the camera.

'So we never forget who we were at the start of summer,' Matilda said bossily, turning the camera around and pouting at the lens.

'*Cheeeese!*' we chorused, our faces squished together.

Once Matilda had tucked the polaroid photo into her small keepsake tin, she took my hand in hers and pulled me along the beach. I forgot all about being cool as we ran and cartwheeled through the sand, giddy with excitement as a whole new summer lay ahead.

Chapter Four

Now

Sophie

Without the usual distraction of work, the day stretches out uncomfortably before me. I find myself wondering how I used to fill my time, in the years before work became so all-encompassing.

After reminding myself how to replace the gas canister and getting the stove working, I pour a coffee and decide to get on with making the hut habitable. My appointment with the estate agent isn't for a few days yet, so I have time to get everything ready for the sale. As unsettling as it is to be back here, I owe it to Mum, to all the happy years spent here, to get a good price for it.

It is one of the larger huts along the sandbank – the long ribbon of beach that juts out from the mainland – but unlike many of the other hut owners, my family was not especially wealthy: back in the eighties my then-childless parents were hiking across one of the headland trails and came across the burnt husk of a hut following a gas explosion. It was at the very end of the row, closest to the rugged headland separating the sandbank from the coastal road and main town on the other side. Gripped by the idea they could own this small slice of freedom on the Jurassic coast, they shunned their existing dream of buying an apartment in Mallorca and bought the half-destroyed shell. My dad – a rumpled mortgage advisor by day – spent two years learning carpentry from a book and lovingly renovating it. Like me, my parents became different people when they were down here. No suffocating ties, no school runs: they left all that behind.

Despite the years of neglect since it was last used as a rental, the hut is still postcard perfect. Resting upon three-foot stilts, it is a bright, cornflower blue, with double doors out onto the wide deck. The timber frames are painted a soft, cotton white and a porthole window sits proudly above the doors. The original window blew out in the explosion, but instead of replacing it with plain glass, my dad sourced a piece of glass in a kaleidoscope of colours: when the sunlight filters through it sends pinks, blues and greens rippling across the room. Inside, there is a main living area complete with sofa-bed, table and small kitchen. Under one of the side windows is a cushioned bench where my mum spent hours absorbed in the romance novels that Dad teased her about. There is a curtained-off area at the back with tall cupboards and the bunk beds where Anna and I used to sleep, reading *Goosebumps* with our torches late into the night and swatting away the mosquitoes that buzzed around our heads.

As the morning wears on, the beach fills with the shrieks of children paddling in sun suits and the hum of boats, off to fish or explore the small coves. I busy myself within the confines of the hut, not ready to face the brightness of the outside world.

By midday, I've filled the water tank and managed to remove the worst of the grime inside the small under-counter fridge. In need of a break, I pick up my phone from the windowsill, but there is a movement in my periphery, as though someone is on the deck. I cross to the doors and open them, but the deck is deserted. My neck prickles. I'm sure I saw something. I step down onto the sand and peer through the passageway between my hut and next door's. Just as I decide that I am imagining things, a shadow shifts across the sand at the back corner of the hut.

'Hello?' I call. The shadow doesn't move; it remains a stain on the golden sand. I swallow and take a step forward.

'Hello?' I repeat. *You're being paranoid.* But there is still no answer and adrenaline propels me forwards. I tip-toe towards the back of the hut.

'Hel—'

Rounding the corner, I find no one. No hidden figures, no shadows. Just me, feeling like an idiot.

Annoyed, I walk back to the hut, my nerves jangling. I jump when my phone starts buzzing on the windowsill, but my face breaks into a smile for the first time in days when I see the name on the screen.

'Hey, Anna Banana.'

My younger sister gives a reluctant laugh at the other end of the phone. I find myself pressing the phone harder against my ear, as though it will somehow bring me closer to her.

'You didn't call me yesterday, you total shit. I've been worried sick. I kept telling Mike you'll have gone and drowned yourself and it would be all my fault for not coming with you.'

'Don't be silly, I'm fine.'

'*Are* you fine?' She sighs and I know she's thinking about Nick, but thankfully doesn't mention him. 'I still don't know why you've gone down to that place.'

'Who else was going to sort out the sale? You're on the other side of the world, Mum's disappeared to Spain with Phil . . . I didn't have a choice.' I try to make it sound matter of fact, but the words come out bitter. There is a long pause on the other end of the phone.

'Dad always handled this kind of stuff,' Anna says eventually.

'I know,' I murmur. I run my finger along the coating of sand on the windowsill. It is almost thirteen months since he died, but I still struggle to think about it for very long.

'What's it like down there, anyway?'

'It feels very surreal . . . hardly anything has changed. Not even Harry.'

Anna gives a snort.

'That old perve still hanging around, is he?'

'Anna! He's not a . . . he's nice enough.' A lump has formed unexpectedly in the back of my throat. Recently it has felt as though someone is snipping away at each of the strings that tie me to the life I had defined for myself: husband, *snip*. Dad, *snip*. I don't even have work to distract me, at the moment. With Anna in Australia and Mum in Spain, I have felt an increasing sense of unbalance, wondering if any more strings are going to be cut away, leaving me to buffet in the wind. Perhaps that's why I decided to return to the place where I spent my childhood before it, too, is gone forever.

'Have you seen Gary and Sheila?' Anna asks suddenly.

I swallow.

'Why would I have seen them?'

'Well, you've not been back to the hut since it happened. I thought you might have wanted to see them.'

'Anna, I'm just here to sell the hut. That's all. I doubt they're even still here.'

'Well, you should find out. She was your best friend—'

I cut her off. 'It's been twenty years, Anna.'

'So?'

'So, I'm not here to stir up the past. I've got to go; say hi to Mike for me.'

Anna sighs, clearly deciding not to force the issue.

'I will. Take *care*.'

Chapter Five

Now

Sophie

After hanging up the phone to Anna, I sit out front with a fresh mug of coffee. The early afternoon sun is now high in the sky, bathing the deck in a warm, buttery glow. I slip a cigarette from the pack in my handbag and light it. Nick thought I had given up, but I often snuck a couple outside the office on more stressful days.

Scanning the beach in front of me, I try to really *see* it: light, almost creamy sand; rolling waves topped with white caps; beds of seagrass around the dunes that lean gracefully into the wind – but if you get too close, they can slice open your finger.

This focus on my surroundings is something the doctor insisted I try, so-called *mindfulness-based cognitive therapy*.

'You need to learn to relinquish *control*,' she said sternly, after I told her there was no way I could take time off work. 'To let *go*. The world around us cannot be controlled or managed. If we try to conquer the ocean, we will drown.'

Nick had apparently decided he no longer wanted to drown.

We had first met in a coffee shop off one of Holborn's busiest roads. It was edgy enough to attract a lunchtime crowd of twenty-somethings with cropped fringes and laptops but cramped enough to deter the hordes of tourists and families making their way towards Covent Garden. It was April and the rain had appeared out of nowhere, hammering onto the pavement. I ran into the café, dripping wet, and hurriedly ordered a coffee. Turning away from the counter, I quickly realised that there were no tables. I found myself irrationally annoyed at the barista for not warning me. *What am I meant to do, just stand here and drink it?*

There was a man by the window, perched neatly on a window bench with a book in his hand. He caught my eye and, apparently registering my harried expression, took his bag off the bench next to him and shifted over. He looked back down at his book as I walked over and sat down on the bench next to him, peeling off my damp trench coat.

'Thanks,' I muttered.

He looked up, his expression unreadable. Behind him, the window was steamed up and a line of condensation trickled slowly down the pane.

'You're welcome.' His eyes returned to his book while my eyes stayed on him. Tall, slim frame. An academic type, from his neat, checked shirt to his suede desert boots. But there was an edge of something else, too. Perhaps it was the length of his stubble: a touch too long to be conservative, or the faint piercing scar in his ear, still just visible.

My phone pinged and I glanced at it instinctively: in the PR world, you couldn't afford to miss a thing. It was a message from my assistant.

Here First has cancelled. Trying to reschedule.

I groaned. Here First was a hugely influential talk show: negotiating an interview for one of our author clients had taken the best part of a year. The client was desperate for the coverage. I picked up my coffee, debating whether to pay the Hear First offices a visit rather than wait around for them to reschedule.

'Dammit.' The coffee was almost stone-cold. I scowled at the barista who had served me, ready to get up and request a new one, when the man next to me spoke.

'Bad day?'

I looked up, alarmed he was speaking to me. His face was completely passive, but I thought I saw a shadow of a smile at the edges of his mouth.

'You look stressed,' he added, by way of explanation.

I wasn't *stressed*. I was annoyed. There was a difference.

'I'm fine. Just work.'

He was looking at me a little too knowingly and I turned back to my phone, ruffled. After a couple of seconds, however, I began to feel awkward about my abruptness. Casting around for something to say, my eyes landed on the book in his hand.

'What are you reading?'

He flipped the book over to show me.

'*Shoedog*,' I read aloud.

'It's about the founder of Nike. Have you read it?'

I hesitated. I had been on enough dates in London to know that a poor knowledge of books often came with a big fat *uncultured* label. But this wasn't a date. And I got the impression the man next to me would know if I tried to lie.

'No,' I said. 'I think the last book I read was when I was a teenager. Jaqueline Wilson, probably.'

Instead of turning away in disgust, the man leant forwards slightly. My neck grew unexpectedly warm.

'Why not?'

No one had ever asked me that question before. My phone pinged again, but I ignored it.

'Work.' I shrugged. 'And . . .' I hesitated, feeling slightly embarrassed. 'I don't like not knowing how things end.'

For some inexplicable reason, this comment made him smile.

'Well why don't you start on the last page? Then you'll always know the ending.' He held out his hand. 'I'm Nick, by the way.'

Without thinking, I put my hand in his.

'Sophie.'

A seagull squawks loudly overhead, bringing me back to the beach. I stand abruptly, the chair legs scraping on the patio slabs. If mindfulness therapy means my mind has to be full of Nick, I can do without it.

Chapter Six
Now
Sophie

For the next two hours I work on sorting the contents of the hut. Whenever the temptation to check my emails or see if Nick has messaged arises, I double-down on my cleaning efforts so that by the time I stop for a break, sweat is trickling down my forehead and my back aches. It feels good to do something physical: I haven't had time to hit the gym in years and I find myself engrossed in the task. My dad's old wind-up radio is blaring country classics, and all the doors and windows are pushed open, flooding the hut with sunlight. It exposes all the cobwebs and stains, but it also casts light onto the glass wind chimes my mum strung up along the central beam and onto the bowls of deep orange and pearly-pink shells we collected over the years.

So far, I have only tackled the back section of the hut, where Anna and I used to sleep. Every single cupboard or box that I open contains decades of trinkets and knick-knacks: half-finished boxes of matches, bits of twine, bottles of sun cream with the lids crusted over, pairs of binoculars left by eager bird-watching renters.

Finally, only one box remains. At the end of every summer, Mum and Dad would insist on Anna and me putting all our 'beach' possessions into our boxes. It was largely pointless: anything worth keeping, like sweets or scented gel pens, would come home with us, so the boxes ended up being filled with rubbish we couldn't be bothered to take to the bin, or things that we were bored with. At some point I had covered my box with plastic glow-in-the-dark stars.

The box sits on the top shelf of the cupboard and has been pushed right to the back over the years. I eye the flimsy wooden chairs in the kitchen. I'll have to hunt down a ladder if I want to retrieve it without breaking my neck. *Just leave it until tomorrow.* The bottle of gin I bought yesterday is calling to me, ready to be mixed with cold tonic in the setting sun . . . only I hate leaving anything unfinished. I know I'll only sit there, unable to enjoy my drink, while the final unfinished box drives me insane.

Telling myself it won't take long, I walk outside and around to the back of the hut in search of Dad's ladder. My bare feet, so beach-hardy when I was a teenager, flinch against sharp stones and the spiky leaves of sea holly.

The three-foot gap at the back of the hut between the sand and the hut's underbelly was mostly used as a place to store surfboards, and the ladder my dad used to maintain the roof and solar panels. Crouching down, all I can make out is the red and white stern of my dad's small sailing dinghy, just visible among the shadows. I shudder. Even as a child, the low, dark space spooked me.

Unable to see anything in the approaching twilight, I tap the torch icon on my phone – briefly entertaining the thought of how my dad would react to me using an app instead of an actual torch – and peer into the darkness. The air underneath the hut is dank and cool. Various cracked buckets and empty gas cylinders meet the light of my phone, but no ladder. Crawling into the gap, I hold my phone out with one hand. Something moves to my left and I jerk backwards. *Snakes?* They aren't uncommon down here. I wait a moment, but everything remains still.

Taking a deep breath, I move the phone methodically from left to right. It is a relief when, finally, the light falls upon a metal ladder leg. It's shoved right back, so I have to lean the phone against a bucket and crawl further forward to reach it. Clearing a rusty paella pan off the top of the ladder, I tug on the legs. The ladder shifts towards me slightly, but it is wedged underneath the bow of the dinghy. I try again, but only manage to drag it a few more centimetres. Groping around in the darkness, I reach for the wooden rim just above me that runs around the perimeter of the hut's underbelly. Gripping it tight in order to brace myself, I hold onto the bottom rung of the ladder with my other hand, pulling as hard as I can. It works: the ladder dislodges itself from the boat and slides towards me through the sand. At the same time, my hand slips from the wooden rim above me. A sharp stab of pain pierces my wrist and I yank my hand away. As I do so, my hand hits something balanced on the rim. Whatever it is falls to the ground with a soft thud.

'Dammit!'

In the half light, my jumper sleeve is torn, blood beading where I caught my wrist on a rusty nail. I reach for my phone, shining it around on the sand to see what fell. I am about to give up, when the torchlight falls on it.

It can't be.

Everything around me seems to disappear as I stare at the small, silver tin.

Twenty years ago the police were looking for that tin. Twenty years later, it sits silently in the sand before me.

What I don't know is how it got there.

Doors open. Blinds pulled up. Bin bags in piles on the deck. They glint in the sun like oozing, black slugs. The binoculars press against my eye sockets.

Perhaps, then, you're not hanging around after all, Sophie? Perhaps you're just sucking the life from the hut before you sell it on to some of your shiny, puffed-up friends from London who want to 'renovate' the hut for their Instagram accounts? They'll put in a bathroom, geometric kitchen tiles, a memory foam mattress, and claim they are adventurers. As long as you're gone from this sandbank, Sophie, I don't care what you do.

The pinch mark on my arm has faded, the skin red and mottled now.

A fellow birdwatcher passes me, binoculars bumping against their chest. We smile at one another, before I raise the small binoculars to my eyes once more and return to my target.

Fly away, Sophie.

Chapter Seven

Then

Sophie

'I'm *bored*,' Matilda sighed, tapping her feet on the decking. As always, her camera was next to her and she picked it up, squinting at me through the lens.

'Smile, Soph.'

I stuck my tongue out as the camera clicked. I was so used to Matilda taking photos I barely registered it anymore.

'Do you use toothpaste on your spots?' I asked, returning to my magazine as Matilda reached for the tin she kept her photos in.

'I don't have spots.'

'You have, you've got—' I stopped. Matilda was looking at me, the tin and photo still in her hand.

'I've got what?'

My face grew hot.

'Nothing.'

As I said it, my eyes involuntarily travelled up towards the angry red spot in the middle of Matilda's forehead. There was a long pause, then Matilda fell about laughing. Relieved, I started laughing, too.

'It's . . . so *big*,' I spluttered, which made Tildy laugh harder.

'I . . . know,' she gasped. 'Everyone who talks to me keeps looking at it. They go cross-eyed.'

We collapsed into giggles, too busy laughing to notice the shadow that fell on the wooden decking.

'What's so funny?'

Kip, Matilda's cousin, leant against the wooden rails, his bodyboard tucked under one arm. I stopped laughing and sat up straighter, sucking my stomach in. Just the sight of him made my heart beat faster. He looked so beautiful, his white-blonde hair dripping, his eyelashes dark and wet.

'Sophie was laughing at my giant spot,' Matilda announced.

'Harsh, Soph,' Kip said, laughing. Panic rose within me like a snake. *I wasn't harsh!*

'It was a joke,' I said hurriedly. 'Matilda thought it was funny, I wasn't being harsh. It was a joke,' I repeated. *Shut up, shut up* my brain yelled at me.

Kip held his hands up.

'Relax. You're so easy to wind up.'

I bit my lip, my insides burning with embarrassment. Kip was only sixteen, but he seemed like an adult already. I, on other hand, couldn't even string a sentence together.

No. I told myself. *This is your summer, remember? Be more Fee.* This is what I told myself to get myself out of 'Sophie' mode and into 'Fee' mode, where I was cooler, funnier, more confident. *Be more Fee.*

I gave a gentle laugh and, remembering what my magazine said, ran my hand slowly through my curls. To my astonishment, Kip's eyes travelled down to my bikini top, like the magazine said they would, where the movement lifted my top slightly.

'You're right, I *do* need to relax.'

I stood up, ignoring the look Matilda shot at me, and walked casually down the deck steps past Kip.

'I'm going to grab a beer at mine,' I said. 'See you later.'

Without looking back, I started walking across the hot sand. *Oh my god.* My pulse was racing. I couldn't believe what I had just said. Did I sound like an idiot? Was Matilda exposing me as an impostor right now, telling Kip the only alcohol I had ever drunk was some wine at New Year's Eve and it was so gross I didn't even finish it?

I had only gone a few feet when Kip called out to me.

'Hey, Fee, we've got some beers here, if you fancy one?'

It worked! And he called me *Fee*, not Sophie. I paused like I was deciding, but really I was trying to swallow my eagerness so I didn't mess up.

'Okay,' I turned and shrugged. 'Thanks.'

Kip smiled and turned towards his hut, which was next door to Matilda's canary yellow one. Matilda looked completely baffled but, like a true best friend, didn't say a word and picked up her magazine. Kip dropped his bodyboard and slid open the doors, beckoning me in. Ignoring the pounding of my heart, I followed him.

I'd never been inside before. It was much fancier than our hut: my dad called it *pretentious*, because they had a hot water tank and a proper coffee machine. The kitchen stretched along the whole back of the hut, with solid wooden countertops. There were neat benches lining the hut walls on either side, positioned under the open windows. They were proper, professional benches as well, not the ones my dad made which splintered the backs of your calves. There was a nautical theme to the whole place: white paint and expensive throws in blue and white stripes.

Kip was rummaging around in the small under-counter fridge, bottles clinking.

'What do you drink? We've only got Budweiser, Heineken or Castlemaine.' He examined a bottle in that inexplicable way grown-ups did. Shit, I'd forgotten the names of the beers he had just said. What if I pronounced them wrong? I decided to rely on my new tactic and gave a relaxed shrug.

'Whatever you're drinking is cool.'

Kip nodded and pulled out two green glass bottles, popping the caps off as though he had done it a thousand times before.

Was I really going to do this? What if I threw up? What if Mum and Dad walked past, or Anna, and she dobbed me in?

Kip handed me the cold bottle and crossed over to one of the benches, patting the space beside him. 'Come sit, Fee.'

Sitting down next to him, I was suddenly very aware that I was only in a bikini top and shorts. Our legs brushed and I was pleased that I had used my special moisturiser that gave my skin a dewy, golden glow. I knew I should say something, but my brain seemed to have stopped working. I had never got this close to a boy before. Being alone with Kip was all I had fantasised about for the past two summers, but now I was here I didn't know what to do with myself. We had always skipped over this part in my daydreams. My stomach squirmed. *Was this how it was supposed to feel?*

Kip had already taken a good few swigs of his beer and I brought the bottle to my lips, praying I didn't do something stupid like throw it straight back up again. The beer was cold and bubbly: I felt it explode behind my nostrils.

Looking over, I saw Kip was studying me.

'What?' I blurted out.

'You're different this summer. There's something about you that's just . . . I don't know, different.'

'Like what?' I asked. *Like you've grown up. Like you're beautiful. Like I'm finally noticing you.*

Kip's shoulder was pressed against mine. I tried to breathe shallowly, in case I had beer breath. He was so close. He opened his mouth to speak.

'Kip!'

We looked up. Caitlin was in the doorway. Framed by the sun, she looked like an angel: her long blonde hair fell in perfect waves and her beaded crop top showed off her flat brown stomach. My heart sank.

'What's all this?' she asked, in a would-be-joking voice, but there was a hard edge to her tone. She eyed the bottles. 'Since when do *you* drink, Sophie?'

'Sophie drinks,' Kip said, getting up. 'Beer?'

He went to fetch Caitlin a drink and she dropped down onto the bench opposite, so confident in Kip's service she didn't bother to reply to him.

'Grown some tits this summer, I see.' She said it quietly, so Kip couldn't hear. 'Didn't your mum ever tell you, less is more?'

She looked pointedly at my skimpy pink bikini top and I forced myself not to fold my arms across my chest. After daydreaming so often about being inside Kip's hut, the urge to get out was now overwhelming. Caitlin's fury was palpable: even though they had never officially been a couple, it was obvious she liked Kip. She had just turned sixteen, so she was closer to his age than I was.

'Caitlin can have my beer.'

I stood and placed the bottle on the countertop, then turned and walked miserably towards the doors. Just as I stepped back down onto the beach, Kip called out behind me.

'Come back later, Fee. We're going to have a bonfire at Tom's.'

I turned and saw Caitlin shooting him a furious look, but I didn't care. I smiled at Kip, my heart soaring.

At last: I was invited.

Chapter Eight

Now

Sophie

The tin sits innocently on the countertop, a silent bomb, as I pace up and down the hut. Outside, the sun has sunk below the line of the water and mosquitoes buzz around my head. My phone lights up across the room, more work emails, but for the first time in years my attention is elsewhere.

The tin's silver has dulled over time, speckles of dark orange rust dotted around the hinges. Most of the lid is covered in surf brand stickers, now faded and peeling away at the edges. I pick the tin up and hear the muffled *tat-tat-tat* of polaroid photos inside. The day Matilda was found swims before me: the frigid police station interview room, the fear, the questions that never seemed to end.

'What can you tell us about Matilda's camera, Sophie?'

'Gary – her dad – gave it to her because she thought it was cool. It was big and black. She . . . s-sorry . . .'

'Take as long as you need.'

'She's had it for like, years. She never goes . . . never went . . . anywhere without it.'

'What about her tin? The one she kept her photos inside?'

'Her dad gave her that, too. She said she needed to keep the photos in some place dark so they would develop. And she hated getting sand on them.'

'Did she always keep the tin with her?'

'Pretty much, yeah.'

'Do you know where the tin is now?'

'No, but she had it with her last night. Why?'

'We've been unable to locate it. It wasn't found with her.'

'I . . . I don't know, then. It's always with her.'

'Sophie, some of the other witnesses from last night said you and Matilda argued recently.'

'I . . .'

'A pretty bad fight, apparently. Matilda wasn't one to argue, according to her family.'

'It wasn't . . . I didn't . . .'

'Were you angry at her, Miss Douglas?'

Dad: 'That's enough.'

I begin to pace around the hut, trying to push the memory of that day away, not wanting to relive the horror, the grief, of it all.

Why was the tin under my hut? When was it put there?

The shallow rim beneath the hut would not be an impromptu or opportunistic hiding place for someone who didn't know it was there. It can't have been an accident . . . *can it?*

For the first time since my arrival, I cross to the doors and look to the right, towards the jagged rocks that curve around the base of the headland and out of sight. Matilda was found among them, her skull fractured.

Rumours circled like sandflies in the hours and days following her death. Whispered conversations through open windows about Gary and Sheila Hall, some claiming Sheila hadn't cried enough, others saying they had always known there was something off about Gary. Fingers were pointed at us, too, the teenagers that were there that night.

It was almost impossible for the police to investigate what had happened in the two-hour window Matilda was thought to have died: back in 1997 there was no CCTV, no phones, no useful forensics. Just a dead girl with a catastrophic head injury and a police investigation that slowly petered out. It became an unsettled mystery that never went away.

In the weeks and months following Tildy's death, I barely left my room. Every time I closed my eyes, my actions from that night played out in front of me, like a horror film on repeat. The guilt engulfed me, drowning out all other emotion. I became a different person: someone always on high alert, who stayed in her shell. Tildy was gone and so was Fee.

I stop pacing and put the tin down. Perhaps it doesn't mean anything; perhaps there's an innocent explanation for it being hidden. After all, most people just accepted Tildy's death was an accident once the investigation went cold. *I* had accepted it was an accident, not wanting to consider the alternative.

Then why am I not opening it?

Chapter Nine

Then

Sophie

'What about this one?' I asked Matilda, twisting this way and that to try and see my outfit better in the window's reflection. Clothes were strewn all over Tildy's hut, our duffel bags for the summer wide open and empty.

'That one looks good, too. They've *all* looked good,' Matilda replied from the window seat.

'You're not even looking!'

'Soph, it's just a bonfire. They have them every night. It doesn't matter what you wear.'

'But this is the first one we've ever been *invited* to.'

I looked again at my reflection. The ripped denim skirt with diamantes along the pockets just looked a bit . . . *trashy*. It's what the girls at school wore, but down here the cool girls wore tiny board shorts and hoodies that artfully framed their salt-scrunched hair. Last year Caitlin had made her own dreadlock with wax and she had woven gold thread through it. My own hair was sticking up in every direction, refusing to do anything I told it to. It wasn't fair that Anna got straight hair like Dad's, whereas I got a stupid bird's nest.

Matilda seemed to have taken pity on me.

'What about my pink shorts with the Hawaiian flowers? You can wear them with your white crop top. And I'll plait your hair the way you like it.'

'With the two plaits? And kind of loose, not too tight?'

Matilda laughed, swinging her legs down from the window seat.

'Like I said, the way you like it.' Suddenly, a cushion came flying at my head. 'Anything to get you to shut up.'

The hut door opened and Matilda's mum and dad walked in.

'You told me they were *real*—' her mum was saying in an annoyed voice. She had red spots on her cheeks.

'They *are* real, Sheila,' her dad replied, sounding exasperated.

'*Rolax* is *not* a real watch brand, I've had Joyce on the phone—'

Gary and Sheila looked up and saw us standing there staring at them.

'Oh! Sorry girls, didn't see you there,' Sheila said. She walked quickly over to the kitchen and started rummaging around, pulling out a wine glass. Tildy's dad Gary beamed at us. His thick hair was sticking up all over the place from the wind.

'Off out are we, girls?'

'Yep,' I said. 'Going to a bonfire.'

'Well, make sure you don't break *all* the boys' hearts,' Gary chuckled. He went over and put an arm around Sheila, but she shrugged him off. Tildy rolled her eyes.

'Come on,' she said. 'Let's do your hair at the table.'

An hour later, we were walking along the sand towards Tom's hut. I had dithered for ages in the doorway to Tildy's hut, not wanting to arrive too early but also desperate to leave. Eventually, Matilda had dragged me out of the door.

As we walked, I was distracted by one of the huts along the beach: it was painted in pink and white stripes, which reminded me of raspberry ripple ice cream. The lights were low in the hut and it almost looked like no one was home – until I realised there was someone sat in the window. For some reason the hairs on the back of my neck stood up: the person sitting in the dark wasn't moving but their head was definitely turned out, looking towards us.

'Who is that?' I asked, nudging Matilda as we walked past the hut. She looked in the direction I was nodding and shrugged.

'Dunno.'

As we carried on walking, I grew more and more nervous. Matilda might not care about hanging out with Kip and Caitlin, but *I* did. No matter what I did or wore at school, I had never been accepted by any of the groups that hung out every Friday night, drinking cider in the park, or sneaking into nightclubs with fake IDs. My Friday nights were spent eating popcorn in front of a film with my parents and Anna, constantly wondering what the others in my year were doing. Wondering when I would experience my first kiss. This bonfire invitation was a big deal to me, an indication that maybe things were going to change this year. That maybe I wasn't quite so lame, after all.

Tom and Kip were already gathered around the fire, chatting to a lanky, dark-haired boy and a girl I didn't recognise.

I didn't know much about Tom, except that he was a bit of a bad boy and he was older – eighteen or nineteen. The same age as the boys that hung around the school gates in their Ford Fiestas, waiting to pick up the popular girls. Tom's parents seemed to be out of town all the time, leaving him and his brother James to do pretty much whatever they wanted. To my relief, Caitlin was nowhere to be seen.

Kip looked up, then, and saw us walking towards them.

'Hey guys,' he said, waving a beer can. His smile was genuine and I relaxed a bit. It didn't look like he regretted inviting us. Next to me, Matilda still seemed completely unfazed, even though we hadn't met the other two around the fire.

'Hiya,' she said, plopping down next to Kip, who shuffled over to make way for her. I quickly copied and sat on her other side, not wanting to draw too much attention to myself.

The actual bonfire wasn't quite as magical as I had imagined: it was just a small pit dug into the sand that someone had chucked a load of logs and fire starters into, but the flames still looked pretty and the crackling was nice in the background. We were sat on the sand in front of Tom's hut, no blankets or chairs or anything. A dented white cool-box was next to Tom and he reached in, pulling out two cans of beer.

'You drink?' he asked, even as he leant over with the alcohol. Matilda shrugged and reached out to take a can from him.

'Should you—' Kip began but Matilda cut him off.

'Shut up, Kip. Don't try and lecture me.'

He shrugged, laughing.

'Got it. No dad chat.'

'You?'

Tom was still holding out the beer to me, his eyebrow raised. Condensation dripped off it. For a moment, I didn't know what to say. No, I didn't want to drink: beer tasted gross. But I *did* want to fit in.

'Sure,' I said, eventually. 'Thanks.'

'This is Fee and my cousin, Matilda.' Kip introduced us to the others. 'That's Tom, Amy, and Dev.' He pointed to the lanky dark-haired boy. Closer, I realised I had seen Dev around before, sometimes accompanied by strict, unsmiling parents, but we had never spoken. His dad was some sort of local politician. Dev nodded at Matilda and me, but his eyes flickered straight back to the fire. Amy, however, looked over at us and smiled. She was drop-dead gorgeous and my stomach constricted with envy. She had curly, blonde-brown hair and wore ripped denim shorts, a baggy Vans T-shirt and a shell choker. Her wrists were thick with beaded bracelets. My make-up and plaited hair suddenly felt childish and over the top: I resisted the urge to tug the plaits loose.

'Hi,' she said, and I smiled back, trying not to hate her. *Did Kip like her?* I peeked across at him under the pretence of opening my beer. He looked so hot: his blonde hair was messy like always and he wore a long-sleeved baseball top, white with red sleeves. He caught my eye and I looked away quickly. Trying to cover the moment, I took a hurried gulp of my beer, but I wasn't ready and the frothy liquid flew down my throat too fast and bubbled painfully up my nose, making me splutter. To my horror, the others all fell about laughing, Tom hooting the loudest.

'Haven't you ever had a beer before?' he said, snorting loudly.

No, no. It was all going wrong. My face burned with embarrassment. Even Amy was laughing. *Oh god, they saw through me.* Only Tildy shot me a sympathetic look. Heart in my mouth, I had a sudden vision of walking past them all for the rest of summer, hanging out together while I was laughed at, or worse, ignored.

I stood up. The words came out of my mouth from somewhere completely disconnected to my body.

'Come on, then,' I challenged Tom, my voice breathless. 'See who can down a beer the fastest.'

Tom grinned and jumped up. He was huge and towered over me, his smile one that probably made girls fall at his feet, but not me. He wasn't Kip.

'You're on, kiddo.'

We moved to the side of the fire while the others whooped and cheered. Matilda was the only one who remained silent, standing up next to me and muttering 'what are you *doing*?' in my ear. I gently elbowed her away. She wouldn't understand: she was smart and funny and beautiful and she was also Kip's cousin. She had a free pass into the group whenever she wanted. I didn't have that luxury and I wasn't going to let them kick me out. Not when I was this close.

'On the count of three,' Tom said. 'One . . . two . . . *three.*'

I threw my head back, closed my eyes and downed the beer faster than I possibly thought I could. The group exploded with cheers and claps and yells of 'Go Fee!' Grinning and licking the froth from my lips, I held my empty can up triumphantly. Tom stopped when he saw I had finished.

There was a long pause and I wondered, fleetingly, if he was going to be mad.

'Not bad, kiddo.' He held his large hand out, and I grinned and shook it.

'Not bad yourself,' I said.

Later that night, I walked back to Matilda's hut with her, completely euphoric, my head swimming from the two extra beers I had drunk. We had all sat and laughed for hours about stupid things: the time that Tom's dad had tried to cut both Tom and his brothers' hair himself and they had to go to school with bowl haircuts, the time Amy had kissed a boy with braces and her lip had got stuck. Even better, Caitlin hadn't shown up all night. I had steadily grown more confident, chipping in with jokes that the others all laughed at. Tom kept grinning at me and even Dev said 'see ya, Fee,' when we had to leave, knowing we would be in trouble if we left any later.

'That was the best night *ever*,' I gushed, skipping along the sand. It felt like I was floating above my body, looking down at the silvery waves. 'Did you *see* Tom's face when I downed that beer—'

'Yes, I saw,' Matilda said shortly. My body came floating abruptly back down to earth.

'What's wrong?' I asked, coming to a halt. Matilda stopped, too. There was something off about her tone, that I hadn't noticed until now. She had, I suddenly realised, been super quiet all night.

'Didn't you have a good time?' I asked.

Tildy sighed and scuffed at the sand with her toe.

'It's just . . . I mean, didn't you think it was a bit . . . *boring*?'

I looked at her in dismay. *Boring?* It had been one of the best nights of my life. For once, I had been part of the inner circle; not outside, looking in.

'What do you mean? Which bit was boring?' I couldn't understand her. It had been a great night. I swayed slightly as I looked at her, the beer making it hard to think straight.

'All of it! Tom – how *old* is he, by the way – with all his *hilarious* stories; Amy going on and on about all the people who fancy her . . . it was just . . . a bit boring, wasn't it?'

'I didn't think so.' My voice sounded small. 'I thought they really liked us.'

Tildy looked at me in a way that was almost pitying.

'Did you really enjoy all that? Being called *kiddo* all the time? You didn't think they were full of themselves?'

I shook my head, slowly. Matilda sighed.

'Fine. It was good to do something different, I guess. Are you coming back to mine so we can go fishing tomorrow, or are you going to be too hungover?'

I grinned.

'I'm staying with you. Your mum makes the best pancakes.'

We linked arms and sang Spice Girls' 'Say You'll Be There' the whole way back to Tildy's hut.

Chapter Ten

Now

Sophie

After staring at the rusted tin for what feels like hours, I finally decide to deal with it in the morning. I am exhausted: weeks, *months*, of dealing with one thing after another has rendered me incapable of making another decision. I carefully shut the tin away in a drawer and climb into bed. Tomorrow my head will be clearer. I just need a good night's sleep.

Only the good night's sleep never comes. I lie awake, staring at the ceiling, trying to shut off my thoughts, but everything is colliding: the tin, the summer of '97, work, Nick. I turn over, trying to get comfortable, still not used to having a whole bed to myself. Closing my eyes, I try and focus on my breathing, in and out, but my mind keeps turning over, a scab being picked at.

Around midnight my phone lights up on the windowsill and I reach for it, glad of a distraction. Perhaps an emergency at work will take my mind off things. Perhaps I should just pack up and get back to London, to hell with the sick leave. I need to be busy, I need structure to my days. Only when I check the screen, it isn't work. '*Three Year Wedding Anniversary*' has popped up cheerfully on my calendar, with a little wedding ring emoji. It's like a bad joke. I shouldn't even *be* here, thinking about Tildy. Nick and I should have been together, on a very different beach somewhere, drinking cocktails and napping on white sun loungers. For one mad moment, I consider calling him. Asking if he had remembered it was our anniversary. Telling him about the tin. Admitting that I want him here, in bed next to me, helping me pack the hut up. But then I remember why he isn't here. And the choice I made.

Before

It was March, a time for things to start budding. The beginning. For the first time in weeks, I left the office before midnight, arriving home just as the colour drained from the London skyline.

I found Nick in the kitchen, finishing dinner with a glass of wine. Across from him was a second place-setting.

'Hi babe,' I said, shifting my handbag out of the way so I could kiss the top of his head. His curly hair, flecked with grey at the temples, was ruffled and he smelt of pepper and sandalwood.

'Hey. Dinner's on the side.'

'I'm not hungry,' I said, putting down my bag and pulling my phone out. 'Thanks, though.'

I poured myself a large glass of wine and sat down opposite him, quickly refreshing my emails. My assistant still hadn't sent across the notes I needed for an 8am meeting with a particularly tricky journalist and I gritted my teeth.

It wasn't exactly a difficult task. It was late to call her, but I expected the report hours ago.

I noticed, then, that Nick was hunched over his plate, his eyes downcast.

'You okay?' I asked, thinking he must have had a bad day at work. He hadn't been mentioning work much the past few weeks, usually a sign he was finding it challenging.

He slowly put his fork down.

'I—'

My phone buzzed and I automatically scanned the message. My heart sank when I saw that my client, a best-selling author, had been interviewed on a popular podcast and apparently made some disgustingly sexist remarks.

'*Shit*,' I muttered, when I saw that the episode – and his worst quotes – were already going viral. My chest tightened. 'This is going to need damage control.' Sure enough, my boss Keith started pinging me frantic messages.

'Miranda's offered me a promotion,' Nick said. I looked up, only half-paying attention as my phone continued to flash with messages.

'That's great babe! Well done.'

Keith's latest message read: '*We need to get on this NOW. Call in 10.*' I quickly started typing a response back.

'It's in Japan.'

I laughed in surprise and looked up.

'Why would they do that? You don't have clients in Japan.'

Nick's face coloured and he shifted awkwardly.

'Nick? Why would they offer the job to you?' I asked again. Something wasn't adding up, but my screen was lighting up with messages and I was struggling to concentrate.

'I applied for it.'

My stomach jolted.

'What? When?'

'Last year.'

Last year? I stared at him. My phone, clutched in my hand, began to ring but I didn't answer it.

'I don't understand.' My brain was playing catch-up, unable to process what Nick was telling me. 'You applied for a job in Japan without telling me?'

Hurt seeped hotly through me as I worked through the bombshell Nick had just dropped and what it meant. This wasn't part of the plan. We were finally settling down, ready to live our lives.

'I'm sorry, Soph. I didn't think anything would come of it; I did it on a whim and it turns out they think more of me than I realised.'

'How long is it for?' I asked, not wanting to hear the answer.

'I don't know. Indefinitely, at least at the beginning.'

There was a long pause. I waited for him to tell me it was a ridiculous idea. That of course he wasn't thinking about taking it.

'Please, Soph, just think about it. Take as much time as you need, we don't need to make any decisions right away. Just have a look at the package. It's seriously generous, it could be a whole new adventure for us.' He managed a half-hopeful smile. 'I think you could love it: think of the cherry blossom.'

'I'm not coming with you,' I snapped. Nick's smile vanished. 'My life is here, *our* life is here.'

'Can't we at least talk about it?' Nick asked, his face colouring. 'It's an incredible opportunity for me. I deserve a conversation, at least.'

'*What* conversation?' I stared at him incredulously. 'We can't just uproot to Japan out of nowhere, you know that. My job is here.'

'A job you *hate*,' Nick said, a hint of anger in his voice, now. 'A job that keeps you up every night, unable to sleep. I could understand if I thought it made you happy, but you're not, you're miserable.'

'I'm not miserable.'

He laughed uncharacteristically harshly.

'Are you happy?'

Happy? I am successful. I am well respected. I have a good income.

'Of course I am.'

I pushed my chair back, needing to work off some energy, still struggling to process what was happening. Eventually I stopped pacing and looked at him.

'Do you *want* to take the job?' I asked. *Please say no.* Nick didn't move from the table. He rubbed his eyes under his glasses. I'd picked out those glasses for him, telling him the clear, round frames made him look like a young Steve Jobs.

'Soph, we've always put your career first and I've never resented that. I knew when I met you that your career was your child. But while you're climbing, I'm stagnating. I need to push myself, find a new challenge.'

'So you chose *Japan*?' I stopped pacing and pressed my hands across my eyes in frustration. 'Why didn't you just talk to me? Not go behind my back making plans without me, not lying to me for months. We're *married* for god's sake!'

'I've tried talking to you,' Nick said, his voice rising. 'I told you we needed change, *I* needed something to change. None of this would be a surprise if you had listened.'

This was getting out of hand. I took a deep, calming breath I didn't feel and tried to keep my voice level.

'Look, why don't we sit down and properly talk about it? If a challenge is what you need, why don't we see if Miranda can offer you something in London that really develops your skills?'

'So you want me to turn the job down? Before you've even looked at the offer?'

I didn't say anything. I didn't know *what* to say. We looked at each other for a long time. I stood waiting, my heart beating too fast. After a while, his shoulders sagged.

'Okay. I'll talk to Miranda.' He pushed his chair back and stood up. As he passed me, he gave me a wooden smile.

The relief I should have felt didn't come; I just felt sick. It didn't matter that he had agreed to speak to Miranda; something had changed. I now knew he wanted to go to Japan, and I couldn't unknow that. If he went, I would be unhappy. If he stayed, he would be unhappy. Either way, one of us was going to lose.

'Mum called earlier by the way,' Nick said from the doorway, in an overly polite voice. 'She said she's booked the restaurant for eight o'clock tomorrow so you don't have to rush after work.'

Shit. It was his mum's 60th tomorrow night. I hadn't told him, yet; but the look on his face said he had already guessed. He didn't even look surprised.

'You're not coming, are you?'

'It's a dinner with a potential client we really need to land . . . I couldn't say no.'

'No,' Nick said stiffly. 'I know you couldn't.'

I opened my mouth angrily, hating the look on his face, but at that moment my phone started ringing again. I hesitated, torn between the conversation we were having and my ringing phone.

I turned away from Nick to answer it. A minute later I heard the front door close.

Now

It is still early when I leave the hut the next day, the quiet morning air edged with a misty chill. The sand is smooth, not yet disturbed by footprints.

After struggling to get thoughts of Tildy and Nick out of my mind, eventually, in the pre-dawn light, I had drifted off. But when I slept, I saw Matilda's pale, lifeless face and I woke up sweating. Climbing out of bed this morning, my head throbbing, I had decided what to do. Carefully, I take the tin out of the drawer and tuck it into my cardigan pocket. It feels good to have a plan, to take back control.

I slide my feet into my sandals and leave the hut. In stark contrast to my frayed nerves, the waves this early are a soft silver, gently folding onto the shore. The noise is soothing and I realise how much I've missed it.

After a few minutes, I reach my destination. The yellow beach hut makes my chest ache. It looks so neglected; the once sunshine-yellow paint faded almost white. I don't want to see it like this. How often did Matilda and I sit on that front deck in the shimmering heat, reading *Bliss* magazine, our teenage equivalent of the Bible? How many sleepovers up on the mezzanine level, burrowed in our too-hot sleeping bags, giggling at Gary's rumbling snores?

To my left, a white hut with pink stripes catches my eye. The blind twitches, as though it has just been snapped shut. A surge of unease runs through me.

Focus.

Slowly, I walk forwards across the soft sand and climb up the deck steps to the front doors.

The tatty, daisy-print curtains are drawn. I don't even know whether they will still be here, or how they will receive me after all this time. My parents took Anna and me back home the day Matilda's body was found and refused to let me attend the funeral, convinced it would be too traumatic. I'm not sure if I could have faced it, even if they had let me. I was only too willing to hide from Gary and Sheila's grief.

Taking a long, deep breath to calm my nerves, I raise a fist and knock.

There is no answer.

I try again, a little louder this time, straining my ears for any noise from inside. It occurs to me that the only thing worse than an answer would be no answer at all. I want this over with; but there is still no stirring from inside.

Reluctantly, I turn and walk back down the steps to the deserted beach. I pause for a moment, just in case someone emerges from the hut: but it stays stubbornly silent, and after a minute I decide to walk to the toilet block.

The huts along the sandbank are split into two rows, standing back-to-back: those on the right face out over the beach, those on the left overlook the harbour and distant town. The closest toilet block is positioned about fifty yards along the row, on the harbour-side, so I cut past Gary and Sheila's yellow hut, emerging into the narrow passage between the two rows.

The air is cooler in the passageway, where the huts block the early sunlight and leave the sand cold underfoot. It is eerily quiet, even for this time of the morning; no squealing children or burbling radios floating through open windows. I pull my cardigan closer against the chill and pick up my pace.

I am only a few yards from the toilet block when something emerges in front of me. Before I can process what is happening, something hard slams into my stomach. I stumble to the ground, completely winded. *What the hell?*

'God, I'm so sorry, are you alright?'

There is a dripping sensation on my forehead. *Am I bleeding?* As the realisation that I am not about to be attacked slowly sinks in, I look up warily. In the half-light I can just about make out light blue eyes, full of concern, resting above a broad, sun-freckled nose. Blonde hair is plastered to the stranger's forehead, apparently the cause of the dripping on my head. A surfboard lays discarded on the sand next to him as he looks down at me.

'I'm fine,' I choke, still winded.

'I'm really sorry,' the man says again. 'I was jogging to my hut and wasn't looking where I was going. There aren't usually people lurking around here.'

'I wasn't *lurking*,' I say, irritated. 'I was on my way to the toilet. *Not* jogging.'

Rather than taking offence at my tone, the man just laughs.

'You've got me there, headmistress.'

There is something oddly familiar about his voice, but before I can think about it, he bends down and hoists me unceremoniously to my feet. We stand facing one another in the shadows for a moment, and I feel a strange stirring in my stomach; a nervousness I cannot place. Just as I open my mouth to speak, he glances down at the sand next to his surfboard.

'You've dropped something.'

Too late, I realise Matilda's tin has fallen from my pocket. Before I can reach it, the man is already bending down, picking it up.

'Oh, thanks.'

Hastily I reach for the tin, but pause at the look on the man's face. He is staring at the tin with intense disbelief.

He knows what it is.

Chapter Eleven

Now

Sophie

Before I can protest, the man steers me between the two huts on our right until we are back out into the early morning sunlight.

'Get off!' I pull away from him, staggering a little on the sand.

'*Sophie?*' the man says aghast. Squinting up at him, I finally place the blonde hair, blue eyes, lean frame. Matilda's cousin Kip stands in front of me, two decades after we last saw each other.

'What . . . I mean, what are you *doing* here?'

'I'm selling the hut. I've been clearing it out.'

Kip blows out a long breath. He rubs the back of his head with his palm, still looking at me incredulously.

'I didn't think I would ever see you back here.'

A flicker of defensiveness flares within me, as though Kip is insinuating that I have the least right to be back here. *As though I was the most guilty.*

'I've got as much right as anyone else. And I didn't exactly expect you to still be hanging around here, either.' My tone is waspish and Kip looks taken aback.

'That's not what I meant. I meant because she was your –
you were the closest. After all this time, I just never expected
to see you again.'

Oh.

'Sorry,' I mutter, embarrassed.

There is a strange charge between us: the last time we
stood in front of one another was the night of Matilda's
death and we . . . *no, I don't want to think about that.* Now we
are as good as strangers.

'Sophie,' Kip begins. He looks wary now, as though he,
too, has realised we no longer know each other. 'What are
you *doing* with this?'

I glance around: other hut owners are starting to emerge
onto their patios. The smell of bacon and sausage wafts
across the beach from a nearby hut. We are standing near
the white and pink beach hut: inside, something moves.

'I don't want to talk about it here.' I walk a little further
down the beach, towards the shoreline. Kip follows, still
looking at the tin in disbelief. As soon as we reach the shore,
he turns on me again.

'How do you have this?' he asks, again. 'It was *lost*.'

'I found it last night. It was . . .' Suddenly, I am over-
whelmed with relief that I can share the burden with someone else. 'It was under my hut. *Hidden*.'

'What do you mean, hidden?'

I explain about looking for the ladder, finding the tin
tucked onto one of the beams.

'I don't think it could have been put there by accident,'
I finish. 'Someone must have hidden it.'

We move out of the way slightly as a jogger runs past us, nodding good morning.

'Have you looked at what's inside?'

I shake my head.

'I was going to show it to Sheila and Gary and then take it to the police.'

Kip chews his lip, turning the tin carefully over in his hands. His next question takes me by surprise.

'Is that such a good idea? Taking this to the police?'

'Kip, the police looked everywhere for this tin. The photos might, I don't know . . . help with the investigation. Why else would they be hidden?'

'What investigation? There was barely any investigation, even back then.'

'I *know* that,' I reply, slightly exasperated. 'But those photos didn't just magically appear under my hut. I can't just decide not to show the police. And Sheila and Gary have a right to know about them.'

Kip doesn't answer. He just stares at the tin, as though it will somehow tell him what to do. A shadow passes over his face, like the darkness of a shark as it cuts through the water. He is suddenly further away than ever from the fresh-faced surfer boy I knew as a teenager. He seems to be deciding what to say; perhaps deciding whether or not he can trust me.

'Look, Sheila's been completely broken since Tildy died. She still comes down to the hut on anniversaries and just sits staring at that spot on the shore.'

So they do still own the hut.

Our gaze moves simultaneously towards the spot. That section of the beach is forever tainted, as though the waves were made of dark red blood. It is also one of the most beautiful spots along the shore.

'*Did you tell Miss Hall to meet you on those particular rocks?*'

'*No – well, sort of. Yes. I suggested it and she agreed. We used to go there a lot.*'

'*If you used to meet there, you would know it would be wet and slippery at night, wouldn't you?*'

'*I—*'

'*Is that why you told her to meet you there, Miss Douglas?*'

'I don't know how she'll react to seeing this,' Kip says. 'It'll bring all the memories back. Gary's been trying to help her come to terms with what happened . . . seeing this could hurt them both all over again.'

This pulls me up for a moment. Selfishly, it hadn't occurred to me how Sheila and Gary would react when I presented them with the tin. Shame pools hotly in my stomach.

Sheila and Gary were a constant presence in the background of my summers growing up, whether it was Sheila giving us advice about boys or Gary fixing our crabbing nets. They bickered like most parents, but there was an impenetrable solidness to them. Sheila was from a wealthy family, slim and fair-haired. She had a soft voice that always knew the right thing to say. Gary was friendly and broad-shouldered, with a loud laugh that boomed across the beach and dissolved us into fits of giggles. Matilda was their whole world.

My thoughts are scattered. *I need coffee.* I had anticipated this being over by now, that I would have handed over responsibility to someone else. This isn't what I wanted when I came down here. Selling the hut, distracting myself from Nick with good old-fashioned elbow grease. *That* was what I wanted.

Breaking away from Kip, I make my way across the untouched ripples of sand to the edge of the water and sit down. I draw my knees up, resting my chin on them, and watch the waves for a moment, wishing I could press pause. I sense, rather than see, Kip sink down beside me. The tin still in his hands, his fingers tracing the curled edges of stickers.

'What are you suggesting we do, then?' I ask. 'I can't just pretend I didn't find it.'

'We could open it.'

I look across at him.

'It's not ours to open,' I say firmly. 'It might be police evidence.'

'We don't know that.' I open my mouth to protest but Kip cuts me off. 'We *don't*, Sophie. We have no proof that this has anything to do with what happened to Tildy that night. But if we involve the police, the whole thing gets dragged up again. Except this time there's the internet, there's Twitter . . .' He rubs the back of his head again, a gesture I suddenly recall he did when he was younger.

'All I'm saying,' he continues, 'is that we might cause a total shitstorm for no reason. For all we know, there are just a few innocent photos in here.' Kip turns fully towards me now. His knee brushes my leg. 'I know how hard Matilda's death must have been for you. Christ, it completely messed me up, too. But it almost *destroyed* Sheila and Gary. Gary's been desperate to leave, but Sheila refuses to sell the hut.

When she comes down here, she watches that bit of shore as if she might actually *see* Matilda coming out of the water one day.'

Tears blur my vision and I blink them away quickly while Kip is talking. The blue in his eyes is bright, like the blue of driftwood flames.

'The last couple of years, Sheila seems to be . . . not *better*, but more accepting, I guess. She reads more, she talks a bit about Matilda. It's like they both know it's been twenty years and now they just want to try and remember her the way she was when she was down here.'

I understand what Kip is saying. The consequences of taking this tin to the police without any idea of what is inside could rip open old wounds. Wouldn't it be better to know what was inside it, before showing it to Gary and Sheila?

Kip is looking at me expectantly, warily.

'Okay,' I say. 'Let's open it.'

Chapter Twelve
Then
Sophie

I opened my eyes to the sound of Dad's snores coming from the other side of the curtain. The early morning sunlight lit up the back section of the hut: Anna and I had fallen asleep last night before shutting the blinds. Outside, I could hear the breaking waves and the usual anticipation ran through me.

Leaning down from my bunk, I looked through my upside-down curls to see Anna still fast asleep, her fringe plastered to her face and her mouth open. I had to resist the urge to poke her to scare her awake.

Pulling myself back up, I shuffled to the small window at the end of my bunk. Slowly, I pushed it open, wincing as it squeaked. I paused for a second, but Dad's snores still rumbled through the hut. As fast as I could, I wriggled out of the window, landing in a neat crouch.

Jumping up, I hurried down the side of the hut and pulled my bikini and wetsuit off the nail I always hung them on to dry. My wetsuit was still a bit damp from the day before and by the time I had pulled it on and zipped up, I was hot and sweaty, even in the cool early sunshine. Tucking my white and pink surfboard under my arm, I tore down the sand towards the shore.

It was the same nearly every morning: come rain or shine, Tildy and I would meet to surf, unless something catastrophic got in the way like a thunderstorm or period cramps. We didn't even care if the surf was rubbish, which it often was. We just liked being out at sea on our own. Today, the swell was perfect: the waves broke high and slow, with almost no wind and the water looked glassy.

Right away, I spotted a head of bright blonde hair bobbing among the waves. Wrapping the surfboard leash around my leg, I waded into the cold water.

'About time!' Tildy greeted me as I paddled out to join her. 'The waves have been amazing!'

As she spoke, my eyes were trained behind her, on the next set of waves about to roll in. We looked at each other and grinned. Excitement fissured through me: when I surfed, it was like I grew with the wave, becoming a giant, ready to take on anything. Tildy yelled at me to go first, but she needn't have bothered: I was already face-down on my board, paddling furiously as the force of the swell sucked me backwards. Just as the wave began to lift me up, I popped up and skimmed along the wave, weaving this way and that.

Once I had slowed down in the shallows, I jumped off and turned to watch Tildy riding the next wave, crouching low with her long blonde hair plastered to her head and shoulders. As she approached the shallows, I cheered and waded over to high-five her.

'That was awesome!' I cried breathlessly.

We immediately paddled back out again, my muscles already warming up in the cold water. As we sat straddling our boards and catching our breath, two figures walked down the sand towards the shore. Once they were closer, I could see they both held bodyboards and flippers. My heart sank: it was Kip and Caitlin. They looked perfect, walking together side by side, like Barbie and Ken dolls. She was even wearing one of his hoodies over her bikini. How could I have ever fantasised about him liking me back?

'I don't think he fancies Caitlin, you know,' Tildy said quietly. I looked over to see her watching me. She looked sad. I shrugged like I didn't care, but I felt a bit sick.

'Even if he doesn't fancy her, it's not like he's interested in me. Why would he be? I can barely talk around him.' I prodded my belly, which was all rolls because I was sitting down. 'And I'm fat.'

'Don't be stupid!' Tildy said loudly. 'You're not fat. You've got a Mariah Carey body.' She paused. 'Without the voice.'

'Hey!' I cried, splashing her with water. 'You're supposed to be cheering me up.' I was smiling, though.

'What about you?' I asked, wanting to get the attention off me. 'Do you like anyone down here? That boy Jack a few doors down looks quite fit these days.'

'He's thirteen!'

'That's not *that* young.'

'Girls can't date guys in the year below them, you know that.'

'Fine,' I conceded. 'Anyone else?'

For some reason Tildy looked a bit odd: she stared hard at the water, the sides of her mouth pulled downwards.

'What is it, Tild?' I asked, manoeuvring my board closer to hers. Tildy tore her eyes away from the water and looked at me for what felt like a long time. She opened her mouth to speak, but then she closed it again.

'Nah, I don't fancy any of the boys down here, they're much better at school. Plus,' she said, pushing her wet hair out of her eyes and patting the bobbing pink buoy beside her, 'buoys,' she cupped her boobs, 'before *boys*, remember?'

It was a stupid saying we made up when we were kids and I rolled my eyes. I was *sure* she was lying about something and I opened my mouth to say so, but suddenly Tildy was lying down and paddling furiously: seconds later she was riding a wave away from me.

What was that about?

For a moment I sat watching her. Then I shrugged and began to paddle for the next wave. It was probably nothing.

Chapter Thirteen

Now

Sophie

The midday sun climbs higher as Kip and I walk towards my hut, picking our way over sharp pieces of shell and avoiding a jellyfish washed up on the shore. Flies crawl steadily across its thick, translucent skin.

As we walk, I grow increasingly conscious, despite the situation, that I am next to my childhood crush for the first time in twenty years. I looked Kip up, once. It was only the one time, shortly after I first met Nick. It was a stupid, silly thing to do and I could never adequately explain it to myself. But the boy with the blonde hair and wet eyelashes had somehow swum in the back of my mind for years. His memory had the quality of the sun: only visible when I wasn't looking straight at it. Kip represented the summer I could have had, the person I could have been, had Matilda not died. The girl who loved to surf and try new things. My search for Kip hadn't taken long: all I managed to find was the website for his watersports company, Wavelength, and a scant Facebook profile. The profile photo was of a teenage Kip, grinning from a kayak; for some reason I had slammed my laptop shut.

'Do your parents come down much?' I ask, to break the silence.

'No, they sold our hut.' Kip glances over his shoulder in the direction of the impressive green hut his family used to have. I vaguely recall Kip inviting me in, once, back when he was the only thing I dreamt about. 'They moved to Cornwall when they retired and didn't see the point in keeping it. I couldn't afford to buy it off them.' He shrugs, but I sense his disappointment. The huts are special.

'What about you? You said your family is selling up, too?' Kip asks.

'Yes. My parents stopped coming down the summer Tildy died. They rented it out for a while, but Dad passed away almost two years ago and Mum decided it was time to sell.' My breath comes out a little shorter as we navigate the sloping dunes. 'I offered to sort everything out for her. Thought I could use some sea air.'

I don't add that my time off work wasn't exactly voluntary, or that I am already regretting my decision to return. Foolishly, I had thought time away from London would outweigh the pain of being back on the sandbank.

'And then what? I heard you moved to London?' Kip is showing no signs of being out of breath as he strides along next to me, the tin clutched in his hand. He looks incredibly fit and healthy, all the better for the passing of two decades: his calf muscles below his board shorts are strong and pronounced and his shoulders strain against the fabric of his light-blue rash vest. Suddenly, I am very aware of the fact that I am wearing the same lilac cardigan as yesterday, which has a coffee stain on it. Nick bought it for me, because he said that it matched the colour of the blossom on the cherry tree in our garden. It didn't match, but I loved it anyway.

As I look out across the waves, where random patches of water shimmer in the sunlight breaking through the clouds, regret washes over me that I never shared this piece of my past with Nick. Growing up in Chiswick, he had never even *seen* the seaside, unless it was from some penthouse window in Dubai during a client meeting. I told him that wasn't the *proper* seaside, the one that smelt like crabs and seaweed, where you could hear the sounds of boats dinging in the harbour. He'd laughed and thrown our local Chinese take-away menu at me, claiming the only seaweed he wanted to smell was crispy.

'Sophie?'

We have reached my hut and Kip is looking at me with an expression of concern. 'Are you alright?'

'Sorry. Got lost in thought for a moment.'

The inside of the hut is a mess of binbags and boxes. I quickly push as much as I can into the curtained-off area at the back as Kip follows me inside.

'Coffee?' I ask, while Kip settles himself at the kitchen table and rubs at his damp hair. 'I don't have anything else. Except wine.'

Kip chuckles. The sound transports me back twenty years to when I would have given anything to hear the warmth of his laugh.

'Coffee sounds good.'

For a moment there is silence as I search the cupboards to find clean mugs. Eventually I uncover two faded leopard-print mugs from an old Woolworths set. The disorienting feeling of not knowing where everything is sets my teeth on edge. As I scoop coffee into one of the mugs, the spoon hits the china rim and coffee grounds spill across the work surface and floor.

'Dammit.'

'Don't worry,' Kip says, seeing my tight jaw. 'It's just coffee.'

'It's . . . I just . . .' *Get a grip.* 'I'm not usually like this.' I gesture irritably to the spilt coffee.

'Like what?' Kip asks, sounding amused, which only aggravates me more.

'Clumsy. Disorganised. Whatever. I'm just tired. Out of routine.'

'What *are* you usually?' Kip asks. His blue eyes are searching, and I turn away, ignoring the inexplicable pull in my stomach.

'I don't know what you mean.'

I busy myself putting the hot water on the stove and carefully brushing the coffee grounds into the bin. I can't remember the last time I spent time with a man that wasn't Nick, and it's Kip Turner: the only other person I really fell for. *Only I'm not fifteen, anymore.*

'I mean, it's been over two decades. I know nothing about the grown-up Sophie.'

Christ. Is he asking me for a bio? A rundown of the last twenty years? *Let's see, my husband left, my own boss has forced me to take time off, and I've started having panic attacks. Have I missed anything? Oh, I've started drinking more than is socially acceptable.*

Instead, I shrug and say, 'I'm not too far different, to be honest. I've taken some leave from work, so after this I might visit my sister, Anna. Do you remember her? She lives on the coast, near Perth, now.'

Kip raises his eyebrows, impressed.

'Wow, I've always wanted to travel around Australia. She was cheeky, your sister, I liked her.'

I smile and nod as I carry the coffees over to the table. We are on safe ground now and I find myself relaxing slightly as I sit down next to Kip.

'She still has that effect on people.'

Growing up, I always admired how Anna didn't just dance to the rhythm of her own drum: she kicked the drum clean out of the way and marched on. Even under the beach's spell, she knew exactly who she was. Unlike most younger siblings, she never whined, never trailed me around or threw a tantrum when I wanted to go off and hang out with friends. Now she is a five-foot-two force of energy, already tipped to become the youngest principal in her architecture firm. Her husband Mike is just as energetic, if not more so: they are a whirlwind of ideas and DIY projects. Mike reminds me a little of Dad.

'And . . . you're married?' Kip asks the question hesitatingly, in the way that people always do when they're trying to avoid making it sound like a come-on. His eyes flicker down to the large yellow sapphire engagement ring and wedding band studded with tiny, perfectly cut diamonds. I touch the sapphire with the tip of my right index finger, feeling the smoothness of the stone.

When Nick had presented me with the ring, down on one knee on the tiny terrace of the first flat we owned together, I thought it was the most beautiful thing I had ever seen, for more than just its appearance. Whenever I was on the Tube or in the shops in the weeks afterwards,

I would make little movements to show the ring off, unnecessarily brushing my hair back, holding my hand out over the fruit at the supermarket as though I was making up my mind about apples. Really, I was trying to make the sapphire catch the light so I could watch it sparkle. I *liked* the looks that other women cast me, imagined the envy from those with a bare ring finger. What better symbol to show you belong, that someone wants you, than an engagement ring? Even though I am now technically separated, I haven't been able to take it off, paranoid that its absence would somehow scream to strangers that my marriage had failed.

'I, uhh . . .' I flounder, embarrassed. 'I'm separated. I just haven't . . .' I lift my left hand lamely, but Kip nods.

'I get it. When my ex and I split up it took me ages to sort out all the admin and stuff, I just couldn't face it. Then I got mugged and she was still my emergency contact.' He is grinning and I stare at him, wide-eyed.

'What happened?'

'Well, it was a bit fucking embarrassing. A *year* after we break up, she gets a phone call to say I got knocked out by two teenagers and can she get to the hospital. She turned up with her new rugby-player boyfriend while I was lying there in a hospital bed like a total idiot.'

I cover my mouth to smother my laughter, but Kip is laughing, too.

'He was actually alright, her new guy. Not as good as me,' he wags a mock-stern finger in my direction, 'but alright.'

As I laugh, my gaze lands on the tin, which Kip placed on the table when we arrived. I immediately stop laughing, astounded at myself for sitting here chatting with Kip when the tin is sat right by us, unopened.

'Kip . . .'

'I know.' His eyes are on the tin.

'We have to open it.'

'I know,' he repeats.

He stands and crosses to the doors, closing the faded checked curtains against the warmth of the June sun. He does the same with the curtains hanging over the windows either side of the hut, so that the only light comes from the thin halos of sunshine that squeeze their way through the gaps around the curtains. I get up from the table and switch a couple of lamps on, casting a warm glow around the wooden hut. We don't discuss the reason for shutting the world out: it doesn't need to be said. Kip picks up the tin and we sit on the small window box, the table in front of us.

'Ready?'

Am I?

I nod.

Chapter Fourteen

Then

Sophie

'Ready?' Tildy grinned at me, her white teeth flashing in the sunshine.

'Ready.'

'One . . . two . . . three . . . GO!'

Tildy slammed down a Queen of Hearts and I immediately followed with an eight of spades. Over and over again we slapped cards down onto the pile in quick-fire succession, until:

'SNAP!' I yelled triumphantly. Tildy groaned just as Sheila emerged from the hut.

'Put on some mozzie spray, girls,' she said, throwing Tildy the bottle. Gary followed behind Sheila, carefully balancing a tray with four steaming mugs on it. Tildy and I eagerly eyed the squirty cream and chocolate shavings. Gary handed out the mugs and started pushing squishy marshmallows onto sticks to roast over the barbecue.

It was evening and the sun was just setting, bathing the beach in a golden glow. The tide was low, exposing piles of seaweed and the sandy mounds of burrowing sea-worms. The best mussels could also be found when the tide was out: I made a mental note to go down with Tildy, before it got too dark.

Just as I took a sip from my hot chocolate there was a burst of laughter and chatter along the beach. Glancing left, I saw a group of five: Dev, Tom, Kip, Caitlin and Amy. They were walking in our direction. My stomach dropped. I hadn't seen them since the bonfire and they hadn't asked us to hang out, again. *They didn't like you, after all. You must have made an idiot of yourself.*

Hurriedly, I looked away and took a big sip of my drink, but it was too hot and the liquid scalded my tongue.

'You okay?' Tildy asked. I looked up to see she was watching me, her eyebrows pulled together.

'I'm fine,' I lied. 'Great hot chocolate, Mr Hall!'

My voice was overly false and I was hyper-aware that the others were approaching right at that moment. I looked down at my mug, waiting for them to hurry up and walk past.

'Hey! Kip!'

My head snapped up: Matilda was calling to Kip. She had a weirdly determined look on her face, like when she was being stubborn over something. Before I could ask her what she was doing, Kip had looked over. He stopped when he saw us out on the deck.

'Hey Tilds! Hey Fee.'

I managed a small mumble, wiping my mouth quickly in case I had cream on my lip.

'Come *on* Kip,' Caitlin snapped, clearly torn between wanting to walk off but not wanting to leave Kip. The others had stopped now, too.

'Where are you off to?' Tildy asked, ignoring Caitlin.

'The headland. Wanna come?'

I thought Kip looked across at me quickly, but then I blinked and his eyes were back on Matilda, who was standing up.

'Let's go, Fee!'

I shot her a quizzical look. She didn't like hanging out with Kip and his friends, she had made that clear. But Tildy gave a small jerk of her head towards Kip and raised her eyebrows.

'Come *on*,' she whispered.

She was doing it for me. My heart swelled like a balloon.

Abandoning our hot chocolates, we jumped down from the deck, hand in hand.

'Pass us the bottle,' Tom slurred. Kip handed him the bottle of vodka, laughing.

'You are *hammered*, dude.'

'Not fuckin' hammered,' Tom said, spit flying from his mouth. I stifled a giggle.

'What are *you* laughing at?'

My back stiffened and I felt my face going red. Across the fire, I caught sight of Caitlin smirking. Tom leered at me, leaning forwards on his bit of log.

'You got something to say, little girl? *Huh?*'

'Leave her alone, man,' Kip said. His voice was calm as he leant casually back on his elbows, but he didn't take his eyes off Tom. I felt a small flush of pleasure and had to remind myself not to get too excited. Kip was nice to everyone, after all. Tom just scoffed.

'I need a piss.'

He heaved himself up and staggered towards the trees where everyone went to pee or make out. I glanced at

Matilda. Even though she had been enthusiastic about coming up here, she hadn't said much since we had arrived.

We were at the highest point of the headland, near the old broken sign that read *DANGER CLIFF EDGE* in large red and black letters. Beyond it, the water was turning steadily darker as the last of the sun sank beneath the headland. Somewhere nearby was the old quarry where the Romans used to mine for iron, or something. The school trip we took to the headland was fuzzy in my head. My seven-year-old self, with my perfectly organised pencil case and neatly brushed ponytail, would have been shocked to know that one day I would be sitting among the dirt and brambles, swigging stolen vodka and passing around a joint. I felt a small thrill: it was exactly what I was hoping for this summer and, thanks to Matilda and Kip, it was finally happening.

Kip threw more sticks onto the fire and turned to talk to Dev about some unreal surf that was meant to be coming in the next few days.

Dev's younger sister, Chetana, was next to him on the log: he had apparently been tasked with babysitting her but all he had done was ignore her. She looked absolutely petrified: her dark brown eyes darted around the small clearing. She was small and skinny and her thick black hair was pushed back with a velvet headband, the kind that made the bit behind your ears ache. Despite the muggy July air, she wore a long-sleeved T-shirt and leggings.

'Here,' Tom had re-emerged from the trees and was leaning over the fire, holding out the vodka bottle for Dev to take. Dev accepted the bottle and took a swig, managing not to screw his face up as he swallowed. He ignored Chetana and went to pass the bottle across to me, but Tom held out a hand.

'What about your little *sis*?' He carried on the 's' noise so the last word came out in a hiss. Dev quickly shook his head as Chetana looked up, startled. Caitlin stopped talking to Amy and began watching the others, her eyes excited.

'No way, man. She doesn't drink.'

A slow smile snaked across Tom's face and I had to fight the sudden urge to push him hard over the edge of the cliff. I was starting to wonder why the others hung around with him. Maybe it was because he was old enough to buy alcohol.

'Has anyone asked *her* if she wants a drink?'

Chetana shot Dev a sideways look. For a second, he looked nervous. Then he straightened up and glared at Tom.

'No one needs to ask her. She doesn't drink.'

Dev was tall for sixteen, but skinny, and not only was Tom two years older, he was big and stocky with it. A prickle of tension crawled up my spine and I wished that the conversation could move on, but I didn't want to say anything in case it drew Tom's attention back to me. Next to me, Tildy looked apprehensive but she, too, remained quiet.

Tom stood up and walked around the outside of the circle. For a moment, he became lost in the shadows but then he reappeared at Chetana's shoulder. He dropped down onto the log next to her.

'Leave her alone,' Dev muttered, but he didn't meet Tom's eye. My stomach was starting to churn, the beers and vodka I had drunk bubbling up in the back of my throat. Tom ignored Dev and put his arm around Chetana, who looked as if she might be trying not to cry.

'Don't worry, babe,' he cooed to her, 'I'm not gonna hurt you. I just want to help you relax.'

He gave her a hard squeeze and a whimper escaped her mouth. Tom was no longer slurring, but somehow that was even scarier. Dev's hands were clenched into fists but he still hadn't moved. *Why wasn't he doing anything?* Tom was intimidating, but Dev was her older brother. He was supposed to protect her, wasn't he? Kip was still leaning back on one elbow, but he was clutching his beer bottle so hard, his knuckles stood out white in the light from the fire.

Tom's arm was still tight around Chetana's shoulders. He waved the vodka bottle under her nose, resting the rim against her lower lip; her nose wrinkled at the smell.

'Here, why don't you ignore your brother and try a bit, beautiful?'

'I . . . I don't . . . want to,' Chetana whispered, pulling away. 'Thank you.'

Dev looked relieved but a flicker of annoyance crossed Tom's face.

'You've not even tried it. *Here*,' he pushed the bottle rim a little harder against Chetana's mouth and she jerked her head backwards.

'It might make you loosen up a bit. Take off some of these baggy ass clothes.' Tom plucked at Chetana's leggings, with a loud, cruel laugh. 'What are these for, covering up your hairy brown man legs?'

Chetana let out a small sob. There was a sudden movement next to me: Matilda was on her feet.

'That's *enough*!'

Her voice carried across the headland, despite the waves crashing against the rocks below. She marched over to Chetana and snatched the vodka bottle out of Tom's hand before he had time to react. For a moment it looked as though she was going to throw the half-empty bottle over the edge of the cliff, but instead she bent down and smacked it hard into the ground so that the clear liquid sloshed around. Tom didn't move; he looked shocked.

'Come on.'

Matilda stood in front of Chetana and held out her hand. Chetana looked up at Matilda, the tears in her eyes glistening in the firelight. There was a long silence while everyone stared, completely taken aback. Then Chetana reached out her hand and allowed Matilda to pull her to her feet, out of Tom's grip.

'Arseholes,' Matilda spat at the group around the fire. 'What is *wrong* with you?'

Matilda turned and her eyes found mine. She raised her eyebrows. I knew what she was asking, what she was waiting for, and the awful realisation dawned on me at the same time it dawned on her: I wasn't going to move.

Giving me a look more disgusted than she had given any of the others, Matilda pulled Chetana away from the fire and they disappeared into the darkness together.

Chapter Fifteen

Now
Sophie

Kip digs his nails under the edge of the tin and peels off the lid. My mouth is dry and for once I am grateful that someone else is taking charge.

What am I hoping to see? Something that will resolve Matilda's death, once and for all? Or to explain why Matilda had hidden the tin, if that's what she had done?

Kip leans forward and my breath catches at the small stack of polaroid pictures. Even though I was certain they were in there, seeing them all these years later feels surreal. Kip carefully plucks the first polaroid out of the tin and places it on the table in front of us.

I immediately recognise the photo as one of me and Matilda in front of her hut. Despite the age of the camera, the quality of the image is good. It is an original selfie in every sense of the word: Matilda has turned the camera around and my face is pushed up next to hers, curly brown hair alongside straight blonde. I pull the photo towards me to get a better look.

The girl in the photo with the curly hair is unrecognisable to me. I look free in a way that I have never felt since. My cheek is squished against Matilda's and I am laughing loudly, my face pink from the sun. The fringe I had tried to experiment with is just growing out, so that it flicks upwards above my eyebrows. My teeth have not yet been straightened and whitened: they are still slightly crooked and their normal, unpolished shade. I look *happy*. When was the last time I laughed like that? I think of my company headshot: my salon-straightened, chin-length cut, my subtle but expensive make-up, the stiff, professional expression that says *I am fair, but firm*. Matilda would never have needed to fix her hair or her teeth; she was the stereotypical magazine-ready golden girl. In the shot, she is laughing, her thick blonde hair falling in front of her face, navy-blue eyes scrunched up against the sun. Matilda tanned much more easily than me, her skin a deep tawny brown. Behind us stands her bright yellow hut, freshly painted, the doors flung open in welcome.

'You look so happy,' Kip says quietly, echoing my thoughts. I don't respond. Being confronted with my sun-drenched, freer past, makes my stomach churn uncomfortably. It is almost impossible to comprehend that the girl is me.

'What is it we're looking for again?' Kip asks.

'I don't know . . . anything that might give us a clue about why she hid these. I can't see anything weird about this one, though.'

'Me neither.'

Carefully picking up the photo, I place it to the side as Kip removes the next photo from the tin.

This one is a shot of Matilda and her parents. Sheila is smiling, one hand on her hip. Next to her, Gary sweeps Matilda up in his muscular arms, his copper hair windswept, while she grins and waves at the camera. Whoever the photographer was had accidentally put their thumb over the lens so that there is a reddy-pinkish haze in one corner.

Kip leans forward to inspect the photo. For the first time, he looks sad.

'God, look at them. My dad says Sheila hasn't smiled again since that summer.'

'Your dad is Sheila's brother, right? I've forgotten his name.'

'Paul,' Kip supplements. 'Our families were always close. It's part of the reason my parents sold the hut, they couldn't stand the memories. Paul isn't my biological dad,' Kip adds. 'My mum was married for a bit to my actual dad. But he's as good as. He adopted me when I was five.'

I look at him in surprise.

'I didn't know that. So you and Tildy aren't blood related?'

'Not technically, no.'

Kip pushes the photo towards me so that I can study it closer. Sheila really is beautiful, her slim legs encased in frilly white shorts, one hip cocked like a professional model.

'Do you remember how uninterested the newspapers were in Tildy's death?' Kip asks suddenly, his eyes still fixed on the photo. 'I don't even think it made the front page. I remember how angry my dad was about it.'

Kip is right: it was surprising, really, the speed at which Matilda's death disappeared from the local news. How quickly the police and white-suited SOCOs had slid away, leaving nothing but boot prints in the sand and the fluttering edges of police tape, still clinging to wooden posts. For whatever reason, Tildy's death just wasn't quite *sensational* enough for the papers. Perhaps it was the lack of any juicy leads. Perhaps it was the suggestion that her head injury could have been caused by a fall after drinking too much. Or perhaps it was because Princess Diana died soon after and no one had any grief to spare for another beautiful blonde girl.

I look back at the photo in front of me and feel a sudden overwhelming ache for my childhood best friend. What would life have been like had she still been here? If I hadn't messed everything up that summer, and we had remained best friends into adulthood? Would we have bounced our babies out on our hut decks? Would it have been Tildy, rather than a bottle of wine, that picked me up after Nick left? Or perhaps he would never have gone; perhaps having Tildy around would have meant that my soft edges wouldn't have sharpened so much over the years and he wouldn't have ended up on the other side of the world.

'Let's carry on,' I say hurriedly, not wanting to think about *what ifs*.

The next photo is a blurry shot, of what looks like the sandbank at night. The moon is just visible, a tiny white dot, and to the right are the hazy flames of a bonfire. It is underexposed and oddly eerie; but there is nothing else to be seen in the black shadows of the shot. After squinting to check for hidden figures or clues, we move on.

The next photo is of Matilda and Gary, this time inside their hut: their daisy-print curtains can be seen in the background. Unlike the other photos, this one is slightly crumpled, as though it has been clenched in a fist. The camera is turned and held high, selfie style, showing only part of

Matilda, lounging on the sofa-bed, her blonde hair loose. In the background, a shirtless Gary has his back to the camera, seemingly oblivious to the photo being taken.

'That's my old shirt,' Kip says, pointing at Matilda's arm. The rolled-up shirtsleeve is an orange checked cotton, like an oversized lumberjack shirt. 'She was wearing it when she was found. I think the police still have it.'

'Did they ever find anything on it? Any DNA?'

Kip shakes his head as I place the photo onto the discarded pile.

'They tried back in '97, but they didn't find anything useful.'

'How do you know?'

'I've got a friend in the police force.'

'Have you?' I ask, interested. Kip nods.

'I used to ask for updates. The case is still technically open but because the police pretty much decided it was an accident, it hasn't been touched for years. I mean, it's not like they ever found anything suspicious, is it?'

I doubt the photos would be classed as suspicious: so far, there has been nothing to suggest anything untoward happened to Matilda. The choice of photos in the tin are apparently just a random collection from that summer.

Kip plucks another photo from the pile and places it in front of us. To my surprise, the photo is of Chetana. I try to quell the rising emotions that seeing her face brings. Chetana is standing in a hut kitchen. She appears to be unaware the camera is on her. Her thick dark hair fans out around her as she turns and her mouth is open, as if she was speaking when the picture was taken.

'That's Dev's younger sister,' Kip says, looking down at the photo.

'Yes. That's Chetana.'

Seeing Chetana's face stirs a sea of uncomfortable emotions. I don't want to think about why Matilda grew close to Chetana that summer, apparently feeling the need to find a new friend that wasn't me. The shame washes over me as though the whole thing was yesterday, not two decades ago. Determined to push those thoughts away, I reach for the tin at the same time as Kip does; his hand knocks against it, sending it skidding off the table and onto the floor with a clatter.

'Shit, sorry,' Kip says, as we both jump to our feet, looking around for the tin; it sits upended near the corner of the sofa, its lid gaping open like jaws. One polaroid has fallen to the ground. Kip reaches down and retrieves the tin and the photo.

'Is that all that was left?' I ask anxiously, walking around the table and looking around on the floor, but seeing no other fallen photos.

'I think so.'

As I straighten up, the room suddenly shifts sideways. My stomach lurches and small pinpricks of light burst in front of my eyes.

'Woah,' says Kip quickly, reaching out a hand to steady me. 'You've gone pale. Sit down.'

He helps me to the window seat and eyes me warily as I take a few deep breaths in and out to get rid of the nausea.

'I'm alright. Just stood up too fast.'

Kip doesn't look convinced.

'No offence, but you don't look great. What have you eaten today?'

The look on my face gives me away.

'Nothing? Right, let's get you some food.'

'Wait, what about the last photo?'

This could be it, I think. *The clue.* My heart pounds and for a moment, I hesitate. What if it reveals that Tildy's death wasn't an accident, after all? What then? Did I walk away from the sandbank all those years ago without even considering the possibility someone might have hurt her?

Kip sits down next to me, holding out the photo, which is now speckled with grains of sand.

It is a group shot from the summer of 1997. There are six of us sat outside Kip's green beach hut: me, Amy and Tom are at the front, our legs dangling over the edge of the deck. My face looks full of nervous excitement, flushed with the pleasure of being included. Behind us, Kip stands in front of the hut doors with his arm around Caitlin. Despite her grumpy expression, she still looks like she has stepped off the set of an old Levi's photoshoot. Dev is sat on a sun lounger, lifting a peace sign towards the camera. I feel a slight sinking feeling looking at the image: there is nothing here that would help find out what happened to Tildy, or indicate why the photos were hidden. Nothing but a reminder of what I hoped my whole summer would look like that year.

'There's nothing here, Soph,' Kip says gently, reflecting my thoughts. 'Come on let's get you some food.'

Swallowing against the lingering nausea, I pick up my handbag and slip the photos inside. Then I gingerly stand up and start moving around the hut, unplugging my phone charger and picking up my lip balm.

'What are you doing?' Kip asks.

'Getting ready,' I say, popping the lip balm and charger into my bag and making sure my purse and hairbrush are also in there. I open my purse to double-check the cash I have.

'Sophie, you're not climbing Mount Everest,' Kip replies, sounding slightly exasperated.

I look up automatically, my mouth already open in a waspish retort. Then I stop. Kip is standing in the doorway, looking exactly like Nick always did when he wanted to get on and I was triple-checking everything. Instead of arguing, I slip my phone and purse into my pocket and leave my handbag under the table.

As I follow Kip out of the hut and down the deck steps, I try to shake the uneasy feeling that has clung to me since I discovered the photos. The feeling that something was missed all those years ago.

And that twenty years later, the shadows have awoken.

Chapter Sixteen

Then
Chetana

Matilda slammed the sun-worn cards down triumphantly.

'BULLSHIT!'

I pressed a hand to my mouth to stifle a giggle.

'Shh, my parents will hear you!' They were meant to be on the water-taxi right now, going to the big supermarket in town, but I was still afraid they could be back at any moment.

'Oh please, they're going to be gone for ages,' Matilda said with all the confidence I would never possess. She dragged the messy pile of cards towards her and started reshuffling them for the next game. I watched her, still unable to believe she was really sat in my hut, or that she had come to my rescue last night at the bonfire. After leaving the headland, we had chatted for a while on the beach; Matilda had sworn loudly about Tom, which made me giggle. I knew Tom's comments should have upset me, but I was too grateful for Matilda's attention to care. If anything, I was thankful to him. This morning I had woken up assuming the night before would be a one-off, that today I would be back to being alone, but Matilda had turned up at my hut holding a pack of cards and settled herself at the table.

'Drink?' I asked, pushing my chair back.

Matilda nodded without looking up from shuffling, her tongue sticking out.

'Got any of that cherry fizz stuff left?'

'Yep.'

I rose from the table and headed across to the kitchen to get glasses and ice. I had noticed Matilda liked ice in her drinks. The three o'clock sun warmed the hut, sending long shafts of golden light across the floorboards. Inside, I felt equally as warm: having spent summer after summer alone, watching through the glass as others played and swam together, I couldn't believe Matilda was choosing to spend time with *me*.

As I was bashing the ice tray against the counter to get the ice cubes out, I spotted a familiar head of thick, brown curls walking along the beach. She was walking away from her own hut, towards Matilda's which was further along from mine. *Was she looking for Matilda?* I felt a surge of anxiety at the thought that my time with Matilda might be about to end. Would Matilda leave as soon as Sophie Douglas wanted to hang out with her?

I'd watched them both from afar for years, laughing and surfing together. Their friendship seemed impenetrable, a golden bubble. They never noticed me, looking out of the window at them. No one ever did.

As Sophie passed, she glanced up and saw Matilda sat in my hut. Matilda's eyes were still down, carefully dealing the cards into separate piles. Sophie's eyes flickered across to me, standing there holding two glasses. Her eyebrows raised in surprise and I suppressed a slight twinge of annoyance.

Would it be that much of a shock to see Matilda hanging out with me? *Yes, it would. And you know it.*

Matilda still hadn't looked up and Sophie seemed to be hesitating, apparently trying to decide what to do. *I could turn away, pretend I haven't seen her.* Too late: Sophie was already jumping up onto the deck and my stomach sank like a stone. She knocked lightly on the glass but stepped inside without waiting.

'Hey,' she said, glancing first at Matilda, then me.

Matilda looked up. A range of emotions flickered across her face when she saw Sophie, like a miniature movie screen: surprise, awkwardness . . . *guilt?* Then her face set coolly.

'Hi.'

There was a long, painful silence. My heart started beating uncomfortably. Sophie didn't seem to know what to do with herself, apparently not expecting this response from Matilda. I felt a sudden surge of guilt: Matilda was Sophie's friend, too. Maybe we could all be friends, like I had always wanted. I smiled at Sophie.

'We were just playing cards. Do you want to join? Do you like cherry fizz?'

Sophie looked at me with something akin to confusion. *Oh no. I've asked too many questions.*

'I'm fine, thanks. I was just looking for Tildy.'

Tildy. The sweet nickname rolled off her tongue so naturally, almost possessively. It was like an unspoken warning: *you are not in this club.* To my horror, my chin wobbled slightly. Suddenly, I felt like an intruder in my own hut, but there was nowhere else to go and I didn't want to draw any more attention to myself. Anxiety started to build, making my chest constrict: I shouldn't have tried to be friends with Matilda, I was out of my depth.

'I'm sorry about last night,' Sophie suddenly said. I looked up, surprised, but saw that she was looking at Matilda, not me. 'Tom was being a dick.' *Wait. Hadn't I been the one Tom was nasty to?*

'He *is* a dick,' Matilda said shortly. There was a silence for a second, but then a reluctant smile spread across her face. Sophie returned the smile, looking relieved.

'I was just going to go down to the shop,' Sophie continued. 'You coming?'

Please don't go.

'Sounds good,' Matilda replied, standing up. She looked over at me. 'Do you want to come?'

For a moment, I hesitated; but then I saw the unenthusiastic look on Sophie's face. It was obvious she hadn't expected Matilda to invite me, too. I turned and started putting the glasses and ice tray away, clumsy in my haste.

'No thanks . . . my parents will be back soon and they'll want me to help with dinner,' I said, trying to sound cheerful. Matilda would have got bored and left eventually, anyway. Maybe it was best she left before I got too used to having company.

'Okay . . .' Matilda said slowly. But she was watching me, as though trying to figure out what I was thinking. Sophie was looking impatient, but slightly triumphant, too. I took a deep breath and plastered a smile across my face.

'It was nice to see you.' *Nice to see you?* I sounded so formal, so . . . The word the boys all called me at school flitted horribly through my mind.

87

Frigid.

Matilda walked across to where Sophie stood.

'Are you *sure* you don't want to come too, Chet?'

Chet. An actual nickname. There was nothing false about my smile, this time. It was as though the sun had burst right inside the hut and into my chest.

'No, honestly, it's fine. I've got stuff to do.'

But as I watched them go, arm in arm, looking like a perfect set of beach girls, the happiness from Matilda's nickname faded. I looked down at my own arms, where goosebumps had appeared across my skin. I pulled one of the black hairs on my forearm, so hard that it stung.

Walking across to the table where Matilda had sat, I slowly gathered the two piles of cards she had dealt into one, solo pile. As I did, the door opened. I turned around, hope springing up that Matilda had returned – but it was Dev. I hadn't seen him since the night before and what had happened at the bonfire hung awkwardly in the air between us. I was hurt that he hadn't defended me, but I wasn't really surprised. He slouched over to the fridge and pulled out a Coke can.

'What were those two doing here?' he asked, opening the can which gave a low hiss.

'Just hanging out,' I replied. It was half-true. Dev raised his eyebrows in surprise.

'So you've actually managed to find some friends? You won't be following me around anymore?'

'I didn't *follow you*,' I snapped. 'You know I didn't want to be there last night. It wasn't my fault.' Mum had forced Dev to take me with him, completely oblivious to what he and the others actually got up to on the headland.

Dev only shrugged. 'Whatever. Just don't mess it up and act all weird. It's hard enough fitting in down here without you being socially incompetent.'

Hot, embarrassed tears bubbled to the surface. I knew Dev wanted to fit in, but I did, too. I sniffed, not wanting Dev to know he had upset me, but I had already lost his attention: he was focused on something outside, his expression suddenly softer. I glanced out of the doors and saw Caitlin walking along the beach in a yellow bikini, her blonde hair rippling behind her.

'You'll never have her, you know,' I said coldly, gripped by a sudden desire to hurt Dev back. 'Dad will never allow it.' She was too blonde, too provocative. She wasn't Hindu, her dad was an *alcoholic*. Dev turned to look at me, his eyes steely.

'I've got more chance than you,' he replied.

Chapter Seventeen

Now

Sophie

Kip and I emerge from my hut and the afternoon sun momentarily dazzles me, so that small fiery suns are branded on the inside of my eyelids. It is a beautiful day we have been missing, tucked in the darkness with Matilda's tin of photos. The smell of charcoal drifts across the beach as we step down from the deck and start walking along the sand.

We walk in silence for a few minutes until we draw near Kip's old sage-green hut, standing alongside the Halls' forlorn yellow one. I avert my gaze, but Kip stops.

'Hang on, I just need to change.'

He gestures to the board shorts and rash vest he's been wearing since we bumped into each other this morning. Instead of his hut, however, he approaches the Halls' hut.

'Why are you going in there?' I ask sharply.

Kip looks over his shoulder at me, confused.

'I told you earlier, my parents sold our hut, so Sheila and Gary let me use theirs whenever I need it. They don't stay much anymore. You can hardly blame them.'

Kip takes the deck stairs two at a time and unlocks the doors as I stand awkwardly on the beach. Although Kip had told me his family had sold their hut, it never occurred to me he would be staying *here*.

'Come in,' Kip calls over his shoulder. I open my mouth to protest, but Kip has already disappeared inside the hut.

Slowly, I walk up the steps, my hand on the deck railing. The paint is peeling away and small flecks embed themselves into my palm. I try not to look too closely at the deck, at the many hot chocolate stains and the scuff marks from when Tildy and I begged for scooters and tried to practise jumps on the deck.

My chest constricts as I step inside the Halls' hut. It is the first time I've been inside since Matilda's death and the disorientating feeling of time having not passed is overwhelming: the hut looks almost exactly the same as it did twenty years ago. The ornaments lining the windowsills are all the same: painted rocks, pearly shells, Matilda's old hacky sacks in the shape of puffins. The puffins all have little grey halos of dust on top of them, as though they, too, have grown old. The butterscotch paint Matilda insisted her parents use on the inside of the hut looks tired and dated. I swallow a lump in my throat.

'Are you okay?' Kip asks quietly, pausing on his way to the mezzanine ladder towards the back of the hut.

'Yes.' To my embarrassment, my eyes start to burn. 'It's just – it's like it never happened. Everything looks the same.'

'I know. I've tried for years to get Sheila to redecorate, but she doesn't want to change anything.'

'How can you stand to stay here?' I ask, without thinking. I immediately regret opening my mouth, but Kip looks unruffled; he simply shrugs.

'It wasn't easy, at first, but I got used to it.' He looks around, with a sad sort of smile. 'The huts aren't meant to stand empty and neglected, they're meant to have people in them. I don't have my own hut anymore and I don't want to see it fall into disrepair just because Gary and Sheila are never here.'

I nod, as though I understand, but I don't. Kip might want to remain at the beach, but if that means living out of a hut that doubles up as a shrine, I would have left a long time ago.

Kip disappears up the ladder and I can hear him getting changed on the mezzanine level above, while I stand unmoving, still trying to take it all in. Matilda feels so *close* all of a sudden, like I could reach out and touch her. Everywhere I look brings up a new memory: the table and chairs where we spent hours and hours playing Gin Rummy or making jewellery. One year, we begged our parents for glittery electronic secret diaries and sat on the window box, typing our deepest thoughts into them. We called them *sea-crets* because we were by the sea and thought it was clever. My face heats up when I think about how many of mine involved Kip, even at that age. Then, as we got older, we would sit out on the wooden deck with books and magazines, trying to make our hair blonder with lemon juice. Nights would be spent wrapped up on the sofa-bed in our pyjamas, watching Gary's tiny portable TV because we didn't want to miss the *Fresh Prince of Bel Air*: especially since we had learnt all the words to the opening song. I never had another friendship like the one I had with Tildy. She was fierce, funny, loyal. Everything I wasn't.

Kip emerges, now dressed in a navy T-shirt and cargo shorts. He stands next to me as I look at a photo on the windowsill of me and Tildy, clutching our first surfboards when we were eight. All of a sudden I can't breathe.

'I need some air.'

Crossing to the doors, I hurry out of the hut and gulp in the fresh, salty air. A movement catches my eye: further down the beach, the doors of the pink and white striped hut have slammed shut.

Kip appears behind me.

'She's still here, you know,' he says, looking in the direction of my gaze.

I don't need to ask who he means. Chetana hasn't left the sandbank.

Chapter Eighteen

Now

Sophie

Kip insists on getting something to eat from the Boat House, the only restaurant on the sandbank. We are given a table outside on the wraparound deck, overlooking the quiet harbour. The afternoon sunlight glints off the smooth expanse of water, dotted with dinghies and thin, graceful kingfishers. It is stunning, but I can't concentrate.

Kip gestures at my burger with his own, half-eaten one. 'I promise you won't get better than that in London.'

I have no appetite, but I reluctantly pick up the burger and take a bite. He isn't wrong: the burger is seriously good.

'When was the last time you ate?' Kip asks.

I try to think back to when I last had a proper meal, but the past few days are one exhausted blur. It is surreal to think I have only been back on the sandbank for two days.

'I don't know,' I admit, swallowing a bite of burger. 'I ordered sushi the other day . . .' I don't add that I got called into a last-minute meeting and the sushi remained untouched on my desk.

'You Londoners,' Kip shakes his head. 'The only sushi you'll get around here is when Ben forgets to cook the scampi properly.'

We eat in silence for the next few minutes and before I know it, my plate is empty. For the first time in days, I am pleasantly full, and I lean back, stifling a yawn. I watch the water-taxi slowly chugging across the harbour with a few late visitors to the sandbank and wonder if I should ask Kip about his life. He mentioned an ex, the emergency contact when he was mugged, but is he still single? Married? Surely not, or else he would have mentioned them by now, wouldn't he? I've not seen him with a phone, texting anyone. Before I can say anything, however, Kip leans forward and speaks in a lowered voice.

'So, what do you think about the photos? Do you still think they were hidden on purpose?'

'I don't know,' I admit. 'They *do* seem innocent. Just us guys, hanging out. But . . .' I tail off, trying to decide what I want to say. 'Do we even know what we're *looking* for? I mean, what if the police know something that we don't? Something they might spot in the photos?'

'I'm not sure,' Kip replies. 'The police never seemed to have a clue about anything.' He squints against the sun, then glances across at me. 'Let's face it, I'm not sure a selfie of you two is going to solve the case.'

'So you think there's a case?'

He knows what I am really asking, what we have been dancing around all day. Whether Tildy really did slip on those rocks, or whether there was something more to that night . . . something we all chose to turn our back on. Kip leans an elbow on the table and rests his chin in his palm.

'Honestly, Sophie, I don't know. That's been the hardest part of all this. Gary and Sheila have never known whether they're supposed to be moving on from a tragic accident or hunting for a killer. Everyone decided it was an accident, but no one knows what actually happened.'

'What do *you* think happened?' I press. Kip looks out at the harbour. It's a few moments before he replies.

'I don't know. There's never been any reason to think someone might have hurt Tildy. But . . .'

'But what?'

He meets my gaze and his blue eyes, older than they were but just as bright, are creased with frustration and pain. Realisation dawns on me that I was so buried in my own pain, I hadn't thought about the effect Tildy's death must have had on someone like Kip, a family member who loved her as much as anyone else.

'She knew those rocks better than anyone,' he says, simply.

We pay the bill and walk slowly, silently, back to my hut. The sun has lowered in the sky, casting a golden glow across the beach and making the windows of the huts flash. It suddenly occurs to me I haven't thought about work once all afternoon. The slight headache that often stabs behind my eyes around this time in the afternoon is also absent.

When we reach my hut, I push down the handle and the door swings open. The moment I step inside, I know something is wrong.

At first glance, everything looks the same as when we left; but there is a rumpled look to the scene, as though the entire hut has been lifted up and shaken. The chair has moved a fraction, the woollen blanket carelessly flung across the window bench.

'What's wrong?' Kip asks from behind me, as I stand stock-still just beyond the threshold.

'Someone's been here.'

My voice is low, afraid they could still be concealed somewhere. Straining my ears, I listen for the creak of a floorboard, the sound of someone else breathing.

Slowly, Kip steps past me into the hut and reaches carefully for the chunky black torch that lives on the windowsill. The batteries will be long dead, but I don't think Kip needs it for its light. He grips it in his right hand and silently creeps towards the breakfast bar. I want to whisper to him to be careful, but my throat has closed up. Rooted to the spot, I watch as he peers slowly around the corner of the breakfast bar.

A second later Kip exhales softly and I know there is no one crouching in the kitchen, waiting to pounce. He starts moving to the room at the back, his footfall surprisingly light. There is no door, just a curtain. Kip reaches out and pulls back the curtain a fraction. He pauses for a moment in the threshold, then sweeps the curtain right back.

'There's no one here.'

At these words, I let out a shaky breath. Once my heart has stopped racing, I start moving around the hut, turning on lamps as quickly as possible so as to chase away the shadows.

'Tea?'

'Have you got anything stronger?' Kip asks, as he puts the torch down. I nod and reach for one of the wine bottles I brought with me to the hut.

'Why did you think someone was here?' Kip asks, leaning against the breakfast bar as I pour the wine into two glasses. My hand trembles slightly, making the bottle neck clink against the rim of the glass.

'I don't know, I just got this weird feeling . . . things just seemed a little out of place.' Handing Kip his glass I look around, frowning. 'I'm sure that's not where I left the blanket.'

Saying it out loud sounds stupid, like I'm being overly obsessive. But I have an eye for this kind of thing. I *know* where things were last left, where I put things.

'Was the hut locked?'

'No, you saw, I just—' I stop.

'What?' Kip puts his wine glass down and moves around the breakfast bar towards me. 'What is it?'

Pushing past him, I pull my handbag out from under the table and feel inside the front pocket. My fingers scrabble against the silk lining but find nothing.

The pocket is empty. The photos are gone.

Chapter Nineteen

Then

Sophie

I flew up to the hut from the beach, finding my parents and Anna sat on the deck playing Monopoly.

'Hi love,' Mum greeted me as I skidded to a halt in front of them. She was sipping peppermint tea, the teabag string fluttering in the breeze.

'What's the rush?' she asked, taking in my red face.

'The waves are huge!' I said breathlessly, already reaching for my rash vest. Pulling it over my head, I looked down at the board scattered with houses and property cards.

'Who's winning?'

'I am,' Anna said, seriously, 'but Dad keeps trying to cheat.'

'I do not!' Dad cried, in mock outrage. 'All I'm saying is that I deal with money for a living, there are better investments to be made . . .'

'It's a *game*,' Anna said slowly, as though she was talking to a child.

I felt a sudden rush of affection for my family. They weren't the richest, or the most exciting, and we had curfews and rules that annoyed me, but they were kind of cool, in a weird way.

'I'm going to get Tildy,' I said as I wrestled with my wet-suit. 'She'll want to see this surf. By the way, Kip's mum is having a birthday party next weekend. She said to invite you. All the parents are going. Gary and Sheila are going to bring *lobster*!'

'Oh,' Dad said, frowning down at the board. 'Sorry, Soph, I'm back at home next weekend. Got some work to do.'

'No you're not,' Anna interrupted. 'You were going to take me kayaking next weekend, remember?'

Dad hesitated and his face turned weirdly blotchy.

'Right. Well, we'll see how next week looks, okay?'

He looked up and saw me staring at him. His face softened.

'I just prefer spending my time with you guys. Not drinking with a load of newbies.' He winked across at Anna.

'Dad, they aren't *newbies*, they've had their hut longer than *you*,' I interjected, annoyed that he would criticise Kip's parents.

'I know, I know,' Dad said, picking up his wine. 'I just mean they don't do it properly. All that fancy furniture and kit. They have a hot water tap, for heaven's sake. It's basically like being at home.'

'Can we *play* now, please?' Anna asked, annoyed. 'This game already takes forever.'

Picking up my board, I left them to it and ran along the beach towards Tildy's hut. When I arrived, I dropped my board on the deck and hurried through the open doors to the yellow hut, not bothering to knock.

'Hi sweetie,' Sheila greeted me. She was standing at the kitchen island preparing some sort of salad with fresh prawns and lemon juice. A bottle of white wine was open next to her. It wasn't even the *afternoon* yet: adults got to do whatever they wanted.

'Hey, Mrs Hall.' I looked around the sunny hut. 'Where's Matilda?'

'I think she popped to the toilet; she'll be back in a minute. Are you staying for lunch?' Sheila asked, rinsing off the prawn slime under the tap. I shook my head.

'No thanks, I was just coming to get Tildy for a surf.'

'Well, what are you doing later? Why don't you stay for dinner?'

'Oh . . .' I shuffled my bare feet on the floor uncomfortably. 'Thanks, but I, uhh, have plans.'

Sheila raised an eyebrow.

'Plans that involve the headland?'

I looked up in surprise. *How did she know?*

'Is that wise? It's steep up there.'

I had to stop myself rolling my eyes.

'It's really safe, Mrs Hall. We just get a good view of the beach.'

'Hmm . . . and the inside of a beer bottle, I imagine.'

My face flushed with the accuracy of Sheila's words. I floundered for a moment, unsure of what to say. My mum would never actually *say* it, just openly like that.

Sheila finished washing her hands and turned back to face me.

'Look, hon, it's not my place to tell you what to do. God knows I got up to all sorts at your age.'

Her expression was worried, her brow creased.

'I just want you to be careful, okay? You're like a daughter to us and I know you've been hanging around with Kip and some of the older kids . . . Kip's a good boy, but I just want you to be careful—' Sheila was interrupted by Gary walking into the hut.

'Sophie!' Gary said, giving my shoulder a squeeze. He was wearing the bright yellow T-shirt Matilda got him for his birthday, emblazoned with the words '*Mad as a Hutter*'.

'Hi, Mr Hall.' I turned to Sheila, itching to get out to the sea now.

'Thanks for the offer of dinner. Maybe tomorrow?'

I waved at them both and hurried out of the hut. I would have to try and hunt Tildy down. It was our rule: when there was good surf, we had to make sure the other one knew before we even *thought* about stepping into the water.

Jumping down from the deck, I left my board on the sand and ran all the way to the toilet block. To my disappointment, it was empty. *Where was she?* I turned and raced back along the beach. A few seconds later, I spotted someone walking towards me with a surfboard under one arm. *Tildy!* Even from this distance, her hair stood out like liquid gold under the sun.

I ran towards her, arriving so fast I sprayed sand everywhere. She looked surprised, but she smiled.

'Hey, Fee.'

'I've been looking for you everywhere!' I cried. 'Have you seen the surf? We've got to go!' I reached out and tugged on her hand, about to pull her along with me, but she didn't move. Her smile faltered slightly.

'Sorry, Fee. I'm meeting Chetana. I was going to teach her how to surf.'

My stomach gave a weird flip and I dropped her hand.

'Oh.'

Matilda looked uncomfortable.

'I just assumed you were with the others.'

There was a long pause.

'Why don't you come, too?' she asked, brightening. 'It'll be fun, and you're a really good teacher. Chet'll be standing in no time.'

I plastered a smile on my face.

'That's okay, I, uhh actually haven't had lunch so I'll get some and maybe join you later if you're still out. Bye!'

I hurried away, trying to ignore the sinking feeling in my stomach. Something felt different, as though the tide was changing, pulling us away on different currents. *Stop being dramatic,* I told myself as I walked along the sand. *You can see her tomorrow.*

Even though I didn't want to, I turned and looked back at Tildy. She was on the deck of Chetana's hut, chatting to her. Suddenly, Chetana's large dark eyes locked with mine over Matilda's shoulder. For a moment, I stopped, unable to move. Then I tore my gaze away and carried on alone down the beach.

Chapter Twenty

Now

Sophie

'Someone knows.'

Turning away from the drawer, I start upending the hut, searching under the sofa cushions and blankets for any sign of the tin. *We must have missed something.*

'Sophie, calm down—'

'No, Kip! Someone's been here, they must know something!'

The thought that someone has been in my hut while I am gone, their hands moving through my things while they search for the photos makes me feel sick.

'Someone's been watching us,' I say, turning back to Kip. He stares at me for a moment, as though he is only just realising the magnitude of the situation.

'Shit. You're *sure* you left them in your bag?'

'I'm positive.' Still, I go around emptying out kitchen drawers of all their various contents, even though I know I didn't leave the tin in any of them: rolls of twine, yellowing Sellotape, spare padlock keys scatter across the work surface. No tin.

'I knew I should have taken them with me, I *knew* it,' I glare at Kip, furious at him for his suggestion that I only bring my purse. *This is what happens when you're careless.*

'What about Gary and Sheila's hut?' Kip asks. 'Maybe you had them with you when I was getting changed and you didn't realise.'

'I didn't, I'm sure . . .'

Am I? Did I definitely put them in my bag, or was it my pocket?

We hurry outside and along the darkening beach towards the Halls' hut, where Kip is staying. Deep down I know it is pointless, that I left the tin in my bag, but there is still a burning hope, as with all lost things, that I am wrong. That I left them in the Halls' hut and somehow forgot.

Five minutes later, we are left panting and empty-handed. The tin is nowhere to be seen.

'Someone's taken them,' I say, pressing a hand to my temple, which has started to throb.

'We don't know that—'

'Yes, we *do* Kip! Don't try and tell me it's a coincidence that the photos were hidden and the second we find them, they've suddenly disappeared again!' My voice is shrill. *How could I have left the hut unlocked?* For some reason, Kip's calm attitude is making me even angrier.

'We should have just taken them to the police,' I say furiously. 'I *knew* we should have done.'

'Sophie, stop. You're jumping to all sorts of conclusions here. There could easily be an innocent explanation for all of this. You could have dropped them, it could have been kids stealing stuff—'

'It's a designer bag and there was cash in it, there's no way it was a random break-in! Someone wanted Tildy's photos and now they've got them. What are we going to do? Kip?'

But Kip isn't looking at me anymore: he is looking past me, his eyes wide. Turning, I inhale sharply.

Sheila Hall is standing in the doorway, her face shadowy in the twilight behind her.

Chapter Twenty-One

Now

Sophie

Sheila slowly steps into the hut, not taking her eyes off me. 'What photos, Sophie?' she asks quietly. Her voice is throaty: a worn-out version of what it was before, when she would pretend to scold me and Matilda for treading wet sand into the hut or for leaving our wet towels on the sofa.

Panicked, I glance across at Kip for help, but he has a resigned look on his face. Sheila doesn't wait for my response.

'You found her tin, didn't you?'

I nod. Sheila's hand flies to her mouth.

'You've found it,' she whispers, 'after all this time.'

For a moment I think she is going to fall; she touches a hand to the windowsill. But then she walks forward and reaches out, wrapping her arms around me tightly. Kip catches my eye across Sheila's head, looking as uncomfortable as I feel. I give Sheila a small pat on the back. She always had a delicate frame, but now she is even smaller, like she could blow away.

'It's so good to see you again,' Sheila says, breaking away from me. She holds a trembling hand to my cheek. 'I missed you for a long time . . . afterwards.'

I don't know what to say, but Sheila doesn't seem to need me to say anything. She starts walking around the hut and turning on the lamps, giving everything a warm, sedate glow. A moth flickers around one of the bulbs.

Sheila sits down at the table and gestures for us to do the same. 'What are you doing back here? How did you find her tin? Please . . . tell me everything.'

With another quick glance at Kip, I start telling Sheila about returning to the hut, about looking for my dad's old ladder and finding the tin balanced on the rim under the hut. As I speak, she reaches for a small bottle of medicine on the table and shakes two pills into her hand, before popping them into her mouth.

The hardest part is explaining how the photos are gone. Sheila's eyes widen and she absent-mindedly bites down on her thumb.

'But *who*?' she croaks, looking between us both. 'Who would do that?'

'We don't know. Anyone could have been watching us, seen the tin. Anyone with a connection to Tildy, or that summer.'

'Or it was just a random theft,' Kip interrupts pointedly. I glare at him, then turn back to Sheila.

'We didn't know what to do next.'

'It's obvious, isn't it?' Sheila says, her eyes fixed on me once again. For the first time, colour has risen in her pale cheeks, two spots of pink high on her cheekbones.

'You have to find the photos. If someone took them, it could be because they know something about what happened to her.' Her voice trembles and I shoot another look at Kip, who walks over and kneels in front of Sheila, taking her hands in his.

'Sheila, I understand why you want to find the photos, I really do. But we *saw* them. They looked innocent to us. Please don't get your hopes up that this might give you answers.'

'Twenty years,' she says, looking down at Kip. '*Twenty years* of not knowing, of wondering what happened.'

'It was an *accident*,' Kip begins, but Sheila is shaking her head.

'No, everyone just *wanted* it to have been an accident. They wanted me to be quiet and move on, because that was easier for everyone else. But all I could think was what if it *wasn't* an accident? What if someone hurt her? Why else would her photos have gone missing?' She pulls her hands from Kip's and looks out at the beach, at the gold-flecked waves.

'I was asleep, did you know that?'

Confused, I glance at Kip: he, on the other hand, looks slightly frustrated, as though he has heard this story many times before.

'The night she died,' Sheila continues. 'She was later than usual and I was waiting up for her, the same way I always did.'

I feel a cold stab of guilt, thinking about Sheila waiting up for Tildy. About why she was out later than usual.

'I was sat right over there, on the sofa, looking out for her. Then . . . I fell asleep. I didn't care enough about my own daughter's safety not to *sleep*.'

She presses a hand against the side of her head, still staring out at the waves.

'At night, I see her just before she died . . . my poor brave girl, alone out on those rocks in the darkness. I knew I was right not to leave here. I *knew*.'

She looks up, her eyes black as coals.

'Promise me,' she whispers. 'Promise me you'll find whoever took those photos.' Her eyes slide back to the waves. 'For her.'

Chapter Twenty-Two

Now
Sophie

I leave Kip to look after Sheila and step out of the yellow hut, my mind racing. It is a warm, sedate evening; the sky over the beach threaded with pinks and golds. All along the sandbank, smoke from barbecues and fires curls slowly into the air. For a moment I long to be part of the barbecuing families, whose only concern right now is when the coals would be hot enough to cook on, or how late their children should be allowed to stay up. I can't get Sheila's face out of my head. Kip had said she was starting to move on, but all I saw was a broken woman. A woman who wants me to find her daughter's photos. *Am I willing to do that?* I wasn't planning on staying down here for more than a couple of days, but Sheila's words cling to me, the way smoke clings to clothing after a bonfire: '*Promise me you'll find whoever took those photos. For her.*' I failed Tildy once already, that night. If I leave, will I be failing her again? More than anything else, though, I am afraid. I don't want to lift the veil and find out that Tildy's death wasn't an accident: that I had disappeared, got on with my own life, without bothering to question what happened.

The striped pink and white hut is to my right as I walk along the beach. The hut is in perfect condition, exactly as it was twenty years ago. The paint is fresh, the wooden deck's railings are smooth and varnished, no chips from surfboards or scuffs from the dragging of feet. It is a hut that I never even noticed until the summer of 1997.

As I draw alongside, I spot a lone figure in the window. I remember Kip's words.

She's still here, you know.

She is seated at the table inside, reading a book. Though her head stays bowed, I notice a shift in her posture as I get closer. Emotion surges through me at the sight of her: anger, bitterness, guilt. Everything I used to feel about her, convinced she was stealing my best friend away. Convinced that she was the reason that things had changed between Matilda and me.

Before I am even conscious of making the decision, I am walking towards the hut and up the deck steps. My heart racing slightly, I knock on the door.

Inside, Chetana carefully folds the dust jacket around the page she was reading and places the book on the table before standing and opening the door.

'Sophie,' she says quietly. Her voice is light, almost childlike.

'Chetana, hi.'

She gives me a long look.

'You remember me, then.'

'Of course I remember you,' I reply. *How could I have forgotten?*

Chetana looks almost exactly the same as she did when I last saw her. Still small and petite, birdlike in her delicacy.

Her thick hair is longer, pulled back in a low bun, and she wears a loose T-shirt with linen trousers.

There is a long pause. It is obvious that Chetana does not want me here.

'How are you?' I ask, eventually.

'I'm fine, thank you. I saw you were back . . .' she trails off, not looking at me. There is another long, painful silence while Chetana remains standing in her hut, me on the threshold. Eventually, she seems to sense that I am not going anywhere.

'Do you want a drink? I've got some wine somewhere, though I don't think it's chilled.' Her tone is half-hearted, no doubt hoping I will say no.

'That would be great.'

Chetana turns and disappears inside the hut without inviting me in. I move across to the edge of the deck, looking out over the horizon. Seeing Chetana again is as awkward as it was between us as teenagers. If I felt on the edge of the social periphery, Chetana stood even further back than I did.

Chetana returns to the deck a moment later with the drinks, in tumblers. She places them on the table and we both sit down. There is another long silence while I try and think of some way to question her without being obvious.

'I'm sorry I'm being so rude,' she says suddenly, her voice slightly breathless. 'I sort of hide away down here outside term time and apparently I've forgotten how to talk to another human being.'

I pick up the tumbler and take a sip. Though the wine is tepid, it slips easily down my throat.

'Are you staying for long?' Chetana asks, not touching her own drink.

'Just a couple of days.' Do I imagine it, or does relief flash briefly across Chetana's face? If so, it is gone by the time I lower my tumbler.

'I'm just here –' I hesitate for a moment, trying to remember *why* I'm here, why I thought any of this was a good idea, '– to clear out the hut, ready to sell. My parents haven't been down in a long time and there's a lot of things that need sorting.'

Chetana nods and takes a small sip of her drink. Even that reminds me of a robin or a starling, taking small sips from a bird bath.

'I was sorry to hear about your father,' she says. 'Harry told me. I remember him from when we were young. He was very friendly.'

My throat clenches unexpectedly.

'Dad was definitely friendly,' is all I can manage. I take another large gulp of my drink.

'Was it an illness?'

'Yes.' To my relief, my voice sounds steadier. 'Bowel cancer. It was quick.'

'I'm very sorry,' Chetana says again.

We silently watch a group of birdwatchers pass by the hut, binoculars dangling from leather straps around their necks, books in hand. One of them says good evening to us and the rest all smile and nod. How normal the scene must look to them: two friends sat outside with drinks, enjoying the evening air.

'You said term time . . .' I venture, trying to get Chetana talking. 'Are you a teacher, now?'

Something in Chetana's face shifts, as though the sun has just emerged from behind a cloud: clearly, she loves her job.

'I'm a lecturer in orthopaedic biomechanics.' The pride in her voice is evident, something that was non-existent in the meek girl from twenty years ago.

'That's impressive. Your parents must be proud.'

'They are,' Chetana nods, then gives me a wry smile. 'Then again, Dev is a barrister now.'

'Your brother?' I ask, thinking of the tall sixteen-year-old boy.

'Don't you remember him?' Chetana asks. 'I'm surprised. You spent a lot of time with him . . . that summer.'

The atmosphere suddenly becomes charged. I look over at Chetana, my scalp prickling uncomfortably. The topic hangs over our heads like a storm cloud. I wonder if Chetana is goading me: reminding me how I chose Dev and the others over Matilda.

'We did hang out,' I say evenly, 'but it was such a long time ago, and we weren't close. Just in the same group, for that one summer. Does he come down much?'

Chetana shakes her head, unsmiling.

'Almost never. These days he's more of an all-inclusive resort kind of person.'

This surprises me: the teenage Dev was the epitome of a beach bum, just like Kip. Then again, we all seem to have changed.

There is another long pause, during which the silence seems to balloon between us like the perfect swell of a wave before it breaks. Chetana's eyes give nothing away, but her hand clutches her tumbler. *Does she know something about the tin? Or that summer?*

'I saw Sheila Hall just now,' I say, studying Chetana for a reaction. 'She doesn't seem to think Matilda's death was an accident.'

This has the desired effect: Chetana stops drinking and stares at me.

'Not an accident?' Her voice is strained. 'What makes her think that?'

I shrug, trying to sound casual. 'She just has questions over what happened that summer. I think lots of people do.'

'I don't understand . . . the investigation ended twenty years ago.'

Chetana looks agitated. My heart beating faster, I take another sip of wine.

'I just thought maybe over time they would have re-examined it, you know?' I reply. 'They do that a lot with unsolved cases.'

'It was an accident. There would be no need to re-examine it.' Chetana puts down her almost full glass: it hits the table too hard, clanging against the wrought iron.

'I forgot,' I lie, keeping my voice even. 'You knew Matilda a bit, didn't you?'

There is a long pause where Chetana stares at me with an unfathomable expression.

'Yes. I knew her,' she says, eventually.

I open my mouth, about to ask what she remembers of that summer, but Chetana stands abruptly, her chair scraping behind her.

'Sorry, but I've really got to get on. Good luck with the hut sale.'

Her tone leaves no room for argument. Reluctantly, I get up, too.

'Thanks for the drink.'

She doesn't reply. I turn and walk down the deck steps, leaving her standing there. After a moment, she disappears inside her hut and the blinds snap shut.

I walk slowly along the beach, replaying the conversation. That wasn't a normal reaction, I am sure of it. *Is it because she's hiding something? Or simply because that summer left scars on her, too?* One thing is certain: Chetana might look almost exactly the same as the girl from my past, but something has changed. There is a hardness now, that seems to radiate from her. Chetana might still be alive, but the girl from that summer is as dead as Matilda.

I watch her silhouette through the curtains as she gets into bed, then turns the light out.

Slowly, I turn to the tin resting on the table. It is cold to the touch. My skin prickles. I thought it was over. I thought any evidence was gone. At least, I reason, I can finally get rid of it. I no longer need to worry about it being discovered. It's a good thing, really.

My hands tremble slightly as I prise open the tin. The lid swings open and I pluck the first polaroid from it, the edge as sharp as a knife.

Five minutes later, I am left staring down at the tin. It isn't here. There is a ringing in my ears. I know it was in here, watched her put it in here that day.

So where is it now?

Chapter Twenty-Three

1982

Sheila

'I spoke to Clive this morning,' Gary said as he entered the hut, running a hand excitedly through his copper curls. His hair flopped immediately back to where it was, catching the sunlight and turning molten amber. I felt a familiar creep of foreboding. Not another business idea. Not that Clive, *again*. My chest began to tighten; I glanced at the small bottle of pills I always kept on the counter.

'What did he say?' I asked reluctantly, because I didn't really want to know. Clive never had anything to say that benefited Gary or our family. I continued chopping the peppers for dinner, focusing on the crunch as the knife sliced through the flesh.

'He's got a great new venture lined up, Shiels, something really exciting.'

That's what he said about those rare snakes. And the un-labelled meat joints. I kept chopping. *Should I roast, or fry the peppers? Salt, or marinade?* The tightening in my chest was getting worse.

'Mattresses. He's got a load of stock from a mate whose business burned down. Some of them are a bit damaged, but they're top of the range, you won't get them cheaper.'

I finally looked up from the peppers: Gary was fired up, his eyes wide and excited. He wasn't asking my permission, not really. He was just telling me. He started explaining in detail about the mattresses that Clive had somehow wrangled from his desperate mate.

Gary's enthusiasm was what first stole my heart: he'd arrived on my doorstep one day in the middle of February, selling a magazine subscription. It was pouring with rain and when I opened the door, he was dripping wet from head to toe, his coat soaked through to his shirt. I knew immediately from his briefcase that he was a salesman, and I tried to think of a polite enough excuse so I could shut the door, but something stopped me; despite his sodden appearance, Gary didn't seem to notice anything except me: the customer. Beaming at me, he explained all about the magazine in one minute flat. As he spoke, I noticed the strong line of his jaw and his bright, piercing eyes. Eventually, I relented and let him in to dry off. Despite tracking muddy footprints across my mother's antique Venetian rug – and despite the magazine being *Petrolhead Weekly Digest* – we sat on the squeaky Chesterfield sofa for hours. I was completely smitten, though my mother and father were less than thrilled.

It was that same passion I saw in Gary as he stood before me, the same passion he had for *all* our decisions and adventures. It was why I loved him so fiercely: I knew he would be this enthusiastic about what to have for dinner, what to name our children. The problem – as my mother liked to sniffly point out as she handed over another cheque – was that '*passion doesn't pay the bills, dear*'.

'. . . do you think? It'll be different this time. I've got a really good feeling,' Gary finished, looking at me expectantly.

Maybe he's right. If at first you don't succeed, try, try again.

Behind him, the evening tide was just starting to wane, receding from the shoreline. I put the knife down and slowly wiped my hands on my apron. Then I walked around the tiny breakfast bar and put my arms around him.

'I think it's a great idea,' I said, standing on tiptoe and kissing his smooth-shaven cheek. I loved how his skin smelt down at the beach: it was different somehow, like it had absorbed the sweet saltiness of the sea air.

'Ahh, you're one in a million, Shiels, you know that?' Gary pulled back and looked down at me, his eyes blazing with something else, now. 'I'm the luckiest guy in the world.'

I flushed with pleasure and ducked my head. Gary leaned in and began trailing kisses along my neck.

'Any . . . news?' he murmured into the soft spot behind my ear.

'No,' I replied, feeling a slight flicker of annoyance interrupt our moment of happiness. 'I told you; we've got to do it during a really specific window and we keep missing it.'

'I'm sorry, honey. I'll make sure I'm around more. Work can wait,' Gary mumbled as he kissed his way along my shoulder. 'Come on. Practice makes perfect.' He gave me a reassuring squeeze, before closing the curtains and leading me towards the small sofa. I wasn't ovulating, but I didn't say anything: I needed this. I needed *him*.

Later, Gary opened the white linen curtains again and we lay on the sofa, my feet in his lap. We smoked roll-ups and drank white wine in a happy, sun-dappled haze. The many photos Gary had taken of us over the years on his beloved polaroid camera were displayed on an old, cracked cork board on the other side of the hut. They made me smile every time I passed them. I loved it here; the hut was a wedding present from my parents. Gary had seemed surprised when I first brought him down to this simple stretch of beach and presented him with our new hut. After all, I could have chosen anywhere: a cabin overlooking a Canadian lake, a villa in the Canary Islands, an apartment in the heart of Florence. But I knew we didn't need fancy. I loved the juxtaposition between luxury and simplicity: days and nights spent in a simple wooden chalet, drinking champagne on an almost deserted beach. I knew we were privileged, thanks to my parents. It's why I could afford to allow Gary to chase his business dreams, no matter how many times they failed.

'What time is it?' I asked, thinking of the half-chopped peppers on the side. Time seemed to stand still at the beach, schedules as fluctuating as the tide.

'Nearly eight.' Gary patted his stomach. 'What time's dinner?'

I was already jumping up, ignoring him.

'We're going to be late!'

'For what? *Please* don't tell me your parents are coming down.'

'We've got drinks with the new neighbours, the ones we met yesterday.'

'*Bollocks.*'

Half an hour later we were hurrying along the sand, me trying to twist my white playsuit into place, Gary clutching a bottle of warm white wine. My heart was fluttering; I loved meeting new people down here, away from the stuffiness of town. Most people didn't know about my family's wealth, which was how I liked it.

'What were their names again?' Gary muttered, as we approached the hut right on the end of the sandbank.

'David and Susan.'

The new neighbours' hut was still a long way from being finished, but the work they had already done was impressive: most of the burnt structure had been replaced with brand new, untreated wood and the debris had been cleared away, leaving bits of ash and glass behind. It would be nice not to have the sad, burnt remains of the old hut ruining the view, anymore.

I spotted David, the husband, fiddling with some wires inside the hut, frowning in concentration. I felt an odd twinge of embarrassment: Gary and I were both useless at DIY. Our hut had been renovated from top to bottom by professionals – it had even featured in an upmarket travel magazine about 'back to nature retreats' – and here they were, doing everything themselves.

David looked up and his face broke into a smile. He had a Nordic look about him: tall and broad-shouldered, with thick blonde hair he wore long and parted in curtains. His perfectly straight teeth were a bright, natural white. As we greeted David, his wife Susan emerged from the back of the hut wearing a loose, floaty kaftan. She was the opposite of her husband: short and curvy with dark curls and a long, almost Grecian nose. Her smile, however, was as broad as

David's, as they invited us up onto the deck and started bringing out bowls of crisps and wine which – unlike our poor postcoital offering – had been chilling.

The conversation flowed easily and I immediately liked this happy, upbeat couple. Susan laughed freely and often, pouring Gary more wine and reaching across to move the lantern closer, as the warm evening wrapped itself around us.

'What do you do, Gary?' David asked.

I glanced down at the tablecloth.

'I'm in sales,' Gary said, straightening up.

'I thought you seemed like a charmer,' David laughed. 'What kind of sales?'

'Well, funny you should ask actually, I've got a new venture that's just come up—'

'What about *you*, David?' I asked hurriedly, cutting across Gary. My face was burning: he was *not* going to try and sell some old mattress to David and Susan.

'I'm a mortgage advisor,' David replied, turning his bright blue eyes to me. 'It's not exactly the fast lane. Don't worry though,' he winked, 'I won't go on about interest rates.'

I laughed too quickly, my face still warm.

'No kids tearing about?' Gary asked, before I could stop him. I wanted to scold him for being rude, asking personal questions of our new friends, but Susan and David didn't seem to take offence and Gary never listened to me, anyway.

'Well,' David replied, taking a swig of beer and glancing at Susan. 'Not *yet* exactly.'

Susan smiled and placed a hand on her stomach, as though in answer; I saw, then, that beneath the floaty kaftan she wore, there was a neat bump.

'A bit sooner than we were expecting,' David explained. 'There goes the honeymoon period.'

Susan shook her head and nudged David playfully, her hand still caressing her bump. I felt an unexpected kick of jealousy in my own stomach towards this happy, down to earth couple. For Susan's pregnancy. For David's steady, sensible job, and DIY skills. They wouldn't have a Clive hanging about, flashing his silver fillings when he got drunk and laughed too loud. A fierce, unexpected wish to be like David and Susan rocked me. We might have my parents' money, but it didn't buy the things I desperately wanted. Children. A husband who could always be relied on.

Breathe, I reminded myself. *Our time will come.* I knew my own impatience was the real issue and I was determined to push it to one side. I wasn't going to let petty jealousy get in the way of our new friendship with David and Susan Douglas.

Chapter Twenty-Four

Now

Sophie

Returning to my hut after seeing Chetana, I immediately pour myself a large gin and tonic at the breakfast bar. I try not to think about the fact that someone has been inside the hut, but I can't help it: it's as though the shadow of the intruder remains. After a few minutes, I carry my drink outside to the deck.

In-between sips, I chew on my thumbnail and replay the conversation with Chetana in my head. She was tense, strange even, when I mentioned Matilda's death. I couldn't get a read on her at all. But, other than my own personal misgivings about her behaviour, there was nothing to suggest Chetana would have taken the photos. If breakable, thirteen-year-old Chetana had had anything to do with Tildy's death, why would she have remained here all these years, at the scene? I sigh, frustrated. I don't know *what* to think. Perhaps Kip is right: that Sheila is a broken woman looking for shadows in the sunlight and there is nothing sinister about what happened to Tildy.

The generous measure of gin slowly starts to swim through my bloodstream; my head feels like it is floating away from my neck. Before I know it, the glass is empty. As

I retreat inside to pour myself another glass, my phone rings from its spot on the table where I upended my bag looking for the tin.

'Hello?' I answer without looking at the caller ID, focused on pouring the tonic.

'Hey, Soph. How are you?' Nick's deep voice greets me through the speaker and my stomach tightens. I haven't heard his voice in what feels like years. It sounds at once achingly familiar and somehow completely foreign. I place the tonic bottle down, trying to think past the alcohol in my system.

'Uh, I'm fine, thank you.' I don't want to ask him how he is, afraid to hear that he is okay, or even good. A seagull cries overhead, spotting some unseen prey.

'Where are you?' Nick asks, sounding confused, his voice stuttering through the poor signal.

'I'm in Dorset, at my parents' beach hut.'

'That cabin thing?' Nick asks, his surprise resonating through the phone. 'I thought you hated that place. Didn't you say it doesn't have a toilet?'

'It doesn't.'

'Why are you there?' He sounds concerned now. 'Is everything okay?'

'Everything's fine, Nick,' I say, exasperated by his gentle tone. 'It's going on the market and I didn't want some random estate agent chucking all Dad's stuff away, okay? And I *do* like this place. I like the beach.'

There is a long pause. Nick loved my dad almost as much as I did, and my parents doted on him; he would understand my need to say goodbye properly. At least Dad never lived to see us separate. He would have been devastated.

'I'm still allowed to worry about you, Sophie,' he says quietly. 'If you want help clearing it out, I—'

'Why did you call, Nick?' I ask, suddenly exhausted. It's too painful to hear his concern, to be reminded of his kindness. I want to lay out on the deckchair outside and close my eyes, forget his voice. The voice that once promised to love me until death did us part.

'My flight is tomorrow night so I'm going to the house tonight to pick up the rest of my things,' Nick is saying. 'I didn't want to tell you over text.'

My stomach twists painfully at the thought of returning to an empty house, devoid of all Nick's things. Our forever house, that I fell in love with as soon as we walked through the door. I could picture our lives in the house so vividly: the large granite kitchen island we would sit at on a Sunday morning eating yoghurt smothered in berries and honey from the farmer's market in town; the landscaped courtyard where we would string fairy lights and grow trellises of honeysuckle and jasmine and host drinks; the wide steps up to the ink-black front door with the burnished brass knocker where I would hang a huge holly and fir wreath at Christmas. Only I never visited the farmer's market or hung up lights and wreathes, because I was always too busy. My chest aches.

'Thanks for letting me know,' is all I can manage through the lump in my throat.

'At least you won't be tripping over my shoes, anymore,' Nick says in an attempt at a joke. 'I'll let you know when I'm done and I've locked up.'

'Okay. I guess that's it then,' I say. A brief phone call and it's all over.

I miss you. Just say it. Tell him.

'There's one more thing,' Nick says and my heart lifts with hope, despite the hurt. 'The insurance policy is about to expire, so make sure you get yourself some cover. Use the same one we had before, it's the best one. Your ring . . .' He clears his throat. The muffled sound of a door closing echoes through the phone and I wonder where he is. *Why would he need to close the door when he lives alone?* 'You need to make sure you get it insured. I'll send the receipt and valuation papers over in a minute so you can sort it all.'

My ring. I look down at it. The glow from the lamps catches the surrounding diamonds, throwing bright refractions of light against the hut wall. I know how much this ring will have cost Nick. He can afford it, but that isn't the point. How can I keep a gift that represents a promise that wasn't kept? He is still talking, rushing through the awkward moment.

'That's it, then. Good luck with clearing out the beach hut. And . . .' he pauses, as though he is trying to decide what to say, '. . . don't work too hard, okay?'

He doesn't know that I have been signed off, that I would have all the time in the world for him, now that he is about to fly to Japan.

I open my mouth to tell him, to admit how low I feel, but either the signal cuts out or Nick is already gone. It is only then I realise how much I had relied on him always being there.

Afterwards, I pour myself another gin and tonic. Then slowly, I slip the beautiful sapphire ring off my finger. It comes off easier than I expected after three years of wearing it, like it never really fitted there in the first place. The delicate, matching diamond band eases off next. Placing them both inside my purse, I hold my hand out in front of me. There is a slight tan line now, advertising to everyone that something is missing. *It's fine*, I tell myself. It'll fade. It'll all fade.

Chapter Twenty-Five

Then

Sophie

*T*onight is the night. The night Kip notices me.

Sucking in a deep breath, I smoothed down my dress. The only mirror I had was the small round one inside my blusher, so I held it out and travelled it up my body. My hair was pulled back in small butterfly clips and the new white dress was one I had been saving for a moment like this. It was soft and ribbed, with daisies linked together as shoulder straps. It was the prettiest thing I owned and it showed off my tan. It was also the shortest thing I'd ever worn and I chewed my lip, wondering if I was going to draw too much attention to myself. *That's the point. This is a Fee dress.* Yes, it was. And I wasn't going to be afraid. I was going to walk down to the beach and laugh and talk with Kip. Maybe he would finally pay attention to me and give me my first kiss. Apparently, Tom had got a bottle of tequila and we were going to have *fun*!

Barefoot, I tip-toed through the hut; the doors were open and only a couple of candles were lit. A mosquito hovered in front of me and I swatted it away in case it bit my face. The kitchen was deserted; Mum and Anna were back home tonight because Anna had a dental appointment first thing in the morning. Dad was down on the sand, where he had moved the table and chairs. He didn't know I was inside; I had slipped back to the hut to get changed, hoping he wouldn't see my dress. He thought I was going to be out with Tildy until late. The truth was, I hadn't seen Tildy all day. I was still stung that she had chosen to surf with Chetana instead of me: we never surfed with anyone else; it was just the way it had always been.

I heard a cork popping and then the glugging sound of my dad pouring wine. Sensing my opportunity, I tugged my dress down and quickly slipped out of the doors onto the deck. It was dark outside and I could only just make out the outline of my dad, further down on the sand. He had his back to me. I hurried down the deck steps and rounded the corner, waiting for a minute, but my dad didn't shout after me: he hadn't seen. *Phew.* I gave my dress one last tug and had just turned away, when I heard Dad speak. I froze, my footsteps silent on the sand.

'No. *Stop. You* listen.'

I could barely make out what he was saying over the breaking waves, but it was obvious he wasn't speaking to me. His voice was low. *Who is he with?* I hesitated, torn between wanting to turn around and see what was going on and not wanting to be caught. Someone spoke and I tried to make out who it was, but suddenly my dad was speaking again in a voice I hardly ever heard him use. It was his angry voice and it came out like a hiss.

'You can't do this. It's not just about you. What about me? My family?'

Then there was a voice back at him, an angry voice. It sounded like a woman; it was definitely female. But Mum and Anna were back home, forty-five minutes away. Who was he talking to?

'People are going to start asking *questions*.'

I listened hard for anything else, but between each roll of wave, there was only silence. The other person had apparently left, their footsteps as muffled as mine.

My heart was thumping. *Who had Dad been talking to?* He hadn't sounded like my dad, he sounded like a man I didn't know. What did he mean '*people are going to start asking questions*'? What questions? Something was very wrong with that conversation, but I didn't know what to do about it.

In the distance, I heard a shout of laughter. The others were probably already walking up to the headland. Through the laughter I heard Kip's voice, and I remembered my special white dress. After a moment, I tip-toed away into the blackness. I would worry about the rest later.

Chapter Twenty-Six

Now

Sophie

I wake with a hangover.

Last night I finished the bottle of gin on the deck, then moved to the woody warmth of the hut when my blanket could no longer keep the chill at bay.

The longer I drank, the easier it was to pretend I didn't care. I convinced myself that Nick would hate Japan and regret ever leaving. I looked out at the navy-blue horizon and up at the perfect, bright stars, planning all the solo trips I would take to discover myself. I scrolled through mine and Nick's messages, the screen slightly blurry. But then the word '*online*' popped up beneath his name and I had to put my phone down.

Before opening my eyes, I give myself a quick once-over. My head is pounding and my throat is dry, as though I'd been drinking sand. My stomach roils dangerously and I take a few, deep breaths to steady it.

I've not showered since arriving on the sandbank so, deciding that a wash and some breakfast is probably the best cure, I gather up my toiletry bag and start hunting around for the key to the showers. The showers are for hut owners only, with one master key given to every hut. Eventually,

I find it buried in one of the kitchen drawers. The large silver key is attached to a key ring from one of Anna's childhood collections: a tiny troll, with a shock of green hair standing up on end.

Not wanting to walk along the beach and risk seeing Chetana or possibly Sheila, I step down from the deck and head around the back of the hut towards the main path.

The harbour side of the sandbank is beautiful this early in the morning; the sun hasn't fully risen and the tops of the huts are bathed in pearly morning light, the fronts still in shadow. Small ripples from skimming dragonflies are all that disturb the glassy harbour water.

There are very few people out yet, only the odd family with children up at the crack of dawn. Outside one hut, two little boys are playing in the sand in front of the path, smacking spades onto buckets. Their parents watch sleepily from their sofa-bed, sipping from painted mugs. The scene is so perfect that I stop, clutching my shower bag.

I have never wanted children, never had any inclination. Even when people handed me their brand-new babies, looking on in exhausted rapture, I never felt the urge. I had made my lack of maternal instinct clear to Nick when we first met and never regretted it. No, it isn't the children making my insides shrivel with envy, it's the perfect sense of *belonging*. The whole scene is blanketed in peace and routine: the way the husband gets up to pour more coffee without his wife even asking; the way one of the children, a blonde boy with a long fringe and crocodile pyjamas, turns his head towards his mother, who is already throwing his jumper out to him.

As I watch, the husband settles himself back onto the bed, dropping a kiss on the woman's head. His eyes find mine and I suddenly realise how I must look: lone woman, bloodshot eyes and matted hair, staring at his family. Though his face is quizzically polite, he stills like a wild animal, sensing a threat. Hastily dragging my gaze away, I hurry on, my cheeks flaming with embarrassment. *Is this how it will be from now on?* Feeling painfully aware of other, happier, people?

After a few minutes, I arrive at the showers. When I was younger, there were two individual stone huts to shower in, exclusively for hut owners to use. I had hated the smell and the spiders that crawled up the rough walls, preferring to use a bucket and a sponge on the deck, or just the sea. The two stone huts are still here, but next to them now stands a modern, communal shower block.

Relieved I don't have to use one of the old stone huts, I approach the new block, pulling out the shower key. It is immediately obvious, however, that the key won't fit: it is far too large for the lock on the new shower block door. Mum and Dad must have used a different set of keys for the families who rented the hut during the summers. I hesitate: I could walk back to my hut and hunt out the right set of keys . . . but now that I am here, I am desperate for a shower. With a sigh, I resign myself to showering in one of the stone huts.

Approaching the closest hut, I unlock the door. The inside is as claustrophobic as I remembered it: a narrow, dank space with an ancient shower head and mildewy, tiled floor. The only natural light filtering in comes from cracks in the stone walls. I shudder before reluctantly stepping inside. As the door swings shut, the hut plunges into darkness. *Just a quick rinse, then coffee and food.* I fumble for the light cord but when I locate and pull it, nothing happens. Just an impotent *click*, with the shower remaining as dark as before. My head pounding worse than ever now, I decide to grit my teeth and get it over with.

After hanging my bag up on the only hook, I turn and press the cold silver shower knob. After a few seconds, lukewarm water cascades over me, teetering just on the brink of being hot enough. I tilt my head back and close my eyes. Finally, my muscles start to unwind, the tension easing from my neck and shoulders.

Five minutes later, feeling somewhat refreshed, I finish showering and dress awkwardly in the small space, keen to get out of the dark hut. My mind now on breakfast on the Boat House deck, I push the handle.

Nothing happens.

I push down again. The handle doesn't budge. Swallowing a flutter of panic, I take a breath, then try again. The rusted silver handle remains completely stiff. *Did I leave the key in the lock?* I don't remember what I did with it after I unlocked the door. *It must be in my bag.* In the semi-darkness, I fumble inside my shower bag, feeling bottles and a hairbrush, but no key or plastic troll key ring. *Shit.* Hopelessly, I look around in the gloom. There is nothing but the shower and single hook on the back of the door. The narrow hut is entombed when the door closes: no windows, *nothing*. My heart starts to race, my throat constricting in the damp air.

Don't panic. I am not the panicking type. It's proudly referenced on my CV: '*Able to keep a cool head under pressure.*' There is always a logical solution to any problem. Someone will walk past in a minute and I can shout to them to unlock the door. Simple. I just have to wait until then.

Only I can't ignore the creeping question: *what if no one comes?* This, I know, is the claustrophobia talking: the showers are right near the huts and the main walking path. This early in the morning, I might have to wait awhile for someone to walk past, but someone will come. The second, more terrifying question, is harder to answer.

What if no one hears?

Stop it. Of course they will. As if to emphasise my fear, the cubicle is silent but for the hollow sound of water dripping from the showerhead.

I try the handle again, but it doesn't move. I bang on the door, but it has no effect: my curled fists thump dully against the thick metal door. Fear begins to squeeze the air from my lungs. *Think, Sophie.* The door is somehow locked. I can't hear anyone and I don't know if anyone can hear me. *Are the showers checked at night?* They must be. A trickle of relief runs through me, until I remember that the residents have twenty-four-hour access to the showers: anyone coming to check would probably just assume the shower was occupied. *Do they even check the old shower huts?* The thought sets panic ringing in my ears.

'Help!' I shout, slamming my palms against the door, over and over again. Silence. Nothing but the final drips from the showerhead.

Wait. *My smartwatch*. My phone is back at the hut, but I can still use my watch to call emergency services. *Why didn't I think of it before?* Hurriedly, I tap the screen. It doesn't respond. I tap it again, more impatiently, but the screen remains blank. I fiddle with the dial on the side, but it's no good: thanks to my drunken pity party last night, I didn't bother to charge it.

Sliding down the stone wall to the wet floor, I bury my face in my knees. I am trapped.

Chapter Twenty-Seven

Now

Sophie

My worst fears come to me over the next few hours. I think about Nick, turning and smiling at a faceless woman walking down the aisle towards him. Of him cradling a baby boy in a blue hat. I picture my dad as he was about to die, taking his last, hollow breath in the hospice. I think of Matilda, not accidentally slipping after all, but facing an attacker alone that night. Pleading for her life.

Images of what I will look like if I am not found for weeks and weeks taunt me, white and emaciated. Teeth jutting out of my head. The human jaw is only attached to the skull by ligaments and muscle: when they decompose, the jaw breaks away. Then, suddenly, I think of Anna, on the other side of the world. Losing her dad and only sibling in less than two years. The thought pulls me up, breaking through the fog of despair. I can't do that to her.

I get to my feet and start banging on the door again. When nothing happens, I hammer on the round keyhole. I try pushing my finger through the keyhole, attempting to reach where the key would be, to push it out. Maybe someone will pay more attention if they see the key on the floor, or maybe they'll have more chance of hearing me through an open keyhole.

'Fuck!'

The keyhole is too small, my finger won't fit. I can just about make out a tiny speck of light on the other side. Pain radiates through the heels of my hands. I let out a small sob.

And then it happens. There is a movement on the other side of the keyhole. Something blocks the light momentarily.

'Hello?' I cry, my voice hoarse. I jiggle the handle over and over, frantically willing someone to hear me. *Please.*

Nothing.

'*HELP!*' I shout, at the top of my lungs.

Just as a desperate wave of hopelessness threatens to drown me, there is a loud *click* and a sliver of light breaks through the darkness. I throw myself at the door and stagger out into the searing brightness of the sandbank.

'*Sophie?*'

Kip is standing there, looking shocked.

'Kip,' I croak. 'I—' The relief of being outside, of seeing a familiar face, is overwhelming and I start to shake uncontrollably. He approaches me, his face creased with concern.

'What happened?'

'I don't know. I've been trapped for hours.'

On trembling legs, I open the door to the shower and quickly pull my shower bag off the hook on the back of the door.

You're okay, I tell myself. *You're out.*

'Let's get you to the Boat House,' Kip says, firmly. 'It's closer and you need sugar for the shock.'

I let him take my shower bag and steer me towards the main path. We have taken just a few steps when I remember.

'Do you have my key?' I ask.

Kip looks at me, puzzled.

'What key?'

'My shower key, the one that was in the lock. It has a little troll on the key ring. With green hair.'

Kip shakes his head slowly.

'No . . . I jimmied the lock.'

'Why would you do that? Why didn't you just use the key?' I ask, coming to a halt. Kip looks at me as though I have completely lost my mind. He opens his mouth and somehow, I already know what he is going to say. I just don't want to hear it.

'Sophie . . . there was no key in the lock.'

Chapter Twenty-Eight

Then

Sophie

'Ask me something else,' Anna ordered from the sofa. I chewed my lip as I sat on the window box, trying to dreadlock my hair. So far, all I had managed to do was get wax all over my fingers.

'Am I going to marry someone rich?'

Anna shook the black plastic bowling ball.

'It says no.'

'Oh. Okay then, am I going to marry someone good-looking?'

Anna shook the ball hard again, frowning down at it. The strands of hair between my fingers were turning into a slippery, mushy mess. Nothing like the delicate dreadlock Caitlin had managed last year.

'It says no,' Anna announced. 'Maybe try something that isn't about marriage.'

'*Fine.* Am I going to be happy?'

Anna shook the ball, then shook her head.

'*It doesn't look good.*'

'Let me see that!' I jumped up and snatched the ball off Anna.

'I *knew* it!' I cried, looking down at the small window in the ball where the answer showed. 'It says "*yes*", you little—'

I stopped when Mum and Dad walked into the hut.

'I *hope* you aren't going to finish that sentence, young lady.' Mum's eyebrows were raised and her nostrils flared. I looked irritably down at the floor while Anna grinned behind Mum's back.

'Right, well *if* you think you can both behave for five minutes, Dad's taking us to the Boat House for dinner,' Mum continued. I looked up, my grumpiness immediately forgotten; I *loved* going to the Boat House for dinner. I had a new skirt I hadn't worn yet and maybe we would see Kip and his family, too.

'Only if you *behave*!' Mum called after me as I scrambled up and raced to the back of the hut to get ready.

It was a Friday evening and the Boat House was already rammed. Parents that worked away from the beach during the week would come back on Fridays, crossing the water-taxi to the sandbank in their suits which always looked really weird.

As we waited at the doors to be seated, I craned my neck to look around the restaurant. Kip was nowhere to be seen, but my parents waved at Shiv and Rushni Chawla. The Chawlas waved back, then returned to their dinner. Dev and Chetana weren't with them and my stomach knotted with jealousy: was Chetana with Matilda, again?

'Good evening,' the waitress smiled at my parents, pink in the face from the hot restaurant. 'We're quite busy tonight, I'll be with you in a moment.'

I stood on tiptoe and tried to see out to the deck, in case Kip was out there. Next to me, Anna shook her magic ball.

'Does Kip know Sophie exists?'

'Hey!' I snapped, turning on her. Anna shook her head.

' "*Not a chance.*" Sorry, Soph.'

I resisted the urge to shove her.

'Moron,' I muttered, instead, so Mum couldn't hear.

The waitress returned, still smiling.

'Are you all together?' she asked, gesturing past my parents. Confused, we all looked around and saw Matilda and her mum and dad walking up the steps behind us.

'No,' Dad said quickly. 'We're not together.'

As Matilda approached, I felt slightly anxious. I was so used to spending every moment of my summers with her that, for the first time ever, I was unsure of where we stood. But to my relief she smiled at me, her face totally normal.

'You've got a dreadlock,' Matilda said, reaching out and tugging at my hair.

'Oh, not really,' I said, ducking my head in embarrassment. 'It's just . . .'

'I like it,' Tildy said firmly. 'It looks cool.'

A rush of gratitude swept over me. I had worried Tildy was going to start going off with Chetana and not want to speak to me, but she seemed to be exactly the same.

'I like your top,' I said. It was a blue crochet crop top that made her skin look even more tanned. Tildy grinned and linked arms with me.

The waitress was studying her clipboard.

'I can seat you all together, if you want,' she said, looking around at us. 'I've got a large table available right now.'

Tildy and I turned to our parents, who were standing silently next to each other.

'Can we?' Tildy asked, eagerly.

'If they get to sit with each other, I want a dessert,' Anna demanded.

'No,' Sheila said. She wasn't smiling. 'This is family time. Thank you,' she said to the waitress. 'We'll wait.'

'She's right,' Dad said to us. His face had gone all red and blotchy. 'We aren't going to interrupt the Halls.'

The waitress shrugged and made a note on her clipboard.

'No problem. It'll be a couple more minutes for the smaller tables.' She walked away and everyone went quiet while Anna kept shaking her magic ball, her tongue sticking out. I wanted her to put it away: it was so *childish*. I looked around the Boat House again, hoping I might have missed Kip the first time, but instead noticed Caitlin, who was walking towards us, a takeaway milkshake in one hand. She wore a tiny pair of denim shorts and a rainbow bikini top so small her boobs were almost out. As she walked past, she smirked at us, tossing her hair over her shoulder, before sauntering out of the restaurant.

'Goodness gracious,' Gary muttered. Anna giggled. There was another long silence.

'We should get the boats out,' Gary said to my dad, after a few minutes. 'Go fishing. It's been too long.'

'Sounds great,' Dad said. His voice sounded higher than normal.

'Will we be seeing you at Amber's birthday party next weekend?' Gary asked.

'Of course,' Mum said.

Dad glanced across at her. I remembered he hadn't been keen on going to Kip's mum's birthday party with the *newbies*.

No one spoke until the waitress arrived and told my parents she had a table ready for us. Tildy walked with me a few steps, out of earshot of our parents.

'Parents are so *annoying*!' I hissed at her. 'Why can't we just sit together?'

'I know,' Tildy muttered. 'They're so weird. They just stand around like goldfish.'

I giggled and did an impression of a fish, opening and closing my mouth with a *pop*.

'Let's just make sure,' I said, as Mum and Dad waved at me to join them, 'that we never end up like that.'

Chapter Twenty-Nine

Now

Sophie

'Talk me through it again,' Kip says. '*Slowly.*'

We are sat out on the busy Boat House deck, surrounded by loud families and barking dogs, but I am still mentally locked in the shower, deaf to the chaos around us. I don't register the waitress as she sets mugs of coffee and pastries down on the table. Kip pushes one of the mugs towards me and I wrap my hands around it, welcoming the searing heat against my palms.

I go over it again: entering the shower, hanging my bag up, then not being able to get out.

'I just assumed something had happened accidentally, like someone wanted to check whether it was occupied and then didn't realise they had locked it. Or it was just stuck. But if there was no key in the lock . . .'

'There wasn't,' Kip says firmly.

'. . . then someone tried to trap me in there.'

Just saying it out loud sends a chill through me.

'Are you sure?' Kip asks. 'You're sure the key isn't in your shower bag?'

'I'm sure, Kip.'

'But why would someone do that to you?' Kip asks.

I give him an incredulous look.

'Isn't it obvious? Because of the photos. Someone was trying to scare me, or worse.'

'That's pretty extreme.' Kip doesn't look convinced and I grip my mug tighter. 'I mean, it's not as if locking you in a shower would actually hurt you, right?'

You weren't there, I want to say. *You don't know how the walls closed in.*

'I had a conversation with Chetana yesterday,' I say quickly. 'After I left you and Sheila.'

Kip looks up in interest.

'Did you learn anything?'

'Nothing specific . . . but she acted really weird when I mentioned the summer Matilda died. And then she immediately wanted me to leave.'

'Hmm.' Kip bites his lip, thinking. 'Are you sure you didn't just misinterpret it? Sheila probably shook you up.' He gestures to the pastry on my plate. 'You need to eat. Just force what you can down, you'll feel better.'

I pick at a fat, flaky croissant, my stomach too knotted to eat.

'How did you find me?' I ask. 'I didn't think anyone would for ages.'

Kip shifts slightly in his seat.

'I came by to see you this morning and you weren't in your hut. After what happened with Sheila last night, I wanted to make sure you were okay. Your hut was open and your phone was inside, but I couldn't find you anywhere. I just had this strange feeling, like something was wrong, especially after last night. I checked the showers but then realised I hadn't checked the old ones . . . when I got near the door, I thought I heard something, so I decided to break the lock, just in case.'

What might have happened if Kip hadn't found me?

'Something strange is happening, Kip,' I say, putting down my pastry. 'The photos . . . the shower . . . I think someone's afraid.'

'Look,' says Kip, leaning forwards. 'Sheila probably just has us on edge. She's never got over what happened; she's determined that someone hurt Tildy and she'll cling on to that idea. I don't want you to get dragged down in it all when you've only just come back for the first time in years.'

My head is swimming from the events of the past twenty-four hours. I just want to sleep, or leave, or both.

'What if she's right?' I ask. 'What if something really *did* happen to Matilda? Chetana was acting strange . . . she could easily have locked me in the shower.'

'Think who you're talking about,' Kip says, shaking his head. 'It's *Chetana*. She would have been, what, twelve, thirteen? Matilda was her only friend; she wouldn't have hurt her.'

'Is there anyone else still around from '97?' I ask.

'My aunt and uncle,' Kip replies, raising an eyebrow at me.

I nod, knowing that neither Sheila nor Gary would be likely suspects. The police looked into them, like they looked into everyone else, but they were both in their hut at the time, asleep.

'What about the others?'

Kip shakes his head. 'Tom's family sold their hut a few years ago and Amy's family were just renting a hut that one summer. Caitlin's family still owns their hut, but she's not been back since Matilda died. I don't know where she is now.'

This surprises me: Caitlin loved the beach, I can't imagine her not coming back down, even after what happened to Tildy. They weren't exactly close.

'Okay, so not Caitlin, Amy or Tom. Who else?'

'There's no one else that I know of, Soph. And I'm more worried about you, to be honest. You look exhausted.'

Kip looks as though he is about to take my hand, but he stops himself. Our eyes meet and my face grows warm. Attempting to cover the awkward moment, I suddenly remember something he mentioned yesterday.

'Didn't you say you've got a friend in the police force?'

Kip looks as though he knows exactly what I'm going to say.

'Yeah, I do. But—'

'We could talk to them about the photos, right? Get some advice?'

'I don't really think that's a good idea.'

'Please, Kip.' I lean forwards across the table. 'They'll know more about this sort of thing than us.'

Finally, he sighs.

'Okay. I'll see if Charlie will meet us.'

Chapter Thirty

Then

Sophie

I sat at the edge of the bank, my feet in the water. The July heat warmed my skin and I watched the water flashing in the sun like fish scales. The old ironstone quarry, nestled in the headland, had always been mine and Tildy's escape from our parents and any jobs we might get lumbered with if they saw us doing nothing. The quarry was dammed years before to create a miniature lake, filled with freshwater and smooth, terracotta rocks. Recently, I had started coming up here more and more: it was somewhere quiet, where I could just be myself. I had brought a couple of magazines up with me, but they sat untouched by my side: I wasn't in the mood for reading.

There was a noise behind me, but I ignored it. Sometimes people walking the trails came across the old quarry; I hoped they would keep walking so I didn't have to share the quiet with anyone.

'Hey.'

I turned my head to see Tildy standing behind me. My mood immediately lifted.

'Hey, Tilds.'

Matilda walked over and flopped on the bank by my side, kicking off her flip flops.

'Not seen you in ages,' Tildy said, glancing over at me. I didn't reply; I didn't want to give away that I had seen Tildy out on the water with Chetana twice recently and I had avoided them. Tildy, however, glanced at the untouched magazines next to me and raised an eyebrow like she knew.

'She's really nice, you know. Chetana. You could try and get to know her.'

I didn't want to get to know her; I wanted her to go away. I wanted Matilda to *want* to be part of the other group, so that we could have the perfect summer I had pictured.

'How come you're up here, anyway?' I asked, trying to turn the conversation away from the friendship divide on the beach this summer. Tildy shrugged.

'Looking for you. Wanted to get away from my hut.'

I registered a vague pleasure that Tildy had come looking for me, but it was quickly replaced with concern.

'What's up?' I asked.

'Mum and Dad are arguing, again.' She picked up a handful of pebbles and began throwing them into the quarry pond. 'It's doing my head in.'

'What were they arguing about?' I asked, watching a particularly large pebble curve into the air and plop into the glassy water below.

'Money, as always.'

'But you've got loads of money.'

'*Mum* has loads of money,' Tildy corrected. 'Dad doesn't have any, I don't think. He's always got some sort of "deal",' she lifted her fingers into air quotes, 'going on, but I don't think they ever go anywhere. He's got some weird mate called Clive who Mum hates because she thinks he's, like, a loan shark or something. None of their ideas are real jobs.'

'But if your mum is loaded, why does it matter?' I asked, not understanding.

'Dunno.'

Matilda started pulling at the long grass next to her, letting it run through her palm over and over again. 'I don't think my dad likes it that all the money comes from nanna and grandpa.'

I chewed on my bottom lip, unsure what to say. The thought of parents talking about money made me feel uncomfortable. There were some things, like boys, that parents just weren't supposed to talk about.

'They're not going to break up, or anything?' I asked, suddenly worried.

'Dunno,' Matilda said again, sounding miserable.

'Hey.' I shuffled closer and put my arm around her. She rested her head on my shoulder, her thick blonde hair tickling my chin.

'It'll be okay,' I said, trying to sound confident.

We sat in silence for a while, watching underwater ripples of sunlight on the submerged rocks. Tucked away on top of the headland, the sounds of the beach below no longer reached us: all we could hear was the rustle of reeds surrounding the bank. *I've missed this. Just being us.*

'Do you ever think that there's one person for everyone?' Matilda asked suddenly, lifting her head from my shoulder.

'You mean, like, are your parents meant to be together?'

Matilda hesitated, her large navy-blue eyes wide. I had always envied her eyes: they looked like sapphires.

'I guess. You and me, too, though. Do you think there's just one person?'

She turned towards me. She looked nervous. We had always spoken about everything under the sun, but this felt different. Was she really that worried about her mum and dad? I wasn't sure how to respond. It wasn't something I had really thought about before, other than vaguely hoping to one day meet someone who would like me for me.

'I don't know if there's one perfect person for everyone . . . but I think there's one person who you can decide is perfect for you. I mean,' I continued self-consciously, already aware I was messing up what I was trying to say, 'it's just about being happy isn't it? You could end up with a right minger, as long as you're happy.'

This made Matilda giggle and I felt relief wash over me. She turned away from me and smiled out across the water. She had grown prettier than ever recently: her hair shimmered past her shoulder blades and her skin seemed to absorb the sunlight, so that she glowed.

'You're right.' Matilda nodded, her jaw set. 'It shouldn't matter what people think about who you love. As long as you're happy, people should understand, shouldn't they?'

'Well, yeah,' I began, immediately confused again. 'I guess . . .' I was about to say, *depends who it is*, but Matilda turned to face me, crossing her legs and twisting her hands in her lap. She took a deep breath in.

'I need to tell you something. I've wanted to tell you for ages . . . but I didn't know how you'd react.' Her words came out in a rush, tumbling on top of one another. 'The thing is, I—'

'Alright, Fee?'

We looked up. Tom and one of his friends, Jamie, were standing a few feet away, kicking at the reeds. Jamie worked with Tom at the same garage in town and he was staying at Tom's hut for a few weeks. He was shorter than Tom, and stocky like a rugby player.

'Hi,' I replied, trying not to look flustered.

'We're going out on Caitlin's donut, you coming?'

My stomach flipped in excitement. I had never been invited to take part in the group water sports before. Had they come over specially to ask me?

'Shall we go?' I asked, looking eagerly across at Matilda. To my surprise, she looked angry, her mouth a thin line. 'Tildy?'

'You go,' she spat.

'What's the matter? *Tildy!*' Before I could reach out to her, she had stood up and was walking off through the long grass.

'Come *on*, Fee,' Tom was saying impatiently. They were already starting to walk away and I got up and quickly hurried after them, not wanting to be left behind.

I couldn't understand what was wrong with Tildy. *I'll talk to her later*, I told myself. *It'll be okay.*

I'd never been on a donut before and I was a bit nervous, but it was the exact kind of thing that the old, scared Sophie would have said no to, or would never have been invited to in the first place. I was going.

Kip, Amy, Dev and Caitlin were all putting on lifejackets when we arrived. Everyone else greeted us, but Caitlin just rolled her eyes and turned her back on me. *Why did she hate me so much?*

'Here you go, Sophie.' Amy was offering me a lifejacket. I smiled gratefully at her and accepted the red and yellow jacket, which was still waterlogged from a previous outing.

Glancing around at the others, I couldn't quite believe I was hanging out with people who were about to go into sixth form. All I had wanted at the start of the summer was for Kip to look my way; I had never once dreamt I would be included in such exclusive beach activities.

I pulled on the lifejacket and started trying to grapple with the buckles, but they were stiff. My heart gave a nervous flutter, sure that Caitlin was about to loudly point out that I was a fraud.

'Come here.' Kip had quietly approached. He clipped the buckles together, adjusting them here and there. He pulled slightly on the vest to tighten it and the force propelled me towards him. I kept my gaze focused on his tanned hands, not knowing where else to look.

'There,' he murmured. 'That should be fine.'

I dared, then, to look up at his startling blue eyes – barely distinguishable from the blue sky behind him – and saw that he was gazing right back at me. My mouth went very dry.

'Alright you two, let's go,' Tom shouted. With a jolt, I realised everyone else was already in the boat, crammed onto the white leather seats. I felt a thrill of fear when I caught sight of Caitlin's mutinous expression and was grateful to be wedged at the far end of the boat, well away from her. Kip ended up next to her, though, and she started talking to him straight away, her head playfully cocked to one side. My stomach sank. I didn't understand the two of them: if Caitlin wanted to be with Kip so much, why weren't they together? And if he had said no, why did she keep trying? I imagined what Mum would say: *love isn't that simple, darling.* For some reason, Dev, seated next to Kip, looked as unhappy as I did.

Tom gunned the engine and the boat roared away, bouncing off the crest of the waves and crashing down again so we were all sprayed with cold, salty water. Everyone started whooping and I couldn't stop myself laughing, too. My worries momentarily forgotten, I lost myself in the glittering sea.

The donut, a bright orange inflatable ring with soft straps attached to the back of the boat by a long rope, only seated one person, so everyone took it in turns to swim out to it and clamber on. No one lasted very long when one of the boys was navigating the boat: they went so fast, the rider was flung into the sea. The nerves started to build as I waited my turn, watching everyone else. I kept letting others go before me, putting off the moment I would have to go.

Finally, everyone else had gone and it was my turn. I stood up on slightly shaky legs. *What if I can't get onto the donut? What if my bikini bottoms slip, with everyone watching?*

Kip looked over and gave me an encouraging smile. Slowly, I clambered down the hot metal ladder and swam out towards the donut. Goosebumps erupted across my skin and I tried not to think about everyone watching as I heaved myself into the donut. As I settled myself into the donut and held tightly onto the straps, I looked up to see that Caitlin had taken the wheel from Tom. She turned and smirked at me. My stomach gave a horrible lurch: *what was she going to do?* I clutched the straps harder and closed my eyes as the engine roared back to life and I was yanked through the water.

To my surprise, Caitlin didn't go too fast, or turn too many sharp corners. The wind whipped across my face and adrenaline flew through my veins as I clung on, half-laughing, half-shrieking in delight.

Incredibly, I managed not to fall off and instead of being fished out of the water, the boat came to a gentle stop while everyone cheered. Grinning from ear to ear, I slipped awkwardly off the donut and started swimming back to the ladder on the back of the boat. *I did it!*

Still smiling, I reached for the bottom rung of the ladder, but the engine suddenly thundered into life, the steel blades churning right in front of me. A blast of water shot from the engine and I was forced backwards, somersaulting under the surface. A flash of orange flew past me, something hard hit my leg . . . and then it was quiet.

Fighting my way back to the surface, I emerged, spluttering. My hair was plastered to my face and I pushed it out of the way as I looked around. The boat was gone and I was a very, very long way from shore. The current was already pulling me further out.

That bitch! I screamed in my head. Caitlin did that on purpose, I *know* she did. I treaded water, unsure what to do, until I heard the sound of an engine and saw the white of Caitlin's boat appear from behind a bend in the sandbank. Despite my anger, I forced myself to stop spitting out water and tried as best I could to look nonplussed, while my heart continued to beat painfully hard under my life jacket.

'I'm so sorry!' Caitlin cried as soon as I was helped back into the boat by Tom and Amy. Caitlin picked her way over and gave me a hug, but I stayed stiff.

'I thought I saw you back in the donut and you wanted another go. I can't believe I did that, Sophie, I am just so sorry. You could have been killed!'

Yes, I could! I wanted to shout at her. *And you knew that, you psycho!*

'Don't get upset,' Amy said soothingly, rubbing Caitlin's arm. 'You didn't mean to do it. Look, Sophie's fine, aren't you Soph?' Everyone turned to look at me, with concerned eyes. I took in a deep breath.

'I'm fine,' I replied, forcing a smile. Caitlin met my eye as everyone settled back down again. She smirked. Tom turned the boat in a graceful arc, speeding us back to shore. I sat looking out at the waves, trying hard not to cry. I wanted to be as far away from them all as possible.

After what felt like forever, we approached the shore. As we came to a stop in the shallow water, I spotted Matilda walking along the beach with Chetana. They were chatting happily and I breathed a sigh of relief. I wanted nothing more than to spend the rest of the day with her, away from Caitlin; I would even make an effort with Chetana. Matilda looked across at the boat as Tom cut the engine and everyone started jumping into the shallows.

For a moment, mine and Matilda's eyes met. I started to move towards her through the ankle-deep waves, but then she turned away. She said something to Chetana and the two of them walked up the deck steps towards Matilda's hut, closing the doors behind them.

Chapter Thirty-One

Now
Sophie

The Ship pub sits on the town-side of the harbour, overlooking the water. It has been around for as long as I can remember, serving town locals and those waiting to catch the water-taxi across to the sandbank. It was Kip's idea to meet here to introduce his friend Charlie, the police officer.

As I approach the doors, someone exits the pub; I automatically step to the side to let them pass but whoever it is suddenly stops.

'*Sophie?* Is that you?'

The face is familiar, though I haven't set eyes on it in more than two decades. Gary Hall looks completely different to the last time I saw him, the day Matilda's body was discovered. Gary was once strong and charismatic, always laughing. Now his red hair is thinning on the crown and his former athletic build has softened. But it's his face, more than anything, that has changed. The wide smile has gone, along with the brightness in his eyes, replaced with puffy shadows and a hangdog expression. He is wearing a rumpled shirt and blue chino shorts with chunky-soled running trainers.

'Sheila said you were back,' Gary says. 'I couldn't believe it.'

I nod. 'I'm selling the hut for Mum. She's moved out to Spain.'

Gary's eyes roam over my face for a moment, as though he is taking it all in.

'I hope you'll forgive me for saying it, but you look so grown up. So sophisticated.'

To my horror, tears cloud Gary's eyes. Despite his words, both of us are shadows of our former selves: the strong, hearty dad, gone to seed; the lively girl who loved to surf, who hasn't slept in days.

'Thank you,' I manage uncomfortably, trying to pretend I haven't noticed Gary's tears. 'Are you off to the hut, now?'

Gary's eyes flicker across the harbour, towards the sandbank on the other side, then he shakes his head.

'I've just left, but Sheila's staying tonight. Thought I would grab a quick beer for the road before I headed back into town.' He nods inside. 'Kip's in there. He mentioned he was meeting you.'

All of a sudden Gary's expression shifts and he looks uncomfortable.

'Sophie, listen. I hope you don't mind me saying something, but I know what Sheila said to you. That she thinks someone took Tildy's photos because it's got something to do with her death. That she wants you to find the tin.'

I nod. Gary sighs and rubs his neck wearily.

'Sheila's always struggled to move on. She's convinced there's some of sort of conspiracy surrounding what happened to Tildy. Who knows,' he lifts his shoulders, 'maybe she's right. But it wasn't fair of her to ask you to get involved. From what Kip said, you've got enough on your plate right now.'

'That's true,' I reply ruefully and Gary smiles.

'You just focus on yourself, right now. I'll look after Sheila.'

My stomach squirms uncomfortably. *Does Gary know Kip and I are meeting a police officer?* I don't want to divide him and Sheila.

'I'll let you get on,' Gary says, before I can reply. 'It's wonderful to see you, Sophie. I'm proud you've made such a success of yourself in London. I bet you're looking forward to getting home.' He reaches out and gives my shoulder a squeeze, then walks off in the direction of town.

For a moment, I stand there watching him walk away. He has no idea how unsuccessful my life in London is turning out to be. *Is that the real reason I'm staying here? Am I using the photos as an excuse not to go home?* Giving myself a mental shake, I step inside the pub.

Looking around for Kip and his police officer friend, I immediately spot him standing at the bar.

'Hi,' I greet him as I reach the long mahogany bar. It smells like cleaning chemicals and stale beer.

'Hey Soph. I've got you a drink. Charlie's over there.' Kip jerks his head towards the corner of the pub. He smiles at me, but something in his expression feels off. Perhaps I am imagining it: my lack of sleep over the past few days has left me hyper alert and jittery.

'Thanks.'

We walk towards the corner of the room, where a single shaft of sunlight cuts across the otherwise dingy table.

'Sophie,' Kip is saying next to me, his voice still slightly strained, 'this is Charlie, the . . . friend I told you about.'

I turn in the direction Kip gestures and, instead of the thirty-something male I was expecting to see, an extremely pretty brunette is comfortably settled into the far corner of the worn booth, an almost-empty glass of wine already in front of her.

Charlie stands up from the booth, her hand outstretched politely. Close up, she looks to be in her late thirties, with olive skin and light brown eyes.

'It's good to meet you,' she says, as we shake hands. Her manner is professional, though not unfriendly.

'Hi,' I reply, trying to read her expression. For one mad moment I wonder if she is about to arrest us. 'So you're . . .?'

'The detective,' Kip says, at the same time as Charlie says, 'the ex-girlfriend.'

I look between the two of them, taken aback for a moment. *Charlie* is the ex? The emergency contact, who arrived at the hospital with her new boyfriend after Kip was mugged?

'Shit, sorry,' Charlie says, though she doesn't look remotely embarrassed. Kip shrugs good-naturedly, looking sheepish.

'To be fair, I did tell Sophie the story of the mugging and how you came to rescue this damsel in distress.'

Kip slides into the booth next to Charlie and I take the seat opposite. I am wearing shorts and the cold leather of the booth sticks to the backs of my legs. Suddenly I feel like an intruder. Things between Kip and I have been so intense the past few days, it is something of a shock to remember that he has a life outside of our temporary bubble.

'I've told Charlie everything,' Kip launches in straight away. 'The photos, the tin getting stolen, you getting locked in the shower. All of it.'

Taking a sip of the red wine Kip handed me, I try to focus. A sense of relief is running through me, like a child handing the responsibility of a secret over to a teacher.

'I'm really sorry to hear what you've gone through,' Charlie says without hesitation. 'It must have been terrifying being trapped in that shower. Thank goodness Kip played detective.' She gives Kip a look that could only be described as glowing. *Did Kip ever say why they broke up?*

'What happens now?' I ask. 'Do we give a statement about everything that's happened? Will they reopen Tildy's case?'

Charlie hesitates.

'Listen, the last thing I want is to sound insensitive,' she says carefully, putting down her glass and leaning forwards the way police do on TV dramas when they talk to the victim's family. 'I know that you were very close to Miss Hall – Matilda – from everything Kip's told me. I completely understand the shock of finding those photos and then having them go missing . . .'

She hesitates, and I realise what she is going to say.

'There's so little funding for reopening unsolved cases, any new evidence has to be incredibly persuasive, especially in a case like this where it's unclear if it even *was* murder.' Seeing the look on my face, she presses on, slightly quicker. 'I can take your statement about everything that's happened of course, but I don't think that the discovery of the photos and an alleged theft—'

'It's not an *alleged* theft,' I flare up. 'Kip was there too, they were stolen!'

Near us, an old man sitting alone glances over. Charlie raises her hands placatingly.

'I'm sorry, that's force of habit, I forget how it sounds,' she says, as though she's speaking to a wayward teen. 'I just meant that the theft hasn't been reported as a crime, there's been no investigation. Of course,' she continues, looking between Kip and me, 'you can report it, if you want? It *is* a burglary, after all. The shower incident too, I can take your statement.'

Her expression is dubious, and I sigh in frustration. I know exactly how it would sound if I reported it. I can picture the police officers' faces, hear the word *unhinged*.

'What do we *do* then?' Through the grimy window, the sun has started to lower over the harbour, turning the sunlight on the table from white to gold. 'I mean those photos might have led somewhere and we lost them! Are we just supposed to . . . live with that?' *What will Sheila say?*

'Kip told me what was in the photos you saw,' Charlie says, calmly. 'I appreciate I haven't seen them, and this isn't me speaking in an official capacity, but they don't immediately sound alarming, at least not in the traditional sense. There was no explicit violence or sexual activity with anyone underage, that sort of thing?'

Reluctantly, I shake my head, but I am not ready to give up that easily.

'What about someone locking me in the shower?' I look between them defiantly.

'Could that have been an accident?' Charlie asks gently. 'Could someone have just mistakenly thought the shower key was theirs? Maybe a kid took it; Kip said it had a doll on it or something, right?'

'A troll,' I mutter, sitting back in my seat and staring down at my drink. This isn't how I had expected things to go: I thought Charlie would take me seriously, believe me. Each event – the photos being hidden, then being stolen, getting locked in the shower – can be explained away individually as accidents, or coincidences. *But it's everything together*, I want to say. *They can't all be coincidences*. And there's the feeling I can't shake, either. The feeling of being watched.

'What if we're wrong though and there is something that was missed back then?' I ask, stubbornly. 'Is there anyone who didn't have an alibi the night Tildy died?'

'It was all covered in the original investigation,' Charlie replies. 'The problem was, it could have been any number of individuals. Anyone on the beach that night had an opportunity,' she raises a slight eyebrow, 'including both of you.'

'But we were all together,' Kip says. 'We were at the bonfire.'

Charlie shrugs. 'You were all drinking, going off swimming. The evidence isn't exactly reliable.'

'So, all of the teenagers out on the beach, basically?' I press. 'That's pretty much it?'

'Well, yes and no. Without phones or any surveillance cameras, even those who said they were in their huts couldn't necessarily be verified unless they were with someone, teenagers and adults alike.' Charlie shakes her head, looking almost impressed. 'A dark beach without signal in the nineties . . . doesn't get much worse than that for physical evidence.'

Kip gets up to go to the bathroom, leaving Charlie and I alone together. She gives me a small smile and leans in, as though she doesn't want anyone to hear.

'Look, about Kip . . .' She hesitates.

'What about him?' I ask, too quickly. 'We're just friends.'

Charlie looks at me doubtfully and my face begins to heat up. I reach for my drink, but in my tired haze I knock the glass of wine over, sending ruby-red liquid spreading across the table and spilling onto the worn carpet.

Charlie jumps straight into action, throwing napkins onto the table to absorb the liquid and jogging to the bar for more. Alone at the table, I yank Charlie's handbag off the floor to save it from the dripping wine. The bag is unclasped and, as I lift it, I notice a thin brown file inside, which now has two blood-red stains spreading across the front. Just as I am placing the handbag on the bench, I catch the label on the file, which has a case reference and a name: MATILDA JANE HALL. I freeze. *She's been looking at the case.* The file isn't very thick, an indicator of how short the investigation was. The shiny edge of a crime scene photo sticks out among the sheets of paper and I recoil, not wanting to see images of Matilda's body. *What else might be in there, aside from photos?* I glance up to see where Charlie is, but she is already making her way over, holding a blue roll of kitchen towel. Hastily, I move away from the bag.

'Here we go,' she says, starting to wipe the table.

There's no way Charlie will let me look at the file, I'm sure of it. But I can't see how I'll get another chance like this. Usually, I wouldn't dream of trying to trick a police officer . . . but recklessness steals over me, an impulsiveness

I haven't acted upon for years. It's as though teenage Fee is calling me.

'Sorry Charlie, but is there any chance you could get me a glass of water? I'm a bit shaken up from everything,' I say, feeling a twinge of guilt at how easily the lie passes my lips. Charlie doesn't seem suspicious, just nods and walks back to the bar. Thankfully, there is a young couple in front of her quizzing the barman about local ales, so Charlie gets her phone out and frowns down at it, not looking in my direction. Kip is nowhere to be seen, but he could be back any second.

Under the pretence of mopping around and under the table, I open the file inside Charlie's handbag and flick through the pages. There are reams of handwritten pieces of paper, statements from those who were interviewed in 1997, before the police decided there was no evidence of foul play. I catch sight of my own name in the top right-hand corner and my heart begins to race. Glancing up to check Charlie is still distracted, I rifle past autopsy and toxicology reports, unsure what I am looking for. Just as the young couple walks away from the bar, one particular page catches my eye. I flick back to it, clumsy in my haste. I've only got a few seconds: Charlie is being served now, the barman reaching for a glass. I scrabble at the page that has stood out, trying to open the file a little more but it is wedged inside the handbag. As Charlie picks up the glass of water and turns away from the bar, I finally manage to open the file an inch further and make out some of the text.

It can't be. I must have misread it.

Charlie starts walking back over and I straighten up, my throat tight.

'God, you look pale as anything,' she says, placing the glass of water down on the table. 'Are you sure you're alright?'

'I'm fine, really. Head rush from wiping under the table.'

Charlie nods, apparently accepting my poor attempt at a lie. She glances over at Kip, who is walking back from the bathroom.

'I've actually got to head off now.' She studies me for a moment, then speaks in a lowered voice. 'Look Sophie, you clearly mean a lot to Kip, and whatever the cause, it sounds like some odd things have happened on the sand-bank. Just be careful, okay? And call me if anything else happens.' She reaches into her pocket and then presses her card into my hand.

I barely hear Kip as he tells me he is late for an appointment in town.

'I'll catch up with you later though, okay?' he says, giving my arm a quick squeeze. I nod, not listening. He and Charlie walk out of the pub together, leaving me alone in the corner.

I slump back against the booth, shock reverberating through me. Dust motes fly up from the worn velvet, tickling my nose. I barely notice; all I can think about is the page I saw in Matilda's file: a photocopy of a handwritten police statement belonging to a DC Blake.

'Before the interview started, I brought Sheila a cup of tea. She was extremely upset and I sat with her while we waited for the interview room to be ready. She asked where Gary was and I informed her he was still being interviewed. Sheila became visibly distressed at this point. I asked if there was a problem and reassured Sheila it was routine for family members to be interviewed first. Sheila then informed me Gary was not Matilda's biological father.'

I watch her emerge from the pub. The sandbank seems to be draining the life from her: her face is drawn and her eyes flit this way and that, as though she is nervous.

As though she knows something.

Blood pounds in my ears. I just wanted her to leave. But she is picking at the scab of this beach, determined to raise the dead.

And what about the part you played, Sophie?

What about what you did that night?

Chapter Thirty-Two

Now
Sophie

I can think of nothing but the police file as I leave the pub and make my way back across the harbour on the painstakingly slow water-taxi. As soon as I arrive on the sandbank, I walk straight to the forlorn yellow hut, grateful that Kip is in town tonight.

Sheila opens on the first knock. Her eyes light up when she sees me.

'Sophie, it's so g—' She stops abruptly when she notices the expression on my face.

'Can I come in?'

'Of course.' She steps back, her own face creasing with concern.

The hut looks tidier than the last time I was here: the floorboards have been mopped and even the ornaments on the side have been dusted. The picture of me and Matilda as children with our surfboards has been pulled right to the front of the windowsill, its glass gleaming from a recent polish. One of the tired honeysuckle walls has been painted a pure white, and a sheet and paint pot sit underneath it.

'What's wrong?' Sheila asks hurriedly. 'Is it Kip?'

'Why didn't you tell me Gary wasn't Matilda's father?'

The words hang in the air. Sheila's face pales and her jaw starts working as though she is chewing, but no words come out of her mouth.

'You asked me – *begged* me – to find out what happened to Tildy, who took those photos, but you didn't bother telling me *anything* about Gary not being Matilda's father.' My voice is tight, working to keep my anger at bay. 'I think someone on this beach is trying to scare me, maybe even hurt me. Don't ask me to put myself in danger and then not tell me the whole truth!'

We stand face to face, unblinking, until Sheila sinks into the nearby wicker chair. Her hands and trousers are flecked with white paint.

'I made a mistake. But it was one I couldn't regret, because it gave me her. I wouldn't take it back for the world.'

'Did Gary know?'

Would the police have seen this as a motive? A way to get back at Sheila? But Sheila shakes her head.

'I told him straight after we heard the news about Matilda. I knew the police would find out and I wanted him to hear it from me, first.'

'So, he wasn't a suspect?'

I glare at Sheila, daring her to lie to me, thinking of seeing Gary earlier today. Kip said he rarely comes down here anymore . . . is it a coincidence, then, that the first time I've seen him is the same day someone locks me in the shower block? What was it he said to me outside The Ship? *'You just focus on yourself, right now. I'll look after Sheila.'* Was he just trying to stop me asking questions?

'Everyone was a suspect, Sophie. But we were both asleep here in the hut when it happened.'

This ties in with what Charlie said about everyone's alibis, or lack thereof. My head swims with fatigue and the overload of information I have learnt over the past twenty-four hours. If Gary didn't even know Matilda wasn't his, where would his motive be? It doesn't fit.

'Did they interview her biological father? Was he a suspect?'

Sheila raises her head to look at me. For some reason, her expression has changed to something that almost looks fearful.

'He was interviewed, yes. I don't know how it ended, whether he was a suspect. I don't think anyone was ever ruled out completely.'

'Who is he?' I ask, thinking that whoever it was could have easily snuck down here at night with the intention of killing Tildy, possibly to punish Sheila.

Sheila hasn't answered, she is squeezing her hands together, her face paler than ever. I feel a strange sinking sensation in my stomach.

'Who is he, Sheila?'

Chapter Thirty-Three

1982

Sheila

'Gary, honey?' I called as I walked into the hut and looked around. The hut was a mess: a jumble of washing-up by the sink, the sofa-bed unmade. I put down the shopping I had just picked up in town and started clearing some space on the work surface, dropping the coffee-ringed mugs into the sink. I had hoped Gary would have cleaned up by now.

As I moved a cereal bowl, I noticed a handwritten note on the side. Gary's rushed, slanted handwriting told me in pencil grey that he was back in Southampton for the rest of the day on business and would stay at home, rather than returning to the beach tonight. I sighed. I was ovulating and had been hoping to try a couple of times, today. I only hoped the business didn't involve Clive. The so-called 'bargain' mattresses Clive was supposed to be getting from a friend had never materialised and I constantly worried about what the next thing would be.

I carried on tidying the hut and putting the shopping away. It was a gloomy, overcast kind of day. Usually I liked these cosy days as much as I enjoyed the sunlit ones, where the dark sky drove away the tourists and you could watch the rain against the window; but today I felt agitated, restless. I increasingly felt as though my life was on pause, waiting for this one, great event, that would finally make everything complete. Perfect. The moment I could watch my parents' faces light up as they unwrapped the tissue paper to reveal a tiny pair of knitted booties, or the day that my friends would throw me a baby shower in a room full of balloons and cake. Even my brother Paul, the self-proclaimed bachelor, seemed to have found a ready-made family in his new girlfriend Amber and little Kip, excitedly buying the hut next door for weekends and summers together. I was ready for it to be *our* turn. Why couldn't Gary have checked with me before he left?

To work off my bad mood, I took my time making a hot chocolate and then settled under the blankets on the window box with a book I kept meaning to finish. It was a steamy romance set in the 1800s, the kind I couldn't read out on the beach without embarrassment.

It took a few minutes before I realised I had read the same page twice without taking any of it in. It was pointless: I just wasn't in the mood for reading. *Maybe a walk on the headland will help.* The expansive view always soothed me, reminding me of my own insignificance. To some people that might sound depressing, but I found it helped put things in perspective.

I put on my flip flops and opened the door. As I closed the hut, I thought of my coat and debated going to fetch it, but decided against it. Already the fresh air was making me feel more alert and I wanted to get on.

The wind pulled at my hair as I walked, head bowed, along the sand. To my right, hut doors were firmly closed with only the hardiest of children still out playing. To my left, the foamy waves crashed onto the shore, the darkest of green-greys on such a dull day. Above me, a low rumble of thunder shook the sky. *Oh, no.*

I was a good five minutes from my hut, the headland in sight, when the heavens opened. Rain came pelting ferociously down onto the sand as the playing children screamed in delight and began running inside. With no coat, my long-sleeved T-shirt and shorts were soaked through in seconds. Shielding my eyes from the rain, I turned around, preparing to run back to the hut, when I heard a voice calling to me. Looking to the left, I saw David Douglas through the rain, waving from the doorway of his hut. Without thinking, I ran onto his patio and into his hut.

'Thanks,' I panted, as David hurriedly closed the doors against the rain.

'What on *earth* were you doing out there?' David asked, shaking his head at my dripping wet appearance. He was clearly trying not to laugh.

'Going for a walk?' I offered, knowing how ridiculous I sounded. David chuckled.

'I admire your dedication. Let me get you a towel.'

I opened my mouth to protest – I felt odd standing in David's hut alone without Susan or Gary around – but one look at the rain outside stopped me. It was so heavy, it would surely pass quickly, and it wasn't like I had anything to get back for.

David emerged from the back of the hut, holding out a pink and blue towel. For a moment, his eyes flickered downwards, to where the wet fabric of my T-shirt clung to my skin. He looked away.

'Where's Susan?' I asked quickly, to cover the moment.
David hesitated.

'She's, uh, got her mum and aunt down for a few days.
They're shopping for a cot.'

I felt a swoop of envy at the thought of Susan and David
excitedly decorating their nursery before the baby arrived in
December, followed swiftly by shame. It wasn't David and
Susan's fault that Gary had barely been around.

'Sheila?'

I blinked.

'I asked if you wanted a beer.' David was smiling warmly
at me, his hand hovering near the fridge. I shouldn't. The
rain would surely stop soon and anyway, I was watching my
drinking. It wasn't good for fertility. Then I thought of my
empty, quiet hut and the unfinished romance novel. *One
drink won't hurt.*

'That sounds good, thank you. Gary isn't going to be
back until tomorrow so I'm all alone tonight.' *Why did I say
that?* I cringed, but David seemed oblivious, already reaching for two beers. I started drying my hair with the towel,
looking around the hut.

'You've done an incredible job with this place. I can't
believe you learnt how to do it all.'

I knew David had done everything himself, right down
to the electrics and plumbing. The soft blue hut looked
breathtaking, all stripped-back plywood cabinets and white
painted floorboards. Like beach huts were supposed to look.
He had added clever little storage solutions as well: benches
that flipped up to reveal bedding and a table that folded
down from the wall.

'Well, it's by no means perfect,' David said, as he handed me a glass of beer. I noticed his sun-tanned hands had smudges of paint on them. 'But it's not fallen down, yet.'

I saw, however, the obvious pride in his expression as he looked around the hut. There was something else, there, too: an emotion I often felt myself.

'You love this place, don't you?' I asked quietly. David looked surprised but seemed to consider the question.

'I do, yes. I suppose it's something to do with the fact that my job isn't my passion, you know? It's just a source of income. Instead of letting it get me down, I decided to make sure that what I do outside of work reflects who I really am.'

I took a sip of cold beer, marvelling at his honesty. David had much more depth than I had given him credit for.

'And you feel yourself down here?' I pressed. I loved talking about the huts with people who shared the same love for them that I did.

'More myself here than in the office,' David said, with a grin. He had a nice smile and I suddenly felt inexplicably shy, being near this tall man who reminded me of a Nordic Viking. *A Viking. What a silly thing to think, Sheila.* It was, however, hard to marry up the man covered in paint, whose broad shoulders strained against his old T-shirt, with something as sensible as a mortgage advisor. 'I just wish I could be here all the time,' he added.

As the storm wore on, I found myself accepting a second, and then a third beer, bypassing the glasses and drinking straight from the bottle. The sky darkened around us and David lit a couple of tea lights. He was easy company and I found myself relaxing, enjoying the undulating flow of conversation. There was something reassuringly solid about his presence. It was rare that I socialised without Gary, who was the boisterous life and soul of any event.

As I took a sip of my fourth beer, I found David looking at me with too-bright eyes.

'I envy you, you know,' he said out of the blue.

I stared at him in amazement.

'What do you mean?' *What could he possibly envy?* He had everything.

'For starters, I envy the fact that Gary works for himself and you get to spend so much time down here. There's no place I would rather be.'

'*I* spend a lot of time down here. Gary . . .' I stopped. The alcohol was making my emotions bubble closer to the surface than usual. I shouldn't be discussing my husband with a man I had only known for one summer.

'What?' David asked. 'It's okay. You can be honest.' His gaze was steady, focused solely on me.

'I don't know whether he likes the hut that much,' I blurted. It was the first time I had ever said the words out loud and it gave them weight I hadn't wanted to credit them with. 'I mean, he *likes* it, but . . . I always thought this kind of thing was what he wanted. It was a wedding present from my parents and I was so excited to show him, but he's never seemed quite as in love with the sandbank as I am.'

When I had unlocked the hut with Gary for the first time, complete with balloons and champagne waiting inside, he had *acted* thrilled: yet something was missing, as if he was just going through the motions. Then, when we were sipping a celebratory glass of champagne on the beach afterwards, he jokingly said 'didn't fancy the villa in Italy then?' I had never quite forgotten those words. Perhaps the problem had been me . . . perhaps I had been trying too hard to prove I was different to the spoilt girls I grew up with that I had missed what Gary actually wanted. I fiddled with my T-shirt, which was still slightly damp.

'Sometimes we're just looking for different things,' David said quietly. 'It doesn't mean you can't have a great relationship. You'll push each other to keep changing, re-evaluating.'

'I hadn't thought of it like that.' Maybe he was right: maybe I had been looking at the situation too negatively, thinking Gary and I were too different.

David gave an unexpected sigh.

'Then again, I'm not exactly one to give advice. Susan and I . . . well, it's just a bit tense at the moment. The whole baby thing happened quicker than we imagined. Maybe *too* quick.'

I stared at him in surprise. Was there such a thing as too quick?

'This hut was supposed to be our dream,' David went on. 'We saved every penny so we could afford it. We planned to have at least a couple of years down here, just the two of us. Only now it's all change. Susan's mum is with us all the time, warning us how things won't be the same again. They're constantly doing jobs, planning baby showers, and I'm just in the way. So I've just been down here, finishing the place off.'

He rubbed the back of his neck and looked out at the sheeting rain, then back at me.

'I know how I sound. It's probably just nerves. But we're all human, aren't we? We all get lonely.'

This is dangerous territory, I thought. We had had a few too many beers. The veil of social niceties that people normally protected at all costs had been drunkenly lifted, leaving a rawness in its place. It was more than that, though. Cloaked in the surrounding darkness, with just the flickering candlelight between us, it was possible to believe that actions didn't have consequences on this stretch of sandbank. That time was suspended: and so was normal reasoning. I thought of Gary, off in Southampton with Clive, always chasing the next big deal to prove to himself and everyone else that he was worthy. Forgetting, when he left, that I already thought he was.

I met David's eyes across the table and my blood heated. 'Yes,' I whispered. 'We all get lonely.'

We held one another's gaze for a beat too long . . . and by then it was too late to look away. David's expression was confused, surprised. Something else. My stomach gave another jolt. I noticed that his eyes were deepest navy, pulling me under.

Chapter Thirty-Four

Now

Sophie

It can't be true. It *can't* be.

'You're saying you . . . you and my dad?' I shake my head. 'He wouldn't. He loved my mum, he loved *us*. He wouldn't do that to us.'

'There was no "*us*" then, Sophie. You hadn't been born. And yes, he loved her, but we were young and foolish—'

'*Young*,' I spit at her. 'You weren't teenagers, you were *adults*.'

The magnitude of what she is saying seems to swell and wrap itself around my head, squeezing until I can't think straight. Sheila and my dad. My wonderful, ordinary, loving dad, who isn't here to defend himself. Matilda: not just my best friend . . . but my *sister*? It's my turn to pace, while Sheila sits there watching my world fragment with her words.

'I don't believe you. Mum would have left, she wouldn't have stayed in a hut *metres* from you.' Mum has never so much as mentioned Sheila or Gary in the past twenty years.

Only, somehow, I know already what Sheila is going to say: my strong, lioness mother would *never* have stayed in the hut, unless—

'She didn't know.'

Sheila's paper-thin hands grip the arms of the wicker chair. Behind her, the beach is full of people walking along the shore, children building sandcastles. One little girl lifts her spade and smashes it down onto her castle.

'I don't believe you,' I repeat. 'I don't. He wouldn't have done this, he wasn't a cheat.'

'Ask Charlie to show you the rest of the police file. Your dad admitted to the police what happened.'

Oh god. I feel sick at the thought of my dad sleeping with another woman, with a woman who treated me like a daughter. While my mum was pregnant. Memories begin to surface; memories of Mum suggesting drinks with Sheila and Gary, of my dad changing the subject. It had apparently never occurred to either me or Matilda that our parents weren't friends: we had been too wrapped up in our own lives to notice something as boring as our parents.

'Sophie, believe me, I *never* wanted you to know about this.' Sheila's eyes fill with tears, her voice growing thick. She reaches up and presses a hand to her temple.

'How long are you saying this went on for?'

'Just once! That was all. We were so ashamed afterwards. I told Gary I wasn't actually that keen on your parents and after a while we all just went about our own lives, with our own families.'

'Why would Dad stay?' I demand. 'If what you're saying is true?'

Sheila shakes her head.

'I don't know, Sophie. Maybe for the same reason I did. This place meant everything. It was worth burying secrets, pretending it never happened.'

I think of Matilda's long blonde hair. Her deep blue eyes. Sheila is blonde, too, but it is a honey-blonde, helped by expensive highlights. Gary has dark red hair and brown eyes. Neither of them has the straight teeth that Matilda had, a feature I now realise she shared with my dad. Anna and I were both born with Mum's dark hair . . . whereas Matilda had the same white-blonde hair my dad had. She was even tall like my dad, far taller than a daughter of Gary's should ever have been. It suddenly seems so glaringly, screamingly obvious, like Matilda herself was parading around like a giant DNA test. I put a hand to my face, squeezing my forehead.

'Who knew?' *Oh god, had Dad known all along?* 'Did my dad?'

'No one, at first. I was going to tell Gary. I had it all planned out, what to say, how to explain. But then he found the test. I had it wrapped in my toiletry bag and he needed something, sun cream, I think? It doesn't matter. He came flying out of the bathroom, asking if it was true . . . by the time I had told him yes, he was already off to buy champagne and talking about names. How could I tell him I was pregnant by another man?'

I want her to stop calling my dad *another man*. Like he was some extra in a scene: if Sheila is telling the truth, Matilda was his baby, too.

'And my dad?'

Sheila hesitates.

'He started to get suspicious that summer . . . her last summer. She had shot up, her hair had grown . . . suddenly she was looking just like him. He confronted me one night, but I ignored him. I wasn't ready.'

'All those years . . . you let Matilda play in our hut, knowing that he was her *dad*.' On the surface I am stony, but beneath I am resisting the urge to start screaming. 'He tried to find out . . . and you *lied*. He deserved to know the truth.'

'I didn't know what else to do!' Sheila cries. 'I didn't know for sure he was her father.'

I almost laugh at this. It's obvious Sheila can't truly believe that: not when the similarities between Matilda and my dad would have been so stark to anyone who knew the truth. So stark Dad eventually picked up on them.

'I would have lost Gary. Maybe Matilda, too. Your parents might have divorced.' Sheila's voice goes up an octave, shrill and trembling. 'You have no idea – *none* – what it's like to live with a secret like that and decide whether or not to play God. Knowing that you might break up two families. I stayed down here because Matilda was happy here. And when your mother had you and your sister, I knew I had done the right thing not telling anyone. You were all so happy. It was better that Matilda was in our family, loved, than the three of you come from broken homes.'

'That wasn't your decision to *make*!' I shout. 'My dad should have had a say! And my mum. She was . . . our *sister*.' My sister. *How am I supposed to tell Anna and my mum about this?*

'I wanted a child,' Sheila says quietly. As though, somehow, that's enough. She leans forward and buries her head in her hands.

'Thanks to you, my dad never knew his own daughter.'

'No,' Sheila whispers as I turn to leave. 'But he also never knew how it felt to lose her.'

Chapter Thirty-Five

Now

Sophie

By the time I walk numbly back towards my hut, the sun is low in the sky and mosquitoes are starting to swarm. I pass old Harry, outside his hut. He raises a hand in my direction as he heads down the beach to the shore, a black bucket in one hand. I hear fish flopping and thunking against the sides of his bucket.

The beach is peaceful at this time of the day: the visitors gone, people on their decks having their first glass of wine, windsurfers returning to shore. It is strange to think that a place so pure, with no traffic, no blaring phones or televisions, can hide so many secrets. *Did Tildy find out about Sheila and Dad? Is that why she was upset that night?*

There is a new slant to all my memories, now. I didn't play with my best friend and hang out in her hut, accepting ice lollies and sun cream from her parents. She was my half-sister, with Sheila watching on, weighed down by her secret. The pain of Tildy's death has somehow intensified, knowing of this connection. There is no doubt in my mind that at some point, we would have discovered the truth. The thought of Tildy meeting Nick, of Christmases together with Anna and Mike, too, taunts me. *It isn't fair that you're gone*. What makes it all worse is that Dad had apparently tried to find out the truth.

When I am back inside the hut, I pick up my phone. Bringing up my mum's number, I hesitate: should I tell her? She seems happy with Phil, and I don't want to upset that. *I'll talk about the hut,* I decide. *See if it leads anywhere.* I don't have to tell her everything right away.

I press call, but almost immediately the phone goes to voicemail. Disappointed, I leave a quick message for her to call me back and put the phone down.

Agitated, I pour myself a large glass of wine. I am heavy-handed and wine splashes over the side of the glass onto the counter. I reach into my handbag and pull out my cigarettes, carrying them and the wine back out onto the deck. I know I need to stop, to start looking after myself again, but tonight, I don't care. I light a cigarette and take a long drag.

Now what? I could call Anna, but I don't feel this is something I can burden her with over the phone. There is, I realise, only one person I want to speak to. The urge is so overwhelming, I am already reaching for my phone. I've never wanted, never *needed*, to speak to him more.

Unlocking the screen, I go to my saved contacts and hover over Nick's name. I wonder, briefly, whether this is a good idea, but the weight pressing down on me already feels slightly lifted just at the thought of talking to him. No matter what has happened between us, he's a kind person and he knew my dad better than anyone. He'll listen.

My thumb presses 'Call': there is no going back now. Straight away I hear the international ring tone. He must have arrived in Tokyo. As the phone rings, my heart starts to beat faster, anticipating hearing his warm voice. How should I start? *Hi, how are you? Nick, I need to talk to you. Nick, I'm sorry. Can we talk?*

Four rings. Then five.

The phone rings and rings, shrill in my ear, and no one answers.

The night steals across the beach as I watch her, out on her deck with a bottle of wine. She puts the phone to her ear. Who is she calling? Does the person on the other end of the phone know what happened that summer? Has she told them the truth?

When I finally fall asleep, I dream about her. I dream about her long, blonde hair. Even in the wind, it seemed to stay perfectly straight, hanging down her back. Her skin, flushed pink from running along the beach, is so real I could almost reach out and stroke the back of her cheek. I can hear her laughing, it echoes around and around in my head. Let me stay asleep forever. Please. I can see the blue of her eyes, shimmering like the sunlight has touched them. Then the blue gets bigger, her eyes get wider, and they become the sea and I am drowning, I can't breathe, I'm sorry, I'm so sorry.

Chapter Thirty-Six

Then

Caitlin

The party fucking blew.

I had known it would: it was a get-together for Kip's mum, for fuck's sake. A boring old barbecue with a load of sandwich platters that kept getting attacked by wasps. But there was always the hope that there would be some booze to swipe, or some drama when one of the parents got wasted. So far, all that had happened was that my mum had dragged me along with her and we had stood around making polite chit chat. I'd been handed a *Coke*.

Mum laughed shrilly at something Shiv, Dev's dad said, and I cringed. It was obvious she didn't have a clue what he was talking about – she didn't follow politics – but she was absolutely desperate to fit in with the *normal* families along the beach. Good luck to her: while the other dads were gathered around the barbecue, my dad was sleeping off a hangover back in our hut. We were never going to fit in.

'Education is incredibly important,' Shiv was saying. 'It is the backbone of opportunity. Schools *must* perform better, or results will keep slipping.'

My mum nodded eagerly then gestured towards me.

'Well, this one got all A stars in her GCSEs! We couldn't believe it, not with the amount of partying she likes to do.'

Shiv looked at me with his eyebrow raised, like he was unimpressed. The other adults in the group, however, were all giving me indulgent, brighter-than-the-sun smiles. It didn't surprise me. I was always getting told I was special: my teachers when I produced top marks, friends of my parents, who would stop and say '*wow, she's a heartbreaker, isn't she?*' I liked it, too. The attention. Some people were born to do great things, be superstars. I just needed to figure out what *my* thing was. Just then, it seemed to be boredom.

Thankfully at that moment, Kip emerged from his hut, followed by his dad. I left my mum to it – she was the one who had wanted to come, after all – and hurried over to him. When Kip saw me coming, he moved away from his dad, grinning at me. He always did that, like he was really pleased to see me, and I felt a jolt of frustrated pleasure. Unlike most boys, Kip was hard to read. I had an on–off boyfriend back at school, but he was so fucking immature it was unreal. All the boys in my year were. Kip was still a boy, sure, but he was much more grown-up than the other kids at the beach. He was quiet, funny and he didn't try and flirt with me, which drove me fucking *crazy*.

'Hey,' I said, hopping up onto the deck next to Kip. 'Thank god you're here, this is *so* boring.'

Kip chuckled. 'Surprised you came. Not really your scene, is it?'

I rolled my eyes at him. 'My *mum* wanted to come. She made me.'

I didn't add that the alternative would mean staying in the hut with my dad, which I always avoided. But Kip gave me a look that said somehow he knew what I was thinking. Kip got me in a way that hardly anyone did. He shook his head at my bitchiness, but he listened when I worried about university applications and tried to distract me from my parents' constant arguing. He just accepted what you gave him without trying to fix it, and I liked that. Not that I would ever have told him, because then he would know how important he was to me. My mum always said that letting someone know you care is like handing them the knife to stab you with. Kip didn't seem like a stabber but I wasn't going to take the risk.

'Well, why don't we spice things up a bit?' Kip muttered, leaning towards me with a conspiratorial smile. 'There's a bottle of vodka out back, I think Tom's brother brought it.' He nodded in the direction of Tom and his family, who were stood with James, Tom's older brother. James had his arm wrapped around the waist of a petite brown-haired girl who wore a glittering diamond ring on her skinny finger and a look of utter smugness.

'No one will notice if we take some,' Kip continued. 'We can hide upstairs for a bit.'

I didn't need asking twice: disappearing upstairs with Kip and a blanket of alcohol sounded fucking perfect. I ignored the thought of my dad, currently flat out after his usual midday drinking session. *I'm not like him. It's not the same. I'm actually going to do something with my life.*

'Wait here,' Kip was saying, 'I'll grab it and then we can escape.'

'Okay,' I said, allowing myself a rare, full smile. Kip disappeared into his hut, while I waited on the deck.

I looked around: Mum was now off talking to Tom's mum, pretending to be full of interest in whatever boring shit Tom's mum would be spouting about being a school governor. To the right, Dev was standing with his parents. He caught my eye and smiled. I knew Dev liked me: it was obvious, even though he had never said anything. Then I noticed Shiv staring at me, unsmilingly. He shot a look at Dev, who quickly pulled his gaze away from me and stared down at the sand. It was glaringly obvious that Shiv didn't approve of me, which irritated me: I hated being told what I could and couldn't do.

Just then, a laugh sounded behind me. I whipped around and saw Kip standing a few feet away with his back to me, his attention apparently elsewhere. When I saw who he was talking to, I gritted my teeth. That sneaky little *bitch*, Sophie Douglas. She had been attached like a limpet this summer. What was Kip *doing*? I was used to getting what I wanted and when I didn't, it drove me insane: especially when the alternative to me was some fat girl with frizzy hair, who was so fucking *try hard*. She did have bigger tits than me though. Maybe that's what Kip liked? Rory at school had called my boobs '*mozzie bites*' in front of all his mates on the last day of term. I had wanted to scream and burst into tears, all at the same time, but instead I just told everyone he had a tiny dick and walked off. He had gone red and all the boys had laughed at him, so I'd felt a bit better. *Well, if that's what Kip wants, he's fucking welcome to her.* I snatched a beer from the table nearest to me, not even caring if my mum saw me, and stalked inside the hut.

Kip's hut was full of buckets of ice, used chopping boards and dirty plates. I dropped onto the window seat in the corner and looked out at everyone else. David Douglas was offering Mum a drink and she kept batting her eyelashes at him. I couldn't really blame her: he was old, sure, but he was really tall with blonde hair and a beard. I sniggered to myself. Bet *he* would never call my boobs mozzie bites. Half the dads along the beach would give their right arm for a glimpse of them. Even Shiv, despite the stick up his ass. I looked at James, Tom's older brother. His fiancée was the walking cliché of uptight: all frilly, high-necked dress and pursed lips. I bet I could show him a *much* better time.

The sound of the fridge door slamming startled me: the beer bottle slipped from my hand and hit the floor, spraying beer everywhere.

'Caitlin! I didn't see you there.' I looked up to see Gary Hall hurrying towards me with a cloth in his hand.

'Sorry,' I muttered. Gary waved away my apology as he crouched down to pick up the bottle and started wiping the beer up with the cloth. The top of the bottle had cracked and a few shards glinted in the sunlight.

'Trying to avoid it all?' he asked, with a knowing sort of look.

'Something like that,' I said, with a shrug.

'Can't blame you,' Gary replied. 'Are you alright? You didn't cut yourself or anything?' His eyes scanned my hands, checking for any injury. He looked genuinely concerned. I suddenly thought of my own dad, mouth lolling open on the sofa back at the hut. Out of nowhere, my throat closed up.

'No, I'm fine.' I suddenly felt cold, despite the warm day. I stood up quickly and left the hut without another word, just as Dev was approaching.

'Hey,' he said, glancing quickly back over his shoulder at where his parents stood. Near them, Kip was still talking to Sophie, but his eyes met mine for a moment. I clenched my jaw and looked away, without smiling.

'I brought you something,' Dev said. His large brown eyes were warm. He held up an orange alcopop he had clearly taken from one of the ice buckets. 'It was the last one left. Mango is your favourite, right?'

I stared at the orange bottle in his hand for what felt like an eternity. It was the colour of sunsets and fire.

'Yes. That's my favourite.'

I sat on the sand for a long time after the party, staring out at the waves. Mum would have left to check on dad before she even noticed I was gone from the party.

I heard him before I saw him: the soft crunch of sand underfoot, the catch of his breath as he finished climbing down the sand dune. I wasn't sure whether it was a co-incidence, or whether he had come looking for me. He sat down a few feet away, awkwardly crossing his legs. From our position, we were blocked from view of the beach huts. The empty shoreline made it seem as though we were the only people who existed on the entire beach.

For the first minute or two he didn't speak. I wondered what he was doing here. He fidgeted with his T-shirt.

'You okay?' he asked, eventually. 'You left the party pretty early.'

I nodded. All of a sudden, I felt unexpectedly nervous, which was stupid.

'I'm not good with stuff like that,' I replied. 'Smiling and being polite. Everyone's just pretending. Showing off. I always think parties would be much better if everyone acted the way they actually wanted.'

He laughed. 'The world would implode if people started being honest.'

There was a short silence before he spoke again.

'Maybe the reason you don't like parties is because people are intimidated by you.'

Great. I knew where this was going.

'Because I'm a bitch?'

I thought of perfect Sophie Douglas, always so desperate to please. If that was what it took for people to like me, I would rather jump off the headland.

'No,' he said, with a frown. He took a deep breath, as though he didn't know whether to say it or not. 'Because you're beautiful.'

My stomach flipped. No one had ever called me beautiful before. Pretty, yes. Hot, yes. Most boys thought telling you they fancied you was enough to make you come running.

I turned to look at him. His eyes were perfect: an amazing colour, with long eyelashes.

'You think I'm beautiful?' I asked. I couldn't help it: I wanted to hear him say it again. It was a thrill like nothing I had ever experienced.

'I think you're the most beautiful girl I've ever seen.'

My heart raced as we looked at one another. There had been a strange atmosphere to the entire day, as though there were a million different stories happening at the same time, criss-crossing through the partygoers. Changing the tide.

He still looked nervous: if anything was going to happen, I figured I was going to have to make the first move. I shuffled closer to him and allowed my arm to graze his, while still looking out at the waves. He didn't say anything, but his breathing became heavier. Slowly, I inched my hand through the sand until it brushed against his. He didn't move it and I took that as a sign. I laced my fingers gently through his, loving the slow pace. He exhaled and a disbelieving smile spread across his face.

'What is it?' I asked, watching him.

'I feel like the luckiest guy in the world right now.'

I tried to hide my smile and we sat in silence for a few moments. His thumb gently rubbed my palm: it felt electric on my skin.

'Can we keep this between us?' he asked, after a while. I nodded. The last thing I needed was my dad finding out and causing trouble, like he always did whenever he caught wind of a boy in my life.

'Our little secret,' I whispered, as he leant in closer.

Chapter Thirty-Seven

Now

Sophie

The night stretches out before me, never-ending, as I wait for Nick to return my call. Anxiously anticipating sharing the burden of Sheila's confession with someone. As each hour slips by with no call, however, my initial anticipation turns into embarrassment. *Fine,* I think, as I pull my phone out from under my pillow for the umpteenth time and see no missed calls, *fuck you.* Lying in the dark, I convince myself it's a good thing he didn't answer. Relying on him isn't healthy. I need to move on.

'It's a *beautiful* hut,' the estate agent, Gina, says as we stand before it. She hugs her iPad to her chest and inhales dramatically.

'You know, I've lived in this area for three years and this is only the second time I've made it to the beach.' She sighs and shoots me one of those long-suffering woman-to-woman smiles. 'Work. Kids. You know what it's like.'

Somehow, I manage to force a polite smile without my face cracking from exhaustion. I had completely forgotten Gina was coming until this morning: I had quickly tidied the hut, trying not to think about Nick, or my dad's alleged betrayal.

Gina can only be mid-thirties at the most. She has highlighted blonde hair, pink nails and a yellow and white polka-dot dress that flares out around her hips. She's all brightness and colour. Even her cheeks have little pink spots on them from the sea air. She circles the hut slowly, making notes on her iPad. She might be sweet and almost motherly, but her eyes are razor-sharp as she observes the hut, taking in every inch.

The morning sunlight hits the blue and white hut, softening its edges and lighting up the soft ash wood inside. It should make me feel happy, officially letting it go on such a beautiful morning; but instead, I just feel confused.

'May I?' Gina asks, finishing her circuit and gesturing towards the doors. I nod, nearly rolling my eyes as she gingerly navigates the deck steps in her nude stilettos, before remembering that I turned up here myself in leather brogues. It feels incredible that it was only a few days ago: time stands still here, as though it catches in the sand dunes.

'It's a beautiful hut,' Gina says again as we walk inside and this time, I give her a genuine smile.

'We had a lot of happy memories here. I was very lucky.'

Gina starts opening cupboards, inspecting worktops and windows, then disappears into the curtained section at the back of the hut while I wait in the living area.

As I stand there with sunlight streaming through the window and warming my face, there is a strange thickening in my throat. For the first time, the reality of losing the hut hits me. It's always been a constant feature of our family, like a tough grandparent or an adored dog. Although things were never the same after the summer of 1997, it was still a huge part of our lives before that time. It's also where Anna met Mike: she came down to stay during the off-season and met Mike, whose parents owned a hut at the other end of the sandbank: two years later, they got married and moved to Australia. The idea that some stranger might repaint the soft blue exterior or replace the coloured glass in the porthole makes my heart ache. My parents loved this hut so much. *I* loved this hut.

Then you ruined it all that summer.

'Are you alright?' Gina's voice cuts into my thoughts. I blink. I had almost forgotten she was there.

'S-sorry,' I mutter. 'I got completely caught up.'

Gina smiles sympathetically at me.

'It's perfectly understandable. You're not just letting go of a property, you're letting go of *memories*. Opportunities. It's always emotional. But,' she says, her fuchsia lips turning upwards, 'I've never had a seller ask for their money back!'

She is so unbelievably perky, I have to admire her. Otherwise I might hit her.

'Well, I've certainly seen enough for now. Shall we have a little chat?'

We seat ourselves at the small table and Gina talks me through her estimates. She tells me it is an advantage that it is the first in the row, closest to the headland. However, it apparently needs work.

'It's dated,' Gina says, with a crisp, but apologetic look. 'You know what it's like nowadays with these huts. People want them to look and feel like a second home, with all the luxuries. I mean,' she gives a little chuckle, 'you don't even have a *hot water tank*.'

This last comment prickles. Is that what I usually sound like, with my need to have the latest coffee machine or industrial-sized fridge? My childhood was no better or worse for not having had a hot water tank. I can hear my dad's voice in my head: '*there's a kettle*'. Then I remember Sheila's confession and push all thoughts of him away.

Gina informs me she can return the next day with the photographer. After seeing her off, I remain on the deck for a moment staring out across the sand dunes, unblinking, until my vision blurs.

A minute or so later, the tall figure of Kip approaches, his hair damp and wearing swimming shorts. Despite my frayed nerves, my stomach does a small flip.

'Morning,' he says, smiling. Ignoring the steps, he jumps straight up onto the deck. 'I'm sorry I didn't come back to the beach last night, I got stuck in town.' He leans against the railings, studying me. 'How are you?' he asks, quietly.

Although I was initially pleased to see him, something about his tone irritates me.

'I'm fine,' I reply. 'Why?'

'You seemed upset yesterday. I know what Charlie said wasn't what you wanted to hear. But,' he continues before I can speak, 'at least we've spoken to someone. Hopefully now we can let this whole thing go.'

Let this whole thing go. He says it so dismissively, so easily and my heart sinks. *Hasn't he spoken to Sheila? Doesn't he know there is more to this?*

'You don't want to end up like Sheila,' Kip says, looking across at me. 'She's never been able to move on, she's obsessed with the idea that there's more to Matilda's death than an accident.'

Anger fissures through me. *Questioning how someone you loved died is not an obsession. It's justice.*

'And if she's right?' I ask tightly, not looking at him. After Nick's silence last night, Kip's words sting almost as much. I thought Kip, at least, could be relied upon. Now I am left with the awful knowledge of what happened between Sheila and my dad, without anyone to talk to about it.

'Don't worry,' he replies. 'There's nothing on the sand-bank that will hurt you.'

I glance at the yellow hut. Sheila might not have physically hurt me last night, but her words have had the same effect as if she had ran through me with a knife.

'Right, well if that's everything?' I say, folding my arms and looking pointedly at Kip. He looks slightly taken aback.

'Well, I thought you might want to get some breakfast—'

'No, thanks. The estate agent is coming back tomorrow so I've got lots to do before I head back to London.'

Without waiting for his response, I turn and walk back into the hut, closing the doors behind me. It is a few moments before I hear him leave.

Chapter Thirty-Eight

Then

Sophie

'Ready?'

Tom's voice drifted up to me from somewhere far below.

'No!' I yelled back. My legs were shaking as I stood at the very edge of the headland, staring down at the fifty-foot drop. The waves seemed angry today, crashing against the rocks below. By my left foot was the broken *DANGER CLIFF EDGE* sign. *Fuck, fuck I can't do this!*

Tom and Amy had already navigated the footholds in the face of the headland with ease and now they were standing on the rocks below, waiting for me. But *they* had done it loads of times: I never had and fear was pinning me to the headland.

'Go on, Fee!' Kip called behind me, where he, Dev, Jamie and Caitlin were all waiting. I could barely hear him through the howling wind. 'The ridge is just below you, under the sign! It's easy from there!'

What was I *thinking*? This wasn't *fun*, this was dangerous! What was wrong with *normal* stuff like fishing or swimming or—

A loud shout of laughter broke behind me: I didn't need to turn around to know it was Caitlin. Gritting my teeth and fighting against the urge to close my eyes, I shuffled forward, so that my toes were hanging off the edge and bent my knees slightly to steady myself. I took one last deep breath and jumped.

For a second, I knew nothing but blind, explosive panic: then my feet slammed onto the narrow stone ridge jutting out from the cliff-face. Instinctively, I crouched into a ball to stop the wind from throwing me off the ridge and let out a shaky sob of relief. *I did it!*

Above and below me, I could hear whoops and cheers. A grin slowly spread across my face as adrenaline surged through me. They had all assured me it was easy from this point on; that the foot and handholds below the ridge were well-worn and deep enough for safety. I tried not to hesitate on the ridge for too long: the sea looked terrifying from this position, grey and churning, the foamy whitecaps swirling furiously. It was partly the reason this particular cliff-scaling activity had been suggested: when the weather was crap there wasn't much else to do. And while I could have thought of a hundred alternatives, I would never have said anything. I turned and slowly lowered my legs over the edge of the ridge, until I was only hanging on by my fingertips. *Where was the first foothold?* I was flailing in the wind, trying to slot my trainer into it.

'Hurry *up*!'

Above me, Caitlin was preparing to jump onto the ridge. Everyone else had waited until the person before them was nearly at the bottom, but she was about to start even though she knew I hadn't done it before. She was showing off, no doubt hoping to overtake me. Before I could move, she leapt off the edge of the cliff and landed heavily, her trainers only inches from my fingers. Stones and bits of clay showered down onto my face, but with my hands gripping the edge of the ridge I couldn't wipe them away. Anger throbbed through me. I *hated* Caitlin. I hated her for the way she made me feel, so small and stupid. I hated her for trying to scare me with the boat. I hated her for being taller and prettier and more confident than me. She had the power to make me feel included, but she never did. Even Amy had started to cool towards me, seemingly fearful of Caitlin's clear dislike of me.

I'm not going to let her win.

Shuffling to the left of the ridge, away from Caitlin's feet, I finally located the first solid handhold: a blunt piece of rock embedded in the cliff-face. Taking a deep breath, I stuck my right foot out and wedged it into the cliff-face. Somehow, despite the blood pounding in my ears, I managed to heave myself off the ridge and navigate the rest of the cliff-face, dodging the soft clusters of rock samphire that could come loose in my hand. Jumping down onto the rocks where Tom and Amy were waiting, Tom gave me a slap on the back.

'Nicely done, kiddo.'

'Thanks,' I muttered, still furious.

'Yeah, nice one Fee!' Amy exclaimed. She glanced quickly up at Caitlin and then leaned towards me. 'You've got some dirt on your face,' she whispered. I hastily scrubbed my face with the back of my sleeve.

Caitlin, Kip, Dev and Jamie all followed in quick succession, with Jamie doing a backflip on the rocks that made

Amy shriek. While the boys high-fived each other, Caitlin pushed past me and sat on the rock to retie her trainer.

'Well done,' Kip said, coming over to stand next to me. 'It'll be easier next time.'

'Next time?' I blurted, without thinking.

Jamie was standing nearby and he laughed.

'I'd catch you,' he winked at me. I quickly looked away, my face hot.

'Let's go again!' Dev shouted. 'See who can do it fastest this time!'

He started jumping along the rocks, back towards the beach and the steps up to the headland. Everyone raced to follow, chatting excitedly. I hung back, reluctant to repeat the cliff-scaling, until I realised Caitlin was behind me, still doing up her laces. Not wanting to walk with her, I quickly hurried along the rocks after the others.

When I reached the point where the rocks met the beach, I saw that Kip was waiting.

'Some kids have covered a hole in seaweed.' He shook his head and pointed to what looked like an innocent-looking pile of seaweed right in front of us on the sand. 'It's pretty deep, so watch out.'

'Thanks,' I said, flushing with pleasure that he had stopped to warn me.

'Let Caitlin know!' Kip called, before running off towards the others.

Clambering down from the rocks, I carefully navigated the wide hole the kids had made. I couldn't see how deep it was as it was expertly covered. *Why didn't the others just get rid of the seaweed?* I hesitated. *Should I move it?*

The sound of footsteps approached from behind. I turned and saw Caitlin jumping along the rocks. I opened my mouth to warn her about the hole, but something stopped me: all of a sudden, it was like sharp poison was flooding my veins. I closed my mouth and stepped out of the way, my heart pounding. Caitlin drew closer, aiming straight for the hole. I watched silently as she stepped forwards, almost in slow motion. With a strangled cry, her arms flew into the air and the bottom half of her body disappeared. I was shocked to see how deep the hole was: only her head was visible as she hit the bottom with a dull thud. There was silence for a second, then she let out an ear-piercing scream.

Within moments the others had come running, along with Tom's dad and, to my horror, Gary Hall. *What if they find out what I did?* Dev and Kip looked terrified and scrambled out of the way of the older men.

Before I had even registered what was going on, the two dads had pulled Caitlin out of the hole and onto the ground, where she writhed on the floor. I felt sick. *Why hadn't she stopped crying yet?*

Gary's face was full of concern, but he bent down and placed a gentle hand on Caitlin's shoulder.

'Sweetheart,' he said calmly and firmly over Caitlin's cries, 'you're going to be fine, okay? It's just a bit of pain and shock. Let's get you looked at.'

It seemed to work: Caitlin's cries softened into a hiccupping whimper as Gary carefully scooped her up into a fireman's carry. As he adjusted his hold, Caitlin let out a sob of pain and clung tighter to Gary, burying her blotchy, tear-streaked face in his shirt. The others looked on, shocked, as Gary and Tom's dad hurried off towards the line of huts with Caitlin. After a moment, Dev ran after them.

Kip came up to me as the rest of the crowd slowly dispersed. I realised I was shaking.

'What happened?' he asked. 'Didn't you tell her about the hole?'

'I . . . yeah, I did,' I lied, certain my voice would give me away. I couldn't look at him. 'She was running, she . . . she wasn't listening.' *What if she was really hurt?* My eyes brimmed with hot tears.

'Hey,' Kip said, rubbing my arm. 'Don't worry, it's not your fault. She'll be fine. It's the kids that dug the hole that'll be in real trouble.' Giving me a final, reassuring smile, he walked off towards the huts.

Kip's right, I told myself. *It'll be okay*. I took a deep breath, deciding to go back to my hut and avoid the beach for the rest of the day.

'Why did you do that?'

I slowly turned around: Matilda was sat on the rocks a few feet away from me, Chetana by her side. My stomach lurched. *How long had they been sitting there?*

'Do what?' I asked, trying to act confused, while my skin prickled with panic.

'You let her run into the hole. You didn't warn her.' Matilda's voice was flat.

'I tried—'

'No, you didn't.' Matilda cut me off. 'We were right here. Kip said to warn Caitlin and you didn't. You *wanted* her to get hurt.'

Chetana was looking down at her feet, but Matilda was staring at me like she had never seen me before.

'You don't understand,' I said, defensively. 'She tried to run over me with a speed boat and then acted like it was an accident.'

'So, you purposefully tried to hurt her back?'

'What is your *problem*?' I snapped, hating the way she was looking at me, hating how shitty I already felt about what I had done.

'My *problem* is that I don't know who you are anymore, Sophie,' Matilda said, her voice rising. 'My *problem* is that my best friend of fourteen years has become an exact replica of the girl she hates!'

'Best *friend*?' I laughed bitterly. 'All you've done the past few weeks is ignore me!'

'I haven't ignored you. If you weren't so self-obsessed you would have realised that by now.'

It was as if she had slapped me.

'Yeah *right*!' I cried. 'It's so obvious you're jealous I've found some friends that aren't *you*.' This was a total lie, but I wanted to hurt her back.

'There is *nothing* about you or your life that I am jealous of,' Matilda said icily. 'I don't think for one moment you're happy hanging around with that lot, pretending you're oh so grown up because you've finally tried a fucking beer.'

'You ditched *me* this summer, remember? You're the one who's fucked off with *her*,' I gestured angrily to Chetana who looked stricken, 'at every opportunity. Bet you've had a whale of a time, playing boring card games with your boring *mate.*' I regretted the words as soon as they came out of my mouth, but it was too late.

We were both breathing heavily, staring at each other.

'I don't even recognise you anymore, Sophie,' Matilda said, at last. 'Not the stupidly small bikinis, not the sucking up. I don't know who you are.'

Tugging on Chetana's hand, Matilda got up from the rocks and walked in the opposite direction to where the others had gone, leaving me standing alone between the rocks and the sand.

Chapter Thirty-Nine

Now

Sophie

After Kip finally walks away, I spend the rest of the morning clearing the remainder of the hut. The radio is on loud and I turn my phone off, stuffing it under the cushions on the window box so I am not tempted to look at it in case Nick calls. Every time someone walks past the hut, I automatically look up, wondering if it might be Kip; but he doesn't return. It doesn't matter. His dismissal of everything that has happened over the past few days said it all.

Gina will be back tomorrow with the photographer and after that the sale process will start almost immediately. I won't have to be here anymore. I won't have to think about Sheila or Kip or anyone left here. I can return to London. Return to work, to my clients. Only that concept doesn't hold the same familiarity and warmth as it once did. For the past fifteen years I have slogged away in the publicity world, giddy when a client said they were impressed with me, thrilled when the firm helped launch a client's career. But over the past few years the industry has changed without me noticing, morphing into something empty and performative. I'm pounding the same route, but the scenery has completely changed. The lack of emails and constant monitoring of followers, press pieces, trending hashtags, hasn't left the chasm I thought it would. Instead, there is a strange sense of detachment.

In the early afternoon, I pause for a glass of wine. Against my better judgement, I pull my phone out from under the cushion and switch it on. Unread work emails flood my screen, but I barely glance at them. No missed calls from Nick or Mum. Putting my phone down again, I look out at the perfect, shimmering sea, overseen by circling gulls. The sun blazes through the glass and beads of sweat gather in my hairline. Regardless of all the secrets, the sandbank is breathtaking.

Once the kitchen counters are done, I move onto the floor. Although it's a small surface area, it takes over an hour to clean; stubborn splashes of spilt coffee and hot chocolate pepper the floorboards. I take my wine with me, shuffling it along the floor by my side as I scrub. Finally, all that is left is the section of floor under the sofa. Dreading the state of the floorboards, I grip the back of the sofa and pull it away from its position under the window. For a small sofa, it is heavy, and at first it barely moves. Finally, with my foot pushed against the wall for leverage, I manage to drag it away from the wall. Behind the sofa, a thick grey line of dust and sand has glued itself to the floorboards. *Great.*

Crossing the room, I drain the last of my drink and reach for the broom. I am just about to start sweeping when I notice something on the floor, among the dust.

I stop. There is no mistaking the small, white square: it is a polaroid photo. I think of me and Kip knocking the tin off the table, the remaining photos scattering across the floor. *We missed one.*

Slowly, I walk forwards and bend down to pick it up. Brushing off the sand and dust, I turn the photo over. It takes me a moment to make sense of what I am seeing; then my heart begins to race.

This is it. The kind of photo that someone would hide under a beach hut. The kind of photo that someone would break into a hut for.

Would kill for?

Chapter Forty

Then

Chetana

My eyes were closed and my head tilted backwards so I could feel the full warmth of the sun toasting my face. Way below the quarry, I could just about make out the sound of waves hitting the rocks and the hum of boats.

Opening my eyes, I saw Matilda watching me. Heat immediately rose in my cheeks.

'What?' I asked.

She looked away, with a small shrug.

'Nothing. I was just looking at your hair.'

I touched it, embarrassed.

'It's so frizzy, isn't it?' I would rather say it myself first than hear Tildy say it.

'No,' she shook her head. Her skin was the perfect, sun-kissed brown. 'It's the way the light catches all the copper and gold in it . . . it's like a badass mermaid tail or something.' She laughed. 'Lucky I'm not going to study English at A-level. I couldn't be poetic to save my life.'

I tried not to show how thrilled I was at her compliment.

'What *are* you going to study? Have you made up your mind yet?' I asked, moving my feet through the cool quarry water.

'Still not sure. Maybe photography. I like social care, too, though. I want to help people, I think.'

'Will your parents mind?' I asked. I was always intrigued by what other parents would say or do. What would it be like, not to have your father narrow the fields you were allowed to study down to the ones he approved of?

'They might. I don't care, though. They always disagree on what I should do. My dad would tell me to go down the business route, become an entrepreneur like him,' Matilda rolled her eyes. 'Mum would want me to do *sensible* topics that would get me a good job. Like a teacher or a lawyer.'

'Why do they always think they know what's best for us?' I murmured. I flicked my feet up and down in the clear water, making the fish scatter. 'How can they know what's best when *they've* never done it?'

Matilda snorted. 'My dad would claim he *has* done it. I'm not sure how he can say that when he's been bankrupt about a hundred times.'

My mouth opened in surprise. Some of the things Tildy said out loud about her parents were outrageous to me. She was so confident, had such strong opinions.

'Your dad's been bankrupt?' I asked. *Bankrupt.* It was such a dirty word. I couldn't believe how casually she said it.

'It's not as bad as it sounds. I mean, it's not *brilliant*,' she added, 'but we've never really needed his money because Mum's family is rich.'

'So . . . your dad doesn't have a proper job?' I watched a tiny terracotta-red crab scuttle along one of the smooth rocks near us, heading for one of the small rock pools.

'I can't imagine my dad doing that. He says it's the man's job to provide, that not providing is shameful.'

My eyes widened in alarm.

'I didn't mean to say your dad is shameful,' I said hastily, 'I-I mean, he works . . . he . . . that isn't what I meant, I'm sorry.' I looked down at my hands, ashamed. *You idiot, Chetana.* The trouble with hanging around with someone as carefree and happy as Matilda was that you started to adopt those mannerisms. I was talking more openly than ever and things just . . . came out. At least before when I never spoke, I never offended anyone. Matilda hadn't said anything. I looked at her anxiously.

'Tildy?'

'Oh, sorry,' she replied, shaking her head. 'I know you didn't mean it like that. I was actually just thinking about Fee. We always used to come up here.'

My stomach dropped. Was she missing her? I bet Sophie would never have called her dad shameful. I was always paranoid that the only reason Matilda was choosing to spend her summer with me was because of their falling out.

'What's up?' Matilda asked. I jumped, realising she was looking at me.

'Nothing.'

'Come on, fretty Chetty,' she said, nudging me. I nearly smiled at the silly nickname. 'What is it? Do you think I should apologise to Sophie?' She sighed. 'I keep thinking about what I said to her.'

Apologise? Sophie had treated Tildy awfully. It made me angry to think she was the one feeling bad about it all.

'You didn't do anything wrong,' I said, before I could stop myself. '*She's* the one who should be sorry. You've been friends since you were born and then she ditches you to go and hang around with those idiots.'

Matilda's face flickered in surprise; but I found that once I had begun talking, I couldn't stop.

'Kip has absolutely no idea how obsessed she is with him, Tom is just *awful* and Caitlin treats her horribly. My brother is no better. Why would she want to be around that? They don't even come *close* to you, how can she not see that?'

I was breathing heavily, my limbs shaky. I wasn't used to talking about people behind their backs. But that wasn't the only reason: Matilda was staring at me and behind the blue of her eyes, I could sense she was putting something together. *Oh no.* I had gone too far. I had given myself away. I rewound back through what I had said – it could all be explained away, heat of the moment anger directed at Sophie. But what if she didn't ask for an explanation? What if she just pulled away and stopped talking to me? My stomach lurched painfully. I couldn't handle that. I opened my mouth, ready to cover up what had happened, to move the conversation on, *anything*, but Matilda was already speaking.

'They don't come close to you either, Chet.'

Matilda's cheeks were flushed and she was avoiding my eye, which was completely unlike her. She was staring straight ahead, as though she didn't know what to do with herself. Suddenly, the air seemed to have thickened and a wild, unbelievable thought occurred to me. *Was it possible?*

For a moment I sat there, completely frozen. Then slowly, hardly daring to breathe, I reached out and laced my fingers through Matilda's slim ones. I waited for her to push me away in disgust, ask me what I was doing, but she didn't.

The surrounding water glinted under the warm sunshine and Tildy kept her hand firmly in mine as we sat in silence, our breathing heavy. I could hear my heartbeat in my ears.

I had wondered, once or twice, about Tildy. Despite fiercely telling myself I was imagining it, I would sometimes catch her looking at me, then quickly glancing away when our eyes met. Other times it was the way she would smile at me, like the sun bursting from behind a cloud. I found myself thinking about her, the way I first started thinking about Annabelle in school. We weren't really friends, but we played netball together, Annabelle always scoring the most goals, people whispering that she was going to get scouted. I had tried to stop thinking about her once I realised that it might not be normal. She had a boyfriend on the rugby team and I found myself peeking across the room sometimes when they kissed, terrified of being caught watching. I started avoiding her, sitting away from her in the common room. I quit the netball team, even though it was one of the only distractions I had from my studies.

But unlike Annabelle, the way Tildy was looking seemed to mirror my own feelings. I hesitated: no one had ever told me what to do in this situation, how to battle past the guilt that I was somehow doing something wrong. Something dirty. But how could it be dirty: two people sitting holding hands under the sun; two people who cared about each other? I'd seen guys shoving their hands up girls' skirts in the park on Saturdays, fag in the other hand. How could this be worse?

Slowly, trying to calm the nerves that threatened to paralyse me, I gently touched the back of Matilda's free hand with my fingertips. I drew feather light circles across the smooth golden skin. Unable to breathe, I looked up at her. Her eyes were wide, her pupils dilated against the ocean blue of her irises. Her mouth was parted slightly, showing the light pink skin on the inside of her bottom lip.

I didn't know how much time had passed, maybe only seconds, but I knew what I wanted. It would be my first time and I had no idea what I was doing; but before I had moved, Matilda's lips were on mine. Blood rushed in my ears like the sound of the ocean and all I could think about was how *she* had kissed *me* – beautiful, fearless Matilda – and I wanted to tell her how in awe I was, but then I stopped thinking. The seagulls cried overhead, the water lapped gently at our bare feet, and for the first time ever, I felt whole.

Chapter Forty-One

Now

Sophie

The beach is quiet as I leave my hut. With each step, I am hyper-aware of the photo in my fleece pocket. *What happened? How did I miss it?*

After a few minutes, I arrive at the pink and white hut. The perfectly swept deck is deserted, so I walk up the wooden steps. Still unsure of what I am going to say, I knock on the patio doors. The blinds are closed against the glare of the sun. I wait for a couple of minutes, then knock again. There is no answer.

'Hello?'

Silence.

Frustrated, I start to move away, but something catches my eye: the key is in the lock on the other side of the door. Either someone is inside . . . or the hut is unlocked.

Walk away.

My palms prickle with sweat. I can't just walk into Chetana's hut. She might be asleep. She might have company. But at the same time, I am desperate for answers to the questions raised by the polaroid in my pocket.

I try the handle. It gives easily and the door swings silently open. *Now what?* Remaining firmly on the other side of the door, I peer into the hut. It takes my eyes a few moments to adjust to the gloom. Like the Halls' hut, the Chawlas' is almost unchanged in twenty years, from the white-wash kitchen cupboards to the bright blue lino flooring. I can just about see the silhouette of a ladder, ascending to the mezzanine floor. The air is still; it is obvious no one is here.

I should turn around and walk back to my hut, return later, or not at all. I should be packing my bags, booking my flight to Australia to see Anna. Instead, I find myself stepping inside the dark hut and quickly closing the door behind me.

In contrast to the bright, sunny beach I have just left, the silent gloom seems to swallow me whole. The hut smells musky and woody. It is also meticulously tidy: there are hardly any personal items lying around, no photos on the wall, no trinkets. The only nod to anyone actually living here is an upturned wine glass on the draining board and a worn pack of cards tied with an elastic band on the windowsill. Oddly, the cards don't seem to have been touched in a long time: a thick coating of dust smothers the Queen of Hearts.

This is a bad idea. Light-headed from the adrenaline, I move further into the hut. A floorboard groans, pulling me up for a moment. I am far enough inside to be difficult to explain, now. I don't know what answers I am expecting to find . . . either way, I need to be quick: she could be back any minute.

The living area contains nothing but empty shelves, so I move straight into the small kitchen and start easing open drawers, looking for the silver gleam of a key, or the green hair of a troll key ring. Disappointingly, the drawers contain nothing but the usual jumble of cutlery, matches and table-cloth pegs.

Turning around, I spot a low cupboard at the back of the hut, made of light ash with a concertina opening. When I open it, I find it full of textbooks and notepads. Frustrated, I straighten up. The ladder up to the mezzanine level is to my left.

Just a quick look. Then I'll go.

I slowly climb the ladder, half-expecting to see someone as my head emerges above the precipice, but it is deserted. It doesn't look as though anyone has stayed up here in some time: the porthole window on the far wall is smeared with grime and dust.

The mezzanine floors are generally designed for children, the sloped ceilings too low to stand up in, so I remain kneeling on the hard floor, looking around. The area is empty except for two faded sleeping bags and a few cardboard boxes, speckled with mildew. I lift the flap of one of the boxes, which feels damp and soft under my hand, and look inside. There is little of interest: old books, a snapped kite, the remains of a friendship bracelet kit with half the sparkly purple beads missing.

I am pulling the other box towards me when a thick, black spider scuttles out from underneath the box. I jump and fall backwards, banging my elbow against the wall. It feels like a sign: *time to go.* As I push the box back into place with a throbbing elbow, something inside catches my eye.

Half-hidden under a yellowing envelope, I spot the unmistakable flash of silver.

The tin.

Carefully, I lift the tin out of the box, too preoccupied to pay attention to the creak of the ladder.

By the time I do notice, it is too late. Chetana is already behind me.

Chapter Forty-Two
Now
Sophie

Chetana stares at me from across the mezzanine floor. 'What are you doing in my hut, Sophie?'

Her voice is icy and her dark eyes bore into mine. In answer, I lift my hand to show her the tin of photos.

'I think you were in my hut, first.'

There is a long pause, where Chetana's gaze flickers between me and the tin. Then she starts climbing down the ladder, out of sight. Slowly, I crawl forwards and follow her down the ladder.

Chetana stands in front of the hut doors, her arms folded, her expression furious. Any pretence at politeness since our last conversation has vanished.

'It was you,' I say. The ladder presses into my back. 'Watching me. Breaking into my hut. You could have just *spoken* to me, but instead you tried to make me feel like I was going mad.'

Chetana ignores me. 'What do you want?' she asks coldly. The venom in her expression takes me aback. I thought she would be scared, apologetic; but she is looking at me as though she *hates* me.

'I want to know what happened the summer Tildy died.'

'Nothing happened.'

'You're lying,' I reply, frustrated. 'I know something happened between you two.'

A flash of something crosses Chetana's face; her folded arms loosen slightly. It's obvious she didn't expect me to know anything.

Things began to make sense after I found the photo under my sofa. Chetana's lonely, closed-off existence. Her reaction when I mentioned Tildy's death. Matilda, too: she could have chosen any boy along the sandbank, but she never so much as mentioned a boyfriend. Her veiled questions to me about love suddenly make sense, twenty years too late.

'I don't know what you're talking about,' Chetana replies stubbornly. She moves away from the door. 'Now get out of my hut.'

'Chetana, I *know*. You took the tin so that no one would find out about the two of you.'

'There's nothing *in* that tin. You've looked, you'll have seen, there's noth—'

I slip my hand into my pocket and pull out the photo I found under the sofa. Chetana freezes, her mouth hanging open slightly. The blood drains from her face, like a plug being pulled.

'How . . . where did you . . .'

'Chetana, the tin, this *photo*, were hidden the night that she died. Can't you see how that looks?'

'That photo had nothing to do with her death.' Chetana's voice shakes. She looks absolutely horrified, her eyes transfixed on the photo in my hand.

'You must know something,' I say. 'You spent all your time together. Did you see her? Before she died?'

Chetana is shaking her head.

'I had an earlier curfew . . . I only saw her that evening, before you all went to the bonfire.'

'Did you tell the police about the two of you?'

'My parents wouldn't let me speak to the police. I never told anyone.'

She looks back down at the photo and the pain in her eyes seems to slice right through me.

'I didn't hurt her,' Chetana says, finally. 'She was the best thing that ever happened to me.'

'It's been twenty years, Chetana. Tell me what happened.'

Chapter Forty-Three

That day
6pm
Chetana

'I love you,' Matilda said softly.

She was looking at me very seriously, her blue eyes even bigger than usual. My heart stopped. *She loved me?*

'Don't look so shocked, Chet,' she laughed, though her voice sounded a bit shaky.

'But . . . why?'

I wanted to be confident and strong and believe that she really meant it. But I couldn't understand what she saw in me. Even Sophie had said it: I was boring.

'Loads of reasons!' Matilda exclaimed, shuffling closer to me on the rock we were sitting on. We were tucked away around the sandbank, out of sight. The water was starting to ebb, exposing more and more of the wet grey rocks. It was getting late: I would have to be home soon.

'You're beautiful. You're smart. You're thoughtful and kind. You do have *shocking* taste in music. But that's okay, I can live with that.'

I laughed and the sound seemed to echo around us, bouncing from rock to rock, so that I was laughing forever. Taking a deep breath, I reached out and squeezed Matilda's hand.

'I love you, too.'

I expected Matilda to make some sort of joke, or tell me she already knew, but instead she just beamed at me and squeezed my hand doubly as hard. My mouth was dry.

'I looked up the trains the other day when I was in town,' Tildy went on. 'It's only two hours twenty minutes to yours. The bus takes a bit longer, but it's still not so bad. I can visit on weekends, and we'll see each other every summer. Only two-and-a-bit years and we can try and find a college near each other.' She was looking at me so hopefully it made my heart ache.

'That sounds perfect, Tild.'

I couldn't believe Tildy really wanted us to stay together, even though we had ages until college and she couldn't tell anyone about us. Every day I waited for her to end it, to real- ise she was too good for me. Yet here she was, still. I didn't know what to say.

Matilda continued making plans while I listened. She spoke about applying for the same university, getting a flat together. A cat. I said very little, just allowing the picture Matilda painted to wash blissfully over me. I pushed down the tiny, creeping doubt that whispered things wouldn't work out the way Matilda was planning. That something would come between us and our fairy tale: my parents, my curfew, the distance. Then there was the other, bigger issue. *Fairy tales always have a prince.*

The water was even lower now, pulling further and fur- ther away from the rocks we were on. Tildy paused for breath and reluctantly, I pulled my hand away from hers.

'I had better go,' I said, miserably. I hated this part of the evening, when I was forced back into the hut with my mother and father, and Matilda would be free for hours more. I would spend the evening peering out of the window on the mezzanine level where I slept, wishing I was around the bonfire with everyone else and worrying that Matilda would make up with Sophie and I would be alone again.

Matilda wrapped her arms around me and kissed me. Shaking off my dark thoughts and thinking only of our future, I reached up and cupped her face in my hands, amazed by the smooth skin of her cheeks. Eventually, we pulled apart.

'Wait,' Tildy said, as I went to get up. 'I want to remember this day. This moment.'

She picked up her camera from the rock beside her. Holding the camera out in front of us, she surprised me by pulling me in and kissing me again, harder than normal. I smiled against her lips as the shutter clicked. Tildy pulled the photo from the camera and tucked it inside her tin as we both got to our feet.

'You go first,' I said, with an apologetic smile. 'Just in case.'

'Okay.'

Tildy gave me one last kiss, then I watched as she started jumping effortlessly from rock to rock. *Maybe one day*, I thought. *Maybe one day there will be no secrets and we can just be us.*

Once she had rounded the bend, I clambered to my feet and made my way back across the rocks. I wasn't as graceful as Matilda and I carefully considered each rock as I picked my way slowly over the safest ones. It was a pretty evening: the clouds across the beach were low, and they were a soft, almost golden, pink. I *wished* I could have stayed out for longer.

As I reached the bend in the headland, just before the rocks met the sand again, I came face to face with a group of people. I jumped in surprise. Dev, Kip, Tom and Jamie were standing huddled together, smoking cigarettes. I froze, my heart suddenly thumping. *Had they seen us? Had they seen what we were doing?* The panic was so sudden, so intense, it seemed to squeeze my head, robbing me of oxygen. After a moment, however, I realised all of the boys except Dev were looking at the retreating figure of Matilda.

'Mate,' Jamie said, shaking her head. 'She is going to be *hot* when she's older.'

'Tell me about it,' Tom agreed. 'She's a right babe.'

'Dude, that's my cousin,' Kip protested. 'And she's *fourteen*.'

Tom shrugged arrogantly. 'They grow up fast these days.'

I wanted to hit him. Tildy was mine and they were talking about her like she was a piece of meat, who would one day be desperate for their attention. Like she would automatically be looking for a boyfriend. *They think that because that's what she should be doing,* said a small, bitter voice in the back of my head. For now, at least, they didn't indicate they had seen anything and my heart rate slowly started returning to normal. *We need to be more careful. Anyone could have walked around that bend and seen us.*

'Come on,' Tom said, dropping his cigarette butt to the ground and stubbing it out with his trainer. 'I'm starving.'

It was then that I became aware Dev was looking at me, unsmiling.

'I'll catch you up,' he said to the others. Alarm bells began ringing in my ears. Dev waited until the others were out of earshot before he spoke.

'I asked you to be *normal*,' he said quietly. 'To fit in.'

He knows. There was a glint in his eye that turned me cold.

'I-I am acting normal. I have friends down here, now.' My voice shook.

'Coming to bonfires is normal,' Dev said. 'Having *boyfriends* is normal.'

He took a step towards me, so that I was forced backwards, towards the face of the headland.

'Dev, I've got to go, Mum'll—' but before I could get past him, he reached out and grabbed my wrist.

'I've pretended not to notice what's been going on because I hoped you would come to your senses. But you haven't, and just then,' he gestured towards the rocks where I had just been, 'you could have been seen by *anyone*.' He squeezed my wrist, just tightly enough to hurt. My face grew hot and I wanted to shout back, to defend myself, but instead I began to shake.

'How can you live with yourself?' he hissed. 'Creeping around the beach. Taking those kinds of . . . photos. What if she shows someone that photo? Starts passing it around her school?'

'She wouldn't—'

'Did you even think about what people would say if you were found out? The *shame* it would bring on Mum and Dad?'

Hot, guilty tears blurred my vision.

'Dev—' I began, desperate for him to hear me, to *see* me. I might not be normal, but I was his sister. He had to know I hadn't chosen this path: it was laid out before I had even known it was there. Dev cut me off before I could articulate any of it.

'End it.'

'Please don't ask me to do that. She's—'

'I don't care what you have to say or how you say it,' Dev said, his eyes boring into mine. 'End it. Or I'll end it for you.'

Without looking at me again, he dropped my wrist and walked away.

Chapter Forty-Four

Now

Sophie

Chetana stops talking, apparently unable to carry on. She turns her head away from me, staring blankly out of the window. I can't think of anything to say. If what Chetana is saying is true, Matilda was snatched away just when they had found each other. And no one even knew what she had lost. I think of her remaining here all these years, with nothing but memories, and an aching sorrow swells within me. The dusty pile of cards, the boxes of friendship bracelet kits . . . everything on pause, just like Sheila. Forever stuck in 1997.

'I'm so sorry.' It's all I can manage and the words sound pitiful. 'I had no idea you felt that way about each other. Tildy never said anything.'

'No one was meant to know,' Chetana says quietly. 'My brother was right, my family would have disowned me.'

There is a long silence while I struggle to piece together the last few days, now I know it was Chetana, all along.

'How did you know I found the tin?' I ask after a while.

'I overheard you and Kip talking about it the other morning through the window.'

'You were following me?'

Her faces flushes angrily.

'No! Not that time. You were talking loudly enough for the whole beach to hear; it wasn't exactly difficult.' She shakes her head and her shoulders drop slightly. 'I didn't want anyone seeing that photo. The shame it would bring on my family, even now. My father wants to be prime minister, did you know that? He might actually do it, too. And I'll be up for tenure at the university in a few years.' She shakes her head bitterly. 'People like to preach tolerance . . . but nothing's really changed.'

'Chetana . . .' I try to choose my words carefully. 'Is there any chance your brother had something to do with Tildy's death? He knew about you two, he was at the beach that night—'

'No!' Chetana suddenly cries, looking at me incredulously. 'Why do you keep trying to rewrite history? Tildy's death was an *accident*.'

'But you said yourself, he knew about the two of you . . . he could have decided it was easier to put an end to it himself.'

'Dev had no reason to hurt Tildy,' Chetana says firmly.

'How can you be so sure?'

'Aside from the fact that he's my *brother*?'

Chetana looks away from me, her jaw clenching.

'I know because I did what he said. I ended things with her that night.'

This pulls me up. She hadn't mentioned this part of the story.

'You . . . what?'

'He would have gone to our parents,' Chetana says. Her face is a mask of pain. 'So I did what he said and I broke

234

up with her that night. At least, that's what I wanted him to think.'

'What do you mean?'

'I needed it to look real when I did it, but . . .' Chetana's voice catches. 'I wrote a letter explaining everything, that I hadn't meant it. That I did love her. I was going to give it to her the next day. I just needed Dev to think I had broken up with her, so we had time to work out a way to keep it better hidden.'

I remember the way Matilda was acting that night, wandering along the beach alone, her eyes puffy. Drinking. It was starting to make sense in a horrible, heart-wrenching way.

'But,' I venture cautiously, 'if Dev didn't *know* you had ended things—'

'ENOUGH!' Chetana suddenly cries and I freeze. Her hair is coming loose from her bun and she advances on me, one slender finger pointed, like a knife.

'My brother had nothing to do with Matilda's death! It was an *accident*. Why can't you just leave it alone? We've all had to come to terms with it and now you want to drag it all up again!'

'I'm not trying to drag anything up Chetana, I'm trying to find out what happened to my best friend—'

She throws her head back and laughs, her eyes wild.

'Your *best friend*? You treated her like dirt! If anyone is responsible for what happened to Tildy, it's *you*!'

I stare at her, feeling a rising sense of nausea.

'Don't . . . don't say that . . .'

My chest tightens horribly as Chetana voices the very thing that has haunted me for twenty years.

'She agreed to meet you at those rocks, even though you didn't deserve one *second* of her time. She waited there alone for you—' Chetana's voice breaks, 'and you were *late*. Even when you did show up, you didn't look for her. She could have still been alive, but you didn't bother looking properly, did you?'

My mouth opens and closes uselessly. Tears trickle down Chetana's cheeks, catching in the sunlight.

'I never got the chance to give her that letter because of you. She died alone that night, believing I didn't love her, because of *you*.'

Chapter Forty-Five

Now

Sophie

She died alone that night because of you.
The words ring in my ears as I leave Chetana's hut and walk back along the beach. What she said is true. It's all true. Tildy was at the rocks alone that night, waiting for me. By the time I finally arrived, it was too late. I assumed she had gone home, never thought to look for her. How close was her body to where I stood? The autopsy said she died from a head injury, but I'll never knew if she was still breathing when I finally arrived at the rocks. Shame crawls across my skin. All this time Chetana has hated me, and rightly so.

As I approach my hut, I spot a familiar figure sat out on one of the chairs. Kip's eyes are closed, his feet propped up on the chair across from him. I didn't think he would be back after how I acted this morning. For a moment, I allow myself to look unrestricted at him. From this distance, he looks almost indistinguishable from the boy of my teen years. What always attracted me to Kip, though I am not sure I fully realised it at the time, was his kindness. There was something innately *good* about him, compared to the testosterone-fuelled boys on the beach and at school. You could trust him.

'Hey.' Kip's eyes are open now, blinking at me against the sunshine.

'How long have you been waiting?' I ask, climbing up onto the deck and unlocking the hut doors.

'Only about five hours.' His tone is light-hearted.

'I'd better get you a drink, then.'

When I have returned with beers and my cigarettes, I light one, curling up on the spare lounger.

'I'm sorry about this morning,' Kip says, straight away. 'I should have . . .' He opens his mouth and then closes it again, shaking his head. 'I shouldn't have compared you to Sheila or assumed Charlie's words had put you at ease. I know you were just trying to help find out what happened to Tildy.'

I don't know what to say. Charlie's words feel like a lifetime ago. Now I know I *was* right to be afraid, that Chetana was in the shadows all along. Kip looks so earnest, I can't stay angry. He could hardly have known.

'I saw Sheila after I saw you this morning,' Kip continues. 'She told me everything. I can't believe it.'

Relieved that I don't have to decide whether or not to tell Kip about Sheila's confession, I let out a breath and nod.

'I don't know how my dad could have kept it to himself.'

'You really don't think your mum knew?'

'Honestly, I've got no idea. I tried calling her, but she didn't answer and she's not called me back since.'

Kip blows his cheeks out. 'All this time . . . you two were sisters.' He suddenly looks up in mock-horror. 'That makes us cousins.'

I almost smile.

'You're not blood-related, Kip.'

'Still, people will talk,' he says with a grin. 'You'll have to keep your hands off me.'

Our eyes meet and my face flushes. *Is he remembering that night, twenty years ago?* I pull my gaze away and we lapse into silence, watching Harry gutting fish on the shore. Above him, seagulls hover, trying to snatch at the bucket of fish. The rocks are stained with dark red blood.

'All these secrets,' Kip murmurs, his eyes still on Harry. 'It's like a bad film. You think everyone is just going about their business, that everything down at the beach is so fucking *pure*.'

I finish my cigarette and take a deep breath.

'There's more.' I tell him about finding the photo of Chetana and Tildy kissing, of their relationship. Kip stares at me as I speak.

'Bloody hell.' He takes a long drink of his beer, his eyes darting across the rocks. 'Poor girl. And Matilda never told you anything?'

I shake my head.

She tried. I didn't listen.

'The night she died, she said she wanted to speak to me. She was upset. She must have wanted to talk about Chetana, the breakup.' My voice breaks, betraying my searing guilt.

'You couldn't have known,' Kip says, firmly. 'Don't start blaming yourself.'

Too late, I want to say.

'Should we give Sheila and Gary the tin, now?' I ask, wanting to change the subject. I left Chetana with the photo of her and Matilda kissing, not wanting it on my conscience.

239

'I guess so. What reason have we got to keep it?' He glances along the beach at the yellow hut. 'Sheila's gone to Wales today. We can give it to her when she's back.'

I lean forwards. There is something I just can't shake, no matter what Chetana said.

'Do you think Dev could have been capable of killing Matilda?'

Kip looks taken aback.

'Dev? I don't know. I don't think so.'

'Why not?'

'He was a sixteen-year-old kid, Soph. With a seriously bright future ahead of him. He wouldn't have had it in him.'

'How do you know that?' I press. 'From what Chetana said, he knew about her being gay, but he never told the police anything about Chetana and Matilda's relationship.'

'He was probably protecting her! Or he was scared. Matilda was *dead*. And anyway,' Kip presses on as I open my mouth again, 'Dev was at the fire the whole time.'

'*You* weren't there the whole time, remember?' I give him a meaningful look. 'You can't know that.'

'Soph, I was barely gone for twenty minutes.' We look at one another, that night ballooning invisibly between us, unspoken.

'What did Chetana say?' Kip asks. 'Did she ever suspect Dev?'

'No,' I admit. 'But she would say that, he's her brother.'

'Listen, if Chetana and Matilda were in a secret relationship, doesn't it make sense that Matilda hid the tin? Maybe she was worried someone would find the photo of them kissing if she kept the tin in her own hut. Then Chetana stole them back the other day because she was afraid or embarrassed or whatever. And if that's what happened . . .'

'. . . Tildy's death could have just been an accident, after all.' I finish.

'Yes.'

Is he right? The photos, the shower key, the feeling of being watched . . . maybe this has never been about a murder, at all. Just a single photo captured two decades ago. A young relationship lost. My head swims with fatigue.

Kip reaches out and gives my hand a squeeze. His skin is warm and it's clear he knows what I am thinking.

'It's better this way, Sophie. No killers lurking out of sight, no hidden motives. I know you feel guilty about why Tildy was there that night, but if you were with her, you might both have slipped, or something. Your parents might have lost you, too.'

Incredibly, the tension seems to ease ever so slightly from my shoulders. Kip's words soothe the knot in my stomach. Maybe it *is* time to move on, to stop chasing shadows and accept Matilda's death for what it was. Try to think more about the happy times we spent here.

'How do you *do* that?'

'Do what?'

'Make everything seem better. You've always been like it. You're so calm and measured about everything.'

Kip takes a sip of his drink, droplets of condensation falling from his glass. As he does so, his scent catches in the breeze and washes over me, minty shower gel and sea salt.

'Well, according to Charlie that was one of my problems. Not enough fire.' He gives a wry smile. 'Maybe it's spending too much time in the water. Makes me all soggy.'

He places his empty beer bottle down and stands up.

'Right. Now we've solved the many mysteries of the sandbank, I've got an idea for something that might take your mind off things.'

I look at him warily.

'What is it?'

'We're going surfing.'

I stare at him. 'I can't go surfing.'

'Sophie, have you even stepped *foot* in the water since you've been down here?'

My silence tells him everything he needs to know. It hadn't even occurred to me to go swimming.

'Then you don't have a choice. Come on, I promise I'm not going to drown you.'

Chapter Forty-Six

Now

Sophie

'Did you see that?!'

Pushing my wet hair out of my eyes, I pinch my nose and pop my ears to get rid of the seawater as Kip whoops in delight behind me.

'That was the best one you've caught all day!'

Hopping straight back onto Kip's spare board, I paddle out to where he is waiting for the next set of waves to roll in. Adrenaline soars through my veins and my muscles feel like jelly, but I don't want to stop.

The afternoon has passed in a blur. After a few wobbly false starts, I managed to catch my first wave in years. It all came back to me in a rush: how nothing compares to skimming across the water, like you're actually flying. I had shouted with delight and promptly fallen off, somersaulting under the surface, but I didn't care. *How could I have forgotten how this felt?*

Sitting up and straddling my board, I watch Kip catch the next wave with supreme ease. He even looks back at me as he slows in the shallows and does a little dance on his board. I shake my head, laughing. My face is tight from the wind and impending sunburn; closing my eyes, the insides of my eyelids blaze red. I want to stay in this moment and never leave. Somewhere, somehow, Fee has returned.

That evening, Kip and I cook spaghetti bolognese in my hut. We move around the cramped kitchen, peeling garlic, chopping the carrots Kip insists on putting in, salting pasta water. Our movements and side-steps are done with unconscious fluidity, a well-practised dance. *It's because we're both used to the contortions of a hut. That's all.* The doors are wide open, inviting the warm evening air inside the hut.

'Try this,' Kip says, holding out the spoon, one hand cupped beneath it to catch the drips. I lean forward to taste the sauce, which is smoky and rich: as I do so, my gaze is drawn outside. The family from the picture-perfect beach hut on the harbour-side is walking past, the mum and dad holding a child's hand each. The little blonde boy is in his crocodile pyjamas once again and a pair of yellow wellies. The dad glances up at me: his face lifts in surprise but almost immediately softens into a smile. *He thinks I have a partner. He thinks that we spend our evenings cooking and teasing one another, sipping wine and dancing to the radio.*

'It's great,' I tell Kip. 'Just needs a little more salt. And fewer *carrots*.'

Kip laughs and pushes me out of the way with his hip.

'More carrots, less salt, gotcha.'

We eat outside, dragging the wooden drop-leaf dining table onto the deck. The beach is a slow bustle of evening activity: boats returning from a day crabbing on one of the longer piers around the bay, freshly washed children sitting at the dinner table, the intoxicating smell of charcoal barbecues. Despite the awful revelations about my dad, despite Chetana's grief and anger, a weight feels as though it has been lifted. The shadows have at last retreated.

'I've just noticed you're not wearing your wedding rings.'

Kip emerges from the hut with the second bottle of Merlot, the first having disappeared quickly.

I glance down at my left hand. Today's sunshine has softened the tan line slightly, but a bone-white band around my finger still gleams.

'Safekeeping?' he presses. I look at him: his expression is unreadable.

'I need to send them back to my husband.' I take a deep, steadying breath. 'My *ex*-husband.'

There, I've said it. The word *ex* is so harsh. Not even a full word, a half-word. As if to remind you: you are no longer part of a whole. Kip studies me for a moment.

'Why did you break up?'

His question is so straightforward, it takes me by surprise. I look out at the water, unsure how comfortable I am talking about Nick with Kip. The tide is slowly ebbing, leaving behind a smooth, shiny expanse of wet sand dappled with pebbles. Maybe it's time to talk about it. I've kept so much buried, from Mum, Nick, everyone. I'm exhausted.

'He was offered a job in Japan.'

'How long for?'

'There wasn't an end date. Permanent, possibly.'

Kip looks confused.

'Sorry if I'm missing something, but why did that mean you broke up? Didn't he ask you to go with him?'

'He asked. I said no.' To my surprise, I realise the anger I have been holding for the past few months is no longer there: instead, I feel nothing but a tired sadness. I look blankly out at the shore.

'Why did you say no?' Kip asks. His tone isn't judgemental, it's curious.

For the first time, I actually try and work out why I said no; the real reason, not the reason that I gave Nick, Anna, my mum.

'I was afraid. I don't like change; I don't like unpredictability.'

'I can't imagine that,' Kip says quietly. 'You always had this air of fearlessness about you, like you were secretly hoping for some sort of dare. You were always brave.'

'I haven't been that person for a long time.' I take a large sip of wine. 'I don't know *who* I am, anymore.'

Unexpectedly, Kip reaches across and takes my newly bare left hand. Heat rises to my cheeks: they must be even redder than normal, fuelled by the surfing and wine. It is confusing, thinking about Nick, while Kip's hand is on mine.

'Sophie, you're still that girl. All you need is to let go and everything else will follow.' He gestures with his free hand to the shore. 'When you surf, the wave doesn't choose you, *you* choose the wave. And if you fall off, you wait for the next set to roll in.'

That night, when Kip steps into the hut, he walks slowly towards me. My body thrums with nervous anticipation as he takes my face in his hands; the calluses from his surfboard brush against my cheeks. He leans in and presses his lips gently against mine. Closing my eyes, I allow myself to melt into him.

Just as I raise my hands to his hair, something makes me freeze. Like an unstoppable wave, the memory of the last time that Kip and I were together comes crashing down around me. A night where my best friend was waiting for me on the dark rocks. Guilt slices through me and I back away from Kip, who looks at me in confusion.

'I'm sorry,' I whisper. 'I can't . . . not right now.'

Kip drops his hands.

'It's okay,' he says. 'I get it.' But his eyes betray his hurt. Before I have time to gather my confused thoughts, he is gone.

Chapter Forty-Seven

Then

Caitlin

The two blue lines on the white stick gradually became clearer and clearer.

No. I can't be.

The puddle of pee next to the tree stump where I took the test slowly trickled down the slope.

I can't be fucking pregnant. I am not that girl. A teen mum.

Dropping the stick to the ground like it was on fire, my stomach turned. Bending over in the gloomy clearing, I heaved, but nothing came up.

This isn't happening. I'd just done my GCSEs, I was meant to be applying to uni, not going to fucking baby classes. There had been talk of a *good* uni too; Durham or even Oxford if I tried really hard with my A-levels. Mum had got all teary at parents' evening when they told her and even Dad was pleased when he got home later, giving me a proper hug.

I sat down among the broken beer bottles and old lighters and pressed my hands against my flat stomach, pressing until it hurt. Something was *in* there. About to ruin my life.

Reaching for the bottle of vodka next to me, I took a few swigs, cringing as the liquid burnt my throat. If it was only really small so far, maybe drinking would just . . . get rid of it? A girl in the year above had got pregnant and she lost it really quick. It isn't as if it would *feel* anything yet, would it? But as I lifted the bottle to my lips again, something made me stop. I suddenly saw a picture of the alternative. Of what life *could* look like. Not a single teen mum still living at home . . . but maybe, instead, a young mum with the kid's dad? Doing it properly, as a family. Someone who was excited about having a kid. I pictured a bright, modern kitchen – really white, shiny surfaces – where my hair was in a messy bun and the baby was eating sticks of cucumber in its highchair . . . when he got home, he would give the baby a big fuss, delighted to have this cute kid, and would then present me with roses and spin me around the kitchen.

The vodka bottle hovered, midway to my lips. The strength of the image shocked me, making my heart ache. Maybe that's what I *wanted*. The thought crept into my mind, calming some of the fear and panic. Maybe . . . just maybe I could *have* that. Surely, he would be happy?

Of course he will. He's crazy about you.

Feeling lighter, I allowed myself a spark of hope. It might be okay . . . I needed to talk to him. But first, I brought the vodka bottle to my lips. One more sip wouldn't hurt.

Chapter Forty-Eight

Now

Sophie

After Kip leaves, I climb into bed and lie there, listening to the rolling waves and snatches of conversation as families get ready for bed and make final trips to the toilet. The beach falls silent just before midnight, but my eyes refuse to close.

The alcohol is contributing to my insomnia, but my mind is also tangled in the events of the day, keeping me awake. The happiness I felt earlier creeps away in the darkness, replaced by a cold, empty feeling. Though I try to think of anything else, I keep picturing the hatred in Chetana's eyes as she had looked at me. *She died alone that night because of you.* Because a boy was more important to me than friendship. And twenty years later, here I am, making the same mistakes with the same boy.

Punching my pillow in frustration, I try to get comfortable and take some deep breaths. *Inhale . . . exhale . . . inhale . . . exhale.*

I feel the first fingertips of pressure against my bladder around half an hour later. Scrunching my eyes shut, I try to ignore it; but the more I try, the more the pressure builds. Finally, I resign myself to the walk to the toilet block.

Picking up my phone from the windowsill, I pull a fleece over my head and slip my feet into my sandals. Along with the lack of sleep, I feel groggy and a little nauseous as the wine slowly ebbs from my system.

The salty night breeze greets me as I step outside. The night sky is completely starless, cloaking the entire beach in velvet blackness. I shiver from the cold and walk quickly down the deck steps, turning and heading towards the path behind my hut on the harbour-side of the sandbank. It is much quicker taking the smooth path than navigating across the sand in the pitch-dark.

As I walk along the dirt-track behind the huts towards the main path, the darkness engulfs me and I reach for my phone to use the torch app. Tapping the screen, the phone remains as black as the surrounding night: I've forgotten to charge it again. My watch, too, is still out of battery. Forgetting to charge my devices is something I would never normally do, another change since I arrived at the beach. I shove the phone back in my pocket and trudge on, trying to make out the track ahead of me.

It is with relief that I reach the main path, where the lights from houses across the harbour make me feel closer to civilisation. Safety. They remind me of holidays to places like Malta with Nick, wandering back from a seafront restaurant, full of beer and whitebait. Moments later, the fluorescent, flickering lights of the toilet block come into view.

I pee quickly, straining my ears for any sound, but there is nothing but the gentle slosh of water against the boats in the harbour and the hum of crickets. *It's over*, I remind myself. *I don't have to be afraid anymore.*

Back inside my hut a few minutes later, I put my phone on charge. Leaving it on the windowsill, I crawl gratefully back into bed.

I am finally, mercifully, drifting off, when I hear it.

Tap.

Tap.

Tap.

My eyes snap open.

I lie there unmoving, every muscle in my body taut.

Maybe I was dreaming.

The hut is silent; there is no other sound except the distant whisper of waves. Wriggling back down under my duvet, I close my eyes and focus on my breathing. *In. Out. In. Out.* Like the waves being pushed and pulled from the shore. At last, my eyes start to grow heavy.

Tap.

Tap.

Tap.

I sit bolt upright, my heart pounding. There is no mistaking the noise this time. I strain to catch it again, but all I can hear is my own pulse, thundering in my ears.

Silence. Then . . .

Tap.

Tap.

Tap.

It is chillingly slow and deliberate. Clutching the duvet in both fists, I look wildly around, but there is nothing. The tapping seems to be coming from the window opposite me, not the doors. Whatever it is stops for a few beats, then continues its agonisingly slow tap on the glass. Could it be a branch, moving in the wind? I already know the answer: there are no trees that close to the hut. The last in the row, there is nothing to the left of my hut except the headland a few metres away and a two-foot gap between my hut and the one on the right.

Tap.

Tap.

Taptaptaptaptaptaptap.

I let out a small sob, clamping a hand over my mouth. The tapping stops immediately. Someone is on the other side of the hut, listening to me.

No. It's just something loose on the roof, or next door's hut. Maybe they've put their windsurf boards down there, again.

I sag with relief at this realisation. *Of course*: next door always leaves their boards and wetsuits down the side of their hut. It'll be something come loose in the wind, a tether from one of the boards or a wetsuit arm flapping.

Except . . . next door isn't here. They haven't been here all week. Unless they arrived after ten, when I went to bed . . . in which case why would they have put their wetsuits out? The tapping starts again, only this time it is at the window above my head. Shaking, I pull the covers up under my chin.

Tap.

Tap.

Tap.

I fumble around for my phone, but when I yank it from the charger and hold it up, the battery icon is flashing, then the screen goes dead. *Shit.*

Trying to think through the fog of panic, I weigh up my options. I can stay here and wait for whoever – *whatever* – it is to either give up or break in.

Or . . .

I can find out who it is.

The thought makes my stomach somersault with fear. But I also don't want to wait for whoever it is to try and break a window. For all I know it could just be some drunken teenager, tapping on what he thinks is his girlfriend's hut. *Or it could be something much worse*. No. I won't think like that. There is no murderer creeping in the darkness. Tildy's death was an *accident*.

Then why am I so afraid?

The faces of those interviewed twenty years ago seem to flicker through the darkness: Sheila . . . Gary . . . Dev . . . Kip . . . Caitlin . . . Tom . . .

There's an innocent explanation. It's something loose. That's all. Just go and check, then you can come back to bed. Pushing the duvet away, I slip out of bed. At the last minute, I grab a large rock from the windowsill, one that Anna painted with a bright, cheerful boat years ago. Clutching the front door handle, I listen carefully.

Tap.

Tap.

There is a soft *click* as I turn the key. Slowly, dreading the hinges squeaking, I open the door. Fear squeezes my throat as I listen out for any sound. It is harder to hear out here, with the breaking waves only a few metres away. Then, as the wind drops for a moment, I hear it.

Taptaptaptap.

A branch wouldn't tap without wind.

Cautiously, I step out onto the deck and down the steps at the front of the hut. My palm is slippery on the rock and

I switch hands, wiping the sweat on my pyjama bottoms. I reach the cold sand in front of the hut without making a noise. Crouching low, I skirt around the front of the hut.

BANG.

Jumping backwards, the rock falls from my hand with a *thud*. I gasp, expecting to see someone lunging at me, before realising it was just the hut door slamming shut in the wind. My heart racing, I turn hurriedly down the side of the hut.

There is no one at the window.

Adrenaline crashes through me. I spin back around in case someone has encircled the hut and come up behind me: but there is no one.

The night air steals over me as I stand in the darkness. The seconds tick by, but nothing stirs.

Finally, I move back towards the hut, scanning the clearing one last time. That's when I see it: a movement halfway up the winding steps leading to the top of the headland. A figure.

Heart pounding, I strain through the darkness . . . but then I blink and all I see is trees.

Chapter Forty-Nine

Now

Sophie

There is no hope of sleep for the rest of the night. I turn on all the lamps and fold away the sofa-bed. Then I bundle myself up in my duvet, wrap my hands around a mug of coffee, and wait.

Was someone trying to scare me? Were Kip and I wrong? Last night I began to believe that Matilda's death really was just an innocent accident ... yet as the dawn steals around me, a feeling of foreboding clings to me like cobwebs.

The lamp light drains away as the sun rises. As the blackness turns from inky blue to pink, I pull the curtains back from the doors and return to the sofa, watching through gritty eyes as fingers of golden sunlight creep across the wooden floor. Finally, when the sun has chased away the last of the shadows, I open the doors and put the kettle on the stove for another cup of coffee.

In the bright light of day, my fears start to lose colour slightly, as though it was a film that I had fallen asleep to, not real at all. I try to cling on to the memory of last night as it begins to trickle away. *Did I imagine it?* No: there was a figure on the headland, I didn't imagine that. *Did I?* Now that the daylight has begun chasing away my fears, my recollection of the night seems to run with it. What if there *was* no figure? What if I got so caught up in my own panic, all I saw was a swaying tree? The kettle whistles on the stove and I pour it sleepily into my mug. Walking across to the doors, I look outside at the beach. It's hard to be afraid, when the morning light shimmers off the waves and a toddler in a frilly swimming costume waddles determinedly across the sand.

My phone dings from the windowsill, reminding me I need to get ready for my appointment with the estate agent. The hut will be put up for sale today; another piece of my past will be gone. With a pounding head, I begin giving the hut a final tidy, pushing my fears away for the time being.

Gina arrives promptly at 9am, this time in a black shift dress with a bright pink scarf wrapped around her neck.

The hut is almost unrecognisable from when I first arrived: I have dusted and polished the remaining sunfaded possessions lining the windowsills, the taps and light fittings are gleaming and the walls are bare except for the old nautical clock and large circular mirror. A bunch of wildflowers from the bottom of the headland sits in a small vase on the table. Sunlight filters through the coloured glass of the porthole, sending rainbow lights dancing around the hut. It looks perfect; Gina even sighs when she walks in.

'Oh, you've done a fabulous job. Just fabulous. Buyers will really see the potential. *In fact*,' she leans towards me and says in a stage whisper, 'I've already set a few tongues wagging with the rumour there's a hut down here for sale.'

I am less and less sure about Gina: something about her unbounded glee, the way her eye travels greedily around the hut as though the wood was made of gold. She starts directing Ash, the dark-haired photographer, around the hut. Finally, after half an hour of rearranging the curtains and table, Gina is bidding me an overly cheerful goodbye.

'I'll be in touch!' she trills over her shoulder, just as my phone rings. Picking it up, I walk outside onto the deck.

My heart sinks slightly at the sight of Anna's name, not Nick's, flashing up on the screen. I try not to think too much into this: the memory of Kip's kiss is still fresh in my mind. The thought of chatting about the hut fills me with dread, but I press answer and force a smile into my voice.

'How's it going?' Anna asks straight away.

'It's fine, the estate agent just left, actually.' Briefly, I fill Anna in on the more boring details of the past few days, wishing that I could tell her more. Anna, in return, tells me about a new client project she has won at work and about Mike's younger brother, Francis, who is over in Australia for a visit.

'. . . totally nuts together, honestly. They keep "fixing" things around the house. I can't seem to find their *off* button.'

I allow a small laugh, knowing she doesn't mean it.

'You sound tired, Soph. Late night?'

Oh shit. Anna's radar is infamous. I can't tell her that I was being kept awake by disembodied tapping. I settle on a half version of the truth.

'Something like that. I went surfing yesterday and cooked dinner with Kip.'

'*Kip? The* Kip, the boy you crushed on for the whole of your adolescent life?'

'I didn't *crush* on him—'

'Nice try, Sophie, you were obsessed. You practised that sticky eye thing on him for days until he asked if you needed to borrow some sunglasses.'

I had forgotten this embarrassing behaviour: Tildy and I had read an article about 'sticky eyes' in one of our magazines the summer before she died. The article firmly stated that in order to lure a boy with eye contact, you needed to look at him for a moment, then drag your eyes slowly away like they were attached to soft, sticky caramel. Tildy nailed it: prancing around the deck with her hand on her hip.

'*Sticky eyes, daaaarling,*' she said, putting on a deep, lusty voice. '*It's all in the eye contact.*' I had tried it and looked like I had some sort of eye defect.

'Anyway,' Anna is saying, 'I was telling Mike and Francis about you being down there and turns out Francis used to know Caitlin Richards.'

'Did he? I don't think I ever saw Mike and Francis down here.'

Mike's parents owned a beach hut in the nineties, too, but I don't remember Anna ever mentioning that Mike or his brother Francis had been at the beach the summers we were.

'No, they used to visit their grandparents in Canada every summer. But they both went to school with her, and Francis was in Caitlin's year. Apparently, she was seriously smart and was meant to go to a top university after sixth form.'

'What happened?' I asked, picturing a ruthless Caitlin in some super successful executive job. It doesn't surprise me that she was intelligent, but I hadn't ever pegged her for the academic type. Like me, Caitlin must have become some-one different at the beach.

'She dropped out of school after that summer; the sum-mer Matilda died. Apparently, she got pregnant and quit school to have the baby.'

'She got *pregnant*?' I rifle back through my hazy teen memory. Towards the end of summer, Caitlin seemed angrier than ever, lashing out and drinking all the time. Was that why?

'Yeah, Francis knew one of her friends at school who said that she got pregnant over the summer. Crazy, right? While everything was happening with Matilda, Caitlin was pregnant.'

'Wow. I can't believe we didn't know.'

Anna starts saying something, but my attention is lost: the doors to Chetana's hut further along the beach have opened. A figure emerges from the hut, too far to see clearly, but still familiar.

It can't be.

My heart starts to beat faster. I'm wrong, I must be . . . the tall, dark-haired figure pauses on the deck for a moment. It looks as though he is tapping intently on his phone. Then he puts the phone in his pocket and steps slowly down from the deck. As he turns to walk down the side of the hut, I get a good look at his face. It *is* him.

Dev is back at the beach.

Chapter Fifty

That day
6.15pm
Sophie

I walked along the beach, staring down at the sand in front of me. In my shorts pocket, the change Mum had given me to go and buy a new magazine jingled softly. She had only given me the money because she was worried something was wrong with me. She was right: for the past three days, I hadn't been able to get the fight with Matilda out of my head. It was making me feel sick.

For as long as I could remember, arriving at the sandbank was the one thing that got me through each miserable school year. But this summer, it had all gone wrong. All I had wanted was to spend time with Kip and know how it felt to be included. To be popular. It had never occurred to me that I would lose Tildy over it, or that I would become a different person.

I realised, then, that I was outside Tildy's hut: for a moment I looked up in anticipation, wondering if I might see her. But the deck was empty and the doors were closed.

'Alright kiddo?' Next to Tildy's hut, Tom was sprawled out on Kip's deck. Jamie was sitting next to him. I raised my hand, shielding my face from the early evening sun.

'Hiya,' I replied, stopping in front of them. Behind Tom and Jamie, I could just make out Dev and Kip inside the hut.

'What are you up to?' Tom asked.

For a moment I hesitated: usually I would have lied about doing something cool, but for some reason I couldn't find the energy.

'Just walking to the shop. You?'

'Fuck all,' Jamie replied, grinning at me, just as Kip and Dev emerged onto the deck.

'Hey, Fee,' Kip said, smiling. *Why did he always have to act pleased to see me?* It was so confusing. He held out a can of Coke to me, while Dev and Tom started rolling cigarettes. 'You have this one, I'll grab another.'

'Thanks,' I said. I looked uncertainly around the deck and then sat down on the edge, my legs dangling over the side.

'What are we doing tonight?' Kip asked, once he was back outside. Tom spread his arms wide, a grin on his face. I suddenly noticed the stubble on his jaw.

'Dude, it's my birthday tomorrow. My brother's bringing a load of booze down tonight. Let's party!' They all clinked their drink cans together and I tried to look pleased: but I couldn't seem to get excited about it. For some reason, hanging out with them no longer seemed so appealing. I was starting to wish that I was back home in my bedroom with my safe, cosy bed and familiar posters on the wall.

'You alright, Fee?' Kip had come and sat down next to me. I hadn't even noticed. 'You don't seem yourself.'

He leant in and nudged me with his elbow. My chest flooded with warmth. I looked into his blue eyes and desperately wanted to tell him everything: about the fight with Matilda; about how I regretted what I said; about how lonely I felt. I opened my mouth, but before I could say anything, Kip's attention was caught by something behind me.

'Caitlin!'

I turned my head, quickly. Caitlin was approaching the deck. She wore small denim shorts and a baggy orange shirt. There was a thick white bandage wrapped around her ankle and my stomach squirmed with guilt. I hadn't seen her since she had fallen into the hole. *Since I had let her fall.*

'How's your ankle?' Kip asked, immediately taking Caitlin's hand and helping her up onto the deck. She looked at me as she passed and her mouth twisted into a sneer.

'It's okay,' she said, turning back to Kip and sighing. 'I've *just* managed to start walking normally again.'

I looked away, swallowing. Even if Caitlin hadn't actually realised what I had done, I still couldn't look her in the eye. Tildy's words from our fight echoed in my head: *I don't even recognise you anymore, Sophie.*

'Gary Hall said it could have been really serious,' Caitlin went on, as if to rub it in. It was as if the whole of Matilda's family were against me, somehow. 'If he hadn't iced and bandaged it so fast, it would have taken way longer to recover, and he says I have to be really careful to let it heal properly.'

'Well, I'm glad you're better. I'll get you a drink,' Kip said to Caitlin, disappearing into the hut.

'Did I hear something about a party?' Caitlin asked, sitting down next to Dev on his sun lounger. He quickly moved to make room for her, almost tipping the lounger up as he did so.

'Yep,' Dev said enthusiastically, straightening up. 'Tom's birthday tomorrow, so tonight it's *on*.'

Caitlin made a show of tucking her injured ankle underneath her on the lounger. Tom and Dev both watched her, staring at her long, tanned legs. Even in an oversized shirt and denim shorts, Caitlin looked perfect.

Kip emerged from the hut and handed Caitlin a glass of Coke with ice and a lemon slice in it.

'Don't get used to it,' he said, handing her the glass and raising his eyebrow at her satisfied smile, 'it's just because I feel sorry for you. You've missed some great surf. *And*,' he added, plucking at her orange shirt, 'I want this back, I was looking for it yesterday.'

Caitlin batted him away, laughing loudly. It felt like a stone had dropped into my stomach. *It's Kip's shirt.* I imagined him wrapping it around Caitlin. *When was I going to stop caring about him?*

'Are you coming tonight?' said a voice to my right. I looked across and saw Tom's friend Jamie, leaning forwards in his chair to talk to me. When our eyes met, he smiled.

Up until now, Kip had had all of my attention, to the point that I had barely even noticed anyone else. But now I was looking at Jamie properly, he actually *was* quite cute: he had floppy brown hair that hung over his eyebrows and nice eyes. They weren't blue like Kip's, they were brown; but unlike Kip's, Jamie's eyes were focused solely on me. He was older, which made me a bit nervous, but he seemed nice. I tossed my hair back and tried to look happy.

'I think so. Are you?'

'I will be, if you are,' Jamie replied.

Out of the corner of my eye, I watched Caitlin smiling at Kip. My stomach knotting, I turned back to Jamie. *Forget about Kip.* Looking up at Jamie through my eyelashes, I gave him a flirtatious smile. He looked surprised, then pleased.

'I'll be there.'

Chapter Fifty-One

Now

Sophie

I peer along the beach towards Chetana's hut, still wondering if I saw correctly. *Was it really Dev? What's he doing here?* My head is sluggish from the lack of sleep. *Where is he going?* From what Chetana said, Dev is rarely down here anymore. I take a deep breath. It doesn't matter *what* Dev is doing here. All I need to worry about is getting the hut sold and planning my next steps.

I go back inside and pick up my phone, determined to start looking at flights to Australia. I have four more weeks of my forced leave: just the right amount of time to visit Anna and Mike. I briefly mull over what Anna told me about Caitlin, that she got pregnant. It was as though everyone on the beach had a secret to hide that summer. Like picking up a pretty rock and finding the underbelly writhing with insects.

Just then, I hear an annoyed male voice coming from somewhere behind my hut. *Could it be?* My curiosity piqued, I jump down from the deck and walk down the side of the hut. Slowly, I peer around the corner and almost immediately I spot Dev. He is striding along the dirt path towards me, in the direction of the headland. His phone is raised to his ear and he is scowling. Though his face is familiar, Dev has undergone a surprising transformation over the years. Gone is the stringy teenager I last saw. Now Dev is muscular and well groomed, his clothes expensive and perfectly tailored. Even his voice sounds different: loud and self-assured.

Why is he so angry? Has Chetana told him what happened between us? Surely not. Even so, I wonder whether he might have found out, which would explain his sudden appearance and bad mood. Is he on the phone to his dad, perhaps? The politician? As Dev gets nearer, I hurriedly retreat down the side of my hut, in case he walks past and sees me watching. Turning my back so that I am facing towards the beach, I wait for him to walk past.

What if Dev was the one tapping on the window last night, trying to mess with me? It seems far-fetched . . . but so much has happened over the past few days, nothing seems implausible, anymore.

After a moment or two, I dare to look around. Dev is a few metres away from me, walking towards the headland steps. His pace has slowed and, though I can't hear what he is saying, he is gesturing forcefully. *I want to know who he's talking to. I want to know if he was the figure on the headland.*

Before I really know what I'm doing, I've run back to my hut for my sandals and I am hurrying after Dev. I try not to picture Kip's reaction if he could see me acting like this, following people around. *I need to know. Just in case.*

I keep a few paces behind Dev as he approaches the headland steps. My foot crunches on some stone and for a second, Dev pauses, the phone still held to his ear. His slick, dark hair gleams in the sunlight as I hold my breath, waiting for him to turn around and see me standing behind him, with nowhere to hide. After a second, however, he starts up the steps. I wait a beat or two, then begin climbing after him. He isn't walking fast, but his legs are long and within seconds he has disappeared around the bend in the headland steps and out of sight. *Shit.* I need to catch up with him, in case I miss some important part of the conversation. I begin taking the steps two at a time. My breathing becomes laboured and sweat gathers as I race up, step after step.

Then, without warning, I round the bend and collide headfirst into something hard and unmoving: Dev is standing on the path. I stumble backwards, my cheeks flaming.

Up close, Dev is even taller than I realised, towering over me. He is looking at me in apparent surprise.

'So, it's true. Sophie Douglas is back in town,' he says in a deep voice. 'And you're into running now? Or just following me?' I start, but his handsome face is amused. None of the anger I just saw.

'I was just walking up to the headland,' I say quickly. It sounds unconvincing, but Dev lets out a short, loud laugh.

'I'm just kidding, Sophie. I'm sure you've got much better things to do than stalk your old friends.' He smiles, showing straight white teeth. I can't believe how different this man is from the boy who seemed so keen to fit in with Kip and Tom. He radiates confidence and polish.

I take a deep breath.

'I've just come back for a couple of days. What are you doing down here?' Far from sounding relaxed, my voice squeaks.

'I've just finished a murder,' he says, leaning against the sun-bleached wooden railing. 'At Winchester Crown Court. I thought it would be nice to have a little break before heading back to London. Not that my clerk seems to agree,' he holds up his phone, with a slight frown. 'I can't even go for a stroll without him hounding me.'

Is that all he was doing? Going for a walk up to the headland? The first stirrings of doubt begin to creep into my mind. *Have I overreacted, again?*

'Oh, right,' I manage. 'Chetana said you don't get down here much.' I watch his face, hoping for a reaction, something to justify my actions in chasing him up the headland.

Dev nods and glances down at his phone, which has started to ring shrilly. He taps the screen, silencing it. 'Chetana told me you two had caught up.'

I nod, forcing my lips into a smile. Above us, a bird of prey circles the sky over the headland.

'That's nice,' Dev continues, 'after all these years.'

I don't know what to say. Dev must know Chetana and I would never catch up solely for a cosy gossip, that we were never friends.

'She also said you're selling up and moving on from here.' Dev glances down the steps, towards the huts. 'I always think that's a good idea. No one should hang around in one place for too long. I keep telling Chetana that. Moving on is healthy.'

I stare at him. *Is he hinting that he knows what Chetana told me? About the photo?* But before I can speak, the smile is back on Dev's face.

'Well, I won't hold you up.' He steps to one side.

'Actually, I—'

'Please,' he gestures towards the top of the headland, 'after you. Chetana will be wondering where I am and I don't want to interrupt your walk.'

I hesitate. If I say I no longer need to keep walking, it'll be obvious I was following him.

Slowly, I begin climbing the steps. As I pass Dev, I tense instinctively; but he remains motionless. Half-expecting him to come after me, I quicken my pace. After a few moments, I look back over my shoulder. Dev hasn't moved; his eyes are watching me. He raises a hand.

Once I reach the top, I wait until I see Dev reach the bottom of the steps and start walking back towards his hut. Only then do I relax slightly. Do I believe his story, that he is here for a break? Or, as I suspect, did Chetana call him to tell him what happened yesterday? *Was he lying about the trial in Winchester? Has he been here all along?* I don't know what to think.

I start walking along the headland. In the distance, a small wooden post looks out over the horizon. I approach it apprehensively. I knew from my parents it was here, but I have never actually seen it. The wood is weathered now but the golden plaque at the top is as shiny as if it were made yesterday.

Matilda Jane Hall, 4th June 1983 – 15th August 1997. A star taken by the dawn. The plaque could not be in a more beautiful place, overlooking the waves, the gold mount glinting in the sunlight. But it should be Tildy, not a wooden structure, sitting here.

I'm sorry, Tildy. I'm so sorry I left you that night. I should have been with you.

For the first time since she died, I allow the guilt to fully wash over me without trying to stop it. I place a hand on the warm gold plaque, my stomach clenched painfully, as the tears come thick and fast. I force myself to finally confront the awful possibility that has eaten away at me like a disease all these years: that, had I been on time to meet her, Tildy might not have wound up dead. Or that if I had actually looked for her on the rocks when I arrived, I might have found her. She could have still been alive. The sea yawns out before me as I cry, wave after wave rolling slowly in from the horizon. *How can somewhere so beautiful hold so much pain?*

My phone rings, making me jump. Sliding it out of my back pocket, I see the name on the screen and hastily answer, wiping my tears on the back of my sleeve.

'Mum!' I cry, suddenly desperate to hear a familiar voice.

'—ophie? Can you . . . hear me?'

'Just about.' I move away from the windy cliff edge, towards the yellow gorse-lined trail. Pressing a finger against my free ear, I try to make out what Mum is saying.

'. . . been out on Phil's new boat with horrible signal. Had to wait until we docked for the afternoon. So many voice-mails!' Her voice is cheerful, buoyant. She is as happy as I have ever heard her.

After Dad died, Mum was unrecognisable for the first few months, just putting one step in front of the other. Then she met Phil at a charity event and they started spending time together, taking hours over pots of tea in their local department store café. At first, I thought it was too soon: Dad had only been gone six months and I didn't understand how Mum could have moved on so quickly. But once I met the warm-hearted Phil, I couldn't help but love him, too. Before long, they had both sold their homes and bought a villa in Spain. It was the kind of thing Dad used to scoff at, but Mum has never seemed more content. I'm happy for her but – though I would never admit it to anyone – sometimes it feels as though I've lost both Mum *and* Dad.

I listen for a while as Mum enthusiastically describes the boat trip and tells me how Phil is. While she talks, I try to decide what I am going to do: how to broach the subject of Sheila and Dad.

'Mum, I'm at the hut—' I begin.

'Isn't that all sorted?' she replies in surprise. 'And you've gone *down* there? After all this time?'

'It was easier than getting a removal company involved,' I say, ignoring the twinge of irritation at her comment, when I'm trying to sell the hut for her. 'Mum, listen, this'll be costing a fortune on that phone plan of yours and I need to talk to you about something.'

'Is everything alright?' Mum's voice is softer now, more concerned. For once, she seems to be properly listening. As much as I hate burdening her, I need to share the weight of Sheila's confession.

'I'm so sorry, I've got something really difficult to tell you . . .' I take a deep, steadying breath, forcing myself to say the words. 'Since I've been back down here, I've found out some things about Dad . . . and Sheila Hall.'

I pause, expecting Mum to interrupt, to ask me what it is. But all I can hear is the sound of her breathing, so I continue.

'According to Sheila, they . . . uhh . . . had an affair. Just once, apparently. But she claimed afterwards she had

Matilda. That Matilda was Dad's. Not Gary's.' My voice is trembling, dreading hearing the shock in my mum's voice, or worse, for her to start crying. Suddenly, I regret telling her. It was selfish, I should have waited until I could somehow verify Sheila's story, or not told her at all.

'I know.'

'*What?*' I didn't hear right. I couldn't have done.

'I already know, Sophie.'

'Since *when?*' She *knows*. I press the phone harder to my ear in disbelief.

'Your dad told me, just before he died.' To my surprise, Mum snorts sarcastically. 'Not exactly brave of him. He admitted to what he had done and said how sorry he was. That was about it.'

'So, it's true,' I say, my voice flat. 'He really did cheat on you.'

'Sophie, your dad . . . well, he wasn't perfect. Trust me. After all, he had the nerve to keep the hut for all those years, knowing what he had done.'

'Why didn't you tell us? *Tildy,* Mum. She wasn't just anyone.'

Mum's voice softens.

'I wanted to protect you, Sophie. Matilda's death tore you apart; I didn't think you could handle knowing that she was your sister, too. And,' she continues, before I can interrupt, 'I wanted to protect the memories you had of your dad. The truth would have only caused you and Anna more pain. I didn't want that.'

Oddly, her justifications echo Sheila's; two mothers, trying to limit the pain for their daughters.

'Oh *Mum*,' I breathe. 'How did you cope with that?'

No wonder she seemed to move on quicker than we expected: her grief must have been tempered by Dad's betrayal.

'I didn't have a choice, sweetheart. If I hadn't got on with things, I wouldn't have met Phil, or moved out here. Life doesn't just stop because something awful has happened. It isn't that generous.'

I think of Sheila, who never learnt to move on, who simply existed like one of the many empty shells scattered along the shoreline. She was young when Tildy died; she could have found a way to get on with life, but she refused. Chetana, too, clinging to the memories of Matilda and that one summer they had together. Am I headed in the same direction? There might be horrors lurking beneath the waters here, but is it my job to find them?

'Get back to London, Sophie,' Mum is saying. 'I don't like you being down there. The sooner we all leave that place behind, the better.'

Chapter Fifty-Two

Now

Sophie

After hanging up the phone to Mum, I message Kip, asking if he will meet me for a drink. I half-expect him to ignore my message, but he replies almost immediately to say yes. I cross the harbour on the water-taxi, unable to stop myself glancing around for Dev every few minutes.

I've only been at The Ship for twenty minutes when Kip arrives. Spotting me, he heads straight to my table which is outside, near the water. It's quiet: midweek, just after lunch. Near the table, fishermen pull crab cages up from the water, dark green seaweed clinging to the bars. The water sucks and slops against the harbour wall as seagulls squabble near the boats, trying to snatch at the black-eyed crabs.

I feel a fissure of nerves as Kip approaches the table, remembering how we left things last night. It's a good sign that he got my message and agreed to meet me, but I don't know how things stand between us since the kiss.

'Hi,' I say as he sits down opposite me. 'You got here quick.'

'I only had a couple of meetings this afternoon, so I blew them off. This was a much more tempting offer.' He smiles and I feel a pang of envy: Kip's existence is so fluid, each moment transient, like the swoop and pull of a kite. I, on the other hand, am the opposite: well-defined development goals at work, strict payments into a rainy-day ISA, carefully considered pension schemes. Always caring more about the future than the present.

I gesture to the second golden pint of IPA on the table. 'That's for you.'

'Are you trying to get me drunk?' he asks, raising an eyebrow, but the look in his eye appears playful: he doesn't seem to be holding a grudge over last night. *When has Kip ever held a grudge?* Then he frowns, studying me more carefully. 'Are you alright? If you don't mind me saying, you look like shit, Fee.'

'Gee, thanks,' I mutter.

He's right, though: tiredness pulls at the skin on my face and my eyes are gritty. I open my mouth to tell Kip about the tapping, about my confrontation with Dev . . . but something stops me. *What if he's tired of talking about it? He hasn't exactly believed me so far, has he?* Kip has been the one thing keeping me sane since my impromptu return to the sandbank. I can't stand the idea of him thinking I am losing my grip. *What if he backs away from me, like Nick did?* The thought scares me more than I want to admit. Deciding to keep the information to myself for the time being, I instead tell him about the conversation with my mum. When I've finished, he blows out a long breath and leans back in his seat.

'That must have been awful. Why didn't your dad just keep it to himself? Surely it would have been kinder?'

Privately, I agree with Kip, though it hurts to think badly of my dad. I don't understand why he decided to put Mum through the pain of his confession, especially when they both knew he didn't have long left. After all, Matilda was dead. Did he consider how selfish it was, unburdening himself of his demons so he could die with a guilt-free conscience?

'I saw that estate agent was back again this morning,' Kip says. 'How's the sale going?'

He doesn't look me in the eye as he speaks, choosing to take another long sip of his drink.

'They took the photos of the hut today. She said they should be up by this afternoon, but she's already had interest, so it'll probably be pretty quick.'

'Right,' he says quietly. 'Then what?'

I look out at the harbour: at the water-taxi making its slow journey back across to the sandbank, at the tourists dotted along the top of the headland. *What's next?* Something has changed since I've been here, some seismic shift in the current of my life. With everything that has happened since the separation and then returning to the sandbank, I no longer know what I want. Nick was right: I hadn't been happy; I had just been in control, keeping myself safe. Now, it's as though I have been presented with a blank sheet of paper but no pen. The idea of taking a surfing trip abroad has been floating in the back of my mind ever since I went out on the water with Kip again. It sparked something within me that had been missing, some connection I haven't felt since I was a teenager. Is there a place for Kip in all of that? Would he want there to be? Then I think of Nick and my chest aches. He didn't know I'd once surfed: I never told him.

'I guess now I need to figure out what I want,' I reply.

Kip sets down his drink. He reaches out and takes my hand in his. It is warm, like him. I haven't eaten today and the beer has gone straight to my head, making it feel pleasantly light.

'What do you want, Soph?'

His voice is low, husky. The fire he always sparks in me flares up again. *Why can't I let this man go?* I point to my empty glass.

'I want another drink.'

Chapter Fifty-Three

Now

Sophie

Sunlight filters through my eyelashes, forcing my groggy eyes open. It takes me a moment to remember where I am: then I spot the surfboards leaning up against the wall on the far side of the room.

I try to probe my memory of last night, but it is hazy and thinking too hard makes my stomach churn. Snippets come back to me, here and there: more pints at The Ship, each going down easier than the last; me and Kip leaning towards one another across the table; talks of surfing the world, leaving England behind; Anna; telling Kip about my life; not mentioning Nick. At some point I think we were told the pub was closing, or maybe it was that we needed food. I had missed the last water-taxi back to the sandbank, so Kip insisted I take his spare room back at his flat in the main town.

Thankfully, when I turn over, I am alone. A quick once-over tells me I am fully dressed in one of Kip's T-shirts and a pair of shorts. Relief pulses through me: whatever I feel for Kip, I need to figure it out sober.

My leggings and shirt from last night are on a small wicker chest in the corner. Pulling them on, I leave the room and walk into the kitchen, finding Kip fiddling with a fancy-looking coffee machine. His hair is wet; it looks as though he has just finished rubbing it haphazardly with a towel.

'Morning,' I say, a little awkwardly. It feels so intimate being inside his home, barefoot. Kip looks up from the coffee machine and smiles. His eyes crinkle in the corners when he smiles, which only makes him look more attractive.

'Hey, how did you sleep?'

'Really well,' I admit. 'I guess copious amounts of beer helps knock you out. Thanks . . .' I shift from foot to foot, embarrassed. 'For letting me stay.'

'No worries. Couldn't risk you swimming back across the harbour. Coffee?' He holds a mug up and I nod, sliding onto a stool at the breakfast bar across from him.

'You look very pretty in the morning,' Kip says, still looking at me with the mug in his hand. With his free hand, he leans across the breakfast bar and tucks a stray curl behind my ear. Then he turns around and carries on making the coffee.

My heart racing slightly, I turn on the stool, looking around Kip's flat. It is light and cosy, with mahogany floorboards and little knick-knacks here and there: tubs of surf wax and a well-worn copy of *Moneyball* doubling up as a coaster. There are other touches, too: paintings of the beach from different angles by local painters – some breathtaking, others shaky – a well-tended miniature herb garden in terracotta pots.

'Do you want to have your coffee on the balcony?' Kip asks.

'Sounds good.'

I am relieved there is no awkwardness in the air this morning. It is something I am growing to increasingly like about Kip: he never takes anything too seriously. We carry our coffee mugs out onto the small balcony, which is sparse, apart from a wooden table with two small benches either side and an old blue bike with a rusted pannier. The shining glory is the view, which overlooks the shimmering harbour and distant sandbank.

'It's funny seeing the huts from this side of the water,' I say, looking at the wooden chalets, neatly positioned like bright monopoly houses. 'They look so peaceful from here.'

'You don't find them peaceful?' Kip asks with a quizzical look. I think about this for a moment.

'I did, once. I used to think they were the only place I could really be myself. The summers and weekends down there were some of the best days of my life.'

'And now?'

My gaze drifts along the huts, left to right, until the point where the sandbank curves out of sight.

'Now all I see is a façade. A cover for all the secrets and lies. And it's worse down there because it's not *supposed* to have darkness, it's supposed to be bright and sunny.'

Kip stares out across the water, towards the huts and the sea beyond them. He looks uncharacteristically serious for a moment, but when he turns back to me, his expression is clear again.

'There were some good bits, though. Remember the summer you and Tildy tried to use olive oil instead of tanning lotion and *literally* fried yourselves?' He shakes his head, smiling. 'You smelt so bad.'

This makes me laugh, surprised that he would remember such a detail.

'My sister threw a massive tantrum because we used up all the oil,' I tell him, 'Dad couldn't make deep-fried chips and calamari rings that night, like he had promised her.'

Kip laughs at this, his eyes dancing; but I suddenly remember what Anna had told me, about Caitlin getting pregnant and dropping out of school. With all that we had had to drink yesterday, I had completely forgotten to tell Kip. His eyes grow wide as I relay the information to him.

'Wow, I had no idea she got pregnant.' He takes a sip of coffee, licking the milk froth from his lip. 'That's such a shame.'

'Did you notice anything at all over the summer?' I ask. 'You were close.'

'Hard to say, she was always kind of all over the place. She had a lot going on with her parents, her dad was drunk a lot. She *hated* you,' Kip admits, shaking his head. 'I never understood why.'

'Kip, she hated me because she liked you,' I say, almost rolling my eyes at his boyish naivety, even at the age of thirty-six. 'She didn't like you giving me attention.'

Kip chuckles. 'Well, I only had eyes for one girl that summer.' Our eyes meet and my stomach swoops. 'Maybe she was seeing someone no one knew about.'

'The one who got her pregnant? Did she ever mention a boyfriend?'

Kip chews his lip, apparently thinking hard.

'No, nothing that I remember. If she was seeing someone, she kept it close to her chest.' He shakes his head. 'Knowing Caitlin, it could have been anyone. My money is on old Harry.'

Kip laughs, but my neck begins to prickle. For some reason, at Kip's words, a seed of something has dislodged itself in the very recesses of my mind.

'It could just be a rumour though,' Kip finishes. 'You know what schools are like. She might never even have been pregnant.'

The dislodged seed suddenly plants itself, its infected roots burrowing deep into my brain. Words I once heard on a dark beach outside my hut come back to me.

People are going to start asking questions.

What about me? My family?

'What is it?' Kip is watching me carefully, his mug hovering in mid-air. He lowers it, slowly. 'Fee, you've gone pale.'

My lips are numb, unable to form words. I had automatically assumed that Caitlin had got pregnant by someone at school or in town, barely giving it a second thought. But what if it wasn't someone from school?

'What if it was someone at the beach?' I whisper.

What was it Mum said? '*He wasn't perfect. Trust me.*'

'What if it was my dad?'

Chapter Fifty-Four

That day
7pm
Caitlin

Ten seconds. It had been ten seconds since I had told him, but it felt like forever. The wooden clock on the wall ticked them off one by one. *Ten . . . tick . . . eleven . . . tick . . .* Did babies grow every second? I stared at the picture on the windowsill closest to me for a minute, not really seeing it: a young girl smiling at the camera with the sea behind her.

I hadn't meant to blurt it out like that: all afternoon I had been putting it off, but as he had climbed out of bed I just *said* it. Now I was sat naked on the sofa-bed.

My stomach – my backstabbing, baby-filled stomach – was knotted as I searched his face for *something*; anything. I had expected him, maybe not to be pleased, but at least to try and make me feel better. To tell me it would be okay. His mouth was frozen in a tight line that started to frighten me a bit. *Why hadn't he said anything yet?* Maybe he was just in shock. In a second he would smile and tell me it was okay. That tomorrow we would break the news to my dad and—

'Why are you telling me this?'

What? I stared at him.

'What do you mean, why am I telling you? I'm pregnant with your *baby*!'

But he was shaking his head as I spoke.

'I've got no proof it's mine.'

I flinched. This wasn't the way it was supposed to go. Where was the person from a second ago, who had kissed me and tickled me under the duvet? Now he looked angry. I had never seen this side of him before: a side other than the happy, carefree one, who was thrilled to be with me.

'I haven't been with anyone else,' I said heatedly. 'It's yours.'

'What do you want from me, then? To help you get rid of it?' He hadn't moved from his position in front of the kitchen counter, but he looked pale. He was wearing my favourite T-shirt, the one that brought out the colour of his eyes. I took a deep breath.

'I don't know if I *am* going to get rid of it.'

He went very still.

'You're not getting rid of it?' It sounded like he was being strangled.

'Maybe not,' I said, standing and picking the denim shorts and shirt I had been wearing up off the floor. I pulled the shorts on, my hands shaking. I hadn't actually decided yet what I was going to do; but the image I had been carrying with me of the bright sunny kitchen and the little girl in her highchair, excited to see her daddy, was slowly trickling away.

Suddenly, he started laughing. I looked up in shock: his mouth was turned up in a smile, but his eyes were chillingly cold.

'You didn't think we were going to have it *together* did you? You thought . . . I would ruin my whole life to have a kid with *you*?' He continued to laugh. The sound rang in my ears. 'Why would I do that? I doubt I'm the only guy you've been shagging.'

Who the hell was this person? I didn't recognise him. To my horror, my chin started to wobble. I had never told him he was my first. The girls at school all thought I had been with loads of guys, but I had never gone the whole way with them. He was looking at me with a mocking smile and I started to get angry. *He thinks he's got a choice in this. The bastard.*

'*Fuck you!*' I hissed. 'I'll make you deal with this. I'm not doing it on my own.' I picked up my shirt and yanked it on.

He made a sudden movement towards me, his face blotchy. There was a flash of something in his eye . . . something that turned me cold. Just then, I heard voices and the sound of flip flops slapping against the deck steps. His gaze whipped across to the closed doors, where the curtains were tightly closed. Seizing my opportunity, I raced out of the back door, leaving him to his lies.

Chapter Fifty-Five

Now

Sophie

Ten minutes later, Kip picks up his keys and phone and walks back out to the balcony. I haven't moved. My cold, half-drunk coffee sits in front of me on the table.

'You stay here as long as you want, okay?' he says, crouching down so he's level with me. He puts a hand on my shoulder, looking worried.

'Try not to jump to any conclusions. There's no reason whatsoever to think your dad is involved in any of this. I'll meet you as soon as I've finished work.'

I nod, barely hearing him. The door opens, closes . . . and I am alone with my thoughts. I get up and pace back and forth along the balcony, running it over and over again in my head.

The photos, hidden under the hut, *my dad's* hut. Anna's revelation that Caitlin got pregnant that summer.

The angry words I heard my dad use on the beach all those years ago come back to me, as though he is hissing them in my ear: *You can't do this. It's not just about you. What about me? My family?* I had thought that the conversation must have been with Sheila, but what if it was with someone else? Someone barely older than me? And if Dad *did* get

Caitlin pregnant . . . what if Tildy had found out about it? Perhaps she came by to see me and caught them together . . . maybe Dad lured her to the headland and afterwards he found her tin and hid it? *No, no, it makes no sense. He would have got rid of the tin, not just hidden it. And he might have had a brief affair with Sheila, but it was just once and she was an adult. He was a good person. You knew him.* Half an hour ago, I thought Dev was the perfect suspect, now I'm wondering about my own *dad* and a teenage girl?

I look out across the harbour towards the sandbank. Distant grey clouds cast a shadow over the coloured huts. Are any of my thoughts legitimate, or is the sandbank driving me slowly mad?

My phone rings. I hurry inside to where my handbag sits on the floor. There are four missed calls from the estate agent, Gina, and two from Nick. My stomach flips. *He called back.* Gina has also sent me a text message: *Hi Sophie, please call me. Exciting news about the hut! Thanks, Gina, Preston & Marsh Estate Agents.*

I put the phone back down. How can I explain any of this to Nick? I shouldn't have called him in the first place; I can't face the idea that he is calling back to ask me to leave him alone. I return to pacing up and down the living area.

Was my dad a murderer? The same man who tied tassels to my bike handles and spent forever adjusting my helmet straps . . . is it possible he could have been both? I suddenly remember how he would sometimes clip the buckle on my helmet too tight, catching the soft skin under my chin.

How do I find out the truth? Dad is gone. Matilda is gone. I can't burden Anna or Mum with this.

Picking up my phone again, I unlock the screen. I've not used the Facebook app in so long, I have to download it again: the small circle closes agonisingly slowly as I chew my thumbnail. Finally, I click on the app icon and type in a name. The results appear on my screen: forty-three of them and none of them is the person I am looking for. I think about what else they might go by. Typing in an alternative name brings up only fourteen results.

Three names down, I find her.

Chapter Fifty-Six

Now

Sophie

The house is small and neat: a detached 1950s bungalow with red roses around the door that don't quite disguise the lack of character. It sits nestled among larger, grander houses on the quietly affluent street. Where the tidy gravel path ends, there is a low ramp leading up to the white front door.

There is a moment, as my finger hovers over the doorbell, when I hesitate. *Do I really want this door to open?* It would be so simple to just walk away. But then it is too late: my finger has pressed the bell, sending an electric *ding dong ding dong* chiming through the house.

Almost immediately, I hear the sound of a door closing and footsteps approaching. The door opens, revealing a tall, attractive woman with a short blonde bob and a serious expression. Without her long mermaid-like hair, it takes me a moment to recognise her. The appraising look in her eyes, however, is unchanged. Thirty-six-year-old Caitlin is as beautiful now as she was when she was sixteen, if not more so. Her face is fresh and free of make-up, and she wears a smart blue jumper and jeans.

'You're here,' she says, by way of greeting.

'Thanks for agreeing to see me.' My voice is high, unsure.

'I didn't exactly have a choice,' Caitlin replies and I feel myself shrinking again, like I used to around her when we were teenagers. For a moment, we just stand there looking at one another, before Caitlin relents.

'I guess you'll have to come in.'

She opens the door wider and is already walking away down a large, airy hallway as I step inside. My first impression upon entering is that everything is well-cared-for and impossibly neat: the marble floor is gleaming; the thick velvet curtains hang perfectly straight. A glass table to the right holds a large vase of peonies. Then I notice that all along the walls are support railings, like the kind you see in a care home.

'Is this your parents' house?' I ask, trying not to sound intimidated as I follow Caitlin into a large, open kitchen with an island in the centre.

'No,' she says shortly. 'I bought it six years ago.'

Six years ago? She must be doing well for herself, to have bought a house like this on such a nice street when she was only thirty.

'It's lovely.'

Caitlin doesn't answer; she walks around the other side of the island and turns to face me, her arms folded.

'You said you wanted to talk.'

Caitlin's body language radiates tension, which only makes me more nervous. Why would she be acting so tense if she wasn't hiding something? Of all the likely people to tell me the truth about what happened, Caitlin would be bottom of the list. But if Anna's brother-in-law was right about Caitlin getting pregnant, her whole life changed that summer, too. She also agreed to see me, today. I clear my throat.

'Yes. I want to ask you about that summer . . . about what happened to you.'

A shadow flickers across Caitlin's unlined face.

'I told you when you messaged me, I have nothing to say to you, or anyone else, about that summer.'

She turns around and starts clearing away the washing up on the side with stiff movements. I feel a flicker of irritation. Caitlin is still treating me like she did when we were teenagers, like I'm someone to be dismissed and spoken down to. If my suspicions are correct, this is bigger than some childhood rivalry. I take a deep breath.

'I know who you were sleeping with.'

CRASH.

The plate Caitlin was holding slips from her hand and clatters into the sink. For a moment she simply stands there, breathing heavily. In the corner nearby, I notice an expensive-looking electric wheelchair. It looks smaller than the average wheelchair and has a Tottenham Hotspurs FC sticker on it. I turn my attention back to Caitlin. She hasn't said anything, still facing the sink.

'Caitlin, you were only sixteen. You didn't do anything wrong.' She was just a *child*. Slowly, Caitlin turns to face me.

'Why exactly are you here?' Her eyes are flinty. 'What possible reason could you have for contacting me after all these years and trying to dredge up memories I've tried very *fucking hard* to forget?'

I take a deep breath. It feels ludicrous to be talking about shadows and secrets in this polished kitchen.

'I'm trying to understand more about what happened that summer. I want to know whether what happened to you was linked in any way to Matilda Hall's death.'

If I expected a reaction, I don't get one: Caitlin looks nonplussed, though I am sure I see a faint flicker behind the blue of her eyes.

'How could it be? Her death was an accident.'

'I'm not so sure about that. I'm starting to think Tildy might have been killed for a reason. Possibly because she knew about you two. But I need your help to prove it. Please.'

'What makes you think she was killed for a reason?'

'It doesn't matter,' I reply, not wanting her to know how little evidence I have, 'I just need to know—'

But Caitlin is suddenly leaning forward across the island.

'*It doesn't matter?*' she hisses furiously, with a glance towards the door. 'You turn up here *unannounced*, dragging up memories from twenty years ago, and expect me to just spill all my secrets to you so you can trot off to the police?'

Shock courses through me as some of her spit lands on my cheek.

'Do you have *any* idea what I went through?'

'I—'

'How fucking *dare* you barge into my life after all these years, demanding answers! You're clearly as self-obsessed now as you were back then!'

Anger stirs within me now, hot and sharp.

'I *deserve* answers,' I snap back. 'She was my best friend. He was my *dad*!'

My hand slams onto the cold, hard, marble countertop, but opposite me, Caitlin stills.

'What did you say?'

'He was my dad,' I repeat. 'I have just as much right as *anyone* to know—'

All of a sudden, Caitlin looks relieved.

'I wasn't shagging your *dad*.'

'But—'

She gives a spiteful laugh, leaning back against the counter with folded arms. 'There goes your little theory.'

'You weren't . . . it wasn't my dad?'

'Of course it fucking wasn't.'

Is she lying? This change in direction has thrown me completely off-course, but there is another feeling: relief. *It wasn't Dad.*

'Are we done here?' Caitlin says, raising a sarcastic eyebrow at me. I am about to nod, when I realise that she hasn't denied that she was involved with *someone* on the sandbank, even if it wasn't my dad.

'Whoever you were in a relationship with might still have had something to do with Matilda's death. Did they ever say anything? Was it Dev? Tom?'

Caitlin says nothing and frustration fissures through me.

'Gary and Sheila deserve answers, even if you don't think *I* do.'

Caitlin's folded arms loosen slightly. For a second, her mouth opens, then closes again. Thinking I might finally be getting through to her, I press on.

'They're still there, you know. At the beach. Sheila's never given up hope of finding out what happened to Matilda. If you know anything, isn't it time to tell someone? Wouldn't you want to know, if it was your child?'

But Caitlin's face is shutting down, again: I've lost her.

'I'm not discussing this with you,' she replies, her eyes fixed on a point over my shoulder. 'If the police want to interview me, they'll have to arrest me.'

Something doesn't feel right. She knows more than she is letting on, I am sure of it. Beneath her hard exterior, Caitlin Richards is afraid. Her eyes flit to the corner where the wheelchair sits. *Has she always suspected that Tildy was killed for knowing her secret? Is that why she never returned to the beach?*

'That summer changed my whole life.' Caitlin's voice is flat.

Surprised, I glance up at Caitlin. She suddenly looks very young.

'I did some stupid things,' Caitlin continues. 'Made some poor choices. And I've had to live all these years with the consequences.'

What consequences?

'How did things end between you and him?' I ask quietly.

Caitlin shrugs, as though it never once caused her pain, but her eyes tell a different story.

'The same way it always does. I wanted more. He only wanted a summer fling. I left the beach and never went back. I had no reason to be there, especially not after Matilda died. No one wanted to be there.'

She's right. I was one of many who never returned after that summer. The beach had been tainted by Matilda's death, the way an oil spill spreads across the ocean.

Caitlin's watch beeps with some sort of alarm.

'I need to get on,' she says.

We walk together to the front door. Just as I am stepping out onto the front path, Caitlin speaks.

'I'm sorry, for what it's worth.'

She stands in the doorway, her hands in her pockets.

'Sorry for what?' I ask, confused.

'For being such a bitch to you. I didn't like you, but I didn't need to be like that.'

If someone had told me when I was fifteen that one day, no matter how many years later, Caitlin Richards would be apologising to me, I wouldn't have believed them.

'It's fine,' I say quickly. 'We were teenagers, it doesn't matter.'

Caitlin gives a small shake of her head. Her expression is almost pitying.

'It always matters.'

Chapter Fifty-Seven

That day
7.15pm

Chetana

I saw her before she saw me: her long blonde hair plaited down her back and her favourite hoody on, sat in front of her hut on a deckchair. It was past my curfew, but I needed to speak to her. If I didn't do it now, I would never be able to. The blinds were drawn on my hut, but I knew I wouldn't have long: I was never late back, and my parents would be watching for me. I ducked past my hut as fast as I could and approached her.

'Matilda,' I said. My voice sounded like a stranger's.

Matilda looked up. When she saw me, she looked pleased, but confused. Her eyes darted towards my parents' pink and white hut.

'Chet,' she said quietly. 'It's past your curfew.'

'I know.' My heart was beating painfully hard, as though fighting against what I was about to do to it. Demanding that I don't break it.

Matilda seemed to realise, then, that something was wrong.

'What's the matter?' She kept her voice low, but got up from the deckchair and moved towards where I stood on the sand in front of her hut.

'I . . .'

You have to do this.

'Chet . . .' Matilda was looking scared now. She jumped down onto the sand and reached a hand out towards me, but I took a hasty step back. I couldn't risk my parents seeing us, or get too close to her and change my mind. From where she stood, I could already smell her light, coconut smell, which tore at my chest.

'Has someone hurt you? Is it your parents?' Tildy's eyes flickered back towards my hut.

I had to say it. But I had never wanted to do anything less.

'This . . .' I gestured limply towards myself and then Matilda, 'has to end. It's wr-rong.' The words tasted like poison on my tongue. But if I didn't say them, Dev would find out and tell my parents. And what then? What about the rumours that could spark fires back home in our tight-knit community, where I would have no Matilda to protect me?

'*What?*' Matilda blurted, her face shocked. I knew she was wondering how things could have changed so suddenly. She took a step towards me. 'Chet, what are you talking about, we just—'

'Stop!' I hissed, hastily taking another step back and glancing over my shoulder at my hut. I was suddenly afraid that Tildy might not listen to me. I needed her to.

'Matilda, listen to me. It isn't right. We're just going through a phase. We're supposed to go to university and then one day we'll marry nice boys and have families, okay?'

We stood facing one another: Matilda's mouth open slightly, my insides crumbling like dust. No one had warned me it would hurt this much. No one had said that doing the right thing would feel like the most wrong thing in the world.

'Chet . . .' Tildy whispered, her eyes brimming with tears. 'Please don't do this.'

Her plea caught me off guard and my own eyes became blurry. She had no idea how badly I wanted to reach out and take her hand. But it was killing me, pretending that I meant any of what I was saying. Behind us, there was the muffled snapping of a blind. I whipped around and saw my mother gesturing to me through the window, her mouth a tight line. She was angry just for my *lateness*. It was the reminder I needed. I had to go.

'That photo . . .' I said under my breath, terrified my mother would somehow hear me, 'I need that photo. I have to get rid of it.' She would know the one I meant. The one she took earlier on the rocks was the only one that would really scare me. I should never have let her take it.

'It's upstairs, in my tin,' Matilda replied, gesturing behind her.

I glanced behind me: the blinds were still up. It was really getting late now. I needed to get back inside. I turned back to Tildy and took a step closer, trying to ignore the tear tracks on her cheeks.

'Get rid of it,' I whispered, quickly. 'Please, Tildy, I'm begging you.'

Matilda's face crumpled and she nodded. I started to move away, needing to get back to my hut so that I could curl up against the tsunami of pain that was bearing down on me, but Matilda spoke.

'You don't mean this, Chet,' she said, her voice trembling. 'I don't know what's happened or why you're saying all of this, but I know you love me.'

I do. I do love you. You'll find out tomorrow why I had to do this.

'I know,' I whispered, my throat thick.

Then I left her on the sand, knowing I had broken her heart and hating myself for it.

Chapter Fifty-Eight

Now

Sophie

By the time I get back to the beach after seeing Caitlin, clouds have started to gather on the horizon, casting a grey shadow across the sand and huts. It looks almost apocalyptic: abandoned buckets and spades lie on the sand, windbreakers flap in the increasing wind, no one to protect. I have only just unlocked the hut as the first rumble of thunder rolls across the beach.

Red sky in the morning, shepherd's warning.

I run inside just as the clouds break and rain starts to hammer silently onto the sand.

The hut is neat, empty. The wildflowers I picked for the estate agent photos have wilted, a couple of fallen petals on the table. There is a faint scent of something familiar in the air . . . like sandalwood and pepper. For once, the tidiness and order doesn't calm me: instead, the hut carries an air of abandonment that fills me with unease. It is an easy choice to pull one of the bottles of red from my carrier bag and fill a glass. Sitting still is impossible: I pace around the hut, then come to a stop in front of the doors, watching the storm rage outside.

I used to chase shadows when I was younger: I would wait until a cloud began to drift in front of the sun, then I'd chase the darkness as it spread across the sand. The shadows flit around my brain now, telling me that something went very wrong that summer. Everywhere I turn, someone is protecting a secret.

What is it that I know?

I know that Matilda was found dead, with blunt force trauma to the head. People say she slipped, but she could climb those rocks as easily as she could breathe.

My dad is Matilda's real father. But according to Sheila, no one else found out until after Matilda was dead.

Matilda was in a relationship with Chetana. Her family would never have allowed it, but Dev knew about it.

Caitlin was sleeping with someone along the sandbank, but it was a secret. She was only just sixteen and, evidently, she got pregnant.

I drain my glass, wanting to take the edge off my jumbled thoughts. I can't link any of the past with the present: the discovery of the photos; the feeling of being watched; Chetana taking the tin; Dev's sudden return. Is this what Sheila has been going through all these years: the constant questions, the nagging doubts? It could all be innocent. It could all be explained by Chetana or simply by a lack of sleep. But what I do know is that plenty of people had a motive to kill Tildy, after all. Motives the police failed to uncover twenty years ago.

I rest my aching head against the cool glass of the doors. The rain drums against the roof, hollow and heavy. Staring out at the grey abyss in front of me, there is a sudden movement near the rocks. *What was that?* I cup my hands against the doors, straining to see through the downpour. My breath fogs up the glass and I wipe it away impatiently.

The beach is dark; heavy black clouds blurring with the line of the horizon. The previously golden shoreline is now a sheet of steel and the waves churn furiously, sending spray flying against the rocks. The minutes pass as I stand, not taking my eyes off the beach.

Is someone watching me? Can they see me standing at the glass?

I jump violently as my phone rings, shattering the silence. With shaking hands, I answer, and put the phone to my ear.

'Soph? Are you there? Can you hear me?'

Anna. Her familiar voice carries through the speaker, but I barely register it. I stare through the glass at the dark beach.

'. . . some news,' Anna is saying.

'Some news?' I repeat, distractedly. 'What is it?' *Does she mean Dad? Has Mum told her?*

'We're pregnant!'

This pulls me up. *Pregnant?*

'You're . . . what?'

'We're having a baby girl! We're actually at the twenty-two-week mark but we had some complications, so we've been keeping it quiet. But Francis knows now and I wanted to call you!'

Anna's voice sounds completely different to her usual deadpan tone. A strange, sick feeling spreads through me that has nothing to do with the figure on the beach.

'I didn't even know you were trying,' I say, prolonging the moment when I would have to start congratulating her. The phone signal is patchy, making it hard to hear.

'. . . not really ready . . . the house . . . work is crazier than ever. But we just thought, why not? When you're there emotionally . . . figure the rest out . . . going to be an aunty, Soph!'

An aunty. Not a wife, or a mother. Ignoring the odd squeezing of my chest, I take a deep breath. This is *Anna*. My sister. This is good news.

'That's wonderful news, An. I'm so happy for you and Mike.' The words sound false. Perhaps Anna suspects it too, because her tone becomes less gushy.

'I know . . . might be a hard thing to hear . . . with everything you've been through. But you're young, you've . . . money . . . you can do anything. Husband, kids, the lot.'

That stings. She knows I don't want children, yet people always assume you'll change your mind eventually.

'Honestly, Anna, I'm fine,' I lie. 'I'm so happy for you guys. It's all just been so . . .' *Easy.* '. . . smooth with you both. Like it was meant to be.'

Anna carries on talking while I stand at the doors, half-waiting for someone to suddenly appear at the window, or smash through the glass. But all I can see is sheets of rain, relentlessly pounding against the windows. *It's just the storm. The sleep deprivation. Isn't it?*

'Sophie?' Anna is saying, slightly impatiently now. 'Is everything okay?'

'Y-yes,' I stammer. 'It's just a bad signal. Anna, I really need to go. Congratulations again, I'll call you tomorrow.'

'Soph—'

I hang up. Anna will be hurt, possibly angry, but I can't focus on that right now. My phone dings in my hand and I glance down automatically. There is an earlier missed call and a WhatsApp from an unknown number. I open the message and register the profile picture: it is of Caitlin standing in front of a night-time London skyline. Her message is brief.

DON'T GO BACK TO THE BEACH. IT ISN'T SAFE.

Chapter Fifty-Nine

Now

Sophie

My breath sticks in my throat. *It isn't safe*. What does Caitlin mean? I press the call button and bring the phone to my ear, only to hear the *beep beep* of no signal.

Frustrated, I try again, but the call still doesn't go through. I glance back at the beach and that's when I see it: a figure, crouching down by the rocks to my right. Just in front of the shore. Unlike the figure on the headland, or the feeling of being watched, this person is definitely real. It could just be a birdwatcher ... though in this weather, it hardly seems likely.

Suddenly the person straightens up and starts to move slowly up the beach, towards the direction of my hut. The figure – it's impossible from this distance to make out whether it is a man or woman – reaches the end of the line of rocks that finish halfway up the beach. Their head looks bowed against the rain. Maybe ... maybe I *am* just being paranoid. Maybe there is a totally innocent reason for them being there. It could be old Harry, having lost some precious fishing equipment.

Suddenly, the figure stops and looks up, directly towards my hut. There is no mistake: they are looking at me. Whoever it is stands there, unmoving.

'—ophie?'

I glance down at my phone: I have finally got through to Caitlin.

'Caitlin,' I say quickly. 'Caitlin, I'm at the hut . . . your message, what did it mean?'

'—ou hear me?'

Caitlin's voice is intermittent and keeps cutting out.

'I can hear you! What is it, what didn't you tell me?'

'—still . . .'

Fuck! Caitlin's voice is breaking up making it impossible to hear what she's saying. Against my better judgement, I move away from the doors, trying to find a better signal.

'—still at the beach, Sophie. You need to leave.'

'Who's still here? Did someone hurt Tildy, Caitlin? Do you know who it is? Is it Dev?' I press the phone to my ear, so hard it is painful.

'—should have told you before. You aren't safe. Get off the sandbank. Come here if you have to. Just get away from—'

The connection cuts out. *Who? Get away from who?* I try calling back, but the signal is non-existent. Running back to the doors, I look out, my phone still clutched in my hand. It's impossible to see through the rain if the figure is still there. *I need to know.* I need to know who is behind all this before the shadows drive me insane. I'm sick of looking over my shoulder, fearing the unknown more than the known.

Without bothering to put on a jacket or shoes, I step out onto the deck. Rain lashes at my face as I clamber down the steps, onto the cold sand. The beach appears deserted; thunder shakes overhead as I stumble across the sand.

'*Where are you?*' I shout into the storm, anger swelling desperately within me.

No one answers.

I approach the line of grey rocks, leading towards the water. Blood pounding in my ears, I pass them one at a time, searching for a hidden figure crouched behind them. At last, I reach the shoreline. Ice-cold water laps at my bare feet but I ignore it: wading further forward into the water, I check rock after rock, convinced there is someone waiting to pounce.

Where have they gone? What do they want?

Then, as I turn to look back at the shore, I spot a set of footprints. The falling rain has begun to blur them, but they are still clearly visible in the hard, wet sand: large prints, almost certainly a man wearing trainers. Further up the beach, the undulating sand obliterates the prints, but it doesn't matter. They lead in the direction of the pink and white hut.

Don't go back to the beach.

It isn't safe.

I wade out of the water and stride across the sand towards the striped hut, just as a jagged flash of lightning lights up the sky. I am barely even afraid, anymore. All I want is for this to be over. The control I prided myself on for so many years is gone, washed away with the rest of the pretence on this beach.

The blinds of the hut are closed and I bang on the doors until they fly open. Chetana stands there, a pair of glasses pushed on top of her head.

'Sophie!' She looks shocked, taking in my wet appearance. 'What are you—'

'Where is he?'

'Who?'

'Dev!' I shout, ignoring Chetana's flinch. 'I know he's here!'

I try and push past her, to see inside the hut, but Chetana raises her hands to stop me.

'What are you doing?! Have you completely lost your mi—'

'*Don't* tell me I've lost my mind! He's been following me, he's been watching me! Where *is* he?'

'Dev hasn't been following you! Why would he?' Chetana cries.

'Because I've been asking questions about Matilda's death! Or to stop me from going to the police about you and Matilda!'

Chetana suddenly grabs my arm: her eyes are filled with panic.

'You *promised me* . . . you said you wouldn't . . .'

'I wasn't going to, but then he started stalking me! He locked me in the shower . . . he could have *killed* me!' I yell. My head whips left and right along the beach, expecting Dev to jump out at any minute and prove me right, to admit that he is the father of Caitlin's child, or that he killed Matilda over her relationship with Chetana.

'Locked you in the shower? What are you *talking* about?' Chetana looks at me incredulously.

'I—' *When was it?* The days are blurring. 'Yesterday . . . no, the day before . . . yes, that's right, Monday . . . he locked me in the shower block and left me in there. At first I thought it was you, but now I realise it must have been him.'

Chetana releases my arm and takes a step back. She doesn't look panicked anymore: now she looks nervous.

'Dev arrived yesterday morning, Sophie. He's been in court the whole time, you can check. And he only came down to visit because his trial was near here. My brother isn't trying to hurt you.'

I shake my head, refusing to listen. Of course, that's what he would tell her.

'He could have snuck down without you knowing . . . he was out on the rocks just now . . .'

I am shivering from head to toe, waiting for the shadow of Dev to emerge behind Chetana, the puppet master, hiding in the background all along. But Chetana is looking at me with something like pity, which only makes me angrier.

'Sophie, Dev left this afternoon for an emergency court hearing. He isn't here.'

I shake my head again, sending droplets of rain from my hair flying.

'You're lying . . . you're trying to protect him . . . protect your family's reputation . . . you don't want me going to the police!' I shout, pointing a finger at her.

'No one is lying to you, Sophie!' Chetana cries, her voice rising angrily. She reaches out and grabs hold of the door handle, so that I am forced out of the way, back onto the deck.

'*Maybe*,' she hisses, her face red and blotchy, 'it's *you*, Sophie. Not me. Not Dev. Maybe *you're* the problem. Now get off my deck and leave my family alone.'

'What do you mean?' I stare at her. 'Chetana what do you—'

But Chetana slams the door.

'Chetana!' I bang on the glass repeatedly, but she refuses to open the doors. Finally, I give up, walking back down onto the beach. The rain is so heavy now, I can only see a foot or so in front of me. The sea and sky are one blurry mess of grey as I run back along the beach to my hut.

Maybe you're the problem.

I clamber back onto my deck, looking back out at the rocks for any sign of movement.

Am I?

Suddenly there is a sharp creak on the deck behind me. I whirl around, arms flying up to protect myself. Kip is standing there, his blue raincoat dripping wet.

'What's going on?' he shouts through the storm. 'What are you doing out here?'

The relief at seeing him there is so strong, I can't speak. Just the sight of him halts the spiralling panic, the thud of my heart. Slowly, I become aware of my bare feet, the goosebumps erupting across my skin. Sensing my shock, Kip gently takes me by the arm and leads me inside the hut where he deposits me on the sofa-bed.

'First things first,' he says as soon as he takes his coat off. 'Tell me where to find some spare clothes.'

I try to speak but my mouth opens and closes and no words come out.

Maybe you're the problem.

As Kip emerges from the back of the hut with a towel, I finally start to calm down. For now, at least, I am safe.

'Listen to me, Fee,' Kip says, moving forwards and crouching down in front of me. 'I don't know what's going on, but whatever it is, we can figure it out, okay?'

I desperately want to believe him. But I can't.

Not until I know what happened that night twenty years ago.

Chapter Sixty

That day
9.15pm
Caitlin

He doesn't want you. He never did.

Tucking my knees further under my chin, I took another swig of beer. Two of the six bottles in the pack were already empty. I probably wasn't supposed to be drinking, but I didn't care. What I wanted was for it all to go away, to *fuck off*, just for a minute.

What now?

The sun had set in the time I had been here, hidden in my secret spot among the ferns halfway up the headland. It used to be somewhere other kids hung out: there was a grimy old rope swing hanging from one of the trees in the clearing and broken lighters on the ground. No one seemed to come here anymore, though: the ferns had grown up and around the clearing, blocking it from view unless, like me, you knew where to look.

My eyes were tight and swollen from crying, something I never did. It made me angry that I cared about him enough to cry. No one had ever made me feel like that before. So loved one minute and so insignificant the next. I should have known I wasn't special, after all.

'You fucking *idiot*,' I hissed, downing the rest of the beer so quickly I almost threw it back up again. Without even considering it, I picked up the next bottle, prising the lid off with my teeth. The beer was disgustingly warm: I'd had to nick them from the back of one of the cupboards instead of the fridge in case my dad noticed.

My head was starting to swim from the booze. Slowly, I put a hand underneath my top and rested it against my belly. It was still flat. No sign that anything was wrong, yet. I had hoped that maybe the test was wrong because it was one of those early ones; but my period was nowhere to be seen. I felt different, too; or maybe that was in my own head.

For a minute, I tortured myself with everything I would lose if I *was* pregnant and didn't get rid of the baby: I wouldn't be able to go to sixth form with the rest of the girls. You got to wear your own clothes to sixth form and everyone played pool in the common room during free periods. There would be no Oxford University for me. No backpacks full of textbooks, no partying or living with other people. I tried to tell myself that was okay. Loads of people were successful without going to uni. Plus, the brochures had looked kind of stuffy: all the girls looked like proper nerds and it was miles from the beach. It was just that for a brief period of time, I had seen a future I hadn't really been expecting: one where I was going to discover what *my* great thing was. What I was capable of. *Just get rid of it, then.* The idea terrified me: that kind of responsibility. But if I thought too hard about it, it made it real and I couldn't deal with it right now.

I clenched my jaw to stop my bottom lip from wobbling. The worst part was that I already wanted to see him. I had been so *sure* he would want to be with me. It hadn't really occurred to me what would happen if he said no.

I pulled out the photo from my shirt pocket. He didn't know I had taken it: I had spotted the camera nearby and secretly snapped it before he saw anything. In that split second I had ached for something physical to hold onto, like a reminder of us. Hot, angry tears blurred my vision. *Fuck you!* I screamed at him in my head. *Fuck. You.* I should get rid of it, burn it or something . . . only I couldn't. It was all too soon. Too painful. Was it possible to love someone and hate them at the same time?

Slipping the photo back into the front pocket of my shirt, I threw back the rest of the beer and wiped my face. I got to my feet and was surprised when I staggered slightly. *Shit.* I was more drunk than I realised.

Tom's party would have started by now. Pushing my way through the canopy of ferns, I emerged back out onto the dark headland steps. As I reached the bottom of the steps, someone grabbed my wrist.

'Hey!' I yanked away from their grip and spun around. He stood in the shadows, but I could see his eyes were round and scared.

'I'm sorry,' he whispered. 'Let's talk.'

My heart soared through my drunken haze, but I wasn't ready to let him off that easily.

'When?' I hissed.

'Later tonight. When no one else is around. I'll come and find you.'

I nodded. 'Okay.'

Chapter Sixty-One

Now
Sophie

After pulling on some dry clothes, I towel-dry my hair and emerge from the bedroom to find Kip rummaging through the kitchen.

'How do you have no food in here? Or fresh milk?' He lifts a carton of orange juice and sniffs it.

'I've been distracted.' Trying not to sound frightened, I ask: 'Was that you outside, earlier?'

'What do you mean?' Kip asks, setting the orange juice down on the side and turning to face me.

'Just now, before you saw me . . . there was someone on the beach, by the rocks. Was it you?'

Kip glances towards the almost-black windows where rivets of rain stream down the glass, frowning.

'No. I came from behind the huts.'

'Well, did you see anyone?' I press. *He might have seen Dev, or whoever it was.* But Kip shakes his head, slowly.

'No. What were they doing?'

'They just . . . they were just standing there.'

He frowns out at the storm.

'Well, there's no one there now.' Apparently realising there is nothing edible in the fridge, he closes the fridge door. 'This is no good. Come on, we're going to Sheila and Gary's. You need hot chocolate. *And* Baileys.'

With no energy to argue, I simply nod.

Half an hour later, we're at the Halls' hut and Kip is handing me a mug of hot chocolate, complete with whipped cream and tiny pink and white marshmallows. I remember this mug, emblazoned with 'World's Best Dad': a gift from Matilda to Gary one Father's Day. As the marshmallows melt, I think of Anna and glance at my phone, which is on the table: I need to call her back. My response to the news of her pregnancy was all wrong. I want to apologise, explain that I can't wait to be an aunty.

'Thank you,' I say, taking a sip. The drink slides warmly down my throat.

'For the hot chocolate?' Kip sits down next to me, giving me a wry smile.

'For everything.'

It isn't just the hot chocolate making me feel warm. Being with Kip is somehow exactly the same as it was when I was fifteen – the giddiness, the nerves – yet also completely removed from those hazy, sunlit days. We are different people; we've been through different things. And yet here we both are, again.

'. . . know you've gone through a lot, lately,' Kip is saying. His eyes are warm, the colour of clear lagoons. 'I don't even know where to begin with all the stuff you've learnt about Matilda, and your dad and Sheila. But,' he takes a deep breath, 'I'm here for you, whatever you want to do. If you still think your dad or Dev might have somehow been involved, let's go to the police, first thing tomorrow. If you want to play Sherlock until you find the answer, I'm with you.' He gives a small, cheesy salute. 'I'm your Watson.'

To my horror, a lump suddenly forms in my throat. Maybe it's the fact that Kip is being nice and I am bone-tired. Maybe it's the fact that he has witnessed me descend into near madness with all of the questions over Matilda's death, yet he is still here, still looking at me in that way. Even after I told him about my encounter with Dev, he just nodded.

'I don't know what to think anymore,' I reply, burying my head in my hands. 'I feel as if I'm losing my mind.'

Kip reaches out and takes my hand in his.

'It's completely understandable, Soph. Even if none of this is connected to Tildy's death, some strange things have happened recently. Stop being so hard on yourself.' His voice is soothing. 'Try to relax.'

'I don't know how,' I say, honestly. This makes Kip laugh, a soft, low rumble. He lifts my hand to his mouth and brushes the back of my fingers with his lips. I stroke the stubble on his jawline, my hand trembling slightly: from cold or nerves, perhaps both. The silence between us is hyper-charged, our forgotten mugs of hot chocolate cooling on the table. He leans in and rests his forehead on mine.

'I'm so glad you came back to the beach. It's like finding the sun, again.'

His lips touch mine and this time, I don't pull away. Pushing all thoughts of Matilda and everything else from my mind, I relax into Kip's warmth. As he slowly starts to undress me, I glance over his shoulder at the darkening beach.

It is deserted.

Chapter Sixty-Two

That day
10.30pm
Sophie

Tom threw another piece of driftwood onto the bonfire, sending bright blue sparks into the air. The night was warm and heavy and I found myself smiling at the flames, my head fuzzy. The three WKDs had turned my tongue blue, and I kept sticking it out, trying to look at it, which was making Jamie laugh.

There were six of us around the fire: me, Jamie, Tom, Kip, Amy and Dev. We were in one of our regular night-time spots, right at the end of the sandbank near the last few huts. They were used as businesses in the daytime, so at night they were deserted. The flames cast shadows on the hut fronts: they looked like people dancing. Amy had strung some home-made bunting up along the closed huts for Tom's birthday and Tom's brother had given him a load of weed. He started rolling a joint while Amy giggled next to him, already wasted.

Jamie passed me another bottle of WKD. My head was starting to spin, but I took it, not wanting my buzz to fade.

The temperature dropped slightly so I shuffled forward on the log, closer to the fire. The waves were blackening, the sky turning an inky blue. I suddenly wondered where Matilda was. I knew Chetana had an early curfew: did Tildy just stay in her hut during the evenings, now?

'. . . a boyfriend?'

'Huh?'

I hadn't realised Jamie was talking to me. He looked a bit annoyed that I hadn't been listening.

'I asked if you had a boyfriend.'

'Oh. No.'

'Cool. Me and my girlfriend broke up a few weeks ago.'

He shuffled closer, grinning at me, and I suddenly regretted flirting with him earlier. He was acting really interested in me, when all I wanted to do was move away from him. Up close, he wasn't anywhere near as attractive as I had thought he was. I didn't like the wispy moustache on his upper lip *at all*.

There was a sudden rustling in the trees behind us and we all looked up. It was impossible to see anything in the darkness, just the vague outline of branches against the black sky. I looked across the fire at Kip, who shrugged at me.

SNAP.

Everyone fell silent: there was definitely a noise this time. Frowning, Kip picked up a long piece of wood and held it in the fire for a few seconds. When he pulled it out, he was holding a makeshift torch which flickered with blue and pink flames.

'Who's there?'

Tom sniggered in the darkness but there was no answer from the trees. Goosebumps erupted across my arms and the back of my neck. *Could it be a parent? The police?* I glanced at the joint in Tom's hand. Kip made a frustrated noise in the back of his throat and stepped over the log he had been sitting on, walking cautiously towards the trees. Slowly, Dev got to his feet, too.

There was another snap of twigs before a shadow reared up out of the blackness. Kip yelled and dropped the torch, sending bright red embers scattering across the ground.

'Get that out of my face, Kip!'

Caitlin emerged into the light of the fire. She was still wearing Kip's orange shirt and I tried not to care. Kip stamped out the torch with a shake of his head, while Dev watched Caitlin, with a frustrated look on his face.

'She's wasted,' he muttered to Kip, as Caitlin stumbled over to Tom and sat down heavily on the log. Reaching for the vodka bottle in Tom's hand, she looked up. Our eyes met.

'What the *fuck* are you looking at?'

My head jerked back. Caitlin had always been mean, but this was a new level of outward dislike. There was an energy about her tonight that seemed to blaze like the fire between us. A hand reached out and took mine.

'Ignore her. She's drunk.'

I wanted the voice to be Kip's, the hand to be Kip's, but when I turned, it was Jamie looking at me. He put his arm around me and pulled me closer, hugging me into him.

Caitlin got to her feet and walked closer to the fire, throwing back her long blonde hair and lifting the vodka bottle to her lips. As she lowered the bottle, her lips curled into a sneer: this time it wasn't aimed at me.

'Are you lost?' she slurred.

Jamie was saying something close to my ear, but I wasn't listening: I had followed the direction of Caitlin's blurry gaze and there, in the darkness, stood Matilda. Almost immediately, I could tell something was wrong. Even in the darkness, her eyes looked puffy. For once, Chetana was not shadowing her.

'Hey Tildy,' Kip called. He sounded relieved, like he was hoping her arrival would break the tension. 'Come and have a drink.'

Tildy wasn't looking at me. I was suddenly aware of my mini skirt, the WKD in my hand. *I don't even recognise you, anymore, Sophie.*

'Come on,' Kip encouraged, 'I've not seen you in ages.' He patted the log next to him and eventually Tildy sat down stiffly while snippets of conversation resumed around the fire. Jamie was still talking to me but at that moment, Tildy glanced up and saw me looking at her. Her face was impossible to read. Then she smiled a small, almost reluctant, smile and it was as though a dam had burst within me. I grinned stupidly back at her across the fire, my heart lifting. *She didn't hate me!* Even after everything I had said to her and Chetana. I suddenly, desperately, wanted to tell her everything. About Kip. About Caitlin and her nastiness. I wanted to tell her that she was right and summers were better when it was just us.

'You're really pretty,' Jamie's voice was close to my ear. I felt his stubble brush roughly against my cheek. He reached out and placed a hand on my thigh, rubbing it up and down, close to the hem of my skirt. I stiffened. He leant closer and I was worried he was going to kiss me in front of everyone. I didn't want to kiss him; I didn't want my first kiss to be with someone I didn't really know. Looking around in panic

I saw Kip watching. Oddly, he looked almost annoyed; but then the breeze blew through the flames and when I blinked he was no longer looking at me. He turned to the cool-box and offered Matilda a beer: to my surprise, she took one, throwing her head back and gulping it down with her eyes shut before gesturing to Kip for another. *What was she doing?* Tildy hardly ever drank and not like that. *What had happened?*

'Come for a walk with me?' Jamie asked. It didn't really sound like a question. He gestured with his head towards the darkness beyond the huts and started trying to pull me up. 'Let's have some privacy.'

Oh no. I didn't want to. The WKD buzz had worn off and now I just felt tired and a bit sick.

'I—'

Just then, Caitlin started fiddling with the speakers, turning up an Usher song and drowning out all conversation. Jamie's eyes travelled to her as she started dancing slowly around the fire, her face unsmiling, her eyes half-closed. For some reason, I felt uncomfortable watching her. Everything felt off, like we should all call it a night and go back to our huts.

Caitlin lifted her arms up, gathering her hair in her hands as she went. She let her hair fall back around her face as she swayed to the music, her injured ankle apparently completely fine, now. Dev watched her, unsmiling. After a few minutes he got up, walking off in the direction of the toilet blocks. Tom and Jamie, on the other hand, whooped and cheered Caitlin on: Jamie's hand slipped from mine as he turned to clap. Next to Kip, Amy was giggling. Caitlin suddenly opened her eyes and looked around the circle.

'We're going skinny-dipping,' she announced.

'Caitlin, come on, you're wasted,' Kip said, as Caitlin kicked off her flip flops.

'Oh don't be such a *dad*, Kip.' Her voice was hard. She sauntered up to where he was sitting and slowly danced in front of him, so his face was level with her hips. 'You know you want to see this. We all know you like a good time.'

She pulled him to his feet and pressed herself close to him as Jamie watched with his mouth open. I wanted to look away, wanted to go home, but I couldn't move.

'Caitlin,' Kip said, firmer this time. 'I think you need to—'

'I'm game!' Tom said, jumping up so fast he almost staggered into the fire. Caitlin turned around, her focus now on Tom.

'Off,' she demanded, reaching out and yanking at Tom's T-shirt.

'It's my birthday party. You first,' he grinned sloppily.

Me, Tildy, Amy and Kip watched as Caitlin shimmied out of her denim shorts, revealing pale pink lacy knickers. Tom tried to whistle but he was so drunk it came out like a raspberry. Next, Caitlin stripped off her orange shirt, throwing it towards Kip. To my intense relief, Tom grabbed Jamie by the scruff of the neck and pulled him up to join them. The three of them ran down to the water, shouting as they threw off their clothes and jumped in. It occurred to me that skinny-dipping was something Fee would do, even if Caitlin was in a rage. Watching them from afar was the old Sophie, the boring girl I wanted to leave behind this summer. But suddenly, I wasn't quite so keen to be Fee, anymore.

I looked across at Kip and Matilda. It was only then I realised Tildy was shivering, despite the warmth of the fire.

'Here, take this,' I said, starting to take off my hoody, but Kip shook his head and reached for the orange shirt Caitlin had thrown at him.

'Put this on. It's my bloody shirt anyway, Caitlin just keeps taking it. I'll make Tom give Caitlin his when they get back.'

'I'm *fine*—' Tildy began reluctantly, but I shuffled over and took the shirt from Kip, wrapping it firmly around Tildy's shoulders. For a moment, Tildy and I looked at each other. I wondered whether she was going to remember all the horrible things I had said and tell me to get lost. But then she reached out and squeezed my hand. My chest exploded with warmth and I squeezed her hand back, hard.

'Nice to see you two together, again,' Kip said. I smiled. My weird feeling of dread about tonight had been way off: I had my best friend back.

Chapter Sixty-Three

Now

Sophie

Kip drapes a blanket around my shoulders and announces he is going to make dinner. Now that the heat of the moment has passed, I feel slightly embarrassed about being naked on the sofa-bed, covered only by a blanket.

'I need to fill up the water tank,' Kip says, sliding on his flip flops.

'I'll go,' I offer, but he shakes his head.

'Don't be daft. You've barely dried off from your earlier rain dance and I want you to be safe. I'll be back in five minutes. You relax.' He bends down and gives me a quick kiss.

Once the door closes behind Kip, the silence settles around me, like sand after it has been stirred up. Glancing out of the window, the beach is shrouded in darkness: no stars or moon to lay claim to the waves. I can still feel the heat of Kip's skin on mine. What would my fifteen-year-old self think about what we just did? *What happens next,* I wonder. *Will Kip expect me to stay down here after the sale has gone through?* For some reason, I don't want to think about that just now. I am suddenly painfully aware that I am sitting in Gary and Sheila's hut. Matilda's childhood drawings seem to judge me silently from the walls, as though her eyes are on me, watching me with Kip, when she is dead. I wish Kip still had his hut, that I didn't have to be in here.

I get up from the sofa-bed and pull my clothes back on. Then I return to the sofa, watching the door for Kip to return. The seconds tick by slowly as I wait. How long has Kip been gone? Surely it's been five minutes? The water tap isn't that far away; just a few metres away from the hut, by the main path. Where *is* he?

Unable to sit still, I decide to get dressed and make a start on dinner. Kip has already laid the ingredients out on the side so I pick up the knife on the side and begin slicing tomatoes.

After a few moments, however, the thud of the knife against the wooden chopping board starts to bother me. The sound is too ominous in the otherwise silent hut. Reaching across the counter, I flick the radio on. An old song is playing: I remember watching the band on *Top of the Pops* on a tiny portable television right here in this hut. Matilda and I used hairbrushes as microphones to sing the lyrics:

Wherever you go,
Whatever you do,
I'll be watching,
I'll find you.
You can try to run,
But we've not begun,
I'll be waiting,
I'm not done.

For some reason the hairs on the back of my neck stand up. I pause, the knife hovering in mid-air.

326

Wherever you go,
Whatever you do,
I'll be watching,
I'll find you.

I snap the radio off, plunging the hut back into silence.

Kip has been gone for almost ten minutes now . . . has he had an accident? What if – my stomach flips – someone's hurt him? The wind howls outside the hut. The thought of looking for Kip in this weather is an unpleasant one, but I am really starting to worry, now. Deciding to give it another couple of minutes, I open the cutlery drawer in search of a garlic mincer. If Kip isn't back by the time I've got all the ingredients ready, I'll go looking for him.

Finding no mincer in the cutlery drawer, I move on to the drawer next to it. It doesn't budge on the first attempt, but on the second, it creaks open, the rusty hinges protesting. There is no need to move things around looking for a garlic mincer: it is very clearly used as an admin drawer, the kind I just cleared out in my own hut. It is full to the brim with receipts, old corks and elastic bands.

I am just closing the drawer when a familiar flash of green catches my eye. Frowning, I move aside an old notepad, reaching for the object. When I finally pull it out, my mouth goes dry.

No. Please no, not him.

But the little green-haired troll on the key ring is unmistakable.

It is my shower key.

Chapter Sixty-Four

That day
11pm
Sophie

Splashing and laughter drifted through the darkness, where Caitlin, Jamie and Tom were skinny-dipping. Kip shook his head and got up to root around in the cool box for another beer.

I checked my watch: I needed to leave or I would be in trouble. My curfew was earlier than Tildy's, but I really wanted the chance to talk to her. Glancing across at her I cleared my throat. I suddenly felt nervous.

'Do you, uhh, want to walk back together?'

Tildy looked relieved and immediately got to her feet. She picked up her photo tin and tucked it into her shorts pocket, then swung her camera strap over her shoulder. I was pleased our huts were at the other end of the sandbank: we would have a good amount of time to catch up.

'You're leaving?' Kip asked, as he turned away from the cool box.

'Yeah,' Tildy said, with a wave. 'See you all later.'

Was it my imagination, or did Kip frown for a second? Dev didn't return Tildy's wave, but leant over and whispered something to Amy, who giggled and glanced over at us. Weirdly, I wasn't that upset: I'd wasted so much time trying to fit in, and for what? Kip had barely looked my way. I could have been hanging out with my best friend, catching fish and riding as many waves as possible before the sun went down. I was starting to feel embarrassed about the whole summer and the way I had been acting.

Tildy and I fell into step together as we left the warmth of the bonfire. We walked in silence for a while, neither of us looking at the other. The moon was hidden behind a blanket of thick, black clouds. There wasn't a single star in the sky.

I took a deep, nervous breath.

'I'm sorry,' I said, at exactly the same time as Tildy did. We looked at each other properly and started to giggle. Matilda wrapped her arms around me and hugged me so hard the air was squeezed from my lungs. The shirt Kip had given her smelt like bonfire and her camera pressed into my hip.

'I've been a selfish cow,' I mumbled into the crook of her arm. 'Obsessing over Kip. Trying to be someone I'm not. I've missed you.'

'I've missed you too, Fee. And *I'm* sorry. Just because I didn't want to do the same things as you didn't mean we couldn't have stayed friends.'

'I said some horrible things to you the other day,' I insisted, feeling the need to get it all out in the open.

'So did I.'

'I need to say sorry to Chetana, too.'

We broke apart, facing one another. I was about to ask Tildy why she looked upset earlier, but she took a deep breath and spoke first.

'Actually, there's someth—'

'Guys! Wait up!'

Tildy and I both turned to see Kip jogging along the sand towards us. I glanced across at Tildy in surprise. *Why had he left the bonfire?*

'Sorry,' he panted, as he reached us. He looked at Matilda. 'I, uhh . . . didn't get a chance to say goodbye.'

Weird. Why would Kip need to say goodbye to Tildy? He would see her tomorrow. He looked awkward and kept shuffling his feet. Maybe he wanted to talk to Matilda about something and didn't know how to ask me to leave? Despite my resolution that I didn't care anymore, my chest still ached at the sight of him. With a sinking feeling, I turned towards Tildy to tell her I would walk further down the beach and wait for her, but Kip's next words took me by surprise.

'Actually Fee . . . can I have a word?'

Me?

'Now?' I blurted, without thinking. His face fell slightly.

'Yeah, now, if that's okay?'

I looked into his bright blue eyes. It was too dark to see them properly, but it didn't matter: I knew their exact shade off by heart. There was something about the way Kip was acting that began to give me butterflies and for a moment, everything stood still, even the waves.

For as long as I could remember, Kip had been the only boy who had ever turned my head. Even when I was back at school, he swam in the back of my mind and I would half-dread returning to the beach, in case I learnt he had a girlfriend. Now, for the first time ever, he was asking to talk to me. I opened my mouth to say yes, then closed it again. Tildy was by my side. I had chosen Kip and the others over her all summer and here she was, willing to give me another chance. It didn't matter how much my heart ached for Kip, Tildy was my best friend. *Buoys before boys*.

'Sorry, Kip. Maybe tomorrow—' I began, but Tildy cut me off.

'You guys go ahead.'

I turned to her in surprise.

'Tildy, no—'

'It's fine,' she whispered to me. 'He looks like he's finally found the nerve to tell you how he feels. We can talk tomorrow.'

She reached out and gave my hand a squeeze, then turned to go. My heart soared; but it still didn't feel quite right to just let Tildy walk away.

'Wait!' I said. 'You wanted to tell me something.'

'It doesn't matter,' Matilda said quickly.

'It *does* matter.' I chewed my lip, thinking. 'What if we meet by the rocks in, like, five minutes?' She would know where I meant: the flat rocks at the bottom of the headland, beyond our huts.

Tildy glanced at her watch.

'I don't know, Soph. Won't you get in trouble? It'll be past your curfew.'

'That's okay,' I grinned. Being friends again was worth getting in trouble for. Plus, Mum and Dad would forgive me when they found out I had been with Tildy. '*Please*, Tilds. I want to know what you were going to say.'

'Okay!' Tildy grinned back at me. 'See you in a minute.'

As Tildy hurried away across the dark beach, I finally turned back to Kip who was waiting with his hands shoved into his pockets. My heart started beating faster.

'What did you want to talk about?'

Kip rubbed the back of his head, accidentally messing up his hair like he always did.

'Look, Fee . . . we've only got a couple of weeks left before we have to go back to school . . .'

My stomach knotted with dread. Was he leaving early, was that what he was going to say?

'Thing is, I've wanted to talk to you all summer, but I didn't really know how.' He looked down at the sand. 'I mean, we've known each other for years and I didn't want to seem weird. Then Jamie started going on about you . . . I didn't know if you were interested in him.'

'I'm not,' I said immediately. Kip laughed.

'I know, you made that pretty clear tonight.' He took a step towards me, so that we were only a few inches from each other. I felt almost light-headed. *Was this really happening?*

'So if you're not interested in Jamie . . . maybe you could be interested in somebody else?' Kip said quietly, his breath tickling my face.

'Maybe,' I whispered. Kip smiled, looking relieved.

'I can work with maybes.'

Then his hands were cupping my face and he was bending down to kiss me. As his lips met mine, I thought my heart was going to explode right out of my chest. My whole body seemed to completely disappear, becoming tiny granules of sand that mingled with the beach. I knew, then and there, it was a moment I would never forget as long as I lived.

Finally, after what seemed like forever and no time at all, we broke apart, smiling sheepishly at one another. Despite the chilly breeze, I felt warm and tingly all over. *He felt the same! It wasn't all in my head!*

'God, I'm so glad I got to do that,' Kip said, his thumbs brushing my cheeks. 'Can I see you tomorrow?'

I nodded breathlessly, incapable of speech. Kip smiled and gave me one last kiss, before disappearing into the darkness.

Once I was sure he had gone, I hugged myself with glee. It had actually happened! For a few moments I stood on the sand, allowing my heart rate to slow down and letting everything that had just happened wash over me. I had finally got my first kiss. With Kip! I couldn't wait to tell Tildy. *Tildy!* I checked my watch, stunned when I saw how long I had been standing in a daze for.

Turning, I tore along the beach, past mine and Tildy's dark huts, towards the rocks. I arrived five minutes later, with a stitch tearing through my side, but when I approached the rocks, there was no sign of Tildy. She must have gone home. I was late, after all, and it was cold. Catching my breath, I tried to ignore the prickling feeling of guilt that washed over me. I had let her down *again*.

Slowly, I started to make my way back towards the huts. *It would be okay*. I would make it up to her tomorrow and find out what she wanted to talk to me about. Everything would be fine.

It was well past my curfew by now. As I started jumping back along the rocks, skipping the ones that I knew were sharp, the memory of Kip kissing me came flooding back. Would I be his girlfriend now? I grinned happily to myself, buoyed by thoughts of seeing him the next day.

Chapter Sixty-Five

Now
Sophie

Kip. His name is like a punch to the gut. Kind, relaxed Kip. Even now, I am not sure I believe it, but the key pressing into my palm is proof enough. He said there was no key in the lock when he 'rescued' me from the shower. He lied to my face over and *over*. Charlie springs to mind. Was it possible Kip had persuaded her not to take my suspicions about the photos seriously? Caitlin's words on the phone earlier come back to me . . . that whoever it was is *still on the sandbank.*

I've done it again, I realise. Just like my obsession with Kip that summer had inadvertently led to Matilda ending up dead, my obsession with Kip as an adult has led to me being trapped in this hut, failing to see the signs before it was too late.

Why him? What reason would he have for tormenting me these past few days? Has he been trying to stop me from asking questions about that summer, all along? Is that why – my stomach roils – he slept with me tonight? Was he trying to keep me close, to get information on what I know? '*I'm your Watson.*'

No, that's insane. It's *Kip*. He wouldn't have been involved in Matilda's death, he loved her.

The hard plastic of the troll bites into my clenched fist. If nothing else, this key is proof that Kip was lying about the shower. Unless . . . is it possible he found it and forget to tell me? After all, it's Gary and Sheila's hut – Kip just stays here. Could Gary or Sheila have found the key afterwards, and not realised the significance? Just dropped it into this drawer? *I need to get out of here.* Then I can think about what to do. How this might be explained. Because while the key could be innocent on its own . . . other suspicions creep uninvited into my mind.

Kip.

Wanting to see the photos before anyone else.

Kip.

Tapping on my window.

Kip.

Appearing just after I saw a figure out by the rocks.

Forcing my legs to move, I pick up my bag and shove my feet inside my sandals. I am just straightening up when the door swings open, letting in a howl of wind.

Kip stands in the doorway, looking straight at me.

Chapter Sixty-Six

Now

Sophie

My heart hammers against my ribcage. Slowly, casually, I slip the shower key into my back pocket, before he can see it.

'Hey,' Kip says, walking in and shaking the rain out of his hair. 'Sorry I took so long.'

I search his face for some sign that he could be a cold-blooded monster, but there is nothing. *Don't jump to conclusions. Just get out of here.*

'Look who I found lurking around.'

Gary enters the hut, his black coat silvery with rain and his red hair plastered to his forehead. Relief floods through me: Kip and I are not alone. He can't do anything with Gary here. Kip seems annoyed by Gary's presence, even though it's Gary and Sheila's hut.

'Sophie,' Gary greets me with a kiss on my cheek and smiles at me, full of emotion.

'Gary . . . hi,' I manage to stammer.

He moves away and I want to tell him to stay close, not to go anywhere. Thankfully, it is his hut and the weather is awful: it's unlikely he will be leaving tonight. Gary closes the door behind him and shivers.

'I hope you don't mind me gate-crashing dinner, you two.'

Kip's face falls, as though he wasn't expecting Gary to stay, even though it's Gary's hut. My chest tightens; I don't want Gary going anywhere.

'Uh, actually,' Kip begins tightly, 'we were just going to have a quiet—'

I interrupt him hurriedly.

'That would be great, Gary.'

I can feel Kip's eyes on me, but he doesn't say anything. Instead, he walks over to the kitchenette and starts pulling out wine and glasses. Gary begins taking off his coat and shoes, still smiling at me.

'How's the sale going?' he asks, sliding his shoes under the table and accepting a glass of wine from Kip.

'The-the what?' I am hyper-aware of Kip's movements in my periphery, but I am afraid to look at him in case he can read my expression and knows that I have found the key.

'The hut sale, love. Would have thought it would be gone by now,' Gary says. His brow furrows. 'Are you alright?'

I force myself to look at Gary and give a wooden smile. My face feels like it might crack from the tension.

'I'm fine, sorry.' I try to remember what is happening with the sale: the days are blurring into each other. 'I think the agent called . . . there might be some offers, but I've not called her back yet.'

'Not keen to leave, huh?' Gary winks, with a look across at Kip. *Has Kip told him about us?*

'Please don't embarrass her,' Kip protests. 'Or else I won't see her again for another twenty years.'

Gary holds his hands up in apology, then reaches for his wine.

'What are you doing?' Kip asks, looking at the bag on my shoulder. 'Are you leaving?'

It takes every ounce of strength to force a would-be relaxed nod and smile.

'I'm sorry, I'm so tired from everything. I can barely keep my eyes open.'

Does he suspect? Surely, he can see the fear in my eyes. There is a pause while Kip looks at me. Gary seems oblivious: he is still sipping his wine and has pulled his phone out.

Finally, Kip speaks.

'Totally understand, Soph. You've had a long day.'

He looks at me with apparent concern and comes over, placing a hand on either side of my shoulders. I fight the urge to throw his hands off. He is gripping just a little too firmly.

'Are you going to be okay?' he whispers, glancing at Gary who is still looking at his phone, apparently trying to be tactful. 'Do you want me to come and check on you later? I can take a spare key, in case you're asleep?'

A spare key! I almost laugh.

'I'll be fine,' I say, not meeting his eyes. Every cell in my body is screaming at me to run, but I can't let him suspect I know anything. How can it all have changed so quickly? Trying not to recoil, I duck under his arm.

'Bye, love,' Gary says warmly. 'Hopefully see you tomorrow. Maybe we could all have dinner?'

I try to look enthusiastic but all I can think about is getting to the doors.

'Maybe.'

I reach for the door handle, just as a shrill ring echoes around the hut. *My phone.* I've left it on the table. I turn in time to see Caitlin's face ballooning onto the screen. Hurrying to the table, I snatch it up. Kip is frowning: did he recognise her on the screen? With everything that happened earlier, I never told him about visiting Caitlin after he left for work this morning. Without looking at either of them, I return to the door and open it, already reaching into my back pocket for my hut key. With a stab of horror I hear something else land with a *clink* on the floorboard behind me. *The shower key.*

'You've dropped something.'

Gary stoops down and picks up the shower key attached to the green-haired troll. Kip is fiddling with the stove, his back to me. A throb of relief pulses through me: he hasn't seen.

'Thanks,' I mutter, quickly taking the key from Gary. Gary meets my gaze and looks as though he is about to say something, but then Kip moves away from the stove and I turn away, out into the sheeting rain.

As soon as I reach the wet sand, I break into a run. I wait for a hand to pull me back, a blow from behind in the darkness, but nothing comes and soon I am back on my deck. Hastily unlocking the door, I stumble inside and slam the doors shut. After triple-checking they are locked, I check all the windows and close the blinds and curtains in the living area. My sandals are caked in wet sand and I kick them off into the corner of the hut.

Pulling my phone out of my pocket, I try to return Caitlin's call but once again, there is no signal. *Fuck!* I slam the phone onto the windowsill. The wind buffets against the hut, louder than ever, echoing my own turmoil. I can almost *feel* Matilda in the hut with me, trying to help me along.

'What happened?' I whisper into the darkness. Fragments of information flit around me, maddeningly out of reach.

Why now? Why would I be in danger after all this time? What's changed?

The photos. The one thing capable of rewinding the past twenty years and dredging up that summer again. The discovery of the tin was where this whole thing started, the one thing that threatened to upset the long-kept secrets on the sandbank. There *has* to be something I've missed. Something Kip has been hoping to prevent me seeing this whole time.

My bag is by the front door and I retrieve it, relieved to see the tin still buried in the side pocket. I think of Kip, insisting we open the photos together, leaning over my shoulder, and shudder. Lighting the torch app on my phone, I hold the photos up one by one, looking for anything I might have overlooked the first time. There is the photo of me and Matilda in front of her hut, our faces pushed up against each other, standing in front of her bright yellow hut. I can't see anything in this shot, other than our smiling faces. Next is the photo of Matilda and her parents, with the pink thumb mark obscuring the lens. Sheila's hand on one hip, Gary sweeping a younger Matilda up in his arms. It's impossible to tell who took the photo. The third photo is the blurry nighttime shot, with just the bonfire flames and dot of a moon in the top corner. I squint at the black shadows, trying to see something, *anything*. I don't even know why Tildy would take such an underexposed photo when she was so careful with her films. Did she try and capture something, possibly her killer, or whoever Caitlin was with, but the photo didn't develop enough? Next is the slightly crumpled selfie of Matilda inside her hut, with Gary in the background in just his swimming trunks, his back turned. Matilda wearing Kip's orange shirt, the one he gave her on the night that she died. *Nothing.* I move onto the next one: Chetana, turning, seemingly unaware of the camera. Her dark hair fans out around her. Again and again, I come back to Chetana and Matilda's relationship, wondering whether it could be linked to Tildy's death. If not Dev, perhaps his parents? The perceived shame of Tildy's sexuality, jeopardising Shiv's political career? The final photo is the group shot of the summer of '97, taken in front of Kip's sage green hut. Amy, Tom and I sitting at the front, our legs dangling over the edge of the deck. Caitlin looking moody, Kip's arm casually thrown around her shoulders. Is Caitlin's pregnancy the link? Was Kip the father and Matilda somehow got involved? I strain my eyes at the photo, at Kip in particular, trying to see something I might have missed. Just as I decide to go through them again, there is a loud creak out on the deck.

Someone is outside the hut.

Chapter Sixty-Seven

Now

Sophie

The seconds tick by as I stand motionless, listening. Did I imagine the creak? The silence billows around me.

Just as I turn back to the photos, a loud knock makes me jump. There is another knock, then the muffled sound of someone calling my name: only it isn't Kip's voice.

I put the photos down and hurry over to the doors. Peeling back the curtain ever so slightly to look outside, I exhale at the sight of Gary standing on the wet deck. Pushing the curtains aside and unlocking the doors, I usher Gary in from the rain.

'You must be soaking,' I say, watching him stamp the wet sand off his trainers onto the mat. 'What are you doing here?'

Gary pushes his damp hair out of his face and puts down a heavy-looking black torch.

'I came to check on you. Don't worry,' he says, as I open my mouth, 'I haven't told Kip.' He gives me a knowing look. 'I got the impression you two have a few things to work out.'

'Thanks, Gary,' I say, relieved.

'Any chance of a drink for this old man?'

I manage to smile, genuinely now. It is a relief to have the company, to feel safe for a moment. Turning on the lights,

I head across to the kitchen while Gary settles himself at the table.

'I've got tea, coffee, wine or gin,' I say, rummaging around in the cabinet, 'what do you fancy? Gary?'

When he doesn't answer, I turn around, clutching a bottle of wine. *Shit*. Gary is staring down at the photos on the table.

'Are you alright?' I ask softly. Gary's eyes are wide: he suddenly looks like a lost child.

'Are these . . .?' He clears his throat. 'The photos you found?'

His eyes flicker to the rust-speckled silver tin on the table. I nod. Gary reaches out and gently picks up the scattered photos as though he is afraid he might shatter them. Placing the wine bottle down next to the glasses, I go over and sit next to him at the table.

'Look how young we all were,' Gary whispers, picking up the photo of him, Sheila and Matilda outside their hut, with him scooping Tildy up in his arms. The dad in the photo, who always reminded me of a fireman, is a far cry from the man sitting at the table. 'I always imagined life would be just like this.'

I look away as he stares at the photo, feeling like an intruder to his grief.

'It's like getting a piece of her back,' Gary says in a low voice. 'We've seen all the photos she had in her albums and in the hut, but these . . . they're like new memories. Are they all from that summer?' He looks up at me with eyes that look almost desperate.

'Most of them, I think. That's why we thought there might be a clue or something in them because she hid them

343

that night. Something we could take to the police. Is there anything you can see that might help?' I don't want to ask him directly about Kip, at least not yet.

Gary gazes down at the next photo, the one of him and Matilda in the hut. He suddenly goes very still. In the light of the lamps, his face seems to pale. It's as though he has forgotten I am watching him.

'Do you see something?' I ask, with a surge of hope. 'She was wearing that shirt the night she . . . it happened. Gary?' His hands are trembling and I wonder if going through the photos and dragging up his only daughter's death is a good idea. Finally, he shakes his head.

'No, nothing in this one.' He slowly places it down in front of him. 'How about that drink?'

I go to stand up, but Gary is on his feet, motioning me to sit down.

'I'll sort it,' he says woodenly. 'Thank you.'

I don't argue: it's obvious he needs a moment. Gary gets up from the table and walks over to the breakfast bar, where the wine and glasses I got out a minute ago are standing. With his back to me, he opens the bottle and starts to pour. The soft glug of the wine fills the hut. When he turns around and hands me the glass, his eyes are red-rimmed.

'To Matilda,' he says, holding out his own glass.

'To Matilda,' I say, clinking my glass against his. For a moment we are silent as we drink to Tildy. Her memory feels more real than ever with her smiling face looking up at us from her own photos. The atmosphere is finally broken when we both lower our glasses.

'I'll top us up.' Gary takes my half-full glass and returns to the breakfast bar.

While Gary pours the wine, I decide to put the photos away. I don't want to make him any more miserable. Once I have gathered them up and placed them carefully in the tin, I realise there is one left on the table: the photo of Matilda and Gary that shook him up so much. I pick it up and study it one final time.

Matilda is sitting on the sofa-bed, the sheets rumpled, the camera turned around to face her, selfie style. Only the edge of her face is in shot, her blonde hair tucked behind her ear and her long golden legs pulled up under her. The sleeve of her orange shirt is just visible, bright in the afternoon sunlight. In the background, Gary is dressed only in small trunks, his back turned, as though he doesn't know the photo is being taken. There is nothing obviously wrong with the image, but there is something nagging at me. Something I am missing.

I've always skimmed over this photo: its blurriness and mundaneness making it uninteresting. But now I am properly looking. In the photo Matilda is wearing Kip's orange shirt. Only . . . I pause. Kip didn't give Matilda the shirt until the bonfire that night, just before she was killed. This photo was taken in the daytime: the hut is sunlit. I lean closer, my pulse quickening. Now I'm looking more carefully, the blonde hair is wavier than Matilda's, the limbs longer and more athletic. The shape of the face is different. *Why would the sheets be rumpled in the daytime?* That's when it clicks.

The girl in the photo isn't Matilda.

It is Caitlin Richards.

Chapter Sixty-Eight

Now

Sophie

*C*aitlin.

It is as though the world around me has completely stilled. The image in my hand suddenly takes on a new, sickening meaning: Caitlin sitting in the rumpled sheets of Sheila and Gary's bed. Gary behind her, wearing nothing but trunks; which I now realise are actually just a pair of boxer shorts.

It was here, all along, in plain sight. Gary must have been the mystery man who got Caitlin pregnant. She was a *child*: just over a year older than Matilda was. It might not have been illegal, but it was still wrong. And if the photo was inside her tin . . . Matilda must have known. *Is that why she hid the tin under my hut? Is that why she was killed?* Shock pulses through me, so that I can't think straight.

'What are you looking at, Sophie?'

Gary's voice is no longer trembling. For a second, I am too afraid to look up. Then, my mouth dry, I force myself to meet his gaze. Gone is the grieving man of moments ago: he is standing very still by the breakfast bar. His dark brown eyes, so unlike Matilda's, bore into mine. *Act natural. Don't let him know you suspect anything.*

'Just the photo. Trying to find a clue. It's so frustrating not being able to find anything.' I force a smile.

Behind Gary, my phone lights up on the windowsill. I need to distract him, give myself time to work out an escape.

'Shall I get some more wine?' I say casually, standing up. Gary's eyes don't move from the photo in my hand. 'I think the good bottles are in the back.' Before Gary can reply, I get up and duck under the curtain separating the back bedroom from the rest of the hut.

Behind the curtain, I clamp a hand over my mouth. The crumpled photo of Gary and Caitlin is still gripped in my hand. *Gary.* Not Kip, after all, but the man with the loud laugh, who made us hot chocolate and taught us how to read the tides. The man who could charm anyone, only he chose to charm a young girl. He must have heard everything through Sheila since the very beginning, known everything Kip and I had been doing. In some ways, Kip would have been an easier perpetrator to stomach. *How could it be Gary? How is it linked to Tildy's death?* I don't understand. But there's no time to figure it out: I need to get out of here. I need to take this photo to the police.

I should have left. I should never have interfered. Out of nowhere, the desperate urge to be tucked away in my lounge in London with Nick hits me. On the other side of the curtain, I hear my phone as it starts vibrating again on the windowsill, followed by the slow creak of a floorboard.

With Gary in the main section of the hut, the window above the bunk bed is the only way for me to escape without him seeing. Quickly and silently, I climb up the wooden ladder to the top bunk. *How long do I have? Seconds?*

The window looks horribly small, but right now it is my only hope. I fumble with the key that unlocks the window and ease the window open.

Gary's voice carries through the curtain behind me.

'Caitlin Richards is calling you.' His tone is eerily sing-song. 'Why don't you come and answer it, Sophie? It must be important.'

He knows. I'm out of time.

Lying flat on my front on the bed, I push my shoulders through the window. It is a tight fit: for one sickening moment I am horribly wedged, the breath squeezed from my ribcage; then I force the rest of my body through the window. My hips catch on the way down and I land face-first in a crumpled heap. *What now?* I need to get help. Chetana's hut is further along the sandbank: I need to reach it. Pulling myself up, I start across the stony trail behind the row of huts.

Through the darkness comes the crunch of a footstep. My stomach drops: someone is on the stony trail already, blocking my escape. Before I have time to think, bright light blinds me.

'Sophie, stop being ridiculous,' Gary says, pointing the torch at me. 'Let's go inside and talk it all through.'

The hard tone of his voice sends a shiver through me. The path to Chetana's hut blocked, I turn on my heel and sprint towards the only option I have left: the headland.

Sharp stones pierce my bare feet as I run. Within seconds, the wooden steps emerge in front of me, barely visible in the darkness. Luckily, the summer nights spent down here as a child taught me how to navigate the sandbank without thinking. As I sprint up the steps, taking them two at a time, I think I hear someone calling my name through the darkness, but I don't stop.

A stitch sears through my side, my breath coming in short bursts. Pushing on, I know immediately when I have reached the top step: the wind up here is stronger and a gust catches my hair as I stagger across the chalky ground. The sea glints ominously below, the black sister of its daytime shimmer. Pinpricks of light across the horizon are too far to be beacons of safety.

I am alone.

There is a trail to the north of the headland that cuts back down to the main walking path and to the huts. I duck behind a clump of brambles as I get my bearings, listening hard to where the waves are breaking. I am close to the trail, I think: another few minutes in the same direction. *You can make it.* Taking a deep breath, I stumble out from the brambles.

Then comes the voice, cutting loudly through the howl of the wind.

'Sophie, stop.'

It's too late.

Chapter Sixty-Nine

That day
11pm
Matilda

'Okay, I'll see you in five minutes.'

Jogging away from Sophie and Kip, I felt something click back into place, despite how much my heart still ached. For weeks I had spent every spare moment of my time with Chetana: it had been the best summer of my life in some ways, but I had wanted to share them with Fee, too. I was still hurting over everything that had happened between us, but it was a relief to know we were going to talk about things properly. I was going to tell her about Chet, too. Sophie would know how to make me feel better, she always did.

Glancing back, I saw Soph and Kip standing close to each other. It looked like they were finally about to get together. I was happy for Sophie – she had fancied Kip since before I could remember – but I hoped it wouldn't mean she would start spending every moment with him. She had been bad enough this summer when Kip and her *weren't* an item. Would I see her at all now? *You've just spent all summer with Chet, remember?* I sighed. Why did everything have to be so complicated?

Along the dark beach, I could just about make out the orange flicker of the bonfire at the other end of the sandbank. My camera was hanging from a leather strap around my shoulder, so lifting it up to my face, I pointed it in the direction of Soph and Kip. They were impossible to make out from this distance, but I figured Sophie would want something to remember tonight by.

I reached into the pocket of my shorts for my metal photo tin. Dad had promised to get me a new one that could clip onto my camera and be more practical, but I liked this one. It was vintage. I opened the tin and immediately wished I hadn't: there was the photo of me and Chet kissing on the rocks after we had said we loved each other. I came to a standstill under the glow of one of the huts, my heart aching at the sight of the photo. Chet's pink and white hut was only a few feet away: she was probably asleep by now. *Why did she end it?* When I took the photo, things had been perfect. *What could have changed?* A familiar feeling of shame suddenly washed over me. *Did she really think what we were doing together was wrong?* It was crushing to realise that even someone with the same feelings as me thought we were somehow abnormal.

I looked back down at the photo. I knew Chet wanted me to destroy it, but I hadn't been able to, yet. It had been one of the happiest moments of my life, discovering that she felt the same way as me. At least I thought she did. Tears started running down my cheeks and I wiped them away with the back of my sleeve. Crying was pointless: it wouldn't change anything. It wouldn't bring Chet back.

I removed the photo and snapped the tin shut, tucking it back into my shorts pocket. Deciding I would work out what to do with the photo of Chet and me later, I dropped it into the front pocket of Kip's shirt. As I did, my fingers brushed against another polaroid photo, already in the pocket. I paused, confused. Why would one of my photos be in Kip's pocket?

I pulled out the photo and squinted at it in the darkness, but it was hard to make out. Moving closer to the outdoor light of a nearby hut, I held the photo up. As my eyes adjusted, my stomach turned.

Oh my god. Bending over, I retched onto the sand, throwing up bile that tasted like beer. *That's Dad . . . in the hut . . . the orange shirt,* this *shirt. Blonde hair. Tanned legs. My dad, wearing basically nothing.*

What was I supposed to do now? I couldn't go back to the hut. I couldn't face Dad, or risk Mum finding out. I looked desperately around. Fee's hut was only a few feet away, so I ran towards it and circled round to the back. Dropping to my knees, I crawled into the gap underneath her hut. With shaking hands, I opened the tin again and slid the sickening photo, along with the one of me and Chetana, inside. Reaching up, I placed the tin out of sight along one of the beams above my head. Tomorrow I would figure out what to do with it but right now, I needed to talk to Sophie.

Straightening up, I sprinted towards the thin strip of sand and rocks that hugged the base of the headland. Within minutes, the sand had disappeared, leaving just rocks and black water in front of me. The rough face of the headland rose up in the darkness on my right, guiding me around the bend. There were a few larger rocks, out of reach of the water, that were flat enough to sit on. Those were the ones that Sophie would be at. I swung my camera strap around, so that the polaroid camera was positioned against my back. *Dad. And her.* Anger flashed through me and I wanted to scream. How *could* he? What was I going to say to Mum? As I approached the rocks, I heard breathing behind me.

Sophie?

Somewhere, high above, came the cry of a seagull: then everything went black.

Chapter Seventy

Now

Sophie

'I just want to talk, Sophie.'

The light from Gary's torch illuminates his pale features. He was handsome, once. Now his greying red hair lifts in the wind as we face one another. We are right at the top of the headland. I am painfully aware of the cliff edge, only a few feet behind me. The grey rocks lie below us, at the bottom of the headland, where Matilda had met her death.

Gary lowers the torch to his side. It is heavy, metal: lethal looking.

'You know,' he says.

'About Caitlin? Yes.'

To my surprise, my voice is steady. Perhaps it is the relief that, at last, we are here. Now I know the blonde girl in the photo with Gary was Caitlin and not Matilda, the tight knot of secrets is finally starting to unravel. I've been wrong about so much, suspecting all the wrong people. Matilda must have found out about Gary and Caitlin. But to *kill* Tildy over it . . . that is something I cannot understand, even now I know what Gary is capable of. The worst part is that now he is here, Gary looks nothing like the shadowy predator my tired brain conjured up over the past few days.

He looks so *ordinary*. His beige chinos are creased, his grey hoody nondescript. He is staring at me with watery brown eyes, his broad nose tinged with pink from the wind.

Every muscle in my body is taut as I try to assess the situation. Gary could probably catch me if I ran: he is wearing running shoes and I am barefoot. Though the cliff edge is a few feet away, it is not far enough away for comfort. My only option right now is to keep him talking until I can figure out what to do. *He said he just wants to talk. Maybe he means it.*

'You locked me in the shower.'

Gary nods, expressionless.

'Why?' I ask.

'Sheila told me you were back, trying to act the detective. I didn't want to hurt you, Sophie. I just wanted you to stop *interfering*. Stirring up the past. But you couldn't, could you?'

He says it like it's *my* fault we are standing here. My fault Tildy was dead at fourteen.

'Tell me it's not true, Gary.' My voice catches. 'Tell me you didn't kill her.'

'You don't *understand*.'

To my disgust, Gary's tone is almost whiny. 'There were things happening, things you wouldn't understand. You were kids.' He rubs the back of his neck with his free hand. 'I'll never forgive myself for what I did. I still haven't. You have to know that.'

Despite the pleading in his tone, he takes a small, almost casual, step towards me. My stomach clenches. *Keep him talking.*

'You must have been desperate. To go to those lengths.'

'I *was* desperate.'

Gary's eyes drill into mine. His hand tightens on the torch handle, his white knuckles glowing in the night.

'It's incredible, isn't it, how people can change your life completely? Matilda, my baby girl, changed everything. Being a dad was the only thing I was ever good at.'

I feel sick. How can he talk about Tildy so lovingly, about being a good parent, after what he did to her?

'Then that little *bitch* Caitlin,' he spits her name onto the dirt, 'tried to destroy it all. That photo . . . I didn't know she had taken it until I saw it just now. Our relationship was a secret, she knew that. She must have used Matilda's camera without me realising.' He shines the torchlight on my hand, where the photo of him and Caitlin is still clenched in my fingers.

'She got pregnant,' his gaze snaps back to me, his eyes feverish, 'I suppose she told you that? She wanted me to *raise* it with her.' Again, his hand squeezes the torch, the beam skittering across the ground.

'I told her I wanted nothing to do with it. But she told me she was keeping it. That I didn't have a choice. I knew she would tell everyone. I had to stop her.'

But she never did. Why? Why didn't Caitlin ever tell her story?

'I think about her every day,' Gary says. For a second, I think he is talking about Caitlin, but then I look at him and see that he has lifted the torch so it illuminates the wooden post with Matilda's plaque on it. 'I begged Sheila to get rid of that god forsaken *hut*,' anger flashes suddenly in his eyes, 'so we could get on with our lives. But she refused. All I've ever wanted is to take back that night.'

The wind howls around us, whipping through my hair. How long can I keep Gary talking before I run?

'Why didn't you go to the police?' I ask. 'If you felt so bad?'

'I wanted to, Sophie.' Gary shifts his weight from foot to foot. 'But everything happened so fast ... I kept waiting for the police to turn up at our door, for the moment where they had a different look on their face. You know the one, where it goes from grieving father to suspect. But it never happened. Days went by, then weeks. After the autopsy came back, the talk started to turn from murder to accident. Everyone thought that she had just gotten drunk and fallen off the rocks.'

I am shivering all over now, whether from cold or fear, or both, I don't know.

'Then there was Sheila,' Gary continues, still shifting on the spot, 'she was falling apart. Matilda was gone, we were being looked at by others as suspects ... she needed me.'

He says it so simply, as though it should be obvious that Sheila would rather have him there than in jail.

'You don't know the hell I've lived through it,' Gary looks past me into the distance, as though I have disappeared and he is addressing some invisible jury. 'I've served my own prison sentence, in some ways.'

He jiggles the torch in his hand. Slowly, carefully, I take a small step back. I need to know how close we are getting to the edge of the cliff. Turning my head ever so slightly, I try to look behind me, but it is too dark. He has me pinned.

'Sheila told me you know about Matilda not being mine,' Gary says, louder now. 'She was still my little girl, though. I don't care what anyone says. Your dad didn't say a word to us after she died. He didn't even come to her *funeral*.'

While talking, Gary has taken another few steps closer to me. Shifting backwards slightly, my leg brushes against something: I glance down and see the rusting *DANGER CLIFF EDGE* sign.

'How did you get away with it?' I ask, my throat tight with panic. 'You were meant to be in the hut with Sheila the whole time.'

'I drugged her before we went to sleep.'

A shiver runs through me. Is there anything he isn't capable of?

'Sheila's always taken medication. She gets incredibly *worried* about things.' A hint of impatience bites in his tone. I remember Sheila's words when we last spoke, the guilt she felt that she had fallen asleep rather than waiting for Tildy to get home. Gary's actions caused a ripple effect of guilt for everyone who loved her.

'It's strong stuff. She had no idea I had left. Then I went out looking for her.'

The way he says it is so cold that I search his face for some semblance of regret, something of the loveable, silly man with the booming laugh; but there is nothing.

'Sophie, if I could take it back, I would.' The whine is back in his voice: I've never despised anyone more. 'Tildy made life worth living, I would never, *ever* have hurt her.'

Perhaps it's the thought of Tildy's wasted life. Perhaps it's the fact that her murderer is nothing more than a narcissistic coward, desperate for pity even after brutally taking the life of his own daughter; but anger flares up within me.

'But you *did* hurt her!' I shout. 'She discovered your dirty little secret and you decided it was worth more than her life!

Did she know it was you?' I spat at him. 'When you killed her, did she *know*?'

Riling him up is a stupid, dangerous thing to do, but right now I don't care. Rage throbs through me. Her life – *all* our lives – might have been so different if it wasn't for the weak man standing in front of me.

To my surprise, Gary looks as though I have hit him. His jaw hangs half-open, gaping at me.

'I . . . of course she didn't—' He puffs up now, dangerous and red-faced. 'I DIDN'T MEAN TO KILL *HER*!' He screams at me, his voice the yowl of a wild animal. 'Haven't you been LISTENING?'

The torch light skitters wildly across the ground. My throat goes dry.

Of course. I should have realised sooner. He never meant to kill his own, beloved daughter. He meant to kill Caitlin.

Chapter Seventy-One

Now

Sophie

Gary is talking, though the words barely register. It all finally makes sense, the way it hadn't before when I thought it might be Dev, or Kip. Matilda's killer never made sense because Matilda, the victim, never made sense. No one ever questioned whether the right girl had been found on the rocks: why would they?

Gary must have seen Caitlin earlier that day, wearing Kip's orange shirt. How could he have known that Kip would give that same shirt to Matilda later that night? Matilda's hair was longer too, that summer, and she had grown a few inches: from behind in the dark, the two girls would have been almost indistinguishable. Hadn't I made the same mistake when I looked through the photos? *Poor Tildy* . . . she must have seen the photo, found it in the shirt Caitlin had been wearing and then hidden the tin under my hut. I hold back a sob at the awful truth. She would have known.

'I went to find Caitlin that night. At first, I just planned to talk to her. To make her see sense. But as I was looking for her, I started to get angry. She had threatened me, told me I had to deal with her problem. She didn't care what it would mean for me. Sheila would have left.' Gary looks at me as though I could somehow understand. 'I would have lost everything.'

'But you did lose everything,' I say. 'You lost Tildy.'

'I didn't mean to,' Gary bleats. 'They looked the *same*.'

I ignore the plea in his voice. There isn't much time: I need to figure out my next move before Gary runs out of steam and realises that he is in almost the same position as he was twenty years ago. Only when I look back into Gary's sunken eyes, it is obvious he has already come to the same conclusion.

'What's your grand plan then, Sophie?' he asks. 'What happens next?'

'Gary, you need to tell the police. You have to. They'll find out, either way.'

'How? You have no proof.'

I stare at him. 'Of course I do.'

'No, you don't. You have no evidence whatsoever. Why do you think they never arrested me the first time?'

'I have this,' I say, holding up the crumpled photo of him and Caitlin.

'That photo doesn't prove anything,' Gary replies coldly.

'Caitlin, then. She'll talk—'

Gary sneers. 'She won't talk. She's only ever looked out for herself.'

What does that mean?

'I . . . you've just told me what you did! You killed Tildy!'

Dread pools in my stomach as the realisation dawns on me that he is right: I have no proof. Caitlin is the only other person who could explain Gary's motives and she's kept her silence for the past twenty years.

Gary's face is pitying.

'You've proven nothing, after all this.'

'Really?' I counter, trying to look confident. 'Well, I hate to disappoint you, but I've been recording this whole conversation and I'm calling the police right now.'

I put a hand in my pocket, but Gary doesn't look remotely concerned.

'Sophie, we both know you left your phone on the windowsill in your hut. In fact,' Gary reaches into his own pocket with his free hand and pulls out my phone, 'I have it right here.'

With a resigned look, almost as though he is disappointed in me, Gary drops my phone back in his pocket and starts towards me.

'I didn't want to do this, Sophie,' he says hoarsely.

He can't be serious. This can't be happening.

'You said you just wanted to talk.' My voice sounds slower, as though the fear has numbed my lips. Gary continues his advance towards me.

'You can't hurt me like you did Tildy,' I say, backing away, horribly aware of the cliff edge behind me. 'It's different this time. No one will believe anything you say.'

'I won't need to *say* anything, Sophie,' Gary says, quietly. 'It's been obvious to everyone you've been out of your mind with grief. Going through a divorce. Coming back here and running around accusing people of murder . . . it's not hard to believe that you would want to end it all. A simple message from your phone to your sister – Anna, isn't it? – should be enough.'

My stomach drops. He's going to make it look like suicide.

Run.

I try and take a step forward, towards the hiking trail, but it feels as though I am trying to step through water: my leg is clumsy and slow. My muscles are refusing to move properly.

I look up at Gary in horror.

'What have you done to me?' My voice is slower than usual. My lips suddenly feel too big for my mouth.

'You remind me of Sheila, you know,' Gary says. 'She worries a lot. She sees things that aren't there . . . obsesses over Tildy's death. That's why she takes such strong medication.'

Then it clicks. *That's why he insisted on pouring the wine.*

'You . . . you've drugged me.'

'What else was I supposed to do, Sophie? You won't feel a thing. Don't worry.'

Already, I can feel my body growing heavier. It's over: I was never going to be able to run away, he knew that. Gary walks towards me.

'Gary, stop, you can't—'

But he suddenly lunges at me, dropping the torch and grabbing my arms in an iron grip. He is far stronger than me and I struggle against him, trying to push him away, but it's no good. I glance stupidly down: the *DANGER CLIFF EDGE* sign is scraping against my ankle. The photo falls from my fingers and flutters to the ground.

'Why did you have to come back?' he speaks through gritted teeth. He squeezes my arms tighter, shaking me. 'I never wanted to hurt you. Why did you have to interfere?'

'Gary,' my voice is slurred, 'Gary, don't do this . . .'

But he grips my arms even tighter and leans towards me. I am dangerously close to the edge now; the wind billows through the back of my jacket. Inexplicably I think of all the hot chocolates he made us, all the grazed knees he bandaged.

'I don't have a *choice*, Sophie,' he hisses in my ear, glancing at the edge behind me. 'You did this! You just wouldn't *leave*.'

The cliff edge yawns behind me. The silvery sea in my peripheral vision looks welcoming, like it's made of the softest velvet. I barely register the pressure disappearing as Gary releases my arms, or the pain in my chest as he shoves me backwards.

As the wind roars in my ears, I see Tildy, cartwheeling along the sand.

Chapter Seventy-Two
Now
Charlie

'What the hell is *that*?' Jacob asks, looking at my bowl in disgust as he returns from the bathroom.

'It's pasta and tomato sauce, what does it look like?' I reply, trying to wave him away from my desk without dropping the piece of penne off my fork.

'That's not tomato sauce mate, that's ketchup. Uni students eat better than you.'

'Piss off, we aren't all married to a chef.'

Jacob returns to his own desk with his usual swagger while I carry on shovelling my dinner down. It's been a long shift and it's the first chance I've had to eat since this morning. Jacob sits down and pulls some fancy-looking Bento box out of his bag, shooting me a smug look. I roll my eyes. Even though Jacob and his wife Maria have only just given birth to their first kid, Jacob looks as alert and fit as ever; not at all like a first-time, sleep-deprived dad. His skin is smooth and clean-shaven, and his shirt hugs his muscles. I, on the other hand, am a walking advert for the single life: ready meals, sporadic gym memberships and a flat that would give Marie Kondo a heart attack.

Ever since Craig and I had split up, there's been little to prevent me from working around the clock. It's always the way: a few months of dating, then realising one day that just because you enjoy a drink together doesn't mean you want to cook Christmas dinner for his whole family for the rest of your life. Back to square one. It was the same after Kip. That one was harder, though, because I liked his family and being at the beach with him. But his lack of any kind of commitment from day to day eventually wore me down. When he had called me asking to meet up, I thought maybe he had realised what we had lost. But then I turned up to the pub and he introduced me to the dark-haired Sophie with the expensive clothes and vulnerable eyes.

Across the station office, Jacob starts making loud noises as he eats whatever fancy dinner Maria has made him. I fight the urge to throw a piece of ketchup-covered penne at his head, just as the phone rings.

'D.I. Brookes,' I answer automatically. As I listen to the message, my appetite suddenly disappears. When I put the phone down, Jacob is groaning.

'Tell me we aren't needed, I've barely eaten.'

'We're needed,' I say, reaching for my jacket and badge. 'That was Sal, we've got to get down to the sandbank.'

Jacob looks up when he hears my tone.

'What's happened?'

'They've found a body.'

A short time later, Jacob and I arrive at the sandbank. When I was a kid, we came for picnics here and I loved how magical the rainbow-coloured huts looked. Now, at this time of night, the darkness on the beach is near impenetrable.

The beach and headland have already been cordoned off by duty officers. As we start walking towards the base of the headland, a young officer with long blonde hair and a torch walks towards us, her face solemn. Megan, I think her name is.

'Ma'am, Sir,' she greets us with a nod. 'The body is round the bend at the bottom of the cliff. Looks like they either fell from the headland, or jumped. We've got a witness who apparently saw the whole thing.' She shakes her head, lifting up the police tape so Jacob and I can duck under. 'It's really tragic. Apparently it's not the first death on this beach.'

'Thanks, Megan,' Jacob says.

We leave Megan and walk purposefully towards the base of the headland. Inside I'm a bit less purposeful: no matter how long I spend on the job, it doesn't make the sight of dead bodies any easier.

'Charlie!'

A familiar voice carries through the darkness. For a moment I don't know where to look; then I spot Kip standing by one of the floodlights that have been erected. I glance at Jacob who has also seen Kip. He met Kip while we were dating and knows Kip spends nearly all his time down here.

'Find out what he wants. But make it quick,' Jacob says, continuing towards the curve of rocks hugging the headland. I stride towards Kip, who is leaning right over the police tape.

'Charlie, what's going on?' He looks panicked in a way I've never seen before.

'Kip, you know I can't tell you anything. I've just got here.'

'Is it true a body's been found?'

I shake my head. 'I told you, I can't tell—'

'Don't *say* you can't tell me!' Kip interrupts. The fear in his voice is razor-sharp. 'I can't find Sophie, her hut's wide open, she's not anywhere along the beach.' He takes a deep, shaky breath and looks desperately at me.

'I can't do this again, Charlie. Not after Tildy . . . I need to know what's happened. *Please.*'

I tell myself that it isn't because I still feel something for Kip. It's because I'm human, and he'll find out anyway.

'All I know is that a body has apparently been found. That's the only information I have.'

'You don't know anything else? You don't know what happened?'

'No, Kip.' I glance up at the immovable, towering cliff. 'I don't know what happened.'

Chapter Seventy-Three

Now
Sophie

Nick reached across and put his arm along the back of my seat, hugging me into him. I rested my head on his shoulder, just as the lights went down and the audience chatter faded away. The conductor lifted his baton and the sweet, mournful sound of violins fissured through the concert hall. Closing my eyes, I settled back in my velvet seat and let the music sing through me. The orchestra began building to the crescendo of the chorus, the brass section ringing clearer than the rest . . . dum-dum-duh-duh-dum-dum . . .

Beep.

Duh-duh-duh-duh—

Beep.

What was that noise? For some reason, the person in front of me turned around, glaring.

Dum-duh-duh-duh—

Beep.

Now Nick was looking at me. Had I forgotten to switch my phone off? All around us people were turning and looking, muttering angrily. I leant forward and fumbled in my bag.

Beep.

Beep.

'. . . didn't believe her. All this time she was in danger and I just carried on as normal . . .'

'How could you have known? And you *did* try to help, you came to me for help, you were looking out for her—'

'Not enough, Charlie. I *knew* there was something strange going on, but I was too fucking caught up in how I felt about her. I never thought he could be capable of anything like this.'

'Caring about someone isn't a crime, Kip.'

'Sophie?'

I open my eyes. Though the lights are down low, it's immediately obvious that I am in a hospital room. The beeping of the heart monitor continues its steady rhythm, confirming that I am somehow, miraculously, alive.

Charlie and Kip, standing near my bed, are now looking at me in relief. Kip sits down in the chair next to me and reaches out to take my hand. His hands are cold and I have to resist the urge to pull away.

'The doctors weren't sure when you were going to come around,' he says, his face creased with worry. 'How are you feeling?'

I give myself a once over: apart from a throbbing head and a dull pain in my right elbow, I feel okay. My arm is strapped into a sling and it feels heavy: they've put it in a cast.

'I'm fine. My elbow is a bit sore.'

'You've broken it,' Kip winces.

'I . . .' I try to remember what happened, but the memory is blurry. 'I landed on the ridge, I think . . . the one we used to climb down as kids.'

'That's where they found you. Another foot and you would have missed it completely,' Kip says, grimly.

I knew as soon as I saw the *DANGER CLIFF EDGE* sign that the ridge lay just below where I stood: what I hadn't known was that thin shelf of rock would save my life.

I pull myself up against the pillows, wincing against the pain in my elbow. Looking directly at Charlie, my heart starts to beat uncomfortably fast.

'Where's Gary?' I ask.

'He's dead.' Kip glances at the floor, his hand slackening on mine. 'He fell from the cliff after he pushed you.'

Dead. I feel nothing, not even a flicker of relief. Just a dull sense of horror that Sheila will have lost both her husband and daughter, now.

'He drugged me,' I said. 'He drugged Sheila too, the night that Tildy—'

'We know,' Kip says soothingly, rubbing my hand. 'Caitlin heard nearly everything that Gary said. She's already given a statement.'

'Caitlin . . .' I whisper.

As I begin to wake up properly, my memory begins flickering back into focus, full of confused fragments. Lying prone on the ridge. A voice above me. Something flying through the darkness and landing with a sickening *thud* on the rocks below.

'She was worried about you,' Kip continues softly. There are dark circles under his eyes. 'She said she had been calling you and when you didn't pick up, she drove down to the beach. She saw that your hut was empty and then she spotted the torch on the headland. She heard Gary confess to killing Tildy, and then saw him push you.'

'Gary was giving her money all these years,' Charlie says. 'A lot of it. Caitlin's son Ben was born with difficulties and needed a lot of support, but Caitlin says it was to keep her quiet because she was the only one who might have put two and two together. Sheila never realised how much money was going out of their accounts, Gary was very careful.'

'He killed Tildy,' I croak. Tears well up in my exhausted eyes. 'It was him.'

'We know,' Charlie says, echoing Kip's words.

'If I had got to the rocks in time . . . it might never have happened,' I whisper. 'It was just because it was dark that he got confused. She would have still been alive if I had been there, he would have known it was Tildy with me.' Tears blur my vision as the awful truth washes over me. If I had only let her go back to her hut, not insisted that she should wait by the rocks.

'Then a different girl would be dead and Matilda's dad would still have been a murderer,' Charlie says firmly. 'This is *not* your fault. Everything that happened is Gary Hall's fault. Not yours.'

There is a long silence in the room. Charlie and Kip look tactfully away as my body shakes with silent sobs. After a while, I compose myself and wipe my eyes dry on the sheet.

'Sophie,' Charlie begins. Her voice is gentle but there is a firmness there too, reminding me that she is still a police officer. 'You'll need to give an official statement when you feel up to it, but just so that you know, Caitlin reported that after Gary pushed you, he leant over the edge to check you were dead and he lost his footing.'

Charlie looks me directly in the eye. Her gaze is sharp and penetrating.

'Does that tie in with what you saw? Did you see or hear anything else? We need to know if there's something we need to act quickly on.'

For a moment, we look at each other. I think of the voice I heard, just before Gary flew past me and landed on the rocks. It's as though Charlie already knows, but she is asking me to choose the way the tide will turn.

'No,' I say, not breaking her gaze.

Sticky eyes, daaaaarling. It's all in the eye contact.

'There was nothing else.'

Chapter Seventy-Four

Now

Sophie

It is early evening by the time I have finished speaking to the police and am discharged from hospital with strict instructions to rest my broken elbow. I only have the dirty clothes that I was brought into hospital in and a pair of flip flops one of the nurses gave me. As I finish dressing, there is a knock on the door and Kip enters. My stomach clenches uncomfortably.

'Hey,' he says with a smile that doesn't quite reach his eyes. He is looking at me slightly warily, as though he is trying to work out what I'm thinking before I say anything.

'How are you feeling?' He nods to the sling on my left arm.

'I'm okay. Just tired and achy.' Now that the painkillers are starting to wear off, my whole body is sore. But the pain is the last thing on my mind right now.

'Kip, listen . . .'

I need to say it before he says anything else. I hate the idea that I am about to hurt him; but despite everything that has happened, my feelings for the blonde surfer boy from my teen years remain firmly on the sandbank, as though he only exists there. Being with Kip made me stop trying so hard and recapture some of my old confidence; but staying with

374

him would be a holiday escape, when you know that you need to go back to work on Monday.

'You don't need to say it,' Kip says, holding up his hands. 'I already know.' He doesn't say how or why he knows. Maybe he also realised in the cold light of day that what we had was only part-reality.

'I just came to say goodbye. I'm heading to Sheila's place tonight. Not the hut,' he says quickly, seeing my expression. 'Her house. Thought she could use the company.'

I nod.

'Say goodbye from me, will you? And that I'm thinking of her?'

'Sure, Fee. And you keep riding those waves, okay?'

With that, Kip steps forward and places a soft kiss on my forehead, before turning and walking away. I can't help but feel relieved, as though I am finally saying good-bye to that part of my past. The boy from my childhood is right where he belongs: now I need to find out where *I* belong. As Kip leaves, I see Charlie waiting outside in the corridor. She gives him a tired smile and they walk away together.

I leave the hospital room a few moments later and start walking along the corridor, following the *Exit* signs. As I approach the double doors leading out of the unit, I spot a familiar figure sat on the hard plastic blue chairs. I have to blink a few times to make sure that I'm not suffering side effects from the pain medication.

'*Nick?*'

Nick turns his head towards me. His clothes are crumpled and his hair is sticking up at odd angles. Next to him is a small suitcase, still with the airline tags on it. *How long has he been here?*

'Sophie!' He jumps up and starts towards me, then stops. He looks unsure.

'What are you doing here?' I ask.

'I'm listed as your next of kin,' Nick says. His face is heavy with relief. 'I can't believe what you've been through. I've been on the phone to Anna, she wanted me to call as soon as I had any news. Your mum and Phil will be here tomorrow.' He gestures to his suitcase. 'I would have got here sooner but I couldn't get a direct flight.'

He's here. He's actually here.

I hurry forwards, grasping him one-armed around the middle and burying my head in his chest, breathing in his spiced, peppery smell. He makes a surprised noise and for a moment I think that he isn't going to hug me back, but then his arms fold tightly around me.

'It's alright. You're safe now.'

We stand there for a moment, in the middle of the bustling corridor where nurses' shoes squeak along the floor and antiseptic seeps into every inhale.

'I've booked a guest house in town,' Nick says softly, after a minute or two. 'Let's get you some food and rest. Then we can talk.'

The way he says *then we can talk* sets alarm bells ringing, even through the blanket of exhaustion. Perhaps he's already seeing someone else? I push the thought to one side. Even if that's true, Nick has travelled all this way, almost certainly putting off work, to support me. It's enough, even if a part of me wishes it could be different.

Half an hour later, we are sitting in armchairs in the lounge of the guest house. The bay windows overlook the harbour, but thankfully the huts are tucked out of sight: I'm not sure I will ever be able to look at the sandbank in the same way again.

The sun is setting over the water and everything is lit up with slivers of soft peachy gold. I am freshly showered and wearing a pair of Nick's oversized joggers and a hoody. Despite the horror of the past twenty-four hours, I can't deny the ache in my chest that has reared its head since seeing Nick again. It is a different feeling to the one Kip sparked: with Kip I felt reckless, disorientated, like I was squinting into the sun after too many cocktails. With Nick it feels solid yet unpredictable, like riding a wave. I just don't know whether it's too late.

'Drink your whisky,' Nick encourages, nodding at my untouched glass. 'It'll help with the shock.'

I reach for my glass and take a sip. Immediately, the whisky burns a comforting path down my throat and into my chest. Then I take a deep breath.

'What you said before, about me not being happy. You were right. I just didn't realise it at the time.'

Nick listens without a word as I describe growing up on the beach and Matilda, the lively, loyal best friend I had never spoken about. I explain the impact her death had had on me, how my guilt over her death had formed my need to control what was going on around me. How work had become an obsessive outlet. I tell him about Kip and, while Nick's face tightens ever so slightly, he says nothing and continues to listen. I describe the horror of being locked in the shower, the moment I fell from the cliff edge. At this, Nick makes an involuntary movement forward, like he wants to hug me, but he stops himself. I pretend not to notice, although it stings.

'Why didn't you tell me?' he asks eventually.

'I never told anyone. I felt so responsible . . . I just wanted to leave that part of my past behind. I didn't realise I had carried it with me all these years.'

Nick shakes his head, looking horrified.

'I can't believe you lost a friend so young. That would affect anyone.'

My eyes prickle. After everything that's happened over the past few weeks, it seems incredible that I never shared this part of my past with Nick, as though it belonged to a different person. But I am finally realising that our futures don't exist without the ripples of our past: I am both Fee *and* Sophie.

After two more whiskies, Nick looks at me through the glasses I had so carefully chosen all that time ago, his eyes full of sadness.

'I'm so sorry, Sophie. For everything. I should have handled it all differently, spoken to you about Japan. I think I was just reacting, having a crisis. Whatever you want to call it.'

I shake my head, the warmth of the whisky finally starting to chase the demons away as the sun slides away below the line of the harbour.

'If you hadn't made that decision, I don't know if I ever would have ended up back here and faced the past.'

My phone buzzes on the table but I switch it to silent.

'And now?' Nick asks.

So much rests on those two words. We both know it. I look out over the darkening sandbank, thinking of Matilda. Of her energy, her excitement. Her open-hearted acceptance of life. Maybe those are the parts I can keep with me.

'Now I need to move on.'

Nick reaches out and laces his fingers through mine. I squeeze his hand, swallowing the lump in my throat. I don't know what else to say, so I reach out with my free hand and pick up my glass.

'Your hair's curly,' Nick says, as I take another sip of whisky. 'It suits you.'

Chapter Seventy-Five

Now

Caitlin

'Mum, Grandad says you can *surf*!'

Ben is looking at me half incredulously, half admiringly. I raise an eyebrow at my dad, who sits on a faded orange deckchair next to Ben's wheelchair, his stomach round underneath his T-shirt. He holds up his hands.

'How was I supposed to know you never told him?'

'Were you any good?' Ben asks. Since we have arrived at the beach, he's been using his iPad less for speech and making an effort to talk out loud, despite how frustrating it is for him. Mum starts cutting up a burger for him and I shrug.

'I was alright.'

'She was fantastic,' Mum says, tutting at me. She wipes Ben's mouth with well-practised movements and starts feeding him his lunch. 'I don't know why you never took it up again. We've still got your board out back.'

'Aww Mum, will you teach me?' Ben begs, almost impossible to understand with his mouth half-full of burger. It is so rare to see him interested in something other than the TV or his laptop, warmth spreads through my chest.

'You'll have to get better at swimming, first.'

I know he's only joking, but I still have to ignore the pang of regret, knowing that Ben will never get to experience what it's like to catch a wave. His cerebral palsy isn't as severe as it could have been, but it is severe enough that he can't walk and struggles to speak, choosing to mostly rely on the text-to-speech tool on his iPad. Maybe there's some sort of assisted surfing I could look into, or sailing. Not that I'll be able to afford it, anymore.

'Okay,' Ben says happily, turning back to my mum who is looking at him with a gentle expression. She came into her own when Ben was born: they've practically been joined at the hip ever since. Even Dad is soft with him; Ben was the catalyst that finally helped him put the bottle down, though it's never been easy. It was the two of them who persuaded me to keep Ben in the first place. I had been a complete mess and they were worried I would regret such a big decision. I'm grateful I chose this route: I can't even contemplate life without him, now.

It's the first time I've been down to Mum and Dad's hut since the summer Gary got me pregnant. Or the summer I should have died, as I now think of it. For Ben, being at the hut is one big adventure; he's pestered me for years to visit but I always made up excuses. It wasn't hard: expensive wheel-chairs and sand don't exactly mix. Now here we are, out on the deck, barbecuing burgers with my parents like we've been doing it his whole life. And even though there are unpleasant memories for me along the sandbank, there are good ones too. Especially now, seeing the sun tinge Ben's cheeks a light pink.

At last, I'm starting to feel free. It'll be difficult for a while: I've never had a job before, so whatever I do I'll be starting from the bottom. But I'll have Mum and Dad and at least I won't feel shitty anymore. I should never have accepted Gary Hall's money in the first place. Sheila Hall had surprised me by getting in touch a couple of days ago, trying to offer me money for Ben but I had said no. I'd already taken enough from her: I should have said no to anything that came from the Halls years ago.

'Stay here, okay?' I say to Ben, standing up and wiping burger crumbs from my shorts. 'I'll be back in a minute.'

Ben barely even looks at me: he's completely distracted by my dad who is promising to take him fishing this afternoon. I leave the deck and walk along the beach, towards the headland. It's a blazing hot day and all along the sandbank, people have set up parasols and colourful windbreakers in and around the sand dunes. Kids and dogs tear along the sand and windsurfers cut through the shimmering water. To some people, this is paradise.

Then again, there are always sharks in the water.

I walk purposefully up the headland steps without breaking stride. The remains of police tape still cling to the trees and wooden posts the police attached them to. Just like when Matilda Hall died. For some reason it annoys me and I tug at the leftover tape whenever I see it, stuffing the pieces into my pocket. I pass the collection of ferns that obscure my old hiding place without stopping.

Finally, I reach the crest of the headland, where the line of the blue sea meets the sky. There is nothing here that would give any clue about what really happened: only someone who was here would know what to look for. My eyes zero in on the scuff marks on the ground from where Gary held Sophie Douglas before he pushed her.

I walk right to the edge of the cliff and look down at the ridge where I found Sophie, barely conscious. There is a large chunk missing now, which would make it almost impossible to climb down anymore, like we used to. It's probably for the best: we did some stupid stuff as kids.

There is another scuff mark on the ground, right above the ridge. Among the disturbed dirt and stones, it is almost impossible to make out. To some, it might look like the place where Gary Hall stood, right before he lost his footing and fell over the edge of the cliff, but if you knew what to look for, you might see the footprints of someone who was peering over the edge, just before they were pushed.

I stretch out my foot and scuff my sandal against the footprints in the dirt. Then I turn on my heel and walk back to my son. For the first time in twenty years, I don't look over my shoulder.

Epilogue

After

Sophie

The ocean stretches out before me, a great expanse of perfect azure blue. Morning sunlight shimmering on each rolling set of waves makes my eyes water, but I don't want to put on sunglasses and dim the view. Below, the pure white sand is still smooth and undisturbed, dotted with canary-yellow beach daisies.

Leaning back in my chair, I allow the warmth to soak into my skin. It has been such a long time since I allowed myself to just *be*. Deciding not to return to work was the first step. This is the second.

'Here,' Anna appears on the terrace, holding out an iced coffee which I accept with a grateful smile. She carefully lowers herself into the chair next to me. She is getting big now, her hand constantly fluttering to her stomach. It was something of a revelation to realise that, for too long, I had seen her as my cheeky, younger sister; someone who walked just a step behind me as we grew up. But Anna is her own woman, full of surprises that I had missed over the years. Despite the initial shock, she coped with the revelations about Dad and Matilda far better than I did, with Mike holding her hand tightly.

It's been three weeks since I arrived in Australia and my skin is darker than it has ever been, the tan lines from my wedding rings gone. Three weeks of no emails. No client meetings. No targets to meet. Just sitting on the other side of the world with Anna and Mike, watching each new wave roll in. The water looks different, here. Flatter, bluer. There are sharks and other creatures lurking in the depths, but these, I know, are far less dangerous than the secrets that skulk beneath surfaces elsewhere.

'It's beautiful out here,' I sigh.

'You say that every day.'

'It's true, though.'

'Stay here, then. There's plenty of houses along the beach for sale. This little one will need her aunty.' She pats her round belly.

We sit in peaceful silence for a moment before my phone dings with a message.

'Nick?' Anna asks, as I squint against the glare on my phone screen.

'Yes. He's sent me another photo of the cherry blossom.' I turn the phone to show her.

'I bet it looks even better in real life,' Anna replies, eyeing me shrewdly through her dark fringe. I smile and start typing a reply to Nick.

Since the guest house, Nick has been calling me almost every day from Tokyo. Asking about Australia. Impressed at my surfing the Gold Coast. To my surprise he even revealed a long-hidden ambition to become a writer. Perhaps I had never known the real Nick, either. Who are we, when we close our eyes and jump?

In the end, the hut was sold to a young family from Winchester, just in time for the summer holidays to begin. They didn't offer the most money, but after a discussion with Mum and Anna, we felt right selling to them. The husband's family had rented a hut along the sandbank once when he was a child and he had spoken excitedly when we met, of crab fishing and teaching his children to kayak. We felt like they would keep the spirit of the sandbank alive, among the many flashy huts now lining the sand.

I had just handed over the keys to the new owner when he leant in conspicuously.

'When I was here as a kid, they used to tell stories about the murder of a girl on this beach.' He looked around, as though a body might be lying just feet away.

'Did they?' I said, non-committally and he nodded sombrely.

'Apparently she looked like a mermaid and now she haunts the sandbank trying to tell her story, but no one can hear her cries because they sound like a seagull.'

They hear, Tildy, I think.

Someone always hears.

Acknowledgments

I used to think that writing a book took one person: how very wrong I was. There are so many people to thank and acknowledge for creating *The Beach Hut*, the list threatens to be longer than the book itself . . .

First and foremost, to my fantastic agent Rosie at Curtis Brown, whose warmth and enthusiasm and all-round hard work on the edits have got *The Beach Hut* this far. Your guidance has been so invaluable. A huge thank you, also, to Tanja and Anna at CB for handling the additional rights – you are all superstars.

Thank you to the wonderful Phoebe at Hodder: your eagle eye and dedication to the book made me feel completely at ease when I could have been a nervous wreck! Thank you for picking up the book and for getting us so calmly over the finish line. Working with you has been an absolute dream. A huge thank you to the whole team at Hodder Fiction who have made me feel welcome from start to finish.

To the wonderful, gifted Sarah, without whom this book would not be what it is. Thank you for the endless edits, for all the 11pm voice notes, for keeping me sane . . . thank you for everything.

Acknowledgments

Thank you to Si, for being an unwavering source of encouragement and honesty. For the countless dog walks spent discussing plot points and for your patience day in, day out. You are my calm evening tide.

To my beloved Bonnie Bulldog, for keeping me warm all those dark winter mornings.

To my truly amazing Curtis Brown Creative (and now friendship) group: Kath, Anne, Tina, Laura, Sam and Olivia. Thank you for the time spent beta-reading, not to mention making my sides ache from laughing. You are all such wonderful, supportive, talented people.

To the superstar writer Lucy Clarke, for always being so generously on hand for advice. You have no idea how much it meant.

To my chaotic, noisy, family, who have always encouraged creativity and as many beach walks as possible, weather be damned. Thank you for creating an environment where it's always possible to daydream.

Thank you to Sue, one of my first ever beta-readers, and the five flame gals for reading my early work with such enthusiasm . . .

A huge thank you to all of my family and friends who will know exactly who they are: your support, encouragement and understanding has meant the absolute world to me.

And thank you, from the bottom of my heart, to every reader.